The Tarnished Oath

The Tarnished Oath

by

Chet Pleban

Gypsy Shadow Publishing

The Tarnished Oath
by
Chet Pleban

Gypsy Shadow Publishing, LLC.
Lockhart, TX
www.gypsyshadow.com

Library of Congress Control Number: 2017961200

eBook ISBN: 978-1-61950-319-9
Print ISBN: 978-1-61950-320-5

Published in the United States of America

First eBook Edition: November 13, 2017
First Print Edition: November 16, 2917

Dedication

To all who have been victimized by politicians

Chapter One

At 6:03 pm on Monday, February 15, the 911 dispatcher received a call from a hysterical female, barely coherent. Not unusual. Dispatchers are accustomed to dealing with people who have witnessed traumatic events or are in immediate danger.

"911. What is your emergency?"

"My, my, my friend . . ."

"Ma'am, slow down. I need to be able to understand you. Take a breath and speak slowly. Tell me what is going on. Are you hurt?" the dispatcher said, attempting to understand the nature of the emergency.

"My friend . . . on the floor . . . blood everywhere. She's not moving."

"Your friend is on the floor, she is bleeding and not moving. Is that what you're telling me?"

"She's dead. Oh my God, I think she is dead."

"Okay, ma'am. Tell me where you are. What is the address?"

"Oh my God. She is not breathing. Blood everywhere. She's dead. Oh, my God. She was my friend."

"Ma'am, please calm down so I can get you some help. Now tell me where you are."

"I am at her apartment. It's . . . I don't know. It's apartment 2B and it's on Jamison. Can't you figure it out? I can't think straight right now," the unidentified caller said as she attempted to control her emotions.

"Please stay there and I will send a car. Please don't touch anything and just wait for the officer. He should be there soon. Do you understand?"

"Yes . . . yes . . . yes, I understand. But she is dead. My friend is dead. I know she is dead. Oh my God."

"The officer will be there soon. Just calm down."

Robbie Bayer, a uniformed St. Louis police officer, got the call. When he arrived on the scene, he found the front door of the apartment closed but unlocked. After announcing the police presence, he entered the unit and located a woman, presumably the caller, standing in the living room. She was crying. The lifeless body of a white female was on the floor. Officer Bayer called for backup, cancelled the ambulance, and instead, requested that the dispatcher contact the medical examiner in addition to the Homicide and Evidence Technician divisions. Blood on the victim's head, along with dried blood on an object next to the victim suggested that this was a crime scene. He would protect the scene and gather preliminary information while he waited for the others.

"Are you okay, ma'am?" the officer asked, trying to determine whether this individual was in need of medical assistance.

No response; the woman continued to cry.

"Ma'am, do you need me to get you an ambulance?"

"No," the response barely audible.

Directing her to a chair at the kitchen table, Officer Bayer continued with his questions. "I need to get some information from you. Are you up to answering some questions?"

"Yes. I'm sorry. She was my friend, and I have never seen anything like this," the woman said.

"I understand. Will you tell me your name?"

"Becky Smallwood."

"And you are the one who made the 911 call?"

"Yes."

"Where do you live, Becky?"

"705 Pheasant Run Drive in Maryland Heights."

"What is your friend's name?"

"Amy Deland."

"How do you know Amy?"

"I work with her. She is . . . was . . . my friend," she said, tears continuing to run down her face.

"Where did she work?"

"She worked at an ad agency in St. Louis. The Stoner Group is the name of the firm."

"What did she do there?"

"She was an assistant to Roger Carroll, the account executive assigned to our political division. They did mostly political campaign advertising."

"What time did you get here?"

"Just shortly before I called 911, whatever time that was."

"Was Amy expecting you?"

"No. She didn't show up for work today, and that's unlike her. I tried to call her several times, but no answer. I got worried and came over here to check on her," Becky said, shaking her head.

"When you arrived, was the front door closed? Was it locked?"

"The door was closed. I knocked several times and when I didn't get an answer, I called her name. When she didn't answer, I tried the handle. The door was unlocked, and I opened it and saw her lying on the floor over there," Becky said, staring at her friend's lifeless body, still trying to maintain her composure while dealing with the horror of the moment.

"Did she live here alone?"

"Yes."

"Do you know whether it was unusual for her to leave the door unlocked?"

"Yes. Very unusual. She used to live in the country She was paranoid about someone breaking in, now that she lived in the city."

"Did you touch anything or disturb anything?" the officer pressed.

"No. I walked in. Saw her and froze. I couldn't move. I couldn't believe what I was looking at. She was my best friend. There was blood. She . . . She was dead. I couldn't believe it," she said, tears and emotion returning.

"When was the last time you talked to her, Becky?"

"Yesterday morning about 11. She said her boyfriend was coming over later. They were not getting along very well." Anger began to replace the other emotions.

"What is her boyfriend's name?"

"Garner Lee."

"What was the problem? Why were they not getting along?"

"I don't know what the specific problem was this time. But there were many problems. I think that he was probably more involved with her than she was with him. Some jealousy issues. He was pretty possessive. A control freak. Didn't want her looking at any other guys, let alone seeing anyone else. I also know he had a temper. She described fights that they had where he became violent. I told her to dump him, but she didn't take my advice. Now he killed her." The anger and hostility in her voice increased with each word.

"How do you know he killed her?"

"I don't. But look at her. I know she didn't kill herself. She was murdered, the door was unlocked, and she told me that he was coming over yesterday. This bastard killed my friend. I know that as sure as I am looking at her dead body."

"Did he ever physically abuse her, that you know of?"

"It wouldn't surprise me, but I never saw any physical evidence of abuse. But again, I wouldn't rule it out. Understand, I didn't like this guy."

Officer Bayer understood that. "Why didn't you like him?" he probed, searching for any detail that would help explain the cause of Amy's death.

"Look at her. She was beautiful. Blond hair, blue eyes, thin, beautiful body. She was gorgeous. Had a great job and was well liked. He was an idiot who flaunted his family's wealth and status. He was a spoiled little rich kid. A trust beneficiary who couldn't make a living on his own."

"Why did she stay with him?' he asked, for purposes of the investigation as well as to satisfy his own personal curiosity.

"Wealth and status. She was my friend, but I also recognized some of her shortcomings. She was 24 years old and a social climber. Listen. While our jobs are good and interesting, and they pay us pretty well, we are really nothing more than glorified clerks. We are support staff and will never make it to the top of this or any other organization. Our lack of education will keep us down. We have to use the talents we have to make it. Her talent was her beauty. And she used it well. Her parents offered no support. They were divorced. Her mother lived in Los Angeles and her father was in Denver. Neither one wanted anything to do with her. She had to make it on her own."

Officer Bayer wondered where this was going. First, she suggested that the boyfriend killed her friend. Now she was beginning to describe her friend as an opportunist who used men or perhaps anyone else to climb the social ladder because she was on her own.

"A guy like Garner put her on top. He took her places. Bought her expensive gifts. She was photographed and mentioned in the social columns. He gave her what she wanted and what she needed . . . status. For him, she was arm candy. They both fed off each other's needs. But there was a difference. He really did care about her. She, on the other hand, would keep him around until something better came along. And that's what caused their problems," Becky Smallwood continued.

As Officer Bayer listened to the candid explanation of the victim's friend, he could not help but wonder what her enemies were like, if Becky was truly her friend. While he appreciated the insight, he had difficulty wrapping his thoughts around the way this woman used men, if her friend was right. He had only been on the job for a few years and, granted, had not seen it all. However, this was one case he would remember. Not so much because it probably involved a murder, his first, but because this one was different. It gave him a little insight into how people can use and manipulate others to get what they want. Sure, in his line of work, he often saw the dark side of human behavior. But he was the same age as the victim, single, and dated regularly. While he had no money or social status, he could not help but wonder whether someday he might fall in love with a woman who did not share that love. *How sad,* he thought as he continued his questioning.

"Who is this guy, Garner Lee? And where does his family money come from?"

"His father is Winston Lee, a lawyer and a state senator. He is the most powerful politician in the state. If you wanted any sort of political favor, he is the guy that you had to go to. Our firm did his campaigns and handles his PR. His mother is a big shot, blue blood lawyer, a partner at McKenzie and Carter. They have a couple hundred lawyers and offices in several states. But their main office is in St. Louis. Apparently, her grandfather was one of the firm's founders. She is a civil rights activist and is involved in several black causes," Becky explained, the tears now completely gone. "Garner is also a lawyer and works for his mother's firm, along with his father. I suspect that Daddy used his influence at the University of Missouri and got him into law school there."

"How long did Garner and Amy date?"

"I don't know. I want to say six months or so. But it could be a little longer."

"I assume that you have met Garner."

"Oh, yeah. I've met him. I've been out with them and witnessed first-hand some of their arguments."

As Officer Bayer continued to question the witness, his attention was directed to the front door. The Homicide detectives, headed by Sandworth, had arrived and would assume control of the scene. Sergeant Jack Sandworth, a 31-year veteran, had been a detective for 18 years, with his fair share of internal affairs complaints and discipline. In fact, a sustained allegation of verbal and physical abuse had resulted in a temporary transfer to uniform out of the Detective Bureau. He has been assigned to the Homicide Division for the past 13 ½ years. He was an old school cop. Street smart. He was not above taking a shortcut or two if that meant solving a murder. He owed that much to the victim. He owed nothing to the perpetrator. Jack Sandworth would head the investigation into the death of Amy Deland. His partner, Detective Leroy Anderson, a 12-year veteran, had spent the last year and a half investigating homicides. Unlike Sandworth, Anderson played by the rules, all of them. He took no shortcuts, followed the evidence wherever it would take him, and analyzed along the way. He was a rising star in the department, bright and articulate, which is why he was in Homicide, a prestigious and coveted assignment.

Unlit cigar in the corner of his mouth; wrinkled, outdated suit accented by a soiled tie; open collar shirt; Sergeant Sandworth began a visual inspection of the scene, speaking to no one in the process. He had a reputation of enjoying an occasional donut while inspecting a blood and guts murder scene. Eventually, he would approach Officer Bayer to take his statement. But first he had to get a feel for the entire scene, the position of the body, the location of the hands, the feet, the head, the injury that potentially caused death as well any other injuries, the blood, and any item that had the potential to be the murder weapon. In short, he had to see, feel and smell death.

The one-bedroom apartment had about a thousand square feet of living space. The front door opened to a living room, which contained a couch, chair, two end tables, a bookshelf and a television. A wall separated the kitchen from the living room. A small dining area was next to the kitchen and was part of the living room. The body was on the floor between the bookshelf in the living room and the front door.

As he was completing his preliminary inspection, the Evidence Technician Unit team arrived. ETU was the arm of the St. Louis Police department responsible for gathering forensic evidence. In this case, their duties would be defined by Sergeant Sandworth. After photographing the scene, this unit would dust for prints, take measurements, take blood samples and bag potential evidentiary items, making certain to preserve the chain of custody and ensure that allegations of tampering by slick defense lawyers could be avoided.

With the exception of a bloody brass statue on the floor beside the victim's body, nothing else seemed to be disturbed in the apartment. There did not appear to be any forced entry. The body was positioned face down in the middle of the living room, her head and body perpendicular to the front door. A large amount of blood covered what appeared to be a deep laceration visible on the back of the skull. A pool of blood and spatter were observed in various locations, both in the immediate vicinity of the body and several feet away. It did not appear that there had been much of a struggle and clearly, the wounds were not self-inflicted. Sandworth surmised that the victim had some familiarity with her assailant, and was struck from behind without warning, as there did not appear to be any defensive wounds.

After a conversation with ETU, Sandworth was ready to talk to Officer Bayer before he interviewed the unknown female seated at the kitchen table. Officer Bayer began reading his notes to the detective. When he mentioned the name Garner Lee, Sandworth stopped him.

"Garner Lee, you say he was the victim's boyfriend? Senator Winston Lee's kid?" Sandworth asked.

"Do you know him?" Bayer asked.

"Let's just say I know of him. He got into some shit, nothing serious, bar room type fight but he got himself arrested because of his mouth. Apparently, he was roughed up a bit in the process. Mommy is a civil rights lawyer with a big law firm, and not a fan of the police. She claimed that we violated the asshole's civil rights and she threatened to sue. After a few phone calls to the chief and the mayor from Mommy and Daddy, the case quietly went away without any publicity. Now, he might be a person of interest in a murder case, if the victim's friend here is credible. Can't wait to get the call from the chief when we go down this road," Sandworth said as he stared at the lifeless body of Amy Deland.

Bayer filled the detectives in on his interview with Becky Smallwood, and she confirmed what she had told him. Of particular interest to the detectives was her statement about a conversation with the victim the day before the body was discovered.

Addressing Smallwood, Sandworth said, "You told Officer Bayer that you had a conversation with Amy yesterday and she told you that Garner Lee was coming to her house later that day."

"Yes."

"What time did you talk to her?"

"Around 11."

"Can you tell me specifically what she told you?"

"She said that Garner was coming over later."

"Is that all she said?"

"Yes. We didn't talk about him very much. She knew I didn't like him and didn't think he was good for her."

"Did she mention anything about him coming over because it was Valentine's Day? Or that they were going to do something special because it was Valentine's Day?"

"I think she said that they were going out to dinner for Valentine's Day. But again, I hated this guy and really had no interest in talking about him or what they were doing together, particularly at a time like Valentine's Day."

"You hated him or disliked . . . ?" Sandworth asked.

"Hated," Smallwood responded before Sandworth had a chance to finish his question.

"Do you know if they went out to dinner often or if he had a favorite restaurant?"

"I don't know. I think they went to Cunnetto's, Gian-Tony's and Kemoll's a lot. They also would go to some bars in Webster and some clubs downtown. The only reason I know that is because she would call me from the bar or club when he would go to the bathroom to complain that he was behaving like an ass. He also belongs to some country club. He used to parade her around there to show her off," she said.

"Do you know the name of the country club?" Anderson asked.

"I think it was the one in Webster Groves, but don't remember the name. She would talk about the things they did, but again, usually I wasn't terribly interested. More power to her. She was having a good time with this guy, but I knew it wouldn't last."

Garner Lee was now at least a person of interest, if not a suspect in the death of Amy Deland. Merely because someone said that Lee was coming to the victim's apartment did not make him a murderer. In fact, although the crime scene looked like Amy was murdered, that, too, would have to be proven beyond a reasonable doubt. Sandworth and Anderson both knew they had a lot of work to do. And that would not be easy if the evidence pointed to the son of a political powerbroker. After all, they both knew well that politics can change the course of justice.

Chapter Two

McKenzie and Carter was one of the largest law firms in the state of Missouri. 173 lawyers occupy offices in St. Louis, Kansas City and Jefferson City as well as New York, Washington, D.C. and Los Angeles. Garner Winston Lee was a second-year associate assigned to the trial division, chaired by his mother Cassandra Lee. As a young associate in a large law firm, Garner's duties included legal research and drafting memoranda to the senior associates who passed them on to the junior partners for review, with the final product landing on the desk of a senior partner. Typical for big firms. Garner would not see the inside of a courtroom or meet a client for several years, if ever.

At 29, Garner was not sure he wanted to continue in the practice of law. His law school career had been delayed by some four years as he tried to *find himself* in places like Europe and the beaches of California, all of which was funded by his mother over the objections of his father. Trouble had a way of finding him in these various venues. Finally, his parents, weary of funding his fun, insisted he return to St. Louis. Rather than obtaining employment, Garner thought law school would be a good idea. Unfortunately, several law schools did not think he would be a good prospect and rejected his applications. But with the influence of his father, the University of Missouri, a state school, welcomed him. To his credit, he graduated and passed the bar exam, some wondering how each of those events happened. He then went to work for McKenzie and Carter.

Garner's freshman year at the firm was less than exemplary. His legal research and writing skills were below average. His enthusiasm did not make up for his lack of ability. Large firms rely upon billable hours from their associates to pay their bills. Those hours are reviewed monthly, and the associates who fall short are asked to explain. Since joining the firm, Garner had not met his monthly billable quota. Of course, when your work day on average begins at 10 am and ends at 4 pm five days a week, it is difficult to amass many billable hours. His lack of ability, along with his work ethic, were the subject of much discussion among the partners.

Firms like McKenzie and Carter attract top law students from the best schools with large three figure starting salaries, bonuses and promises of partnerships and the good life. Garner Lee was the exception to that rule at McKenzie and Carter. His employment was the result of his mother's intervention. Her grandfather, Andrew Brook, was one of the founders of the firm, a truly remarkable accomplishment at a time when there were few African Americans in the practice. Graduating at the top of his Harvard law school class, he clerked for a Federal Appellate Court judge for a year, after which he joined a prestigious New York firm and then returned to his home in St. Louis to start his law practice. His contacts at Harvard and New York allowed him to partner with some of his colleagues to develop the firm of McKenzie and Carter.

But Cassandra Lee did not rely upon her family name to establish herself in the legal profession. A cum laude graduate of Yale law school, Cassandra was a nationally recognized civil rights trial attorney. As an African American female, she understood racial disparity and discriminatory practices. She talked about those issues, wrote about them, and successfully pursued them through the judicial process. She was no friend of the police, the St. Louis Police Department in particular, having successfully sued both on several occasions.

Garner's father was also a lawyer and a partner at McKenzie and Carter. Although he had an office at the firm in St. Louis, he was seldom there. He wasn't much of a lawyer, and had little interest in the practice. Instead, he had lofty political ambitions which were supported by the firm.

Prior to his election as a Missouri State Representative where he served for 8 years, Winston Lee was the lobbyist for McKenzie and Carter and spent most of his time in the Jefferson City office advocating the causes of the firm's clients. Forced to leave the House of Representatives because of term limits, he ran for and won a state Senate seat. Nearing the end of his second and final 4-year term,

11

he was planning a race for the Governor's office. The current governor was also term limited and it was widely believed that Lee was the front runner to be his replacement. He had money, status, name recognition and support from a variety of special interest groups. As the President Pro Tem of the Senate for the last 5 years, some would say that Senator Lee was more powerful than the governor. Clearly, the road to all political favors at some point went through Winston Lee. Like his wife, as an African American, he also experienced discrimination and was sensitive to those issues. However, unlike his wife, his public support of black causes was tempered by political necessity.

The Lees lived in a multimillion dollar mansion in the heart of a gated community in Ladue, a wealthy suburb in St. Louis County. They enjoyed a lake house in the Ozarks during the summer, which Winston also used in the winter while the legislature was in session. Exotic vacations were the norm. They were members of a prestigious country club, were invited to all the parties and social events where people go to be seen and get their pictures in the paper, regularly dined in the finest restaurants throughout the state, and were active in multiple charities.

Garner, their adopted son, also enjoyed some of the same benefits, although he earned none of them on his own. He was a regular at social events where he would be photographed by several newspapers. After all, he was the only child of some very influential people. During his days at the University of Missouri law school, Garner lived in Columbia, Missouri, about two hours west of St. Louis. Summers were spent with his parents in their home, although he headed for the lake when those all too common family disagreements would occur. When he graduated, his parents bought him a condominium in west St. Louis County to keep peace within the family.

The Lees enjoyed the good life. They had money, status, influence and power. They had everything that anyone could want. That is until February 14th. After that date, their lives would change.

Chapter Three

Senator Lee arrived in Jefferson City on Sunday at about 5:30 pm. He was scheduled to have a late dinner with a lobbyist at 6. His dinner was interrupted by a phone call from his son, which he ignored at first. But when he received a text indicating that it was an emergency, he returned the call.

Speaking incoherently at first, Garner settled down and explained that he was at Amy's apartment, and she was dead. Fearing that someone might intercept the conversation, his father told him to get out of the apartment immediately, go home, lock the door and come to Jefferson City in the morning. In the meantime, he advised him to speak to no one about what he had discovered.

After a sleepless night, he arrived at his father's senate office early Monday morning. His father was already in a meeting, but had instructed his secretary to put his son in a conference room out of public sight when he arrived. Garner paced around that room until his father arrived about 45 minutes later.

"What's this about, Garner?" his father asked.

"I went to Amy's apartment yesterday. We were going out for dinner. It was Valentine's Day. When I got to her apartment around 6:30, I found her lying on the floor. She was dead," Garner began as his father listened without comment or expression. "I didn't know what to do. I panicked. I didn't know what to do. I thought about calling the police."

"But you didn't, did you?" his father finally said.

"No. I called you instead and got out of there like you told me."

"Did you touch anything in the apartment?" the senator asked.

"I touched her to see if she was breathing. I might have touched something else. I don't know. All I saw was Amy lying on the floor, blood all over the place. I couldn't believe what I was seeing. It was surreal."

"Garner, you need to think real hard. Did you touch anything?"

"I really don't know. But what difference would that make? I have been in her apartment before. But I remember having some blood on my hand," he recalled.

"Where did that come from?"

"I suppose from her body when I checked to see if she was alive."

"After you got the blood on your hand, did you touch anything in the apartment?"

"I don't know. I was just interested in getting out of there."

"Did you leave any blood on the doorknob or anything else?" his father pressed, trying to determine if his son had left any evidence that would potentially implicate him in the death of this woman.

"Dad, I really don't know what I did or what I touched. I was in shock. I left, I got the hell out of there. You can continue to ask me that question and I will continue to give you the same answer," Garner said emphatically, in an attempt to stop the cross-examination.

Realizing he was getting nowhere, the senator said, "Okay, let's leave it at that for now. Eventually, the police will come knocking on your door and they will have some questions, given your relationship with this woman. I assume that this will get some media attention and your name will be mentioned as her friend . . ."

Friend, Garner thought as his father spoke. This was the woman he loved. This was the woman he thought he might want to spend the rest of his life with. He was well aware that his parents did not approve of the relationship. But that was his decision, not theirs. Now, he understood that his father was interested in publicity and the potential damage to his precious political career because his son was in love with a white woman. A dead white woman at that. He knew his father was already thinking of the spin.

"I do not want you talking to the police. Say nothing. Do not answer any questions, regardless of how innocent you think the question is. Do you understand that, Garner?" his father continued.

"Why can't I answer their questions? I have done nothing wrong," Garner said, challenging his father's advice.

"Garner, we don't know what happened to her. We don't know how she died. If this was a murder, we don't know who is responsible. Given your relationship with her, you will at least be a person of interest, if not a suspect. We need to hope that no one puts you inside that apartment. Any statement you make can be used against you at a later time . . ."

"Used against me? What the hell are you talking about? I didn't kill her. I loved her," Garner said, interrupting his father.

"Garner, I'm not going to argue with you on this. If you are not going to take my advice, what are you doing here?" the senator said, clearly annoyed with his son.

"I'm sorry. I'll listen to you. I don't mean to be difficult. I am just very upset. She's dead. I loved her . . ." Garner said, his voice filling with emotion as his eyes began to fill with tears.

"All right. I understand. But you also need to understand how serious this could become. Have you said anything to your mother about this?"

"No. I didn't say anything to anyone. I just came down here this morning like you told me."

"Fine. I suggest that you go back home and get some sleep. You look like hell. I will take care of talking to your mother."

"Okay."

"One more thing. As I said, I am sure that there will be some media attention on this and your name will come up. If you get a call from any reporter, the same admonition would apply. Say nothing."

"Fine." Garner said, recognizing that once again his father was more concerned about his image than the death of a woman his only son loved. *Some things never change,* he thought as he left his father's office and began a slow drive back to St. Louis—mindful of the speed limit on Interstate 70 to avoid any police contact. As he drove his thoughts wandered, generating both sorrow and fear.

Who would want to kill Amy? Was this a burglary, a rape? Was Amy raped? Would he be accused of murder? He loved her. He couldn't kill her or anyone else. What did

15

he touch in that apartment? He didn't know. It was all so surreal. It was like watching a movie. He was there but he wasn't there. He knew he was a young man of privilege, but had no idea what he was going to do if he was accused of murder. He couldn't worry about it now. He knew he hadn't killed her and needed to stop thinking about it. Everything will be okay. He turned up the radio and kept his eye on the speedometer.

Once Garner left, the senator contacted his wife to let her know what was going on. His conversation was short, providing minimal details over the phone, saying only that Amy was dead and Garner was upset. He assured her that everything was under control and he would provide more details when he got home.

Chapter Four

Around 8 o'clock, first thing Tuesday morning, there was a knock at the door. Fearing the worst, Garner's immediate thought was to ignore it. *But what if it was the police and they saw him park the car and go inside his condo yesterday? Not responding would not look good. It would appear he was hiding and that would make him look guilty. But he hadn't done anything. There was no reason to hide. It might not even be the police. There was only one way to find out; open the door. Sooner or later he expected a visit from the police. Better to get it over with.*

When he opened the door, he was greeted by two males, one white, one black, both wearing business suits. They identified themselves as St. Louis Police officers and produced badges. "Are you Garner Lee?" one asked.

"Yes sir, I am," Garner replied.

"May we come in?" the white officer asked, entering the residence without waiting for a response.

"I'm Sergeant Sandworth and this is Detective Anderson. We need to talk to you for a few minutes," the white officer said as both officers took a seat on a living room couch.

Uncertain what to do, Garner said, "What is this about?"

"You don't know?" was the quick response from an experienced homicide detective.

"No, sir. I don't know what this is about."

"It's about the death of your girlfriend, Amy Deland. You didn't know she was murdered?" Sandworth asked as he stared at Garner, anxious to see his reaction.

The words *death* and *murdered* rattled around Garner's brain like a steel ball in a pinball machine. He was frozen, speechless. Finally, without any sign of emotion or shock, he was able to utter a simple, "No."

Noting his demeanor and disbelieving the response, Sandworth pressed. "When was the last time you saw her?"

"A couple days ago, I guess," Garner said, ignoring his father's advice.

"You have to guess when you last saw your girlfriend? You don't know?" Without waiting for a response, Sandworth went to the heart of the matter. "Did you see Amy at all on Sunday?"

Without thinking about the consequences of any answer that he might give, Garner immediately replied, "No".

"Were you in her apartment at any time on Sunday?"

"I wasn't there," Garner said emphatically.

"What about yesterday? Did you see her at all yesterday?"

"No," another quick and thoughtless response.

"Were you in her apartment at any time yesterday?"

"I wasn't there," Garner said, repeating his earlier response.

"When was the last time you talked to her?"

"A couple days ago, I think."

"Did you plan to go to her apartment on Sunday?"

"No."

"Did you ever tell her that you would be coming over to her apartment on either Sunday or yesterday?"

"No, not that I remember."

"She was your girlfriend. Right?" Sandworth asked, as he did nothing to hide his frustration with Garner's responses.

"Yes."

"How long had you been dating her?"

"I don't know. Around six months or so, I guess."

"Was it a serious relationship?"

"I considered it serious."

"Did she?"

"Yes, she considered it serious. We were in love. Why all these questions?" Garner said, finally recalling his father's advice.

Ignoring the question and realizing that this conversation might soon come to an end, Sandworth continued, "You don't know, you don't remember, you have to guess about whether you saw her on Sunday or even planned to see this woman that you claimed to love on Sunday, which,

18

by the way, was Valentine's Day. You did know that, didn't you?"

"Yes, I did know that."

"Did you ever have any arguments, fights?"

"Listen, I don't know what this is all about and—" Garner began.

"I told you. This is about the murder of your girlfriend Amy Deland," the detective said, interrupting Garner.

"Am I a suspect? Am I under arrest?"

"Nobody is a suspect, and nobody is under arrest at the moment. We are just trying to gather some information and in particular some background information," Detective Anderson injected, moving to calm the situation in an effort to keep Garner talking.

"Well, I feel like a suspect, and I don't feel comfortable with this conversation."

"Listen, Mr. Lee. As I said, we are trying to get some background information on Amy so that we can have a better understanding of her life, which will hopefully help us find out who ended that life. I assume that you are just as interested in finding that out as we are. Aren't you, Mr. Lee?" Anderson said, trying to engage Garner in further conversation.

"Of course, I'm interested in finding out what happened to her," Garner said, avoiding the use of the word murder. "But you show up here without any notice, barge into my home and ask a lot of accusatory questions. Like I said, I feel like a suspect, despite what you say."

"Should we consider you a suspect, Mr. Lee? Did you have some involvement in her death, Mr. Lee?" Sandworth asked, recognizing that Lee wasn't going to answer any other questions, but anxious to see his reaction.

"I'm going to ask both of you to leave my house now," Lee said, ignoring Sandworth's questions.

As soon as the door closed, Garner was on the phone calling his father. "I just had a visit from two detectives from the city," Garner told his father.

"Well, we expected that. They didn't waste any time getting to you. I assume that you didn't say anything to them," the senator said.

"No, I didn't talk to them. But it was pretty scary. I got the impression that they thought that I had something to do with her death," Garner replied, ignoring the fact that he made several statements that could potentially be used against him.

"What do you mean you got the impression that they thought that you had something to do with her death? What did they say? Did they tell you that you were a suspect or a person of interest?"

"No, they didn't say anything like that. It wasn't so much what they said, but more of how they asked questions. I felt their attitude was accusatory. It may be that I'm overreacting. It's a bit disturbing to have cops show up at your door with no prior notice asking you questions about someone you loved."

"I understand. But as long as you didn't say anything, we should be okay. Maybe we should hire a lawyer for you, just to be on the safe side, particularly since you feel that they might be looking at you. If you're right, they will be back, and the lawyer can deal with that."

"Yeah, I think a lawyer would be a good idea," Garner said, hoping for the best, but fearing the worst.

"I'll talk to your mother about that when I get home. But in the meantime, Garner, keep your mouth shut," his father said, ending the conversation.

Chapter Five

As the detectives drove back to their office, they discussed what they had just seen and heard. Sandworth began the conversation. "That little shithead just flat out lied to us. He said he didn't know his girlfriend was dead. Bullshit. Did you see his demeanor when he said that? No emotion whatsoever. He knew goddamn well she was dead. The question is how he knew that. Did he know it because he was the one who killed her? This asshole has something to do with this, and we're going to find out exactly what that is. Can't wait for Daddy to come to his rescue."

"I saw his reaction or the lack of any reaction," Anderson began. "But it may be that he really didn't know she was dead and he was in shock after we told him, which would explain the lack of emotion."

"Are you kidding? He told us they were in love. If I told you that someone you loved was dead or rather murdered, you would show some emotion beyond a deadpan dumb look, like he did," Sandworth replied.

"Everyone is different, Jack. People react differently to the news that a loved one is dead. At the moment, other than what Becky Smallwood told us, we don't have anything to even consider this guy a person of interest. I know that you have a little history with him and I would hope that incident wouldn't get in the way here. If this guy is involved somehow, we're going to have our hands full from downtown with the political fallout," Anderson cautioned.

"I'm not looking to hang this guy. And believe me, I'm aware that the shit will hit the fan if this guy is good for this. It's true, I'm not real fond of Garner Lee or his cop-hater mommy and power-broker daddy. All I know is what my instincts tell me, and they tell me that he has something to do with this. My instincts also tell me that he lied to us just now. He doesn't know whether he saw the woman that he claims to have loved or even talked to her on Valentine's

Day. That conflicts with what our witness, Becky Small-wood, told us. Remember she told us that Amy told her that she expected this loser to come to her apartment on Sunday. But let's see where the evidence takes, us starting with another chat with our only witness, Becky. I'd like to find some other people who can describe Garner's relationship with Amy and corroborate what she told us."

The majority of the work done by detectives involves developing and following leads, most of which are dead ends. Luck also plays a role in any investigation. Sandworth knew this case wouldn't be easy. He had a dead body and a possible murder weapon. If he was lucky, he might get some forensic evidence. And if he was luckier still, he might find someone who saw something. But, as far as he knew, there was no video in an age where, thanks to television, juries demand such evidence, along with DNA connecting the defendant to the crime. As an experienced law enforcement officer, Sandworth was very much aware of the extensive publicity during the past several years surrounding those who were exonerated by DNA evidence after spending years in the penitentiary. That didn't make his job any easier. But he never was one to look for easy. He loved the challenge, the chase. That's why he got up every morning. That's why he was a cop.

Becky Smallwood was able to supply the detectives with the names of three individuals—Karen Brady, Sandra Weston and Lauren Randall—who would be able to describe the relationship between Amy and Garner. Like her, these people had no love for Garner. Each described him as an arrogant, self-centered, ne'er-do-well. Each claimed to have witnessed frequent arguments where Garner lost his temper.

"I saw him lose it several times," Karen Brady told Sandworth.

"When was the last time you saw him lose his temper?" Sandworth asked.

"A couple weeks ago, we were in a bar downtown and he was upset because she was talking to some other guy. He pulled her away from the guy and was yelling at her, causing a disturbance in the bar. The bouncer came over to settle him down and he got into a shouting match with that guy. Eventually he left, and I gave Amy a ride home. Another time, he threw a plate at her."

"When was that?"

"I don't know. Probably about a month ago. It was at her apartment and they got into an argument about something."

"What was the argument about?"

"I don't remember. They were so frequent, it was hard to keep track. Look, Officer, this guy is bad news, and he wasn't good for her. All of her friends knew that, and I suspect that she did, too."

"Then why did she stay with this guy?" Detective Anderson asked, looking a bit confused by the last comment of the witness.

"He had money, or at least his family had money, and he wasn't afraid to spend it. Aside from the regular arguments, he took her to a lot of nice places, restaurants, trips. He gave her frequent gifts. So, she put up with a lot of his bullshit, at least for the moment."

"What does that mean?" Anderson pressed.

"It means that the relationship would eventually wind down. She would get tired of him and move on to the next guy. I know that sounds harsh. But that's how she was with guys. She was a tease, a flirt. She liked the money and all that it brought. And as far as Garner was concerned, she was arm candy. They both got something out of it. She allowed him to parade her around to these social events and in return, she got her name and picture in the paper, as well as the opportunity to meet the next guy with money."

"In your opinion, was this relationship winding down?" Sandworth asked, obviously looking for a motive.

"Yes."

Although Sandra Weston never witnessed any violent interaction between Garner and Amy, she clearly believed that Amy had made a poor choice in her selection of a male companion, describing him as a *silver spoon, possessive prick*. She did, however, recall arguments in which Garner would express his displeasure whenever Amy would even speak to another man. On occasion, he would accuse her of cheating on him, an accusation that Amy would deny.

Lauren Randall expressed the same concerns and opinions as Sandra and Karen. However, the detectives hit pay dirt when she described an actual assault.

"I saw this asshole take a swing at her," Lauren said.

"When was that?" Anderson asked.

"It was about a month ago. My ex-boyfriend and I were at Amy's apartment, and she and Garner got into an argument and he took a swing at her."

"We're going to need a few more details than that, Ms. Randall," Anderson said.

"Okay. We were in the living room and Amy and Garner were in the kitchen. We could hear an argument and when I looked up, I saw him swing at her."

"Did you see the punch land?" Anderson asked, pressing the witness for more details.

"Yes," Randall said after some hesitation.

When Anderson began to ask a follow up question, his partner waived him off. "Thank you, Ms. Randall, we appreciate your input. We will be in touch. If you think of anything else, please let us know," Sandworth said as he handed the witness his card.

"What the hell was that about?" Anderson asked as they walked to their car.

"What do you mean?"

"You know exactly what I mean, Jack. You and I both saw her hesitation before she said that she witnessed Lee hit the victim. You knew I was following up with that and pressing her to be absolutely sure that she actually saw that punch land. She was light on details and I'm not sure that she saw what she claims to have seen. I'm not sure she is credible," Anderson said, clearly troubled by his partner.

"What difference does it make? She saw him take a swing. Who cares whether it landed? The swing is an assault."

"It makes a big difference, Jack. If she is lying about seeing the punch land, then she could also be lying about seeing Lee take a swing. It's a matter of credibility. If she is embellishing on a critical piece of evidence, how can a jury believe anything else she says? A defense lawyer will eat her alive."

24

"I'm satisfied that she is credible. Let the prosecutor figure it out later," Sandworth replied.

"Okay. You're the lead on this, Jack. But when this comes back to bite you in the ass, don't say that I didn't warn you."

"Noted," was Sandworth's only response to Anderson's warning.

Despite her hesitation, Sandworth had gotten what he wanted from this witness. There was no reason to get additional details, at least not right now. The detectives were looking for someone to say that Garner actually assaulted the victim. That would get them one step closer to putting a murder case on the son of a political power-broker. When they eventually took the case to the prosecutor seeking a murder charge, they would present a police report that would not contain any mention of Randall's hesitation or uncertainty. It would say only that this witness saw Garner Lee strike Amy Deland. Ultimately, the prosecutor would talk to the witness and make the final decision as to credibility and whether the jury would hear her testimony. But in the meantime, Garner would be facing murder.

Chapter Six

They had a statement from Lee, in addition to four individuals who witnessed violent arguments between the victim and the suspect, as well as an assault, but that would not be enough to persuade a jury or the prosecutor that Lee murdered his girlfriend. The detectives needed more. Becky Smallwood said she talked to Amy around 11 am Sunday and was told that she was expecting Lee to come to her apartment sometime later that day. But Lee denied that he was in the victim's apartment at all on Sunday or Monday. In fact, he said that he had no plans to go to her apartment on either day. At the moment, there was nothing to rebut Lee's denial and nothing to put him in the apartment at the time of death.

Although the medical examiner had not completed the autopsy, he told the detectives that he believed the time of death was between 5 and 7 pm, Sunday, February 14. Now they had a window. They knew the body was found in the victim's apartment. The preliminary evidence suggested that someone struck Amy on the back of the head causing her to fall. There was no sign that the body had been moved, and it appeared that she died where she fell. Now they needed someone or something to put the killer in the apartment at or near the time of death. Since the forensic examinations were incomplete, the detectives decided to do another canvass of the neighborhood in the hope that someone had seen something. The canvass done by the uniforms had uncovered nothing of value to the investigation.

The victim's apartment, 2B, was on the second floor at 1104 Jamison in the City of St. Louis, and was one of four units. The building itself could only be entered through a front door on the ground level. The two apartments on the top floor were accessed through a staircase. The building had no elevator.

Janice and Jim Berry occupied 1A. They said that they had been home all day Sunday and didn't notice anything unusual. They knew Amy Deland, but only to say hello. They estimated that Amy lived in 2B for about two years. They recognized Garner Lee in a photograph that the detectives showed them. They would see him at the building from time to time and believed that he was Amy's friend, but never met him. They had not seen any visitors on February 14.

Clara Carson was in 1B. She had not been at home when the uniforms did the first canvass and was not there when Sandworth and Anderson returned to do the follow up. They left a card in her door asking her to call them.

Sam and Andrea Jennings lived in apartment 2A, across the hall from the victim. They, too, had not been at home when the uniform officers were knocking on doors, but were there when the detectives arrived. They told the detectives they had lived in the apartment for about three years. They knew their neighbor, Amy, but not well. They could not believe what had happened to her, and were concerned about safety issues.

On February 14, the Jennings had dinner reservations to celebrate Valentine's Day at Charlie Gitto's On the Hill, a local Italian restaurant in the heart of the Italian neighborhood known as the Hill. This quaint section of the city of St. Louis, rich in Italian tradition, is marked by outstanding Italian restaurants and was the boyhood home of both Yogi Berra and Joe Garagiola. The Jennings left their apartment about 6:30 pm to head to the restaurant, although they were not positive of the exact time. They were certain that their reservation was at 7, and the restaurant was a short drive away. If you wanted to keep your reservation, you needed to be on time at the restaurants on the Hill. As they were walking down the steps of their apartment, they passed a man walking up, presumably going to Amy's apartment. They recognized him as a frequent visitor, but had never formally met him. Both Sam and Andrea identified the man in the photograph of Garner Lee as the person that they passed on the staircase on February 14.

After the detectives left the Jennings' apartment, Sandworth wasted no time saying, "I told you so."

"That shithead lied to us. I knew it. And now we've got him in the crosshairs," Sandworth gloated. "That silver spoon son of a bitch killed that girl and is going to fry. Let's see how Mommy and Daddy get him out of this one."

Anderson was quick to challenge his partner's rant.

"Slow down, Jack. We are at the beginning, not the end of this investigation. I'm as anxious to catch a killer as you are. But I want to make sure that we catch the real killer and not just put a case on somebody to close our file. I get the feeling that you have already tried and convicted this Lee guy."

"I haven't tried and convicted anyone. This guy told us that he wasn't at that apartment. Now we find out that he was in the apartment. He was also there during the period that the medical examiner calculates the time of death. He tells us that he didn't know she was dead, and shows no emotion when we tell him that the woman that he supposedly loved was murdered. It's Valentine's Day, and he has no contact with the woman that he claims he loved. Then there is the matter of his temper. The violent arguments. And if that's not enough for you, there is the assault. This guy murdered Amy Deland. No doubt about it. I suspect that it was the result of another violent argument. Unfortunately, this time it didn't end with some punches. This time it ended with a death. But I agree that we have more work to do to be sure that his family doesn't pull some political strings and get him out from under this."

"Obviously, Garner Lee is our primary suspect. But, for starters, we have nothing that puts him inside the apartment. We have two witnesses who put him on a staircase heading in the direction of the victim's apartment. I suppose it's possible that he knocked on the door and when he received no answer, he left. I suppose it's also possible that he entered the apartment and she was already dead. Remember the estimate of the time of death is just that, an estimate," Anderson said.

"Then why did he lie to us about being at the apartment?" Sandworth asked.

"If I recall, we asked him if he was in the apartment. Maybe, he never went in, so he was telling the truth."

"You're not serious. There is not a jury in the world that would buy a bullshit explanation like that. The door was unlocked when her friend found her, and that was unusual. Are you telling me that it is possible that this guy went to her apartment, knocked, got no answer and didn't try the door to see if it was locked? I assume that you're just trying to piss me off with that kind of bullshit," Sandworth said, clearly becoming frustrated with the direction of the conversation.

"I believe that he lied to us. I think the questions that we asked were quite clear. But that won't stop some slick defense lawyer from twisting and turning our words. You know that better than me. Back to my original point. We need a lot more evidence to get this guy charged and convicted. I think that you should forget who he is and who his parents are and get to work with gathering the evidence. Let's finish the neighborhood canvass."

Sandworth said nothing more. Instead, the detectives went to work knocking on doors and interviewing those who were home and willing to talk. They left business cards in the doors of those who were not home. Although the people who were interviewed expressed concern that a murder had occurred in their neighborhood, no one could offer any additional information helpful to the investigation.

Chapter Seven

Senator Lee arrived home from the state capital Tuesday evening. His wife was anxiously waiting for the explanation that her husband was unwilling to provide over the phone.

"What the hell is going on?" Cassandra Lee asked as soon as the senator entered the residence.

"Amy was found dead in her apartment on Sunday," he said.

"I know that. They had a brief story on the news, but nothing in the paper. They are treating it as a murder. How does Garner figure into this, other than the fact that he dated her?"

"He went to her apartment on Sunday and found her."

"Did he contact the police?" she pressed.

"No. He called me from the apartment and I told him to get out of there immediately and say nothing to anyone. I asked him if he touched anything and he told me that he got blood on his hand when he checked to see if she was still alive. He said that he didn't know if he touched anything after he got the blood on his hand."

"Oh my God. Are you serious? He doesn't know if he left any fingerprint evidence in an apartment with a dead body?" she said, shaking her head in disbelief at what she was hearing.

"He said that he was in shock seeing her on the floor. with blood all over the place. When I first talked to him, he was incoherent, rambling. I had to settle him down. I told him to get out of there, go home, lock the doors, not talk to anyone, and come to Jefferson City in the morning. And that's what he did."

"You know it is only a matter of time before the police come knocking on his door," the senator's wife said.

"They already have. They showed up at his house this morning. He called me after they left. He was upset. He said that he got the impression that they thought that he had something to do with her death."

"What did they say? Did they accuse him of some type of involvement?"

"No. It's not anything that they said specifically, but just how they were acting," the senator said.

"I assume that he was smart enough to keep his mouth shut."

"He said that he didn't say anything. Whether he did or not remains to be seen."

"These lying bastards will say that he made some type of incriminating statement, particularly if they have no other evidence to connect him to her death. Did he tell you what the scene looked like? Did he have any idea of what caused her death? Or who might have killed her?"

"I didn't ask him any questions like that. I was more interested in settling him down and making sure that he didn't say anything."

"How in the hell did they get to him so fast? It was no secret that he was involved with her, but that was quick. I'm guessing that one of her friends put them onto him. I can only imagine what else they said about him," she added.

"I suppose that's possible. But all they had to do was google her name and they would have seen pictures of them together at various social functions."

"I told him to dump her low life ass on more than one occasion. He would complain that she was a flirt and they would continually argue. In fact, he just told me about a recent argument that they had. But no, he had to have it his way and ignore my advice. I was getting push back from people every time his picture was in the paper with her. Well, now it may come back to bite him," Garner's mother said.

"Well, he didn't dump her, and we have to deal with the fact that his girlfriend is dead, murdered, and he may be a suspect. We also need to deal with the fact that there will be media coverage which will impact him and us. But I suppose the first thing that we have to decide is whether we need to get him a criminal lawyer. That's probably not a bad idea. However, we need to consider how that will look when the press starts to run with the story. The public perception will be that only guilty people hire criminal lawyers. And certainly that will be the spin that the media will put on it with the help of our political enemies, at a time that we planned to start the gubernatorial campaign. That won't be good."

"I understand the political ramifications. But I also understand that this is our son, our only child, we are talking about. I'm not sure how a criminal lawyer is going to help right now and, as you point out, may do more harm than good. But before we make any final decision, I think it would be a good idea to talk to our son and see what he has to say. I'm also interested in his answers to some of the questions that you didn't ask. Let's get him on the phone."

Garner's mother made the call on a speaker phone. After a few moments of social conversation, she got right to the point after clarifying the purpose and nature of the call, in case others were listening.

"Your father and I have some questions for you about Amy. But before we begin, I want to say that these questions will be asked in an attorney-client context. At this point, your father and I are acting as your attorneys and this conversation will be protected by the attorney-client privilege. Do you understand?"

"What are you talking about? Why are we talking about a privilege?" Garner asked, confused by the unusual start of a conversation with his parents.

"Because I don't know if other people are listening or may be recording this conversation," his mother, now his lawyer, said.

Cassandra Lee had earned her reputation in the legal community as a fierce litigator, always prepared and always one step ahead of those who dared to oppose her. The preamble to the conversation with her son was but one example. She knew the law and how to use it both as a sword and a shield. Now her son had a potential legal problem, a criminal one at that. She would use her instincts as a mother, her skill as a lawyer, her money, politics and anything else she needed to ensure that nothing happened to her only child.

"Now, with that in mind, tell us what happened on Sunday," she directed.

"I talked to her on Sunday. We were going to go out to dinner for Valentine's Day. We had a disagreement the day before and I thought it would be a good idea to go out, have a nice dinner, celebrate Valentine's Day and put the disagreement behind us. I told Mom about this argument . . .."

"You told me about many arguments that you had with her," his mother added.

Ignoring the comment, he continued, "I got to her apartment around 6:30 or so. We had a reservation at Kemoll's downtown at 7 o'clock. I was looking forward to it. When I got to her place, I knocked on the door, but got no answer. I knocked a couple more times, called her name, but no response. I tried the door. It was unlocked. That was unusual as she always kept it locked. I opened the door and that's when I saw her lying there, blood . . .." Garner said, emotion interrupting his story.

"Take your time, son," his father said, in an attempt to calm the situation so the explanation could continue.

"She was lying on the floor in the living room by her bookcase. Her head was bloody, and blood was on the floor," Garner said as he slowly and deliberately continued his explanation.

"Did you see where she was injured?" Cassandra interrupted.

"Yes. It looked like someone hit her in the back of the head."

"Why do you think someone hit her as opposed to her falling and striking her head on something?" his mother asked, interrupting again.

"Because there was a statue on the floor next to her. There was blood on it. It looked to me like she was walking to the door when someone hit her in the back of the head with this statue."

"Do you know who might have done this to her?" his father asked.

"I have no idea."

"What did you do after you found the body?" his mother asked.

"I tried to find a pulse to see if she was alive. I couldn't find one, and I didn't hear her breathing. I knew she was dead. But I think I knew she was dead the minute I walked in. I then called Dad and left."

"I asked you once before whether you touched anything when you were in the apartment. You said you didn't know. Have you had time to think about that?" the senator asked.

"I really don't know. I was in shock. But what difference would it make? I have been in her apartment before and touched many things."

"That statue that was on the floor next to her. Did you touch that?" his mother asked.

"I don't think so. But again, I was in shock, seeing her lying there."

"And you haven't told anyone about this, other than your mother and me, is that correct, Garner?" his father continued.

"Yes."

"And that would include the police when they came to your house?" his father continued.

"Yes."

"Tell me as best that you can what specifically they asked and what specifically you said in response," his mother said, seeking as much detail as possible.

"It was very upsetting, but I will do the best I can to answer your question. They asked me about my relationship with Amy. How long we were dating. They were trying to see what I knew about her death. Did we have any fights, arguments? Was I interested in finding out what happened to her? When I responded, vaguely or not at all, they became more aggressive and suggested that I really wasn't interested in what happened to her and that I really didn't love her or even care about her. They asked me if I was at her apartment on Sunday and whether . . ."

"Did you answer that question?" his mother asked, interrupting his response and recognizing the significance of that question.

"I told them that I wasn't there," Garner said, hearing the concern in his mother's voice.

"Why in the hell did you do that, Garner?" she asked without any hesitation.

"Because that's what Dad told me to do."

"I didn't tell you to do that. I told you to keep your mouth shut and not answer any questions. I explained to you the harm that could be done if you talked. What is it that you didn't understand?" The senator was now yelling.

"You told me that it was important that no one was able to put me in her apartment. So, I told them I wasn't there. They were very intimidating. I was in shock. I didn't expect them to be at my house that quickly. Don't be so quick to criticize until you have been there."

"You are a total idiot. You can't . . ."

"That's enough," Cassandra interrupted. "This isn't going to get us anywhere. What's done is done. I need to figure out where we are going to go from here. I need some time to think. We will get back to you, Garner. In the meantime, keep your mouth shut," she said, ending the call to her son.

"You're the smart trial lawyer in this family. What are we going to do to prevent this idiot from going to the penitentiary?" the senator asked, truly aggravated by his son's responses.

"I don't know," was her short reply.

Chapter Eight

Sandworth needed something to put Garner Lee inside the victim's apartment. He knew he had a witness that would put him in the apartment building, walking up the stairs heading in that direction. But that was not enough. He had a statement from Lee that his witness would rebut. That would show that Lee was lying when he said he did not see Amy on the day of the murder. But that was not enough. He needed more. A fingerprint. DNA. But even those wouldn't work, because Lee was the boyfriend and had been in the apartment on numerous occasions. His lawyer would claim this type of forensic evidence proved nothing.

In any criminal investigation, involving the son of a high-profile and powerful politician or not, investigators not only needed to gather evidence sufficient to prove guilt beyond a reasonable doubt, but they also had to anticipate potential defenses. How would some slick defense lawyer twist and turn clear evidence of guilt? An experienced investigator like Sandworth knew that the defendant would claim that walking up the stairs toward the victim's apartment did not mean that he entered that apartment. *Because the time of death cannot be established precisely to the minute, Lee will say that he knocked on the door, got no answer and left. Of course, that's ridiculous. This is her boyfriend, the door is unlocked and he wouldn't open the door? On Valentine's Day, no less. Bullshit, fucking lawyers, no wonder people hate them,* Sandworth thought, as he tried the case in his head.

Sandworth was particularly interested in any forensic evidence that the lab people gathered. Visually, the scene had looked clean, except for what appeared to be a bloody print on the front door handle. He didn't know about any latents. Whether the lab had enough to match anything was another question—a question that Sandworth needed answered as soon as possible. Daily calls to the lab did nothing to expedite the process and just aggravated the technician responsible. But Sandworth knew that if he couldn't connect some physical evidence to Lee, he couldn't put him inside the apartment. The best he would be able to do was put him in the building heading toward the victim's apartment at or near the time of her death. Although it was compelling circumstantial evidence, it would not be enough to put Lee where he belonged, in the penitentiary for the rest of his life. Fucking lawyers.

Fingerprints can generally be found on practically any solid surface, including the human body. Prints found on hard surfaces are either visible (patent) or invisible (latent). Visible prints are observed when a substance like blood, dirt, ink and the like are transferred from a finger or thumb to the hard surface. They can be observed on a variety of surfaces, including hardwood floors like the ones found in Amy's apartment. Latent or invisible prints are formed when the body's natural oils or sweat are deposited on another surface. Because they are invisible, these prints are detected through powders or chemicals.

Once the prints are collected at the scene, they are sent to the lab for analysis. There the quality and quantity of the evidence is reviewed to determine if it can be used for comparison. If there are insufficient characteristics, the examination ends there. If, however, the sample contains enough characters to compare to a known print, the examination continues, with the analyst identifying those characters that are suitable for comparison with the amount of standard deviation that will be acceptable. Often, certain unique characteristics are observed, such as a scar which can help indicate where to begin the comparison process.

If the known suspect print is unavailable, fingerprint databases are searched. The FBI's Integrated Automated Fingerprint Identification System (IAFIS) is the largest fingerprint database in the world. Several years ago, it held more than72 million print records from criminals, military personnel, government employees and other civilian employees.

As Sandworth sat at his desk going through the photographs of the scene looking for something, anything, that would put Garner Lee inside the apartment, the phone rang. It was the lab. "I've got good news, bad news on that murder case that you called me 100 times about. Come on over and I'll show you what I got," the lab technician told Sandworth.

Chapter Nine

"That's the fastest I have ever seen you get over here, Sandworth," Jim Barber the lab technician said, as Sandworth and his partner walked into the lab.

"Don't be a smart ass, Barber. Just tell me what you have," Sandworth responded, in no mood for chit chat.

"Wow. The way you have been pushing me on this case, someone may think that you have a personal interest in this one," Barber said.

"Not personal, but this does involve the kid of a high-powered politician," Detective Anderson said.

"Who is that?"

"Senator Winston Lee," Anderson replied.

"Oh. That's some political muscle. Does the chief know about this?"

"There is nothing to tell the chief right now. We don't have anything that puts this kid in the house. But you're going to help us take care of that problem. Right, Barber?" Sandworth said.

"How is Lee's kid connected to this case?"

"He was the boyfriend of the victim," Anderson said, as Sandworth waited patiently for Barber to tell him what he found.

"But, if he was the boyfriend, I would think that his prints and DNA would be all over the place in the victim's house."

"That could be a problem," Anderson said.

"Jesus, Barber, just tell us what you got. We've got work to do," Sandworth said, obviously annoyed by the dialogue and losing his patience.

"Now, is that any way to treat someone who is doing you a favor, Sandworth?" Barber asked, enjoying the fun he was having with the investigator.

"I swear Barber, if you don't tell me what you have in the next five seconds, you won't be talking to anyone anytime soon," Sandworth said.

"Better tell him, Jim. You know what a bad ass he is," Anderson added.

"Okay, Leroy. I'll do it for you. I have good news and bad . . ."

"Will you please just tell us what you have without all of the editorial comments?"

Ignoring the interruption, Barber repeated, "I have good news and bad news. The good news is that I have prints, both patent and latent. Most of the prints are from the victim, lifted in various rooms. No surprise there. I also have a print on the outside doorknob that matches Becky Smallwood. We got elimination prints from her because I understand that she was the one who found the victim and called it in. I got another partial off the outside doorknob, but not enough for a comparison. I got a print off the brass statue. Of course, if it's your suspect's, he can always say that he touched that statue during some other time that he was in the apartment. But I did get something that I think you can use. It may not put your Lee kid in the apartment, but it will put someone who has something to do with this in that apartment. I have a bloody print."

"Is that the one on the inside front doorknob?" Sandworth asked.

"Yes."

"Amy was lying face down with the top of her head perpendicular to the front door. A bookcase on her left. It appeared as though she was walking toward the front door when she was struck on the back of her head with the brass statue. Photographs of the body lying face down taken from the bottom of the body depicted an injury to the left side of the back of the skull, suggesting the killer was left-handed or at least used the left hand to administer the blows."

"Did you get a match on the bloody door print?"

"No. I can't match that print or the one on the statue to anything anyone has on file. I need comparison prints. We also have DNA off the statue. But again, I have nothing to compare it to."

Although he didn't have any matches, Sandworth had something that might lead him to the killer. He was confident that both prints and the DNA would match Lee. *Otherwise, why would Lee have lied about being in that apartment? If he didn't murder his girlfriend, why wouldn't he have called 911 like Becky Smallwood did when he found her?* Sergeant Jack Sandworth was certain that Lee was his guy. But now they had to get his prints and a DNA sample.

On their way back to the office, Sandworth said, "We need to get a set of prints and DNA from Lee. I doubt that he is going to give those up voluntarily."

"Probably not. But what happens if we get a match on the doorknob but not the statue or vice versa?" Anderson asked.

"I would like both, but I'll take one or the other," Sandworth replied.

"Well, let's look at the possibilities here," Anderson, the ever-vigilant and cautious analyst, said. "The bloody print on the doorknob definitely puts someone in the apartment at or near the time of the murder. By itself, that doesn't mean that the person who left the print is the killer. If the same print is on the statue, maybe we have our guy. But if the print on the doorknob is different than the print on the statue, we have a problem."

"What kind of problem?"

"It potentially means that we have two people in the apartment at or near the time of death. It could also mean that the person who left the door print, came in and found the body, but did not do the murder. To complicate things even more, if Lee's print is on the statue but not the door, he could claim that he handled that statue during one of his many visits to the apartment. Nobody disputes the fact that she was his girlfriend. In that case, we may have nothing until we find the person who left the print on the doorknob. In the meantime, we would be back to square one with Lee. And in fact, if his print is not on that door, he may be in the clear. Or, even if his print is on the door, he could claim that he came in, found her, and left."

"Goddamn it, Anderson. You're making my head spin. You think way too much and worry about shit that may never happen. I'll cross all those bridges if and when we get to them. Now let's go get a print and close this case, so my head will stop spinning."

Chapter Ten

She was only 24 years old. Her whole life was in front of her. But someone, for whatever reason, ended it. She has no future. Her dreams were extinguished like a cigarette in an ashtray. Just that fast. A life taken away. Her parents were conspicuously absent at the memorial service arranged by Amy's friends.

One by one, the speakers reminisced about the life and times of Amy Deland. She was beautiful, smart, a friend to everyone, and loved by all. Her coworkers at The Stoner Agency talked about what a hard worker she was, a dedicated employee, always willing to lend a helping hand. Friends recalled how caring she was. The call to a sick friend, a ride when a car was in the shop, babysitting for a friend in need on a Saturday night and on and on.

For this day, in memory, Amy Deland was perfect. No one talked about the flaws. Her friend and coworker, Becky Smallwood did not tell the mourners that Amy was an opportunist, a social climber who used her beauty to climb the ladder until something better came along like she had told Officer Bayer. Today, for Becky Smallwood, Amy had no shortcomings.

Garner Lee sat alone in the back of the church, unnoticed. For him, Amy was perfect, flawless. Although they'd had their fair share of disagreements, he loved her and had wanted to spend the rest of his life with her. He'd routinely fought with his parents, defending her. She had no family members who cared. He was her family. But now she was gone and there was nothing he could do about that. Filled with emotion, tasting the salt from the tears that flowed down his cheeks, he thought only of the good times. There were no bad times, at least not today.

Listening to Amy's friends speak, he felt their pain. He saw it in their faces and heard it in their voices. But he also recalled the many times that these same people encouraged Amy to end the relationship. They'd never accepted him and recognized the love he had for this woman. They made no secret of their animosity toward him. He never understood why they felt this way. Was it him or something he did? Was it his parents? Was it a black man involved with a white woman? All questions that lingered without answers. However, this was not the time to dwell on past issues and problems. Today was a celebration. It was Amy's day.

As the service ended, Garner knew that he needed to leave before he was detected by those who would not welcome his presence. Her friends would not be pleased to see him, and he did not want to add to their grief. He would leave, quietly and unnoticed. He did what he knew he had to do, say goodbye to the woman he loved.

Chapter Eleven

During the ride home, Garner tried to think of something other than the death of Amy. But try as he might, his thoughts continued to return to the realization that he would never see her again. She was gone for good. His emotions were running wild. He was preoccupied to such an extent that he didn't notice an unmarked police vehicle parked in front of his house as he pulled into his driveway. Sandworth and Anderson greeted him as he got out of his vehicle.

As planned, Anderson began the conversation. "Hello, Garner. How are you?"

The detectives were there to get Lee's fingerprints and a DNA sample. The easiest way to do that was through his cooperation, rather than a court order which might attract media attention and the involvement of his father. They were not ready for either at the moment. Both would come soon enough. They thought that it would be better if Anderson handled the situation, since the last visit had not created a warm and fuzzy feeling between Sandworth and Lee. In fact, Anderson suggested that his partner remain in the car, but Sandworth was not having any part of that.

"Fine," Garner said, surprised by the visitors in his driveway.

"I'm Detective Anderson and this is Detective Sergeant Sandworth. We talked to you before about Amy Deland."

"I remember."

"Listen, Garner, as you know, we are looking to find out who killed your girlfriend and we need your help. We know that you didn't have anything to do with that, because you told us you weren't even at her apartment on Valentine's Day. Right?"

"Yes."

Another admission that could be used against him at trial. It's okay for cops to lie to suspects; just part of the game.

"We need to get some elimination prints from you," Anderson said, continuing his friendly tone.

"What's that?"

"Good question. Obviously, before her tragic death, you were in Amy's apartment. We would expect your fingerprints to be there. But we need your prints to match to the prints that we know we will find in there and eliminate those prints. In that way, we can identify the prints of people that may have no reason to be there. Hopefully, that will then lead us to the person responsible for the murder of your girlfriend."

"Did you find some prints in her apartment?" Garner asked.

"No," Anderson said. Another lie.

"Then why do you need my prints, if you don't have anything to compare?"

That was a fair and logical question, but one that aggravated Sandworth. He was tired of playing nice with this guy. He began to say something, but his partner waved him off.

Realizing that he had made a mistake, Anderson began to back pedal. "I didn't mean that there were no prints in the apartment. Obviously, there are prints. We are in the process of eliminating the prints of people that had a reason to be there. We are gathering the prints from Amy's friends, family and people that would have had a reason to be in the apartment. Then, after we eliminate all those prints, we will be able to see if we have a print or prints that can't be eliminated. Do you understand?" Anderson said, hoping he didn't blow it as his partner stared at the suspect waiting for a response.

"I understand what you're saying. But the last time you were here, I got the impression that you were accusing me of killing Amy."

"Let's go get a court order. This is bullshit. Obviously, this guy doesn't want to help us catch the person responsible for murdering his girlfriend," Sandworth injected.

"Listen, Garner. I know that you want us to find the person who did this. And I know that you want to help us.

When we were here last time, this investigation was just starting, and everyone was a suspect. Since that time, we got more information and we know that you are not involved. But let me tell you how this will work. We can get a court order to get your prints. If we have to go down that road, the media may find out that Amy's boyfriend refused to cooperate in the investigation and refused to voluntarily give up his fingerprints. Now, how do you think that will look?" Anderson said.

"Probably not good."

"And the media won't know that these are just elimination prints. And, if we must go this route, we won't tell them. It will then look like you are a suspect and have something to hide. You don't want that to happen, do you, Garner? If the press gets ahold of this, think about what the headline will be. '*Son of a Prominent State Senator is a Murder Suspect*'. How do you think your father is going to like that?"

"He would be upset."

"So, what do you want to do?" Anderson pressed.

Garner didn't answer immediately. He was trying to decide what to do. *Should he call his parents? But if he did that, he would look guilty. If they can get a court order and force him to give his fingerprints, what's the difference? They will get them one way or the other. But he didn't do anything wrong, so how can giving them fingerprints hurt? Plus, they said he was not involved.* Finally, he said, "Well, I guess it would be all right."

"Okay, let's get it done."

"Where do I have to go?" Garner said.

"We'll do it downtown at headquarters and we'll take you and bring you back. It won't take that long."

"I can drive myself," Garner said, hesitant to ride with two police officers.

"Parking is a problem down there and it would be easier and faster if you rode with us. Come on. Let's get it done and get you back here."

"Okay," Garner agreed, still uncertain as to whether this was the right thing to do.

Anderson decided to wait until they got to the station to request a DNA sample. No sense complicating the issue with more than one request. If he agrees to give up his prints, should be no problem getting a little spit.

Chapter Twelve

The fingerprinting process was painless. Over the objection of his partner, Sandworth decided to hold off on obtaining the DNA sample. There was a risk in getting both samples. He wanted to wait to see if they got a match on the fingerprints. If they got a match on the prints, but not on the DNA on the statue, that would be a problem for the prosecution. Sandworth figured they could always get a court order for the DNA if Lee was no longer cooperating later.

As promised, the detectives gave Garner a ride home. But now, he had to make a difficult decision. Should he let his parents know that he had voluntarily given his fingerprints to the detectives investigating Amy's murder? Why wouldn't he provide those things? He was an innocent man. He didn't kill the woman he loved, and he wanted to find the person who did.

"You did what?" the senator yelled.

Recognizing that his disclosure was a mistake, Garner said, "There's no need to yell at me."

"No need to yell? What was it about not talking to these people did you not understand?"

"Dad, I have nothing to hide. I didn't have anything to do with Amy's death. I didn't kill her. I loved her."

"Oh, my God. You really don't get it. It doesn't matter whether you are innocent. They can still put a case on you. And you help them do that when you cooperate and open your mouth."

"They told me that they know that I wasn't involved," Garner said.

"They lie," was his father's quick response.

"That may be. But I know that I was not involved. They also told me that they could get a court order and that wouldn't look good for you or me. They were going to get my fingerprints one way or the other. I thought it was best to do it voluntarily."

"The problem with doing it voluntarily is that you have waived any legal challenge that you might have. Perhaps the court would have ordered you to comply and perhaps not. We could have had a hearing and resisted. But it doesn't matter now. Did you sleep through your criminal law class in law school?"

"They said that a hearing like that would attract media attention and make me look bad, like I was guilty and hiding something."

"We need to get your mother involved in this conversation. I'll call you back after I find her," Senator Lee said, abruptly ending the conversation.

As he waited for the return phone call, Garner tried to figure out where all of this was going. *If his father was right and the police wanted to put a case on him, he could wind up accused of murder. And worse yet, convicted and sent to the penitentiary. If his parents thought he was guilty, what chance would he have with people that don't even know him?* His thoughts were interrupted by the phone.

This time, both mother and father were on the call, with his mother beginning the conversation with less emotion than his father previously. She wanted to know if, in addition to samples of his fingerprints, whether he gave the police anything else. She seemed less than convinced by his denial and pressed the question of whether he made any statements, whether or not he considered them incriminating.

"Where did they do the fingerprinting?" she asked.

"They took me downtown to police headquarters," Garner answered.

"They took you? You rode with them in their car and didn't drive yourself?" she pressed.

"Yes."

"What did you talk about during that ride?"

"Nothing, really."

Garner's mother was a trial lawyer and a skilled one at that. She was not about to accept that answer.

"Garner, I need you to tell me as best you can what that nothing was."

"Why are you cross-examining me? There wasn't much conversation and there was no conversation about Amy. They were being nice to me, to try to get me to talk."

"Please tell me as best you can, the general nature of the conversation. I don't need to know the specifics of what you talked about."

"We talked about the traffic into downtown, the weather and some sports. That's all I can remember. Most of the ride was in silence, other than the chatter from the police radio."

The senator listened patiently to the dialogue. His only concern was whether anyone had seen him going in or out of police headquarters. Garner explained that they went in a back door and used a private elevator.

"You know that I'm planning to run for governor?" his father said.

No response.

"I can't have a headline that you are a suspect in murder case. You do understand that, don't you?"

Still no response.

"He understands," his mother said. "My concern is why they want those prints."

"I was told that they were for purposes of elimination. Since she was my girlfriend, I was obviously in the apartment and my prints would be there. They wanted to figure out which were mine along with others who would have visited Amy. They could then eliminate those and get to the prints of someone who had no business there, other than to harm her. That's one of the reasons that I didn't have any problem giving them what they wanted."

"I'm telling you, Garner, they didn't want those prints to eliminate you. They wanted them to include you. And the more that you give them, the better they can build a murder case against you," she said.

"But I didn't ..."

"Stop," his father interrupted. "You just don't get it. You are ..."

Now his mother interrupted, recognizing that this conversation was going nowhere. "Okay. That's enough. Garner, if you hear from the police again, please call me immediately. There's nothing we can do at the moment. We will just have to wait and see where this goes. In the meantime, please don't discuss this with anyone in the office. I don't want anyone in the firm involved in this. Understand?'

"Yes."

"In fact, it is probably a good idea if you take the next few days off, until we see where this is going. I don't want the police showing up here. We will talk to you soon," his father said as he ended the conversation.

"What do we do now?" the senator asked his wife.

"We wait, and hold our breath."

Chapter Thirteen

The lab wasted no time doing the analysis. What would ordinarily take a week, took a day, probably because they were tired of the phone calls from Sandworth. Anderson was out of the office when his partner got the results of the comparison. Sandworth couldn't dial the phone fast enough to share the good news.

"We got him. We got the little bastard. Let's see his old man get him out of this one," Sandworth told his partner.

"Slow down, Jack, and tell me what we have," Anderson said in an effort to calm his excited partner and understand the new development in the case.

"I just got a call from the lab and we have a match on the print. Lee's print is in the blood on the inside doorknob."

"Didn't we also have a print on that brass statue that we think is the murder weapon?" Anderson asked.

"Yes," Sandworth said unwilling to voluntarily provide any additional information on that evidentiary item.

"Is Lee's print on that?" Anderson pressed.

"No," Sandworth said, again unwilling to expand his answer.

"Whose print is on the statue?"

"We don't know."

"We have a print in blood on the inside doorknob that matches Garner Lee, the boyfriend. But his print is not on the murder weapon. Do I have that right?" Anderson asked.

"That's what we have forensically."

"Well, with that, how can you say we got him?"

"We can put him in that apartment at or near the time of her death. He told us that he was not in her apartment and didn't see her that day. We knew that was false, because we have the witnesses that will put him at least in the building on the day of the murder. But until now, we couldn't put him inside that apartment. Now we can. He lied to us. The only reason he lied about being in her apartment was because he killed her. This little prick is going down."

"Merely because he was in her apartment doesn't mean that he killed her. If, in fact, that statue is the murder weapon, how do you explain that his prints aren't on that, but someone else's are?"

"I can't. But I am not worried about that and it won't be a problem," Sandworth said emphatically.

"In my opinion, we don't have enough."

"What more do you want? Video?" Sandworth said sarcastically.

"No. I'd like a little more evidence that we have the right guy."

"Like what?"

"For one thing, I'd like to know whose print is on that statue."

Sandworth just listened. He didn't respond.

"As you well know, thanks to television, juries these days like to see the science. Yes, he clearly lied to us. But there are many reasons that people lie to the police. That doesn't make him a murderer. Did we hear from the medical examiner yet?" Anderson continued.

"Yes. I just got off the phone with him right before the lab called. A skull fracture, blunt force trauma, brain swell, all of which was caused by the statue. No surprises there. He amended the time of death a little. Originally, he thought 5 to 7 pm on the 14th. But now, he is thinking it could be 4 to 7. I suppose it could be plus or minus either way. The report isn't finished yet. He also said that it looks like whoever did this is either left-handed or used his left hand to cause the injury, because of the angles and locations of the fractures. But I told him that probably doesn't need to be in the report," Sandworth said.

"You told the medical examiner to keep a detail like that out of the report? Are you kidding? Why would you do that?" Anderson asked incredulously.

"I told him that information wasn't relevant for several reasons. First, he told me that was his off the cuff opinion. Second, left-handed or right-handed has nothing to do with the cause of death. She was whacked in the head with that statue. That's how she died. His job is to tell us how she died, and he did that. These medical examiners like to offer opinions about all kinds of irrelevant shit."

"But you'll accept those irrelevant opinions when they are consistent with your theory of the case. You and I both know that the real reason that you don't want him to put that in the report is because we don't know if Lee is left-handed. And if he's not, that's a problem for us. What about the blood on the statue? Do we know if that is a match to the victim?"

"Yes. It's the victim's."

"You're way off-base on this one, Jack." Anderson knew that there was no sense in debating the issue. Sandworth was determined to put Garner Lee in the penitentiary. "I'm going to check out those restaurants that Becky Smallwood gave us to see if Lee made a reservation for Valentine's Day. At least then we'll have some evidence to link this guy to the murder," Anderson said.

Sandworth couldn't resist continuing the discussion. "That's fine. But I think that we have all that we need to move forward with this case. I'm going over to apply for a warrant. I have a prosecutor over there that I know will be friendly," Sandworth said.

"That's a mistake, Jack. I don't think we are ready. You may get the warrant issued through your friend, but at the end of the day, we need to prove the case. I'm opposed to applying for the warrant at this time."

"I know you are. I'll let you know whether the prosecutor agrees with you or me," Sandworth said as he ended the phone call.

Anderson felt strongly that the evidence was insufficient to convict Garner Lee of the murder of Amy Deland. But he also recognized that his partner believed that Lee would be convicted with the evidence they had. He also knew that Jack Sandworth would not tell the prosecutor of their disagreement when he applied for the warrant. Sandworth was the senior investigator on the case. He had more experience than Anderson. While the junior detective could express his opinion and disagree, in the end, Sandworth's decision would control. But Anderson wondered what was motivating his partner in this case. He had worked some other cases with Sandworth, and he was fair and thorough. However, in this case, there seemed to be a rush to judgment, and Anderson wondered why. *Was it because of Lee's family background? Was there some history with Lee's father or his mother?* He was a kid of privilege, but Sandworth had dealt with kids of privilege who committed crimes before and had not pursued those with the same enthusiasm. Regardless of his partner's motives, Anderson just hoped that they had the right guy for this crime.

Chapter Fourteen

When Anderson returned to the office, he made some calls to see if Lee had made any reservations for dinner on Valentine's Day. He started with the country clubs. Becky Smallwood thought that he was a member of a club in Webster Groves. There were two in that area; Algonquin and Westborough. He started with Westborough, but they had no member with the name Lee. Algonquin, however, did have a Garner Lee on their membership roster, but had no record of a dinner reservation.

That left the restaurants that Becky Smallwood had mentioned. He started with Gian-Tony's. But no luck. They had no reservation in the name of either Garner Lee or Amy Deland. Cunnetto's said that they did not take any reservations for dinner. It was first come, first served. But Anderson figured that a high roller like Lee would probably not go to a casual place like Cunnetto's for Valentine's Day. He would want some ambiance to impress Amy, and Kemoll's would be just the place. It was an old established St. Louis restaurant that in addition to fine dining was located on the 40th floor of the Metropolitan Square building with spectacular views of downtown St. Louis, the Arch and the Mississippi River. He was right. Kemoll's had a 7 o'clock reservation for two in the name of Garner Lee on February 14. But according to the manager, the customer was a no show, and Anderson knew why.

Just as Anderson finished his restaurant investigation, his partner returned to the office. Sergeant Sandworth had his warrant. Garner Lee would now be arrested and charged with murder in the second degree. That would not make either Lee or his politically powerful family happy. It also did not make Detective Anderson happy, and he was not shy about sharing his disappointment.

"You persuaded your friend to charge Lee with murder two?" Anderson asked, hostility in his voice.

In the state of Missouri, murder in the second degree carries a punishment of 10 to 30 or life in the penitentiary. In order to convict Garner Lee, the prosecution would have to prove the defendant knowingly caused the death of Amy Deland or with the purpose of causing serious physical injury to Amy, caused her death.

"Yes. It was between that or voluntary manslaughter. The prosecutor thought it would be better to charge the more serious felony, in the hopes of possibly negotiating a plea to manslaughter," Sandworth said.

"This is bullshit. We both know that we aren't going to make either murder or manslaughter stick. We don't have the evidence, and some slick defense lawyer is going to kick our asses. On top of that, his high-powered family is going to kick whatever is left of our asses. You also need to be ready when we are dragged into the chief's office to explain what we have and why we charged the son of the guy that probably was responsible for making him the chief. Did your friend, the prosecutor, make the connection that this is the senator's kid?"

"If she did, she didn't say anything."

"And of course, you didn't mention it either," Anderson said.

"Why would I mention that? I don't care if he is the son of the President of the United States. If he committed a crime, he should be prosecuted, regardless of who he is. There isn't a special law for people of privilege. And my job is to put those people in a cage for a very long time."

"That's more bullshit, Jack. Get off your high horse. I'm not impressed. You mention that this is the kid of a high-powered politician not because he shouldn't be prosecuted but rather to allow the prosecutor to prepare for what will follow. You know that the media will be all over this. That's also the same reason that you tell the prosecutor that the evidence is weak. But, of course, if you did that, you knew you wouldn't get your warrant."

"You and I disagree on the strength of the evidence. No sense continuing to flog that dead horse. Time will tell."

Anderson knew that he was not going to win this argument. His partner had made up his mind and was anxious to proceed with the prosecution of Garner Lee.

"I agree. I called the restaurants to see if I could find a reservation," Anderson said, in an effort to change the subject.

"What did we get?" Sandworth said, a tone more cordial than the prior discussion.

"We got a dinner reservation at Kemoll's for 7 o'clock on February 14. Obviously, Lee never made it to the restaurant."

"That fits with what our witness said. The Jennings said they saw him in the apartment building around 6:45. and it's about a fifteen-minute drive to Kemoll's downtown. That's really a good piece of evidence because now we know that he wasn't just dropping by unannounced, to say hello. He had a known purpose. He was picking Amy up for dinner and going to a nice restaurant. She was expecting him. He wouldn't just leave if she didn't answer the door. He would know that something was wrong. At a minimum, he would try the door if he got no answer. We know that when Becky got there, the door was unlocked and there were no visible signs of forced entry."

"That's good, but it still does not make him a killer. The medical examiner fixes the time of death between 4 and 7. That gives us a pretty small window since we put him there between 6:30 and 6:45," Anderson said.

"These times of death estimates are just that, estimates. Actually, they're guestimates. I'm not worried about that," Sandworth said, again looking at the evidence through rose colored glasses. "Now let's go do our duty and arrest a killer".

Chapter Fifteen

Figuring that Lee would be at work, Sandworth suggested that they go to the law firm to make the arrest. Although he didn't object to that starting place, Anderson suspected that Sandworth had an ulterior motive for going there. That would cause both Lee and his high-profile family the most embarrassment.

When they arrived, they were met by a receptionist who asked a variety of questions that clearly annoyed Sandworth. Do you have an appointment? Is he expecting you? May I tell him why you want to see him? When his efforts to deflect answering those questions failed, he displayed his badge and identified himself as a police officer, demanding to see Garner Lee immediately. The receptionist asked them to have a seat and said that someone would be right with them.

After what seemed like an eternity to Sandworth, a female approached the area where he and Anderson were sitting and identified herself as Mr. Lee's assistant. "What can I do for you, officers?" she asked.

"You can't do anything for us," snapped Sandworth.

Before his partner could say anything else, Anderson introduced himself and told this assistant that they need to see Garner Lee.

"Mr. Lee isn't in right now," she said.

"When do you expect him?" Anderson asked.

"I really don't know."

"You don't know when . . ." Sandworth said, his voice rising.

"Is he out of town or in court somewhere?" Anderson said, interrupting his partner.

"Let me see what I can find out," the assistant said as she walked away.

"This is bullshit. They are giving us the run around. I would stake my pension on the fact that he is back there in his office right now," Sandworth said.

"Relax, Jack. It doesn't do us any good to piss these people off. Then we get nothing," Anderson said.

No sooner had Anderson finished his sentence than a tall, thin, well dressed black female appeared. She didn't introduce herself. She didn't have to.

"Hello, Officer Sandworth. What can I do for you?" the unidentified female said.

"That's Detective Sergeant Sandworth."

"Okay. What can I do for you, Detective Sergeant Sandworth?"

"You can get your son out here," Sandworth said.

"What do you want with my son?"

"Are you going to get him out here, or shall I lock you up for obstructing?"

"Do whatever . . ." she started to say but was interrupted.

"Hi. I'm Detective Leroy Anderson. And you are?"

"Cassandra Lee, Garner's mother and his lawyer. Let me ask again. What do you want with my son?"

"Why do you think your son needs a lawyer?" Sandworth asked

"We would like to talk to him," Anderson said, holding his hand in the air and shaking his head at his partner who began to speak.

"Any time your police department is involved in anything, people need lawyers," Cassandra Lee responded, looking directly at Sandworth.

Hoping to divert further conflict between Lee and his partner, Anderson repeated, "Listen Mrs. Lee, we just need to talk to your son."

"He's not interested in talking to you," Lee responded, again looking at Sandworth, who was now shaking his head.

"Well, that's fine, but we need him to tell us that. You can certainly be with him. Is he here, Mrs. Lee?" Anderson said.

"He isn't here."

"Can you tell us where he is or when he'll be back?" Anderson said, continuing to play the game of ask the right question to get the right answer.

"I have no idea," was the short response.

"Can we agree that you'll make him available to us today?" Anderson said, handing her his business card.

"I will try to locate him."

"Thank you, Mrs. Lee. We'll look forward to hearing from you today."

When they left the plush offices of the law firm, Sandworth expressed not only his displeasure with the way in which Anderson handled the situation, but also his skepticism that Lee's mother would make him available for the arrest. "She's probably on the phone with him right now, telling him to pack a bag and get out of town," Sandworth said.

"That may be true. But there's nothing we can do about it now. The warrant is in the computer and if he gets picked up on a traffic offense, he'll be detained. Until then, the only thing we can do is check his house to see if he's there," Anderson said.

Chapter Sixteen

Lee's mother wasted no time calling her son. "The police were just here and want to talk to you again. I suspect that they'll be heading to your house right now. You need to get out of there."

"Why? I keep telling you that I didn't do anything wrong. I have nothing to hide," Garner said.

"I don't trust you to keep your mouth shut. You need to get out of there now."

"Should I come to the office?"

"No. Check into a hotel until we can figure out what the hell is going on."

"Which hotel?"

"Oh, dear God, Garner. Can't you figure that out? Go to the Ritz in Clayton. In the meantime, I think we need to get you a lawyer. I told them that I represent you, but we are going to need a criminal defense lawyer to handle whatever is going on here. I don't have a good feeling about this. I'll talk to your father and get back to you. In the meantime, stay in your room."

St. Louis has many very good attorneys who practice criminal law. But this case was unique in the sense that the Lees needed a criminal defense lawyer, but one who would be able to handle the onslaught of publicity that would result. One such person came to mind, Jonathan Felbin.

Felbin, as he is known to both his friends and enemies, is not only a skilled defense attorney but he would give the Lees an added dimension. Felbin represents police officers throughout the state of Missouri and in other parts of the country in cases where they are accused of both criminal and departmental misconduct. In his most recent case, he successfully defended a St. Louis police officer who was accused of murdering a suspect he was attempting to arrest.

Bobby Decker, who was white, was indicted for the murder of Julius Thornton, a black young man, on the roof-top of a pawn shop in the City of St. Louis. The prosecution claimed that Decker struck Thornton on the back of the head with a flashlight, causing a massive skull fracture. The case attracted both local and national attention, including numerous protests and the involvement of black activists.

During his political career, Senator Lee had been a vocal critic of the St. Louis Police Department and their treatment of African Americans. He not only supported the prosecution of Decker, but he encouraged, both publicly and privately, the elected Circuit Attorney to bring criminal charges. His outspoken position put him at odds with Felbin during the pendency of the Decker case. The Lees needed to evaluate whether that would help or hurt their son in the court of public opinion. But more importantly for the senator, he needed to decide whether Felbin would hurt his political career, including his intended effort to run for governor.

"I don't know if he is the right guy for this," the senator told his wife.

"Whether or not you like him, you must admit that he kicked our friend Joan Cardwell's ass both in the media and the courtroom," Cassandra Lee said.

Joan Cardwell was the elected Circuit Attorney for the city of St. Louis. She was the one who made the decision to proceed with the prosecution of Officer Bobby Decker.

"That's what bothers me."

"Why would that bother you? Seems like we want someone who can take a prosecutor apart on our side."

"Yes, but we were on Cardwell's side in that case. We encouraged her to prosecute Decker," the senator said.

"You mean we threatened her. We suggested that she might not get a judgeship if she didn't prosecute the cop. So, she did. Her mistake was that she indicted Decker before the autopsy of the victim's brain was completed. And Felbin used that effectively to discredit not only her but the entire prosecution of his client. He told the press and the media that Cardwell prosecuted the case to curry favor with the politicians, and in particular black politicians, to get her judgeship. And it worked for him."

"Actually, you were the one who pressed the issue, because you needed a conviction on that cop to help your civil rights cause and to help you ring the bell for the dead kid's mother who had contacted you to sue Decker and the St. Louis Police Department. I guess you don't remember that. In fact, after the Decker case, you were the one who came to me telling me that I needed to make good on the promise and put her on the bench," the senator said.

No response from Cassandra Lee.

State court judges in both the city and county of St. Louis are not elected, but rather appointed through the Non-Partisan Court Plan. A committee of lawyers and citizens review and interview the applicants and send three names to the governor, who makes the appointment from the list of three candidates. The nonpartisan moniker is a bit of a misnomer. The appointment to these coveted positions is subject to political influence, usually in the form of a blessing from the leaders of the party in power. That might explain why the St. Louis metropolitan area does not get the best and the brightest, but rather the most politically connected in these extremely important positions. When Officer Decker was charged with murder, Senator Winston Lee had controlled the Democratic Party, and thus the appointment of judges.

The senator continued, "You will also recall that Cardwell already lost the high-profile case of the white St. Louis police sergeant, Tom Cannon, who brutally assaulted that black mentally challenged young man in his own home. Remember that Cardwell screwed up the change of venue and allowed the case to be transferred to Kansas City, where a white jury acquitted Cannon. In fact, you were the one who also led the charge about the result in that case. Decker came on the heels of the loss in the Cannon case. There was outrage in the black community, and we couldn't let another case of police brutality go unchallenged and let another cop go free. As you well know and at your suggestion, I had that little chat with Cardwell about prosecuting Decker, and then you had a more aggressive conversation with her," Senator Lee repeated his point and reminded his wife of her involvement in both the Decker and Cannon cases.

"I remember. But I would also point out that it was Felbin who orchestrated the final result, an acquittal," she said.

"I just don't know how this is going to play. One minute I'm complaining about the guy getting guilty cops off and the next minute, I'm hiring him. The press will have a field day with that. I'm not even sure that he'll take the case, given what I have said about him and his police clients."

"What I hear you saying is that you're concerned about how hiring Felbin will impact your political career. You're worried that your opponents in a governor's race will use that against you. This is about our son, not you. I don't know where this case is going. But I don't have a good feeling. We need to get Garner the best lawyer that we can. Frankly, we need to protect our family and our political future. This thing impacts us all. You're the one running, but we all share in the prestige and power. We decided a long time ago, that our family and the firm will get behind your political career. But first and foremost, we need to defend our son and make sure that he doesn't wind up in the penitentiary if he's charged and convicted. I don't know whether Felbin will take this case either. But we are going to find out. Either you can call and get an appointment, or I will."

Chapter Seventeen

The Lees could not wait for their scheduled appointment to see Jonathan Felbin. They had an emergency and needed to see him immediately. Felbin's office was on the top two floors of a twenty-one-story building in downtown St. Louis. The 2nd floor and the 20th floor were joined by a circular staircase. Felbin occupied the corner office on the 2nd floor along with the fifteen other equity partners and their assistants. The 20th floor housed the twenty associate attorneys, their assistants and other support staff. The receptionist escorted the Lees into a large glass-enclosed conference room, one of seven, that had a spectacular view of the Mississippi River, the Old Cathedral and the Arch, the tallest man-made monument in the Western Hemisphere, representing westward expansion. They took a seat at a custom-made marble conference table that matched the marble on the floor and was accented by Queen Anne chairs and furnishings. But the Lees had no interest in the trappings of this law office. Their interest was for their son and his uncertain future.

"Thank you for taking the time to see us today, Mr. Felbin. We have a problem. A big problem. I'm Winston Lee and I believe you know my wife, Cassandra," the senator said.

"It's very nice to formally meet you, Senator Lee. And Cassandra, it's nice to see you." During the course of representing police officers, Felbin had faced Cassandra Lee in the courtroom on several occasions. "What can I do to help you?" Felbin asked.

"Our son, Garner Lee, has been arrested for the murder of his girlfriend," the senator said.

"When was he arrested?"

"This morning. Somehow the police found out that he was staying at the Ritz and went there and picked him up this morning."

"Why was he at the Ritz? Does he live in St. Louis?" Felbin asked, confused by the location of the arrest, but hoping that the explanation would not hurt their son's situation.

"He lives in St. Louis, but I told him to go to a hotel, after the police came to our office looking for him. They said that they wanted to talk to him and I was concerned about that. Frankly, Mr. Felbin, Garner isn't the brightest kid, and I didn't trust him to be alone with the police," Cassandra interjected.

Felbin was surprised, both by the bad advice and the comment about her son. "That could be a problem," he said. "But tell me what you know about the situation."

Cassandra explained the relationship between her son and Amy Deland, as well as what she knew about her death. She also described her son as a playboy who worked for the law firm only because his last name was Lee.

"I assume that the information you have comes from conversations you had with your son and that you have done no independent investigation."

"That's correct," Cassandra said.

"Recognizing that you don't have all of the details of this case, do you have any idea why your son was arrested?"

"They arrested him because of his name. I have been at odds with the police department and have made no secret about that. This is their payback. This is their way to damage me. I can see the headlines now. Garner said that he had nothing to do with that girl's death, and I believe him," the senator said.

"Other than your speculation, do you have any evidence of that?" Felbin asked.

"Not at the moment, but time will tell. Obviously, I'm concerned about the publicity and the damage that it will cause me, my wife, and our firm."

Felbin was struck by the exclusion of his son in the father's damage calculation, but decided to let it pass. "What are you asking me to do?"

"We are asking you if you would represent him in this matter," Cassandra responded immediately.

"My wife feels that you would be the best lawyer to do that, but I have some reservations," the senator added.

"What exactly are your concerns?"

"My concern is your prior representation of police officers, including the Decker case. We were obviously on different sides of that issue and I wasn't shy about expressing my opinion. My wife and I both have been critical of the way that police officers in this town treat black people. And I'm concerned that might get in the way of your representation of our son," Senator Lee said.

"Let me explain it to you this way, Senator Lee. I believe everyone has an absolute right to a fair trial and effective legal representation. I don't care what the defendant is accused of, the color of his skin, or his heritage. Whether that person is guilty or innocent is up to a jury, not me. My job is to ensure a fair trial and provide the best defense that I can. But in the case of Bobby Decker, I truly believed that he was innocent, based upon the information that we obtained. Unfortunately, there were those, including yourself, who only saw black and white and came to conclusions without any factual support. Fortunately, when twelve unbiased people heard all the evidence, they agreed with me and not you and your group," Felbin said.

Cassandra looked at her husband as Felbin continued his response.

"As far as your son is concerned, I don't care whether he is good for this or not. I also don't care that he is your kid, or that I have to challenge the police and their investigation. If you recall, I had to challenge the police department and individual officers in the Decker case. And every time I represent an officer, whether in a criminal matter or internal charges that the department brings, I'm challenging other police officers. My job is not about pleasing my opponents or even getting along with them. It is about defending the person I have agreed to represent to the best of my ability. Does that address your concerns, Senator Lee?"

"It does," the senator said.

"A couple other things, Senator. If I agree to get involved in this case, I will be representing your son, not you or your wife. Frankly, I am not concerned about how the publicity impacts you, your wife or your law firm. My only interest is how it effects your son and his ability to get a fair trial. To that extent, I will need an understanding from you that you will not let your political future prejudice your son. Is that something you can live with?"

Senator Lee looked at his wife as he digested Felbin's comments and demand. But before he could respond, his wife said, "That's agreeable with us."

"How about you, Senator?"

"I will agree."

"Fine, I'll go over to the jail and see your son and then make a decision whether I will agree to represent him, and he will agree to have me represent him."

Subject to the meeting with Garner, the Lees agreed to be responsible for the legal expenses. Cassandra signed the retainer agreement.

Chapter Eighteen

Dressed in an orange jumpsuit, handcuffed and dragging leg irons, Garner Lee was brought into the lawyer's conference room of the jail to talk to an individual who might become his ticket to freedom. Uncertain who Felbin was, Garner eyed Felbin suspiciously, and Felbin eyed him as an introduction was made.

Garner sat at the table across from Felbin, the handcuffs and leg irons remaining in place. He was a good looking, clean cut, young black man. Many times, Felbin sat at that table across from hardened criminals, rapists, thieves and stone-cold killers; people who had no conscience. But Garner Lee seemed different. He was an entitlement child. That much Felbin knew. But today, he was treated like an animal in a cage rather than a person of privilege. And he was scared, as he should be. He was accused of murder and could spend a good portion of his life behind bars. But there was an innocence about him. Perhaps it was his eyes. While first impressions can be important, Felbin had been fooled before. Only time would tell.

"Your parents asked me to come over here and talk to you to see if I would be willing to represent you," Felbin began.

"Sir, I didn't kill anybody. She was the woman I loved," Garner said, carefully weighing each word and still uncertain of Felbin.

Garner described his relationship with Amy as two people who were in love. Although he admitted that they'd had disagreements, he downplayed any significant arguments and certainly none that would serve as a motive for murder. As he spoke, Felbin sensed that Garner's feelings were real, but that there was more to the relationship than he was sharing. But he decided not to press the issue. At least not directly, currently.

"Why do you think the police believe you killed the woman you loved?" Felbin asked.

"I have no idea. All that I know is that I didn't kill her. I came to her apartment on Valentine's Day and found her there lying in a pool of blood, her head smashed in. I saw that she was dead. I was in shock. I panicked, called my father and left the apartment."

"What time were you at the apartment?"

"Around 6:30 or so. We had dinner reservations at 7 o'clock downtown."

"Well, they have something that connects you to this murder." Felbin decided to press him a little on his relationship with his girlfriend. "I realize that you said you had disagreements with her. But when was the last argument that you two had?"

"We had a difference of opinion the day before Valentine's Day. I thought we could go to dinner, celebrate Valentine's Day and settle our differences. But obviously, it didn't work out that way."

"What was the argument about?" Felbin asked, preferring to use the word argument rather than difference of opinion.

"I don't really remember. But it probably involved one of her friends meddling in our business. They didn't like me for some reason."

"What was that reason?"

"I don't know for sure. But I got the impression that they were jealous. Amy and I went to a lot of nice places and did a lot of fun things. I just enjoyed being with her, and had the money to do those things. And she enjoyed that lifestyle, too. Sometimes we would go to parties that the society section of the paper would cover. We would get our picture in the paper, and her friends would see it. I guess that didn't help the relationship I had with her friends. I also don't know whether she was doing some bragging. That would have been a problem, too."

Felbin knew this was going to be a problem. He was certain the police had interviewed Amy's friends. He was also sure they would paint a different picture of the relationship between Garner and Amy; one that might serve as a motive for murder.

"Did you get along with any of her friends?" Felbin asked.

"No," was the quick and simple response, extinguishing the spark of any hope that Felbin had to counter the hostile testimony he expected.

"Did you have any contact with the police during their investigation?"

"Yes. They came to my house."

"Did you make any statements to them when they came to your house?"

"No," another quick response.

Felbin was not satisfied with that response. He knew most defendants responded negatively to that question because they didn't appreciate the significance of what was being asked. Statements by criminal suspects can be used as admissions. Simple answers to simple questions are routinely quoted by prosecutors during the trial and used to support convictions. Another typical misunderstanding is the belief that statements cannot be used if the Miranda warnings are not given. Unfortunately for those who harbor that belief, those warnings are only necessary during custodial interrogations. If the interrogation is noncustodial, no warnings are given because they stifle the free flow of information the police are receiving.

"Let me ask that question in a different way. Tell me about what you talked about with the police," Felbin said pushing Lee to disclose complete details of his meeting with the police.

"Mr. Felbin, you have to understand I was pretty intimidated by that visit. On top of that, the woman I loved was just murdered. So, please forgive me if I can't recall all of the details of meeting."

"Please do the best you can."

"Before I answer, I have a question for you. Are you my lawyer now?"

"I'm trying to decide whether I will become involved in your case at this point."

"Does that mean what I tell you is privileged at this point? Because if it is not, I may not want to continue this conversation. I'm a lawyer but, frankly, not a very good one and I never did any criminal cases. But people keep telling me I talk too much," Lee said candidly.

"This conversation is, in fact, privileged whether or not I agree to represent you in the future. I'm getting the feeling there's something you need to tell me that you're concerned about. I need to know everything, good and bad, about this situation so I can effectively advise and represent you. Don't hold anything back. Do you understand?"

"I understand, and there is something you need to know. I told the police I wasn't at Amy's apartment on Valentine's Day."

Felbin hesitated before asking the next question to allow that answer to rattle around his brain. He was beginning to think this young man's mother was correct when she said he was not very bright and she didn't trust him to be alone with the police. Apparently, she did not realize the damage had already been done.

"Why did you tell them that?" Felbin asked.

"I don't know. I wanted to talk to them because I didn't have anything to hide. I didn't kill her. But my father told me not to talk to them. He told me it would be a problem for me if they could prove I was in her apartment. When they asked me if I had seen her on Valentine's Day or whether I had been to her apartment that day, I thought it would look bad if I just told them I wouldn't answer the question. I told them I didn't see her and wasn't at her apartment that day."

The reason Garner Lee was arrested for this murder was becoming clear to Felbin. The police had credible evidence that would put him in Amy's apartment at or near the time of the murder. His lie would come back to haunt him. But that was an issue for another day. Today, Felbin needed details, the lectures could wait.

"Did you tell them anything else that might be harmful?"

"No. But they did get my fingerprints."

"How did that happen?"

"They came to my house again and asked if I would give them my fingerprints. They said if I didn't give them the prints, they would get a court order and there would be publicity. So, I agreed to give them what they wanted."

"When they contacted you the second time to get your prints, did you have any more discussion with them about the case?"

"No. They didn't ask me anything, and I didn't volunteer anything."

"I think I get the picture. Is there anything else you think I need to know?"

"No. Will you represent me and get me out of this mess? I swear, Mr. Felbin, I didn't kill Amy. I couldn't. I loved her and still do. I hope you believe that and you will represent me."

"I will represent you Garner. We have a lot of work to do. But the first order of business is to get you out of here."

"Thank you, Mr. Felbin," Lee said.

"Drop the Mister, I don't like formality. People just call me Felbin."

As Felbin left the jail, he wondered how he was going to handle the false statement his new client gave to the police. Although rarely putting much stock in the declarations of innocence he routinely heard, there was something different about this kid. Maybe it was the way he said he loved this girl, or the look in his eyes when he denied having anything to do with her murder. It was something he could not quite put his finger on. But he knew his client's lie would come back to bite him in the ass and would be the cornerstone of the state's case. Felbin also knew that if Garner Lee didn't kill Amy Deland, there had to be evidence somewhere that would identify the real killer. He just had to find it. In the meantime, he had to deal with enough circumstantial evidence to put his client in the penitentiary for a long time.

Chapter Nineteen

The Grand Jury took no time returning an indictment against Garner Lee. And the news media took no time letting the public know the son of a prominent politician and his wife, an equally prominent lawyer, was charged with murder. The million-dollar cash bond the defendant posted also didn't help their son's cause. Felbin had no comment, but Senator Lee had plenty to say. He proclaimed his son's innocence and the family's love of Amy Deland. "Garner would not do anything to harm her, he loved her, the family loved her," he was quoted as saying.

Unfortunately, several of Amy's friends disagreed. They unanimously described the relationship as anything but a loving union. "Arguments dominated most conversations and physical as well as mental abuse were the norm," or so they said. When asked about the relationship between Amy and the Lee family, one friend said, "Are you kidding? The Lees hated her. She wasn't good enough for their son. They encouraged him to dump her. The Lees are all about money and power. They viewed Amy as an embarrassment."

Felbin met in his office with Tony Carmine, one of his investigators, to brief him on their new case and await the arrival of the Lees. Carmine would be doing the leg work, beating the bushes, not only to free their client, but also to find the truth, no matter where that led him.

Felbin and Carmine had a long history dating back to the days when Carmine was a rookie with the St. Louis Police Department some 25 years ago. With less than a year on the department, Carmine made a traffic stop that netted a cache of drugs found in the vehicle operated by Felbin's client. The cross-examination at the suppression hearing began pleasant enough, but didn't end that way. Carmine got a refresher course in the rules of search and seizure. While he lost that case, he gained a lesson he would never forget. He would go on to become a well-respected investigator who would be rewarded with prestigious assignments such as the homicide division. Numerous future professional encounters over the years were not kind to Felbin, and Carmine enjoyed kicking the lawyer's ass. Eventually, the two became friends. When he retired, Felbin persuaded him to join his staff and work the other side of the fence.

"We have a guy who lied to the police and probably has a fingerprint that connects him to the murder, and God knows what else," Felbin explained.

"And we have a political asshole who has never been our friend, already shooting his mouth off to the media. Can't wait for this show," Carmine said.

"Well, you'll get to see round one in a few minutes when Garner and his family get here. We need to come to some understanding with him about the public comments. Apparently, he's going to run for governor and I'm hoping he's willing to place the welfare of his son ahead of his political ambitions."

"Good luck with that. I'm betting the good senator's ambitions will come first," the investigator speculated.

"Time will tell on the senator. I wanted you to sit in on this conference because I'm interested in your take on this kid. I met with him and listened to his story. While I think he isn't being completely candid with us about certain things, I don't think he had anything to do with Amy's death. Apparently, her friends are going to do what they can to help the prosecutor convict this guy by providing a motive for murder."

Before Carmine could respond, the receptionist announced the Lees had arrived.

When Felbin and Carmine entered the conference room, they observed Garner seated on one side of the table and his parents on the other. Felbin hoped this was not a preview of things to come.

After introducing Carmine, Felbin got right to the point. "I asked you to come in today so we can have a conversation and establish some parameters, particularly as they relate to public commentary. I also want to discuss the relationship all of you had with Amy Deland. Let's start with that. According to the article in the paper, the Lee family loved Amy. But according to her friends, that relationship was hardly a love fest. Which is it?"

"They hated her and did their best to destroy the relationship," Garner said.

That response certainly explained the seating arrangement Felbin and Carmine found when they entered the conference room.

"Is that true?" Felbin asked, looking at Garner's parents.

Cassandra was the first to respond. "Hate is a bit strong. We didn't hate her. But we also didn't embrace her. Frankly, we thought she was a gold digger, and Garner could do better. We also didn't think she felt the same about him as he did about her. He spent money on her, took her to nice places, introduced her to influential people and treated her like the princess she thought she was. She liked the attention. Garner was just a means to that end."

"And you were wrong about her. You didn't know her and never gave her a chance. You treated her like shit," Garner said.

"What do you mean by that?" Carmine asked.

"When we were at social events, they would ignore her or if they acknowledged her presence, it was with a grunt. At those same functions, they could be overheard complaining to their friends about how she was dressed or how she looked. One time, I heard them refer to her as a whore, and I know she heard it too. Repeatedly, they would tell me to dump her. I couldn't dump her. I loved her and still do. I didn't murder her. I didn't do anything but love her," Garner said, his voice filling with emotion.

"That's because she *was* a whore and was using you. Are you forgetting you would come to me and complain about what she was doing and the arguments you had with her because of her wandering eye? But you couldn't or wouldn't figure it out. And now look at where it got you, accused of murder. Had you listened to us, we would not be sitting in a lawyer's office trying to figure out how we were going to defend a murder case," his mother said, clearly upset by her son's comments.

Attempting to deflect the hostilities between a mother and her son, Felbin wanted to know what they knew about Amy's background.

Silence. Neither the senator nor his wife offered any information.

"What about her family?" Carmine continued directing the question to Garner.

"Her parents were divorced. I never met her mother or her father. She really didn't have anything to do with them. I think they live in another state. She has a brother I never met. I think he also lives in another state," Garner said.

"There you have it. You know nothing about her family because she didn't want you to know anything about them. And this is the love of your life," Cassandra added.

"Fuck you, Mom."

"Okay. That's enough. This back and forth isn't getting us anywhere, which brings me to the second reason I wanted this meeting. We need to address the issue of how the news media will be handled. I would prefer this office handle all media. Senator, you made a comment about the relationship between your family and Amy, and it backfired." Felbin saw no purpose in elaborating on the screw up. "What are your future plans about media communication in connection with this case?" he asked the senator.

"I can't climb into a closet while this is pending. I will soon be starting a campaign for governor. Obviously, this situation will not be helpful. It will come up, and I will do my best to avoid saying anything that will harm the defense."

Felbin was struck by the callous and hostile attitudes of Garner's parents. Clearly, Amy had been a subject of contention and family arguments. Their son did not follow their advice, and that upset them on several levels. But this wasn't a time for finger pointing. This was a time to forget the past and come together to focus on the future.

"I certainly hope you don't say anything that would harm the defense, Senator. Your son's life depends on it," Felbin said.

Chapter Twenty

Criminal cases are assigned to trial judges in the city of St. Louis at random. Or at least that is how it is supposed to work. But Felbin wondered if it was the luck of the draw when he learned Judge Joan Cardwell would be presiding over the case of State of Missouri versus Garner Lee. His relationship with Judge Cardwell, former Circuit Attorney Cardwell, was not a good one. In fact, it was a hostile relationship. He disliked her, and she despised him.

For several reasons, the relationship between Jonathan Felbin and Joan Cardwell was never a good one when she was the elected prosecutor for the city of St. Louis. She prosecuted. He defended. Natural enemies. But it reached a fever pitch when she prosecuted Felbin's client, St. Louis Police Officer Bobby Decker. Felbin built a reputation, in part, on representing police officers, including those who were charged with crimes. But the Decker case was different. Felbin believed Bobby Decker was the sacrificial lamb on the altar of Cardwell's judicial ambitions.

An appointment to the bench in both St. Louis City and County is an arbitrary political contest masked by a process known as the Nonpartisan Court Plan. Under the Plan, a nonpartisan judicial commission reviews applications, interviews applicants and selects three individuals for an appointment to the circuit court bench. The judicial commission is comprised of three lawyers selected by lawyers, three civilians selected by the governor and the chief justice of the Missouri Supreme Court. The names of the three individuals selected by the commission are then sent to the governor from which he selects the winner. On its face to this point, it is seemingly a fair process. But things are not always what they appear to be.

The lawyers on the commission are influenced by fellow lawyers. The plaintiffs' bar influences the plaintiffs' lawyers on the commission while the insurance lawyers influence their side. Meanwhile, the politicians are working the governor's appointments. Supervising the commission is the Supreme Court Justice who is a graduate of this nonpartisan process.

But the real fun begins when the three names arrive on the governor's desk. Now the politicians go to work. While the candidates encourage people to send letters of support to the governor, the real horse trading is done by the political power-brokers who have something to either give or take away from a sitting governor.

St. Louis police officer Bobby Decker found himself in the middle of a political and racial tug of war when he arrested a young black man on a roof top one rainy night. The suspect died from a massive skull fracture. Prosecutor Cardwell rushed to judgment with an unsupported conclusion that the fracture was the result of blunt trauma with a linear object, namely Decker's flashlight, and charged the officer with murder.

Felbin wasted no time launching a public attack on the decision of his nemesis. He claimed the murder charge was filed before the autopsy of the brain was completed. He supported that contention with a newspaper article quoting the St. Louis medical examiner who said the autopsy of the brain would take three to four weeks to complete. He further told the news media that her rush to judgment was a thinly disguised effort to force the medical examiner to conclude that his client's flashlight was the cause of the massive skull fracture.

Felbin also reminded anyone who cared to listen that Cardwell was looking for a judicial appointment and needed to curry favor with politicians, both white and black, to accomplish that. Her reputation in the black community was never good, but reached an all-time low after a white sergeant was acquitted of feloniously assaulting a young mentally challenged black man in his own home. Felbin represented the sergeant in that case as well, and filed a motion for change of venue. After Cardwell failed to file a timely objection to that motion, the St. Louis judge sent the case to Kansas City for trial. An all-white jury acquitted the officer. Cardwell was blamed for a mistake that prevented the trial from happening in St. Louis where the incident occurred. At the time, the black politicians led by Senator Lee were relentless in their criticism. He suggested Cardwell robbed the black citizens of St. Louis of their right to sit in judgment of a police officer who maliciously beat a mentally challenged young man in his own home.

When the Decker incident occurred on the heels of the sergeant's acquittal, Senator Lee came to the forefront once again. He reminded the community of Cardwell's mistakes in the last case that involved a white cop and a black suspect. He threatened extreme consequences to Cardwell for a repeat performance. It was that rhetoric which allowed Felbin to suggest that the prosecution of Decker was motivated by a desire to please people like Senator Lee and had nothing to do with the facts of the case or justice. The public commentary of Cardwell, Lee and Felbin further inflamed an already racially divided city.

Felbin asked his investigator, Tony Carmine, to come into his office. He needed to figure out how to deal with Cardwell. "We drew Cardwell for the Lee case," he told the investigator.

"You're kidding," was the only response Carmine could make.

"I wish I was. Now, what do we do? Disqualify her?"

"How in the hell did she wind up with this case? I thought this was supposed to be random. You mean to tell me with all the judges in the city of St. Louis, it was just a coincidence you wind up with her? Particularly when the Decker case isn't out of the rearview mirror. That's bullshit."

"You and I both know this is no coincidence. But what do we do? We have two choices. Either keep her or disqualify her, and there are consequences to both," Felbin said.

In any criminal case, both sides can disqualify a judge one time without having to give reasons or prove cause for the removal. Felbin knew the prosecutor would not disqualify Cardwell. They never did for fear of retaliation in future cases. Many judges take offense to a disqualification. Since they spent all their time in the courtroom, prosecutors did not want to run that risk. Defense lawyers did what was best for their client at the time, and were content to deal with any future fall out later.

"Obviously, she hates my guts. Probably with some good reason. But will she hurt Garner? Of course, the real question is whether she will intentionally hurt him. We know she can accidentally hurt him because she is stupid and will make stupid rulings and decisions just like she did when she was a prosecutor," Felbin continued.

"She is beyond stupid. But those stupid decisions can also help you in the long run if this case goes south and you need to appeal. She's also new to the bench and will make rookie mistakes, which can also help you in the long run. I think that as a new judge, she is not going to want to make mistakes. Of course, you will have no problem pointing those out. That can be embarrassing, particularly in a high-profile case like this," Carmine said, obviously sharing Felbin's disdain for Cardwell. "That said, you might be able to intimidate her into doing what you want. She knows you wouldn't be afraid to express your displeasure in front of the cameras."

Felbin was not a stranger to the news media. His general philosophy was that the best defense is a good offense, particularly against big government and big business that had unlimited resources. And he had no problem setting that stage through the media, which he viewed as the great leveler. In fact, Felbin would routinely say that Joan Cardwell was the best argument for term limits for elected prosecutors.

Carmine reminded him of another public incident, this time with a federal judge. Those black robes were generally off limits to most rational thinking lawyers. "I am sure you recall the media feeding frenzy in that federal case where the justice department indicted that county chief. And right before one of the recesses, the judge asked you if you could refrain from criticizing her with the reporters until she at least left the bench. Your response, I believe, was that you would try your best."

"Yeah, I remember that. For most of that trial, I wondered whether she went to law school, given some of her rulings. But unfortunately, in this country, the judicial selection system is the by-product of a process where political influence and money rather than ability control. But I think we are up against it in this case. The prosecutor is going to have a lot of prejudicial, circumstantial evidence to inflame this jury. And I really don't need a pro prosecution judge who dislikes me helping their cause. My inclination is to get rid of her."

"But if we get rid of her, we could get someone worse. Another political hack. Different pew, but the same church," Carmine said.

Before Felbin could respond, he was told Garner and his parents were on the phone. When he finished the brief conversation, he looked at his investigator and said, "Looks like that issue is off the table. We were just directed to keep Cardwell. We were also told to get a quick trial setting. I told them they needed to come into the office to have a conversation. They're on their way."

"What's that about?" Carmine asked.

"I hope it's not what I am thinking," Felbin said, obviously concerned that the politicians were going to fix this case. As he stared out his window admiring the beauty of the Basilica of St. Louis, King of France, fondly known as the Old Cathedral, the oldest Catholic cathedral west of the Mississippi, he wondered what he would do if his worst nightmare ever became a reality.

Chapter Twenty-One

Winning or losing any trial, whether civil or criminal, is directly proportional to the amount of preparation. The best trial lawyers don't like surprises. They like to know everything there is to know before they enter the courtroom. The case of Garner Lee was no different. But what was different was the client's parents pressing for an immediate trial with their son apparently in agreement. Usually, a quick trial disadvantages the defense in criminal cases because the prosecution has done its preparation before the charges are filed.

The Lees wasted no time getting to Felbin's office.

"We want this case heard as soon as possible," Senator Lee said with his son nodding in approval. Interestingly, Garner's mom, the trial lawyer in the family, sat silently, neither approving nor disapproving.

"The first question I have is why you want to keep Judge Cardwell? You know she and I are not the best of friends. As the former elected prosecutor, she's also very pro prosecution and that won't help us in this case," Felbin said.

Senator Lee's response was firm and immediate. "I know Joan Cardwell, and I believe she will be fair. She won't help them, and she won't help us. She'll call it right down the middle. If you disqualify her, you may get someone who isn't fair. She's new to the bench, and we can get a faster setting with her because she doesn't have a large docket at the moment."

"Let's address the elephant in the room, Senator," Felbin said.

Lee looked confused by that statement and said, "What elephant?"

"It was no secret that you and she were working together to get Bobby Decker prosecuted. You made no secret about that. I suggested at the time that she prosecuted

Decker to curry favor with you and the black politicians. My question to you, Senator, is this. Did you have anything to do with Cardwell's judicial appointment?"

"I was certainly aware of your accusations, Mr. Felbin. But you had no proof then, and you have none now. You were spinning that tale to help your client. I understand that, and you are very good at that, which is part of the reason we are here. However, you saying it does not make it so. In answer to your question, I had nothing to do with her appointment. In fact, I intentionally stayed away from that after the Decker trial because of your unsubstantiated allegations. We lost the Decker trial and you won. Frankly, there was nothing in it for me to get involved in her appointment. Now can we get on with getting an immediate trial setting from Judge Cardwell?"

Felbin didn't believe Lee had nothing to do with Cardwell's appointment. But the senator was correct. He couldn't prove it and, therefore, had to move on.

"We just received the police reports a week ago, and there are many things we need to investigate. Those reports aren't favorable to us. Putting aside for the moment the fact Garner lied to the police, his bloody prints were found in the apartment, and the victim's friends provide a motive for murder. We aren't in good shape. Why are you anxious to get this tried so quickly? Is that because you are afraid it will impact your political career the longer this case is in the media?" Felbin said, looking squarely at the senator and ignoring his client.

This time his response was not immediate. He waited for the anger to subside. When he finally spoke, Senator Lee said, "I'm concerned about my son. This has nothing to do with my political career, Mr. Felbin. My wife and I read the police reports, and we don't believe the case is very strong. We're concerned that if they are given more time, their case will get better. Right now, it is what it is. Yes, Garner did lie to the police, but he was in shock at the time. Yes, he was in the apartment and yes, his fingerprints were found in her blood. We aren't going to change that unless you have some brilliant plan to alter those facts, Mr. Felbin. But that doesn't mean he killed this girl. And that's what the state must prove beyond a reasonable doubt. If they don't, he will be found not guilty."

Still, no comment from Garner's mother.

I don't have any brilliant plans to alter those facts, Senator. You are correct, it is what it is in that regard. But we need an explanation for why he did what he did. And that explanation may involve expert witnesses and perhaps a mental health examination. And that will . . ." Felbin said before he was interrupted.

"We are not using any nut defense," the senator said.

"I am not talking about a nut defense, as you call it. I am talking about an expert psychologist explaining the net effect of how someone who is in shock impacts the ability to recall. I'm not saying we will put an expert on the stand, but we need to hear what that person has to say after examining Garner."

"No shrinks. No mental exam. No nut defense, directly or indirectly." Senator Lee was clearly a man who needed to be in control and was used to getting his way.

Now it was Felbin's turn to pause before speaking. When he finally spoke, his response was not directed to the senator but rather to his son. "Are you ever going to say anything, or are you just going to sit there taking notes?"

"I agree with my father. We have discussed this at length. I don't think they have a strong case. I did lie, but I didn't murder Amy, as I told you before. I was in shock when the cops came. I don't know how an expert is going to explain that any better than I can. I don't want the stigma of a shrink in the middle of this case. As far as Amy's friends are concerned, I can get you some witnesses who will contradict the lies those people are telling. I hope you understand and will respect my position, Mr. Felbin," Garner said.

"You're the client, Garner. You control your own case. All I can do is advise you. You are free to accept or reject my advice. In this case, I think it's a mistake to shortcut the investigation of potential defenses. Trials are not searches for the truth. They are spin contests. Whoever spins the facts to the benefit of his side and to the detriment of the other side, wins. The fact you didn't kill her, and I believe you didn't, doesn't matter. If the prosecutor can convince a jury you did kill her because you lied, that's the end of the game. You lose. While you get to call the shots in your case, whether good or bad, I get to decide whether to stay in and

85

continue to represent you. And if I think the decisions you are making are harmful to you or you are making them because of undue influence, I get to withdraw as your lawyer. Frankly, Garner, at the moment I am inclined to get out," Felbin said.

Throughout his conversation with the senator, Felbin couldn't help but wonder why his client's mother said nothing. She was an experienced, well recognized trial lawyer and certainly knew how to try a case. Strange that a mother, particularly one who knew the system, would not contribute to the discussion. From past dealings with her in cases where she was suing police officers he represented, Felbin knew she had an opinion. But not sharing that opinion whether agreeing or disagreeing with what her husband was saying, was odd. Thinking her opinion might be helpful and certainly couldn't hurt even if she agreed with her husband, Felbin decided to invite her to comment.

"I believe it's in the interests of my family to resolve this matter as quickly as possible. I agree with my husband that the case is weak and given your skill as a trial lawyer, my son will be acquitted," Cassandra Lee said.

Felbin was surprised by her response. He knew she did not believe what she said. Of course it was in the interest of her family to get this case off the front page of the paper. But not at the cost of having this young man's life destroyed. She knew better than that. Something else was going on. Although his past dealings with Cassandra Lee were adversarial, he had a lot of respect for her. He hoped she was not involved in anything that would jeopardize her law license and her career.

"You won't get out, Mr. Felbin," the senator continued, addressing the threat to withdraw. "I know that, and you know that. You know that getting out of this case with all the publicity it has attracted so far will hurt Garner, and you won't do that. My research about you tells me that is not in your DNA. Have a good day, Mr. Felbin," Senator Lee said and left the office.

Carmine sat through the meeting without saying a word. But after the Lees left, he had plenty to say. "What the fuck was that? Are you kidding me? Did that prick just throw his kid under the bus and guarantee a conviction? I knew we shouldn't have taken this case. We knew exactly what this political hack was all about before he ever walked in here."

"Yes, we did know what he was all about. He has an agenda that's as transparent as Donald Trump's effort to conceal a combover. But we're not representing him. We're representing his kid. And while I thought he would get in the way from time to time, I never counted on him controlling his kid to the extent that bad decisions are made. It almost appears like he wants his kid to be convicted. I'm also surprised by Cassandra's comment. You and I have both dealt with her, and this is out of character. I think the fix may be in, Tony."

"What are you gonna do? Are we getting out?"

"I don't know."

Chapter Twenty-Two

Felbin needed to think. He was between a rock and a hard place. The senator was right, if he got out, he could hurt Garner. But if he stayed in, he might also be part of something that hurt Garner. The decision was not an easy one. When he had decisions to make like this one, he needed to talk to someone. An ear that was not attached to a lawyer, his investigators or anyone associated with the case. He needed the ear of Melinda. Melinda Evans, Felbin's long-time girlfriend and companion, was always there for him in situations like this. She had the ability to separate the forest from the trees, focusing on what was really important. She served as his armchair psychiatrist. And if anyone needed a shrink particularly in times like this, it was Jonathan Felbin.

Felbin and Melinda had been together for several years. They traveled together, spent the winters in Florida together and the summer weekends at the Lake of the Ozarks. But they also led separate lives. They enjoyed the freedom of independence with the comfort of committed loyalty. They were always there for each other in good times and bad.

Melinda was a widow, and Felbin was divorced. His marriage didn't work in part because he was married to his job and the law is a jealous mistress, a receipt for disaster in any marriage. Being married to a lawyer, particularly one married to his job, is a challenge, and Felbin was unable to reconcile the two. Divorce was the best option for everyone. Following the divorce, Felbin experimented with life in the fast, single lane. Parties, dates, bars, listening to bullshit pickup lines and exhaustive mindless conversation. It didn't take him long to realize this lifestyle was not for him. He knew he needed more than his work. The divorce taught him that lesson. But he had no other options; that is, until he met Melinda. She was beautiful, smart and compassionate. She understood him and his life of dedication to his clients. And the best part was that she was not a lawyer or a judge and had nothing to do with the legal profession.

Melinda had her own life and businesses that occupied her time. She owned a dental company that manufactured dental appliances like dentures and crowns. She also had a real estate license and in her spare time sold homes. She lived alone in a 6-bedroom, 5 bath home on two acres in an exclusive area of St. Louis County. Unlike Felbin, her marital life was fulfilling until her husband of 19 years passed way. But like Felbin, she quickly became disillusioned with the single scene.

"Are you free for dinner tonight?" Felbin asked.

"Sure. That would be great. You pick the place and the time. I'm good with any time," Melinda said.

"How about 7 at LoRusso's? I have a couple more things to finish up here. Order a bottle of wine if you get there first. I may need more than one."

When he finished his conversation with Melinda, Felbin asked his administrative assistant, Jan Marshall, to have his driver, Joe Weller, bring the car around at 6:45.

St. Louis enjoyed a reputation of having great restaurants, particularly Italian. LoRusso's Cucina had old world charm and great food and was a favorite of both Felbin and Melinda. The owner would always accommodate the couple with a table with a curtain which separated them from the rest of the diners.

When Felbin arrived, he was greeted by Rich LoRusso, the owner and chef extraordinaire. After an exchange of some pleasantries, Rich walked him to the table, his regular table. Melinda was already there, a glass of wine in front of her and a 2009 bottle of Lafite Rothschild on the table. The curtain at their table was open, but Rich closed it as he was leaving. Melinda welcomed him with a kiss.

"I got here a little early and thought I would start without you," she said, pointing at her glass of wine.

Felbin and Melinda enjoyed wine, particularly French wines, but had also taken several trips to the Napa Valley to sample some of California's finest.

"Tell me about your day," Melinda said as she poured a glass of wine for her dinner companion.

"I have a problem without a really good solution."

But before Felbin could continue, the curtain parted, and the waitress appeared. "I assume you want to wait a little while before you order, Mr. Felbin," she said. Felbin nodded. He needed some libation and conversation before he could even think about dinner.

"My problem is with the Lee family," he continued.

Melinda knew he was representing the son of a powerful state senator. Not only did he tell her he was representing Garner, but it was also a headline.

"I thought you only represented Garner. How can you have a problem with the rest of his family?"

"It seems that his father is running the show. He has decided what is best for his son and how this case should be handled, starting with an immediate trial."

"And you won't have enough time to prepare," she observed.

"Exactly."

"Is the case strong? The press coverage has not been kind to your client."

"They don't have any direct evidence. But they have a lot of circumstantial evidence. For example, at the time of the murder, he was at her apartment. When the police talked to him, he made two mistakes. He talked to them, and his second mistake was that he lied to them. He said he wasn't there."

"How do they prove he was there?" Melinda asked.

"They have people who saw him on the stairs heading toward her apartment, and they have his fingerprint in her blood inside the apartment."

"How do you get around that?"

"He was in shock at the time he made the statement. When the police came to his house shortly after the body was discovered, he felt they were accusing him of murdering her, and he panicked. I obviously need to be able to explain his state of mind and my feeling is I'll probably need a mental health expert testimony to do that. And they don't want any part of that. Or, I should say the good senator doesn't want any part of that."

"Why would he object if it helps the defense?"

"I suspect he thinks that kind of testimony will impact his political career, which involves a run for governor. He wants to put this case behind him as quickly as possible

for the same reason, which is why he wants a trial yesterday. He did most of the talking today while Garner and
his mother just sat there adding nothing to the discussion.
I finally pressed the mother to weigh in. She's an experienced and well-respected trial lawyer who also wants to put
this behind her and her family as soon as possible. That's
odd because she knows what can happen with a quick trial
unless she's involved in a fix," Felbin said as he shook his
head and refilled his wine glass.

"What are your options?"

"Before I get to that, let me add one more concern. Joan
Cardwell has been assigned to hear this case. And I have
been told I can't disqualify her."

"The former prosecutor who pursued that police officer? What was his name? Decker? You didn't have many
kind words for her at the time?"

"That's the one. And I have several concerns about her.
She's not above retaliating against me through my client. I
also assume that generally she'll favor the prosecution. But
more than that, I'm concerned about her relationship with
Senator Lee. I asked him directly whether he had anything
to do with her appointment, and he denied it. But I don't
believe him. And that may explain why he's pressing for a
quick trial without any preparation, because the fix is in."

"What are your options?" she repeated.

"I can stay in the case or I can get out. If I stay in and
can't do my job, this kid will be convicted. And I don't think
he's good for this murder. If I get out, the spin will be that
I abandoned a guilty client, and that won't help Garner. In
addition, I don't want to be a part of any effort by Cardwell
and her friend Lee to fix this case if that's what they plan
to do."

Just as Felbin finished outlining his options, the waitress returned, asking if they were ready to order. Felbin ordered his usual, Mudega, which is beef tenderloin prepared
very rare and topped with fontina in a lemon wine sauce
with garlic, prosciutto ham and mushrooms and a side of
white pasta. Melinda was a fish person. Unlike Felbin, she
was always concerned about eating healthy. She ordered
Salmon Piccata served with white wine lemon sauce, ca-
pers, mushrooms and an off the menu side of Brussels
sprouts prepared specially for her by Rich.

"Sounds to me like you have already figure out what you want to do," Melinda said after the waitress closed the curtain.

"What do you mean?"

"Sounds to me like the risks staying in the case are greater than if you get out. If you stay in, Garner's father will be calling all the shots and you will lose. If the fix is in, you'll have an ethical problem and maybe even a criminal problem. But if you get out, there might be some discussion adverse to the client, but that will be temporary with limited coverage and probably forgotten by the time of trial."

Melinda had way of simplifying issues, getting to the heart of the matter. She would listen to what Felbin would say and then separate out the relevant from the irrelevant. She would never offer her own opinion on any particular course. Instead, she would provide the pluses and the minuses for each option. When she did that, the appropriate course would become obvious. But it had been there all along, just concealed by the fog of confusion caused by misdirected thoughts.

"Thanks for showing me the way once again. Now, let's order another and enjoy the rest of the evening," Felbin said pointing to an empty wine bottle.

"Deal," Melinda said, raising her glass to do a toast.

Chapter Twenty-Three

The next day, Felbin notified his client that he would be filing a motion to withdraw, citing irreconcilable differences and requesting a hearing. Garner was upset, begging Felbin to reconsider. But the decision had been made. Things wouldn't change. The senator would continue to call the shots to the detriment of his son. That was not acceptable to Felbin, not because he didn't want his reputation to be tarnished with a high-profile loss but rather, he couldn't bear to stand by helplessly watching a young man's life be ruined for a crime he didn't commit. That was not his nature. If Garner's father had his way, the case would turn into a slow plea of guilty.

When he finished his call with Garner, Felbin waited in his office for the next call. It didn't take long. The senator was on the phone, and Felbin knew this was not going to be a pleasant conversation.

"What the fuck do you think you're doing, Felbin?" Senator Lee screamed.

"And good morning to you, Senator," Felbin said softly and calmly.

"Don't good morning me, you low life prick. What do you think you're doing?"

"I'm getting out of this case," Felbin said, his voice still unusually calm.

"Irreconcilable differences. What the fuck does that mean? There are no irreconcilable differences. The only difference is that you don't agree with the way your client wants to handle this case. That's the difference."

"Wrong. I don't agree with how *you* want to handle this case. I also don't appreciate your getting between me and my client. You probably would be better off sticking to your slimy political practice and leave the real practice of law and the defense of your son to me. This isn't about your future, it's about his. Unfortunately, you don't want to accept that and have made this about you. Everything is always about you, isn't it, Senator? You first, and everyone else a distant second, including your own son. Is the power of your political office so important to you that you are willing to sacrifice your only son?

"I'm not the one doing the sacrificing. You are. We will object to your withdrawal."

"Fine. And I'll put your interference and the reason you're sacrificing your son on the public court record. Politicians don't like that kind of publicity, do they, Mr. Politician?" Felbin asked.

Felbin knew that this was but an idle threat he couldn't make good on. It would be harmful to his client to say that in the presence of either the prosecutor or the news media.

"Fuck you," Lee said as he slammed the phone down, ending the conversation.

Felbin prepared his motion to withdraw as Garner Lee's attorney, alleging simply that irreconcilable differences made his continued representation ineffective and impossible. As with any motion to withdraw, the lawyer had to be careful to preserve the attorney-client privilege. The specific differences that existed could not be included in the motion for fear of prejudice to the client as the case went forward. But the motion had to contain enough detail to provide a basis for the court to sustain the motion. In the end, the court had the discretion either to agree or to disagree with the lawyer's request.

Felbin was surprised to learn within an hour after his motion was filed, Cardwell's clerk called and said the motion was scheduled to be argued at 8 am the next morning. That was unusual. Dispensing justice was a slow process. Even recognizing, as the senator had, that this new judge's docket was not as full as the others, this was still lightning fast.

In one sense, scheduling this hearing early was a plus, because the courthouse doesn't start to get crowded until after 9. That should reduce the publicity, at least for the moment. But Felbin wondered whether the senator had anything to do with this expedited setting. This was similar to his concern that Cardwell's selection to preside over this case was something other than a coincidence. But time would tell, beginning with tomorrow morning.

Chapter Twenty-Four

The courthouse was empty when Felbin arrived at about 7:45. Neither the judge, nor the prosecutor, was there. But that was not unusual. Most of the time, defense lawyers had to wait for the prosecutors to appear. Finally, a few minutes before 8, the prosecutor, Paul Perrin, arrived in the empty courtroom. He would be the one to try the case, assuming a plea could not be worked out. He introduced himself to Felbin, as the two had never met.

"I guess we are here today on your motion to get out of this case," the prosecutor said.

"Yes," Felbin responded without further elaboration.

"This shouldn't take very long."

"I wouldn't think so. But I was a little surprised to see how quickly this was set. I just filed it yesterday afternoon."

"I don't know when you filed it. They gave it to me at the same time they gave me the setting."

The lawyers sat in silence in an empty courtroom awaiting the arrival of the judge. There really wasn't much to talk about, as Felbin was getting out.

As he sat there, Felbin wondered what kind of a reception he would get from the woman he despised and for whom he had no respect. When she was a prosecutor, they were adversaries representing the interests of opposing parties. They disagreed, fought, sparred, insulted and criticized, all in the interests of advocacy for a client. But now, his nemesis was a judge. She was in control. She was the queen of her castle and set the rules. God help the lawyer who would criticize a judge. Those aren't career enhancers.

Many who made it to the bench were mediocre, at best, when they practiced. But when they put on the robes, it was like they were infused with legal knowledge. You would think they were sitting on the United State Supreme Court after graduating summa cum laude from Harvard or Yale. Felbin reflected on the many boring war stories he was subjected to during his younger days from judges who had either no trial experience or a limited second or third chair roll. "When I was trying cases," the bullshit would begin. As he aged, the bullshit was at least filtered because these blowhards knew Felbin was familiar with their less than stellar careers. Although it is not always about the money, Felbin often wondered why anyone who had a successful law practice would want to trade that to become a state court judge. Maybe it was the power and prestige. Or maybe it was just simply retirement.

Joan Cardwell was a case in point. Seemingly, her goal was always the bench. She was hired as a prosecutor in the City of St. Louis. When her acquittals exceeded her convictions, she had to make a decision. Get a job in private practice somewhere, preferably not as a litigator, or become a candidate for the elected position of the Circuit Attorney for the City of St. Louis. She took the political option which kept her on track for that coveted judgeship. That office would allow her more opportunity to do favors for those who could influence her future judicial efforts.

Finally, her Honor arrived. It was 8:20. So much for an 8 am hearing. But punctuality didn't apply to judges, just the lawyers and everyone else who entered the hallowed halls of the courthouse. The clerk informed the lawyers the judge would hear the matter in chambers rather than in the courtroom.

Before proceeding to the judge's chambers, Felbin decided to check the hall to see if his client had arrived. When he notified Garner of the date and time of the hearing, he said he and his father would be there to object to his attempted withdrawal. Felbin thought it was strange neither was present. *Perhaps they were not going to contest his motion.* Felbin returned to the courtroom and asked the bailiff to bring his client into the judge's chambers if he appeared.

When he entered Cardwell's chambers, the judge was sharing pleasantries with her former employee. She was seated behind a large, empty desk that contained only the Garner Lee file. Behind the desk was her trophy wall. Awards, pictures with politicians and other notables, her law license and law school diploma, dispelling Felbin's belief that she never went to law school. When he took his seat in front of her desk and next to the prosecutor, Felbin noticed she was wearing her judge's black robe. *You have got to be kidding.* Judges customarily don't wear their robes when they meet the attorneys in chambers. Usually, those conferences were informal. But in this case, Felbin assumed she was wearing her robe either because it was early, she was in a hurry and forgot to get dressed or it was her way of subtly reminding him she was in charge. He assumed it was the latter. This was going to be interesting. But he was hopeful this agony would not last very long. She would sustain his motion and he would be out of there and back to the real world.

"Good morning, Mr. Felbin. Nice to see you," the judge began.

Nice to see him? Felbin knew that was bullshit. It was never nice when these two were together. Never had been, never would be. Felbin resisted the temptation to verbalize what he really thought about her greeting. But he decided to play nice. After all, he would soon be rid of both her and the Lee family.

"Good morning. I was under the impression this matter was scheduled for 8," Felbin replied. He couldn't help himself.

Ignoring the reference to her tardiness, Judge Cardwell said, "We are here this morning on your motion to withdraw from this case, Mr. Felbin, is that correct?"

"That's correct," Felbin said, unable to force himself to address her as Judge or Your Honor.

"Why do you want to withdraw?"

"I have differences that cannot be resolved with the defendant and certain others that are influencing him."

This is the area where Felbin had to be careful he did not say anything detrimental to his client, particularly since the prosecutor was present.

"I'm going to need more than that to let you out."

"What are you talking about? This case is in its early stages and certainly this defendant can easily get replacement counsel without any delay. Secondly, you know or at least you should know, I can't discuss details of my relationship with my client in the presence of this prosecutor. If you're serious about needing more information before granting this routine motion, we will need to do it *in camera.* In case you didn't know, that means you and I will discuss this alone outside the presence of the prosecutor," Felbin said sarcastically. So much for playing nice.

In camera conferences with a judge involve only one party to the suit. The lawyer representing the party that has requested the conference meets privately with the judge and presents his position outside the presence of the lawyer for the other party. These conferences routinely occur to allow the court to become fully informed about a particular matter, while protecting the confidentiality of circumstances that might unnecessarily cause harm to one of the parties. Felbin asked for this meeting so he could explain in detail the involvement of Senator Lee and his client's refusal to pursue certain defenses. Obviously, that would be a discussion not meant for the prosecutor's ears.

"You want me to meet privately with you outside the presence of the prosecutor? I won't do that. It would be unethical. Your motion to withdraw is overruled. You're staying in this case," Cardwell ruled.

"You're kidding. I don't know which is worse, the fact you don't know what an in camera review is or that you have no reason to deny my motion other than to be vindictive," Felbin said as he left Cardwell's chambers.

Before leaving the courthouse, Felbin thought he would check the hallways one more time to see if Garner and his father arrived. No luck. But as he was looking, it occurred to him the absence of the Lees was not due to lack of interest. For as adamant and hostile as the senator was the day before, there was no way he'd changed his mind overnight.

Something wasn't right with this picture. Within an hour or less of the time he filed his withdrawal motion, he had a hearing scheduled bright and early the next morning. Neither father nor son appeared at the hearing to object to the motion. What should have been a motion routinely granted, was not. In fact, it appeared Cardwell had made up her mind before Felbin arrived. He wondered whether Cardwell had a conversation with anyone. The only way to find out would be to ask.

Since he was at the courthouse, he thought he would start with Cardwell. The door to her chambers was open and she was sitting behind her desk, absent the robe. No need to impress herself with her authority when no one else was around. Felbin stopped at the threshold and asked, "Did you talk to Senator Lee about my motion to withdraw?"

"Get out of my office and go and prepare for this trial, which I plan to set soon."

"Thanks. You answered my question. Actually, you answered several questions I had," Felbin said as he turned to leave her chambers.

Felbin's next call was to his client's father. "I just left Judge Cardwell's chambers and she said you and she had a conversation about this case," Felbin said, hoping to get an admission, but recognizing that the senator, like most politicians, was a skilled liar.

As expected, the response was an immediate denial. "I didn't have any conversation with her about this case. I already told you that," Senator Lee emphatically said.

"Then she lied to me? Why would she lie to me?" Felbin pressed, trying again to get an admission.

"I just told you I didn't talk to her, Mr. Felbin. And I doubt she told you I did. Sounds like you are the liar. Have a nice day," Lee said as he ended the conversation.

Felbin called Garner to let him know he was still in the case. There was no sense in questioning him about what his father had done. Felbin knew the senator would not trust his son to maintain the confidentiality of this type of issue. And he also knew this politician was attempting to influence the person he put on the bench. But there was one thing Felbin did not know. To what extent Cardwell would allow Senator Lee to influence her in connection with the murder charge his son was now facing. Felbin was concerned.

Chapter Twenty-Five

Felbin asked his investigator to come into his office. "We have ninety days to get this thing ready for trial. I just got the order from Cardwell. And interestingly, I didn't ask for a quick setting, which means she has been talking to the senator," Felbin told Tony Carmine.

Ordinarily, in the state of Missouri as well as other states, felony criminal trials, especially murder trials, do not occur in less than a year. However, criminal trials in federal courts are on a much faster track. Those that do not contain multiple defendants and complex issues can be scheduled in less than six months. But the case of State of Missouri versus Garner Lee was a state court matter.

"You're kidding. I've heard of the rocket docket, but this is ridiculous. I assume the client, or should I say his father, still wants a quick trial and we can't get a continuance," Carmine said.

"That would be correct. We just need to do the best we can."

"I also assume you still can't get rid of Cardwell."

"Right."

"If Lee is talking to Cardwell, is that good or bad for us?"

"I suppose it can be good for Garner, but not necessarily good for us."

"How so?" Carmine asked.

"Her rulings can favor Garner as a payback. But that's a potential ethical problem for us. What do we do if the fix is in? Blow the whistle, which will impact our client? Or sit back and do nothing and let it happen?" Felbin asked, understanding there was really no good answer.

"Well, first of all, we don't know Lee is talking to Cardwell. And if they are talking, we don't know if they're talking about this case. And finally, even if they're talking about the case, we don't know if Cardwell will do what the senator wants. We really don't know anything for sure right now."

"We know that with all of the judges in the criminal divisions, Cardwell is assigned this case. We know that after I filed the motion to withdraw, we got an immediate setting. We know she denied our motion, despite the fact this case is in its early stages. And we know she did so without hearing my position or that of the client, who wasn't there. Finally, she set this case for an immediate trial without any request from me or the prosecutor. That is what we know for sure right now," Felbin said.

"Let's break that down. We can't rule out a coincidence in her assignment to this case. She is a new judge with the fewest cases. The immediate setting on the motion can be explained because her case load is light, and she has the time. She also wants to move the case along and can't do so if the issue of his lawyer is not quickly resolved. She denied your motion because she hates your guts, which may be the real reason."

"That is one thing we absolutely know for sure," Felbin interrupted.

"I suppose she could have denied your motion because you wanted to get out and she wasn't going to give you what you wanted. She didn't care what the reasons were. That was your payback for all those times you embarrassed her. As far as the quick setting without you or the prosecutor asking, I can't explain that. Maybe she is just looking for something to do. But I suspect it is more than a coincidence that the senator wanted a quick trial setting," Carmine continued.

"But if he is talking to her about a quick setting, then he is talking to her about more than that. Unless the fix is in, why would they want a quick trial setting?"

"I don't know the answer to that, other than the senator wants this to go away as quickly as possible. From what I have seen so far, this guy couldn't care less about anyone other than himself, and that includes his kid."

"Yes, but having a convicted murderer in the family can't be a career enhancer. He wants this out of the headlines as quickly as possible, but he doesn't want the kid convicted for his own selfish reasons. And that is why he will call in the favor from Cardwell," Felbin theorized.

Jan Marshall, Felbin's administrative assistant, interrupted the conversation. "I think you are going to want to see this. It was just faxed in," she said.

"What is it?" Felbin asked.

"It is the autopsy report, and it will not help you."

Chapter Twenty-Six

Felbin read the report quickly and handed it to his investigator. He would study and analyze it later. But for the moment, he'd read enough to understand Jan's comment. Amy Deland was pregnant. Felbin asked Jan to contact Garner and get him into the office immediately and alone. Recognizing the significance of the report, Jan had already contacted Garner, and he was on his way.

"I'm not sure whether this helps us or hurts us as to the pending charge. It will depend on how we play it. Obviously, the prosecutor will see this. The question is whether he will want a DNA sample from Garner," Felbin said, surprised by what he'd just read.

"Why wouldn't he ask for one? There doesn't seem to be a downside for him on that," Carmine said.

"That's probably true. If Garner is the father, he could take the position that he didn't want the child and she refused to abort. That led to an argument, which led to rage and ultimately Amy's death. On the other hand, if Garner isn't the father, that plays better for him. Then he has a motive for murder juries clearly understand. The question now is whether we initiate a DNA analysis."

"But if we do that, isn't the prosecutor going to find out about our results?"

"Yes, I suppose so. Technically, we would be required to turn over our results."

"How far along was she according to the medical examiner?" Carmine asked.

"The report says eight weeks."

"If that is all she was, it is certainly possible Garner knew nothing about it. She wouldn't be showing at that point. And certainly, if he was not the father, she wouldn't be letting him in on her little secret. But we also have another problem. Will the prosecutor be adding another charge for the death of the unborn fetus?" Felbin wondered aloud.

Most of the states have fetal homicide laws. In the state of Missouri, life begins at conception. Depending on the circumstances, the death of an unborn fetus can be charged as a criminal act.

Felbin did not have to wait very long to see what the prosecutor was going to do. He was on the phone.

After some brief social conversation, Paul Perrin said, "I faxed the autopsy report over to you."

"I just got it," Felbin said.

"The cause of death is pretty straightforward, skull fracture, brain bleeds and swells, et cetera. But the report contains an unexpected finding. Amy Deland was pregnant at the time of her death. I'm sure you saw that."

"Actually, I just got it and really haven't had a time to thoroughly review it." A small white lie.

"Well, take a look at it. In the meantime, I would like to get a DNA sample from your guy, so that I can establish paternity. Will he consent to that?"

"I don't know. I need to read it first and then make a decision from there," Felbin said, keeping his options open.

"Okay. Let me know. If he doesn't want to do it voluntarily, I'm going to have to file a motion. And since we are on a short leash, I'm going to need to know his decision as soon as possible."

As soon as the conversation ended, Felbin looked at his investigator, who was reviewing the report. "We don't need to make a decision. They want a DNA sample. Now we have to worry about whether they will try to charge Garner with another count of murder. Interesting that Perrin didn't mention that. But I guarantee you they're considering a manslaughter charge for the fetus."

Before Carmine could respond, Felbin was told Garner had arrived and was in the conference room. He was not alone. His father was at his side.

The presence of a third party during an attorney-client conference waives the privilege. Other than the defendant in a criminal case, all who are in attendance could potentially become witnesses subject to subpoena and compelled to testify as to what was said.

The discussion to exclude the senator from Felbin's conference with his client was not a pleasant one. "I'm staying," Senator Lee said.

"Your presence here will potentially make you a witness and subject you to a subpoena," Felbin responded.

"No, it won't, because you're not going to tell anyone I was here."

Felbin knew that this was a no win and continuing this discussion would be a waste of time. The conference would go on with both Lees in attendance.

"Have it your way, Senator Lee. You always do." Turning to Garner, Felbin said, "We just got the autopsy report. Amy was pregnant."

Felbin had decided to break this news without any forewarning. He wanted to see the immediate reaction of both father and son.

"Oh, my God," Garner said, his eyes beginning to fill with tears.

No reaction whatsoever from Senator Lee.

"The prosecutor wants your DNA so he can see whether you are the father . . ." Felbin began before being interrupted.

"I am the father," Garner said immediately.

"Okay. Let me finish. It isn't that simple. We need to make some strategic decisions. We need to decide whether you will give him the sample voluntarily or make him get a court order. And there are . . ." Felbin said before he was interrupted a second time.

This time it was the senator. "We are not voluntarily giving a DNA sample. Make them get a court order," he said.

"With all due respect, Senator, that's not your decision. It's Garner's. And if you will allow me to continue, I will discuss the pluses and minuses of both courses of action."

"We don't need your pluses and minuses. We are not going to volunteer a DNA sample," Senator Lee said.

Felbin knew he had to stay cool and professional. But it would be difficult if this guy continued to give the orders.

Ignoring the senator's comment, Felbin looked at Garner and said, "Would you like me to explain the pluses and minuses, or do you know what you want to do?"

There was no immediate response. Garner looked confused. He wasn't thinking clearly. In his heart he knew he was the father. He didn't want to deny that. But he was being accused of murder and needed advice from someone he trusted. "I guess I'll go with my father's recommendation and won't volunteer my DNA," Garner finally said.

"Okay. I will let the prosecutor know. That's all I have for today. Have a nice day," Felbin said, as he and his investigator left the conference room.

When they returned to Felbin's office, Carmine said, "What happens now?"

"Perrin will file a motion to get Garner's DNA. It is a simple motion that will be granted. Then we'll see if our client is the father of a dead baby," Felbin replied.

That's what happens in an ordinary case. Felbin knew the case of Garner Lee was anything but ordinary.

Chapter Twenty-Seven

Karen Braxton was now the Circuit Attorney for the City of St. Louis, replacing Cardwell when she went to the bench. Braxton had been Cardwell's second in command for the entire time Cardwell was the elected prosecutor. She came from a large silk-stocking law firm that didn't do any criminal work. Consequently, she had no criminal trial experience and knew nothing about criminal law. But she helped get Cardwell elected and this was the payback. She agreed with everything Cardwell wanted to do and was viewed as the Circuit Attorney's lap dog by the real lawyers in the office. As a reward for all her years of dedicated service, Cardwell worked her political magic to ensure Braxton would replace her as the chief law enforcement officer in the city of St. Louis until the next election. Now, in her rookie year, she had a political tiger by the tail.

Paul Perrin needed direction on the new development in the Garner Lee case. He wanted to know whether he could file an additional charge against Lee for the death of Amy Deland's unborn fetus.

Myra Long was the Public Relations Officer for the Circuit Attorney's office. She, too, was a leftover from the Cardwell days and another yes person. Her interests had nothing to do with seeking justice. Her sole responsibility was to make sure Cardwell looked good in the eyes of the public. Now, that responsibility shifted to Braxton. So, it was no surprise Braxton sought the advice of Long on the latest development in the Garner Lee case.

The decision to charge the son of an influential politician with his sights set on the governor's office was not any easy one. After all, Braxton only had the job of Circuit Attorney temporarily to fulfill the unexpired term of Cardwell until the next election. Then she would need political help if she wanted to keep the office. Making an enemy of an influential politician would not help.

Unfortunately, Braxton was not consulted before Garner Lee was charged with murder. Detective Sergeant Jack Sandworth did an end run around the Circuit Attorney by having one of his buddies issue the warrant. And now it would be too late to do anything. The warrant had been issued. After many heated discussions with Detective Sergeant Jack Sandworth, Braxton and Long decided they had no choice but to pursue a charge against Garner Lee. They were both astute enough to understand that a dismissal at this point would result in a media crucifixion for all concerned.

But the question that remained was whether they could get away with a manslaughter charge instead of murder. Doubtful. In the final analysis, any effort to change the murder charge to a manslaughter for the son of a highly influential politician would be seen for what it was. Political favoritism. That, they concluded, would do more harm than good when she ran for her first full term as the chief law enforcement officer of the city of St. Louis. The compromise was murder second degree, as opposed to murder first degree. That, they believed they could sell to both the public and the senator.

Paul Perrin was a young prosecutor. He did not have much trial experience under his belt and wondered why he had been assigned such a high-profile case. He was not included in the discussion which resulted in the decision to keep the charge of murder second degree rather than trying to change it to manslaughter. The rumor around the office was that Braxton had met with Senator Lee before she made the decision to keep the murder charge Sandworth had so skillfully obtained. If true, Perrin thought that was rather unusual. However, although young and inexperienced, he knew politics, and politicians played a role in most things in life.

Now, faced with the prospect of putting an additional charge on the son of this politician, the immediate question to be answered was the depth of the political fallout and what could be done to minimize that fallout. After many discussions and hand-wringing, both Braxton and Long understood that another charge for the death of the unborn child probably needed to be filed. They would not be able to withstand the public outcry when, not if, it was discovered that justice was not pursued for the murder of a little, help-less, unborn child.

This time they figured if a charge had to be filed they could get away with involuntary manslaughter. They thought they could sell that to both the public and the sen-ator. Or at least they hoped they could. But before any final decision was made, Perrin wanted a DNA sample from the defendant. The police had not gotten one when they got the defendant's prints. Braxton and company figured that possibly could buy them a little more time. And maybe, just maybe, if they couldn't get the defendant's DNA, no addi-tional charge would be necessary. Of course, that wasn't the reason Perrin was looking to get the sample. Wishful and convoluted thinking, no doubt. They all knew whether Garner Lee was the father of the child had little to do with an additional manslaughter charge. An unborn child died, regardless of who the father was.

Chapter Twenty-Eight

As promised, the prosecutor filed a motion to compel the defendant to provide a DNA sample. Interestingly, that motion was filed under seal, which means that the public and most importantly the media, did not have access to it. Most judges would not have permitted a motion like that to be filed secretly. But Cardwell was not most judges. And, like the motion filed by Felbin, this latest motion was also scheduled for hearing with lightning speed.

Once again, Felbin was the first to appear for the hearing on the state's motion. He sat at the counsel table in the courtroom to organize his thoughts. Although he had little hope of prevailing on his objection, he would argue his client's DNA was not relevant to any issue in the case. And the prejudicial effect of that evidence would be outweighed by its probative value. In other words, the minimal, if any, value to the state would be disproportionally harmful to the defendant. In the interest of fairness, the evidence should be excluded, and the state would not be harmed by the exclusion.

As usual, Judge Cardwell was late. Apparently, eight o'clock in the morning was not her finest hour. At 8:15, the lawyers were invited into the judge's chambers. Since the matter was filed under seal, the argument of the motion would be behind closed doors, in chambers.

On the way back to the judge's chambers, Felbin asked Perrin to tell him who had the idea to file the motion under seal.

The response was immediate. "Not mine."

Before the argument began, Felbin asked for the proceedings to be recorded. He expected to lose the motion and wanted to make a record for possible appellate purposes. The judge accommodated his request and summoned her court reporter to record all that would be said during the hearing. But like the motion itself, the record of the argument would also be sealed. The only way the motion and the record could be unsealed was on the order of Judge Cardwell.

Paul Perrin began the argument.

"Your Honor, as our motion indicates, during the autopsy of the victim, it was discovered that she was pregnant. We are seeking the DNA of the defendant to determine paternity. We believe . . ." the prosecutor said before he was interrupted.

"Mr. Perrin, this isn't a paternity case. It's a murder case," Judge Cardwell noted.

It is not unusual for the court to ask questions and make comments during the argument of motions by the lawyers. When the jury is present, judges very seldom ask questions and are careful to avoid favoring one side or the other.

"I'm aware this is a murder case, Your Honor. But the point of the DNA is to establish a motive. If the defendant is not the father of the child, we believe this circumstance is a motive for murder," Perrin continued.

"What if the defendant is the father of the child?" the judge asked.

"It can still serve as a motive for murder. We know the defendant and the victim argued regularly. If the continuation of the pregnancy was an issue they argued about, that is information the jury should consider, because it describes the totality of their relationship. And remember, we have alleged that he killed her."

"Do you have any evidence that they argued about the pregnancy?"

"No."

"Actually, Mr. Perrin, do you have any evidence the defendant even knew about this pregnancy?"

"No, Your Honor."

"Sounds pretty speculative to me. Mr. Felbin, what is your position?"

Felbin made the relevancy argument he had prepared prior to the start of the hearing. In addition, he suggested the prosecutor had a sinister motive. Once acquired, the defendant's DNA would be in a data bank to be used in the future without notice. "I believe the court has to consider the privacy issues regarding this fishing expedition.

When those interests are compared, the prudent course is to preserve privacy," Felbin added. He knew his argument was total bullshit. But when you have the law, pound the law. When you have the facts, pound the facts. And when you have neither, pound the table. Felbin was doing a lot of table pounding.

"Your motion is overruled at this time, Mr. Perrin. I believe it is a fishing expedition. If you develop any additional evidence, you can refile the motion," Judge Cardwell ruled.

Felbin stood there motionless. He heard the words, but couldn't believe what he was hearing. He'd now lost a routine motion he should have won and won a routine motion he should have lost.

When she returned to her chambers, Cardwell made a phone call. When no one answered, she left a voicemail message. "They filed a motion to get the DNA sample and I took care of it. No sample will be given."

Chapter Twenty-Nine

As soon as he returned to the office, Felbin told his investigator he wanted to see him. While he was waiting, he contacted Garner and told him about the ruling. To his surprise, Garner said he was near the office and would like to come in.

"Did you get your ass kicked this morning?" Carmine asked when he came into Felbin's office.

"I won."

"You won what?"

"No DNA sample. They lost the motion. They get nothing," Felbin responded, still in shock.

"I thought you said you were going to lose that motion, and Garner would be forced to give a sample."

"I did say that."

"What the hell happened?" Carmine said, confused by Felbin's announcement.

"I have no idea. Obviously, it's not a paternity case, as Cardwell said. But it is a potential piece of evidence that could be used to explain the defendant's conduct, assuming they could prove somehow knew she was pregnant. It was another relatively routine motion that should have been granted. But it wasn't. I doubt any other judge would have denied that motion. They were absolutely entitled to the sample for a lot of different reasons. The question of whether they could use it during the trial is a different issue. But that was not before the court today. That's a story for another day."

"In light of her ruling today, do you think she will keep out any reference to the pregnancy altogether?"

"Yes, I think so as long as they don't bring another charge relating to the death of the child. If they do bring a manslaughter charge, then obviously the jury will hear about the pregnancy."

"Do you think they'll file another murder or a man-slaughter charge?"

"Ordinarily, I would say yes. I would think the press will have a field day if they didn't once it was discovered she was pregnant. Of course, finding that out might be a little difficult since their motion was filed under seal, and the motion was just heard in her chambers with a sealed record. But the way this case is going, nothing would surprise me."

"I don't understand why they just didn't bring the manslaughter charge to begin with. Surely they knew they couldn't just ignore the death of a child. Somebody was going to find out and leak it. And why try to get the DNA first before the additional charge is filed? I don't get it," Carmine said.

"I don't either. But I have to believe Cardwell, the senator, and Braxton are all joined at the hip. I suspect Senator Lee doesn't want to read the headline that his son is a baby killer. Because Braxton is such a bad prosecutor, maybe she thought if she lost the DNA motion and the pregnancy was leaked, she could take the position she couldn't prosecute for the death of the child. Of course, that's ridiculous and probably wouldn't pass the straight face test. But you never know what she and her friend Cardwell could cook up. Look at all the crap they pulled when they were in the Circuit Attorney's office together."

Carmine shook his head in agreement.

"The thing I really didn't understand is why they didn't argue they wanted to get his DNA sample to compare it to the DNA they claim they found on the murder weapon. They have a print and DNA on the murder weapon, yet Sandworth just gets fingerprints from a cooperating suspect. Something is up," Felbin said.

"Do we have all the DNA evidence and the profile off of the statue that we could compare to Garner's?" Carmine asked.

"Yes. We also have all the DNA evidence and the markers from Amy and the child."

Just as Felbin and his investigator were finishing their conversation, the client arrived. This time he was alone.

"Garner, is here," Felbin told Carmine.

"What's he doing here?"

"When I called him and told him about the DNA ruling, he said he was near the office and wanted to come in and talk."

"That's strange. What does he want to talk about?" Carmine asked.

"I have no idea. You know as much as I do. But talking to him and his father is never productive. At least not for us."

"Is his father with him?"

"No, he's alone."

"That's different. He wants to see us without his father controlling the entire meeting. This will be interesting."

"That it will. Let's go see what's on his mind," Felbin said as they both headed for the conference room where Garner was waiting.

Chapter Thirty

When Felbin and Carmine arrived at the conference room, they found Garner standing by the window, his back to the conference room door. They said hello and asked how he was doing. No response. He didn't turn around or otherwise acknowledge their presence. He continued to look out the window. It appeared he was looking at nothing in particular, just staring, deep in thought.

Felbin waited awhile for a response. Still nothing. Finally, concerned about the behavior, he said, "Garner, are you okay?"

"No. I'm not okay," Garner said, continuing to look out the window, his back to the lawyer and his investigator.

"What's the problem? Let's talk about what's bothering you," Felbin said.

Garner Lee had come to talk to his lawyer without his father. That was a first. And now he was upset. Something was troubling him. And apparently, he didn't want his father to know what it was.

"The last time we were here, we talked about volunteering my DNA to see if I was the father of the child. My father said we would not volunteer it and I went along with that decision. I want the DNA test. I know I am the father of that child. But for my own peace of mind, I want it confirmed through the science," Garner said as he turned to face Felbin and his investigator.

Felbin was listening to what his client was saying. He understood it was important for Garner to verify he was the father of the child he lost. He also understood he was representing a kid who loved the woman who died, didn't kill her, and was being pushed in a direction he didn't want to go by his father. But this was a criminal case. Not a civil paternity matter. "It's not that simple, Garner," Felbin finally said.

"It is that simple. The simple fact of the matter is that I loved this woman, didn't harm her, and certainly did not kill my child."

"I understand what you are saying. And I believe you. But, as I said, this is a serious criminal case. I can't do anything which has a chance of getting you convicted. I have explained that the DNA evidence in this case can be a double-edged sword. If you are not the father, they will argue that when you found out, you became enraged and killed her. If you are the father, which I believe you are, they will say you didn't want the child and were upset she was pregnant and became angry when she refused to end the pregnancy."

"But none of that is true. I didn't even know she was pregnant," Garner replied.

"I know. But that is not the point."

"Please listen to me. I loved her. I didn't kill her."

"We know that, Garner," Carmine injected.

"You need to understand something. Since I have been with Amy, my life has been a living hell, and now I'm accused of killing her."

"What do you mean your life has been a living hell?" Felbin asked.

"My family didn't want me to have anything to do with her. They repeatedly told me to dump her. They said vile things about her. She was an opportunist who was using me. She was taking advantage of my social status or rather my family's social status, not mine. And now she is dead, and I'm sure they are happy about that."

"That's pretty strong, Garner. I doubt they're happy someone was killed," Carmine said.

"No. I think it is true. They don't like the fact I'm charged with her murder. But I'm sure they are thinking at least she is out of my life and we don't have to fight about that anymore. And the reason they don't like the fact I'm charged with murder has nothing to do with me and everything to do with them. My father is all about his political image. And my mother is all about her image, the law firm and her blue blood family background."

As Carmine and Felbin listened to this rant, they wondered where this was going. *Did Garner grow a pair overnight and would he now stand up to his parents, and in par-*

ticular, his father? Would he now control this case, rather than continuing to allow his father to make bad decisions? Would he now listen to the advice from his lawyer? Or was he just venting safely outside the presence of his parents?

"I admit that I haven't been a model child. School and a career were not important to me. I was a playboy. And that was not anyone's fault but mine. But then Amy came along. She provided the stability in my life I needed. And that was taken away from me by someone for some unexplained reason. I have nothing left except the memory of a child we made together out of love and I didn't even know we had. Acknowledging that unborn child is important to me. Do you understand what I'm saying?"

Garner began to cry as Felbin and Carmine watched in silence. If this guy was good for the murder of Amy Deland, then this was an academy award performance. But neither Felbin nor Carmine thought their client was acting. They truly believed he lost someone he loved, and that loss was painful. Now he learned he'd also lost a child. And the only way he could deal with what he had left was to embrace a child he never knew existed. But they were lawyers, not shrinks. For reasons that were not completely clear, the court blocked the prosecution's effort to get a DNA sample. That was an unexpected break that could not be compromised.

"We understand your position. But we can accomplish the same thing if we do the test privately without the risks," Felbin said.

"No, we can't. What you don't understand is that I know I am the father of this child, and I want the prosecutor to know that," Garner replied.

"We can give him the results of the private test later."

"That's not the same. It looks like we were uncertain I was the father and that's why we did a private test. I'm not uncertain. Please tell them they can have their sample."

When Lee left the office, Carmine looked at Felbin asked, "How in the hell are we going to get this done without the prosecutor finding out?"

"I have no idea. We need to follow his directions, but not necessarily right away. In the meantime, I'm sure you will figure out something. But right now, we need to figure out how we are going to defend this guy," Felbin said. He left Carmine sitting alone in the conference room.

Chapter Thirty-One

Figuring out how to do a secret paternity and playing armchair psychologist to deal with the mental health of the defendant had to wait. Time was short. Carmine needed to figure out what the prosecution's case was all about, where the weak spots were, and how the defense could capitalize. Those were the priorities.

Carmine already knew from the police reports that Amy's friends had no love for Garner. They believed that he killed their friend, and they were going to do everything that they could to make sure that he paid the price. But what he didn't know was the background of the victim. That is where he would start.

Amy had worked for the Stoner Group, a St. Louis based advertising agency that represented many of the large national corporations throughout Missouri and elsewhere. She was assigned to the political division and was the administrative assistant to Roger Carroll, who headed that division. Carmine thought he would begin with her supervisor.

The Stoner Group was only a few blocks away from Felbin's office in downtown St. Louis. They occupied the 26th and 27th floors of a 40-story building overlooking the St. Louis Arch and the Mississippi River. The reception area was elaborately furnished, typical of a company trying to impress high dollar clients. Carmine was escorted into a large glass enclosed professionally decorated conference room complete with a scenic and impressive view of both the arch and the river.

A short time later, Roger Carroll appeared. He was what Carmine had expected, a professional-looking business man. Carmine estimated his age at around 50, salt and pepper hair neatly trimmed, wearing a starched white, buttoned down shirt with a pink and green striped tie.

Carroll had nothing but high praise for Amy and was clearly upset by her unexpected death. He described her as conscientious, bright and very personable. Usually, the assistants had little if any contact with the clients. But Amy was different. Her personality endeared her to the clients, and she'd had a great deal of contact with them. In fact, Carroll had so much confidence in her ability that he even permitted client contact in his absence.

But Carmine wasn't interested in listening to accolades. Instead, he needed information which would help defend his client on a murder charge. He needed to find out who would have a reason to kill Amy Deland.

"What exactly did Amy do for your agency?" Carmine asked.

"Our company is obviously in the advertising business. We represent most of the large companies that call Missouri home. Apart from the corporate side is the political group which I supervise. Our job is to get political clients elected. We formulate advertising programs with input from the candidates and their staffs. We also do their public relations work. Amy was a big part of our team."

"In other words, you are the spin doctors, and she would help formulate the spin?"

"I am not sure I would put it quite that way. But yes, she had input into the types of ads that would run and when and where they would run."

"Was your political clientele limited to Missouri, or did you also have national candidates or candidates in other states?"

"The company does represent candidates in other states. However, our group is limited to Missouri. We do mostly Democrats who are seeking state-wide office. Although we also do some, but not many, local municipal elections, usually the mayoral races."

"How many people are in your group?"

"In addition to myself, there are five people in our group. All women and, as I said, I'm the supervisor. Amy pretty much ran the show in my absence."

"Do you do any socializing with the staff?"

"Occasionally, I will have a drink with them. But the ladies are all good friends outside of work."

"Have you ever met Amy's boyfriend?"

Carroll hesitated. He wasn't expecting that question.

"You said you wanted to talk about Amy. You wanted some employment history. Why are you asking me about her social life?" Carroll asked.

"Is that question a problem for you, Mr. Carroll?" Carmine responded, answering the question with a question, a trick that Felbin taught him.

"I just really don't feel comfortable about answering any questions about Amy's personal life."

"Okay, fair enough. Thank you for your cooperation," Carmine said, ending his interview.

Becky Smallwood also worked with Amy at Stoner. She had found her friend's body. Unlike Carroll, she was willing to discuss the relationship between Garner and her friend. There were no surprises in what she had to say. Her description of the relationship was consistent with what she had told the police. No love lost between her and Garner. That didn't help.

Before he concluded the interview, Carmine thought that he would take a shot at seeing if she could explain Carroll's refusal to discuss Amy's social life.

"Thanks, Becky. I appreciate your taking the time talk to me. I know this has been really rough on you," Carmine said.

"You're welcome," she replied.

As they both stood getting ready to leave the conference room, Carmine said, "Please tell Roger thanks again for taking the time to talk to me and making you available. Tell him that I didn't mean to upset him or make him feel uncomfortable."

Carmine figured that Becky Smallwood was a person who liked to be in the know and was no stranger to spreading some good gossip. He knew that she couldn't resist asking about the Roger Carroll comment. Her boss upset or uncomfortable? She's in.

"What do you mean?" she asked without hesitation.

"Oh nothing, he just didn't want to talk about the relationship between Amy and Garner. And I thought that he might have met Garner, so it struck me as odd that he refused to go down that road with me."

"Probably because of his father," she volunteered. No question necessary.

"Whose father?" Carmine asked.

"Garner's."

Garner's father? Carmine had no idea what Garner's father had to do with Roger Carroll and the Stoner Group. Then it occurred to him. But he asked the question anyway, just to confirm his thought. "What does Garner's father have to do with this?"

"He's a client of the firm."

Chapter Thirty-Two

"Why didn't we put that together?" Felbin asked after listening to Carmine's recap of his conversation with Becky Smallwood.

"Probably because we didn't know anything about the Stoner Group where the victim worked."

"What does that do for our defense in this case? Does the fact the defendant's father is a client of the advertising agency where the victim worked, help us or hurt us?"

"I don't know the answer to that yet," Carmine said.

"What I find interesting is that neither Garner nor his father mentioned this little detail," the lawyer pointed out.

"Maybe they didn't think it was important."

"Not important? The kid is dating an employee of the firm that represents his father. And both father and mother hate the girlfriend. Yet, father continues to work with the person that both father and mother hate. And that is not important to us in defending their son?"

"Well, apparently the Stoner Group is good at what they do, and the senator may not want to switch to another agency. I did some checking on Stoner. They are well respected and considered to be one of the best, not only here but nationally," Carmine said. "Apparently, there aren't all that many companies that have a political division. Or at least not that many that are any good in St. Louis. If he fired Stoner, he would have to go out of town to get someone just as good, and that would cost more money. And remember, Senator Lee is all about Senator Lee and not his kid or anyone else."

"I hear you. But there is something is not quite right about that situation. I can't put my finger on exactly what it is, but I don't have a good feeling. As a matter of fact, I don't have a good feeling about anything in this case. We wind up with a judge that the defendant's father put on the bench. Then we try to get out of the case and we can't. Then she denies a routine motion for DNA evidence in a case that involves the death of an unborn child," Felbin said.

"I hear you. I just wonder what's next," Carmine said.

"Here's another thing that I don't understand. When Cardwell denied the motion to get the DNA sample, there was no reaction from Perrin. Usually, these prosecutors would be jumping up and down and screaming if they lost a motion like this. Ordinarily, the Circuit Attorney and a platoon of assistants would be in the judge's chambers yelling and threatening if the ruling isn't changed. Hell, they whine when they lose a motion that there is no way they should win. But not in this case."

"Politics," Carmine said. "Once again, politics invades the criminal justice system. From what I'm hearing, Braxton didn't want to pursue this, but she got some heat from the police department. Apparently, Jack Sandworth did an end run to get the case issued and then threatened to go public if they didn't prosecute this kid."

"That's interesting. It explains their attitude. It may also explain how we wound up with Cardwell and her crazy rulings."

Carmine thought about what Felbin had just said. "Are you saying Cardwell is in bed with the prosecutors?"

"I don't know. But I certainly wouldn't rule it out."

"That's interesting. Usually, our clients are the ones getting screwed, not benefitting from the political bullshit. But since this is a whole new world for us, I'm just wondering what that gets us for Garner."

"I don't know where it gets us in the long run. But my more immediate concern is whether they'll be adding another charge for the unborn child. And if your information is correct, I suspect Sandworth will pitch another fit if that charge isn't added. I'm guessing we'll see that charge soon because they won't want to blow the trial setting."

Chapter Thirty-Three

Carmine couldn't worry about politics; his job was to figure out if the state's case had any holes, and time was short. He'd need to visit Amy's apartment and talk to the neighbors.

Sam and Andrea Jennings, a couple in their mid-thirties, lived in apartment 2A across the hall from Amy Deland. They confirmed what they had told the police. Although they were uncertain of the time, they identified Garner Lee from a photograph as the man they had seen walking up the stairs to Amy's apartment at the same time they were leaving to go to dinner on February 14. They had never met Garner, knew him only as a frequent visitor. In fact, they admitted they really hadn't known Amy well. Andrea Jennings also mentioned that periodically, she would see another male visitor. The only description she could provide was a black male who always wore a black baseball cap.

Janice and Jim Berry lived on the first floor of this two-story apartment building. Carmine estimated them to be in their early sixties. They didn't hear or see anything of note on February 14. From time to time, they would see men enter the apartment building and assumed they were visiting Amy. No additional details could be offered as to the identity of these visitors, as the Berrys really didn't pay much attention to the comings and goings of Amy or her visitors. For the most part they kept to themselves. Like the Jennings, the Berrys didn't know Amy Deland very well.

Clara Carson, however, was the self-appointed mayor of the apartment building. As a first-floor resident, Clara knew who was entering and leaving the building. The fact that her easy chair was positioned in front of the window helped. She was able to identify Garner in a photograph.

Clara was a widow and proudly announced her age at 86 years young. Although she was out of town on the day of the murder, she knew all the details. It was a shame poor sweet Amy was murdered by that black boy. Clara wasn't shy about sharing her opinions on any subject whether or not one asked. She was also not terribly fond of political correctness. She had seen Garner going to visit Amy regularly. Although she had never met him, she knew that relationship was not good for Amy. Carmine didn't bother to ask her why she would form that opinion when she had never met Garner. He didn't need to ask. Clara was the product of a different era.

"Did you ever talk to Amy about her friend?" Carmine asked.

"Yes. After I saw him coming here quite a bit, I asked her who he was. She told me his name was Garner and he was just a friend. Well, I knew that wasn't true. I knew what that boy was looking for."

"Did she tell you anything else about him or their relationship?"

"No. She would just tell me he was a friend. I told her he wasn't good for her. This was a while ago. But he kept coming. If she had listened to me, she would still be alive. It's really tragic. Pretty young girl like that murdered."

Clara also volunteered her concern about another of Amy's visitors. She described this individual as a black male who always wore a black baseball hat pulled down, as though he was trying to conceal his face. She was not able to provide any additional descriptive details because *they all look alike.* She readily admitted her eyesight was not what it once was. These visits would not be on any particular schedule, but always at night, after dark which also limited her ability to provide a more detailed description. He would stay for about an hour and leave, hat still in place concealing his face.

"Ms. Carson, if they all look alike as you say, how do you know that this individual was not Garner?" Carmine asked.

"Because that young man never wore a hat."

As Carmine was trying to evaluate the credibility of this witness, she supplemented her answer to his question. "The guy with the hat drove a black car that had a light out in the back. I was going to tell him about it because that's not safe. But I never got around to it. And the other guy, that Garner fella, had a little red car. I think it was red. But

I know for sure that he didn't have a light out in the back like that other guy."

"Which taillight was it, right or left?

"It was on the right side."

"As you are looking at the rear of the vehicle, the light that was out was on the right side, the passenger side?" Carmine asked.

"Yes," Carson said.

"The fella with the taillight out, do you know what kind of a car it was?"

"Well, I'm not real good with cars. But this one wasn't like a regular car. It was more like a van, but it wasn't as big as a van," she said, unable to clearly describe the exact make and model.

"Was it an SUV? Do you know what that is?"

"No, I don't know cars. I have had the same old car for years. But this one looked like a station wagon, but it wasn't a station wagon."

That was close enough for Carmine. She was describing a black SUV with a rear taillight burned out.

"Did you happen to get a license plate number?"

"No. It was a Missouri license plate, but I didn't make a note of it."

"How long had this guy with the burned-out taillight been coming to visit Amy?"

"I wasn't counting, but I know he was coming here for quite a while. Why? Is that important?"

"I don't know. I am just trying to gather as much information as I can about Amy and the circumstances of her death," Carmine said.

"Sounds like a waste of time to me. Everybody knows that black boy killed her."

"Thank you for your help, Ms. Carson," Carmine said, quickly trying to leave the apartment and put some distance between himself and this lady who could be Donald Trump's mother.

Chapter Thirty-Four

As expected, the state added a count of involuntary manslaughter for the death of the unborn child. In Missouri, a person commits the offense of involuntary manslaughter if he or she recklessly causes the death of another person. For purposes of that statute, an unborn child is deemed a person.

Although Felbin and company didn't know exactly what was going on with the prosecutor, the judge, and the senator, they figured the state could not simply ignore the death of the unborn child. They would not be able to credibly explain it, particularly if Sandworth involved the press, which he was likely to do.

The problem now was the paternity test. Surely, Perrin would revisit the issue and ask Judge Cardwell to reconsider her previous order denying his request for a DNA sample. The prosecutor now was in a little better position to obtain the defendant's DNA. He had a manslaughter charge.

Felbin and his investigator needed to figure out a game plan to handle this latest development.

"I assume Perrin will be filing a motion to try to get another bite of the DNA apple," Felbin began.

"No doubt. And is there anything we can do to prevent it?" Carmine asked.

"I would have thought there was nothing I could do the last time he asked for a DNA sample. But, obviously, I was wrong. That idiot Cardwell told him this wasn't a civil paternity case and she wasn't going to order him to produce his DNA. And it is still not a civil paternity case. But it is a criminal involuntary manslaughter case, and that ups the ante. Of course, we will again say it's not relevant for whatever that will be worth."

"That may be worth a lot if the fix is in."

"That's true. Let's get Garner on the phone to let him know about the new development."

Ordinarily, a new charge would give the defense a basis to request a continuance. But Felbin knew his client, or rather his client's father, would continue to press for a speedy trial and would resist any effort to the contrary.

When Felbin spoke to Garner on the phone, he explained the new charge and his expectation of a renewed effort to obtain his DNA. No reaction. Silence on the other end. Finally, Garner spoke. "Good. Now we can get the DNA test done and everyone will see this is my child, which will show how much I loved her."

Now it was Felbin who was speechless. Either his client was delusional or really stupid—or perhaps both.

"Garner, we have been through this before. Putting your DNA in the hands of this prosecutor for a paternity test is a very bad idea. They can use it against you whether you are or are not the father of this child. If they file another motion to get your DNA for a paternity test, I suggest we resist like we did successfully before," Felbin said.

"No. I want the test," Garner responded immediately and forcefully.

"Listen. We can figure out a way to get the test done privately and in the meantime, resist the state's efforts to the test," Felbin suggested.

Once again, the response was immediate and forceful. "No. You don't understand. It's important for everyone to know that this is my child. When they file the motion to obtain my DNA, I want you to consent," Garner directed as he ended the call.

As he listened to his client insist on a course of action that would undoubtedly hurt his efforts to defend these serious criminal charges, Felbin wondered whether something else was motivating him. Felbin knew for whatever reason, Garner's parents disapproved of his relationship with Amy. In fact, according to Garner, they made his life hell. Garner was certain the child was his. Felbin was not as certain. Was this Garner's way of sticking it to his parents? Showing them he and the woman they hated were going to have a child? Black rich kid lawyer from a powerful political family impregnates a white low class nobody. That type of revenge might very well be sweet. But dangerous.

"Does this guy want to be convicted?" Carmine asked.

"If I thought it would do any good, I would file another motion to get out of this case. This kid is on a course of self-destruction. I suspect some of this is payback to his parents for the problems they created for him and Amy. Unfortunately, since I can't get out, I have to follow his wishes. He is the client and has the right to control his case, regardless of where that takes him. We can only advise."

"Do you think it would do any good to contact his father and see if he can help us persuade this kid to get off this paternity test thing?"

"Sometimes I think his father wants to get him convicted, given his behavior. Although I'm not excited about asking him to do anything, I'll give it a shot. We have nothing to lose," Felbin said, his voice lacking enthusiasm.

"By the way, I had an interesting conversation with one of Amy's neighbors that may be helpful. A Clara Carson lives on the ground floor and spends her days monitoring the people who are coming and going in and out of the building. She is a piece of work. An 86-year-old lady who has no time for black people and is firmly convinced that Garner killed Amy."

Felbin was confused. "How is a racist old lady who believes our client is guilty going to help us?"

"She said that Amy had another regular visitor. A black guy who would visit at night and wore a hat that was pulled down as though he was trying to conceal his face. He would stay for about an hour and then leave in a car with a broken taillight."

Felbin was still uncertain how this piece of information was going to help defend Garner Lee. A regular visitor who would show up at night, stay for an hour and leave, while trying to conceal his identity. Obviously, Amy was an active young lady who had more than one friend. Equally obvious was the fact that Garner's concept of the relationship was different than Amy's. But how was that going to fit into this defense? Or would it be better left out of any defense? Felbin had some decisions to make. And none were good.

Chapter Thirty-Five

The media wasted no time running a front page above the fold story that the only child of the most powerful and influential politician in the state's son was a baby killer. The article was brutal. The headline worse. *Garner Lee Accused of Killing a Baby.* The presumption of innocence was completely obliterated. But interestingly, Karen Braxton, the elected Circuit Attorney, declined comment. Unusual for a politician to resist the temptation to grab a headline in the interests of justice. But this case was an unusual pursuit of justice.

It was bad enough that Garner was the son of a politician, and a kid of privilege. All politicians have enemies, and Senator Lee had more than his share, particularly among white people. The chances that some of those enemies would wind up on the jury was high, and Felbin knew that. But now, Garner Lee would also be facing a jury as a baby killer. And all the money, power and influence would not help him in the world of the common people who would be charged with the responsibility of deciding his fate.

As he read the article, Felbin knew it would only be a matter of time before he heard from his client's father. No sooner did he finish the article when he was informed that the senator was on the phone. He thought about ducking the call, but figured that this arrogant prick would appear in his office and it was better to deal with him on the phone than in person.

"What the fuck is going on?" the senator began.

"And good morning to you, too, Senator," Felbin replied, thinking that his day probably couldn't get any worse.

"No, it's not a good morning. Did you read that fucking article? Those bastards butchered me."

"Butchered you? And here I thought it was your son who was pending serious felony charges that would be prejudiced by this kind of article. I didn't know you were defending murder charges, too," Felbin said, struggling to remain professional with this self-centered, egomaniac.

"This thing impacts the entire family. We told him he needed to dump her sorry gold digging ass. She was nothing but . . .

Felbin interrupted the rant. He was in no mood and it accomplished nothing. "Stop. This isn't getting us anywhere, Senator. If you have a question or a concern, I'll listen. Otherwise, this conversation is a waste of my time and yours."

"No, it's not a waste of time, and you will listen. That is what I pay you to do." Anger filled the senator's voice.

Felbin considered hanging up. He really didn't need this bullshit from this political hack. But for the sake of his client, he needed to maintain his cool. He was the only hope Garner Lee had. "Let's get something straight, Senator Lee. You pay me to represent your son in a very serious matter. Nothing more. Now what is it that you want?"

"What I want is to get through this case. Now we have another charge. I suppose now they will be able to get the DNA sample."

That comment took Felbin by surprise. Did Lee know the court had denied the prosecutor's request to get a DNA sample? And if so, how did he know, since the motion was filed under seal and argued in the judge's chambers? The press never picked it up? Felbin decided to press the issue. "What do you mean?" he asked.

"I assume that with the new manslaughter charge they will make another effort to get Garner's DNA, to show he is the father of the child."

It was clear to Felbin that the senator had not spoken to his son about his desire to volunteer his DNA or the court's denial of the prosecutor's effort to get the sample. But he thought that he would ask anyway. "Have you spoken to Garner about the DNA issues?"

"No. Garner shut out his mother and me. He doesn't talk to us about this case anymore. In fact, he doesn't talk to us period, and hasn't for a while."

Although Felbin knew some of this from Garner's perspective, at the risk of encouraging another rant, he wanted to hear how the senator viewed this conflict. He decided to wait on the question of how he knew about the state's sealed motion. He was pretty sure where that information came from. "Why did Garner shut you out?"

"Because we opposed his relationship with this gold digger. We had numerous arguments about this. He didn't listen to us, and look at where it got him."

"Do you think he is the father of that unborn child?"

Senator Lee didn't answer immediately. It appeared he wasn't expecting the question. But when he did finally answer, he said, "I have no idea. I'm guessing she was involved with more men than just Garner."

Since his client was not discussing the case with his father, Felbin would not disclose Garner's direction to volunteer his DNA in his effort to tell the world he was the father of this child. Instead, he decided to take the conversation in a different direction.

"Did you know Amy Deland?" Felbin began.

Another question that Lee was not expecting. And another delay in his response. Lee's response was simple and straight forward. "No."

Felbin knew that was not completely true. Senator Lee was a client of the Stoner Group, an advertising agency. They handled his political advertising, and Amy Deland was an employee of that company. In fact, she would occasionally have supervisory responsibilities in the absence of the manager of the political division of the agency. It appeared to Felbin that Lee would at least know Amy Deland.

"Aren't you a client of the Stoner Group?"

"Yes. But what the hell does that have to do with this?"

"Amy Deland was an employee of the Stoner Group. In fact, she was assigned to the political section of that advertising agency. Are you telling me that you didn't know that?" Felbin pressed.

Clearly annoyed by the question, the senator said, "Of course I knew that she was employed there. But you asked me if I knew her. I knew who she was, but I didn't know her. And I didn't want to get to know her, given her relationship with my son."

"Did Garner know that Amy worked for the agency that did your political advertising?"

"I have no idea what he knew and didn't know. I didn't tell him, and he never mentioned that she told him. My guess is he didn't know. But, again, what does this have to do with anything? More importantly, how are you going to prevent the prosecutor from getting his DNA sample? Whether or not he is the father of this child seems to be irrelevant to whether he is guilty of murder and manslaughter. It can also be prejudicial because either way, it will supply a motive for murder," Senator Lee said, his tone escalating from annoyed to hostile.

Felbin had several more questions to ask the senator about his relationship with Amy, but thought it best to save them for a more cordial moment in the unlikely event that would ever occur. Instead, he just said, "I don't know how I am going to prevent the state from getting Garner's DNA."

Given the current relationship between father and son, Felbin felt Lee could read about what Garner planned to do with his DNA in the newspaper, if and when the issue became public. He could also read that his son was to have a child with the woman he considered a gold digger.

Chapter Thirty-Six

The Circuit Attorney had her own problems. Not only had she charged the son of the most powerful politician in the state with murder, now she had to add a count of manslaughter for the death of a fetus. On top of that, she was only the interim Circuit Attorney replacing her predecessor, Joan Cardwell. When she runs for election, she would need the senator's help and the help of his friends. Making him an enemy by sending his son to the penitentiary would not be helpful. She also knew that declining either charge would be equally problematic when it was election time. Most people shared a complete disdain for politicians these days. But worst yet was an elected prosecutor who fixed a case for a fellow politician.

Karen Braxton saw the Baby Killer headline and read the article. She needed a strategy session with Myra Long, her public relations director. Somehow, they had to figure out a way to get through this prosecution without alienating future political support. If anyone could figure that out, it was Myra. After all, she had been successful in keeping Cardwell out of trouble when she was the elected prosecutor.

"In light of this article, do we need to have another conversation with Senator Lee?" Braxton asked.

"I don't think so. I don't know that it would do any good, and I don't know what I would say to him. We didn't write the article," Long said.

"I know we didn't write the article. But do we need to reassure him that our heart is really not in this prosecution? But the fallout would be worse both for him and me if we didn't pursue the case."

"I already told him that. And I also told him that we assigned the case to a young inexperienced prosecutor. He doesn't like the whole mess, but he understands. He wants to get through this as quickly as possible. As you know,

Felbin is on a short leash. He can't get out of the case and he can't request a continuance to get more time to prepare the defense. The only thing he questioned was the need to get a DNA sample. He knows that we lost our motion to get a sample the last time we tried it and wants to know if we are going to file another motion. He was not happy that we didn't tell him we were filing the last motion. I told him that I would check," Long added, uncertain about the DNA sample question.

Braxton as the Circuit Attorney understood the need to get this case concluded as quickly as possible. She didn't understand why Lee was opposed to a DNA sample, and asked Long if she had any ideas.

"I suspect that because he didn't care for Amy Deland and he doesn't want proof his son is the father of her child. He probably thinks this will hurt him when he runs for governor. As I'm sure you know, this guy is all about himself. Sometimes I wonder whether he cares if his kid is convicted, as long as he can get this case out of the public eye," Long said.

"I'm sure he cares about whether his son is convicted, but only because that will continue to keep this case on the front page and will haunt him in the campaign," Braxton said.

"Politics is an evil game played by people who would go to any lengths to feed their egos and destroy anyone who gets in the way," Long said, recognizing that she was speaking to someone with no political experience who would soon be entering the game.

Braxton said, "I'm wondering if we need to show the defendant is the father of this child. What difference does it make? When he killed his girlfriend, he also caused another death. Let's get Perrin in here to see what he thinks."

Perrin came in and listened to the concerns of the two women. He thought about the question for a moment. He was young and inexperienced, but he was not an idiot. He had been assigned this high-profile case, and it was not because he was the son of Clarence Darrow. He didn't need a house to fall on him to figure out that politics were playing a role in this prosecution. And now this question. Uncertain why his boss would be asking a question like this, he said, "I don't need to prove who the father is in order to prove the crime of manslaughter, if that is what you are asking. The paternity issue goes to the question of motive. I think that's important to this case."

"What do you mean?" Long asked.

Now the public relations person was asking questions. He knew that public relations people shouldn't get involved in advising on trial strategy issues, but answered the question nonetheless. "If he's not the father, then that means she was involved with someone else. In many cases, infidelity is a motive for murder. If he *is* the father and didn't want the child, that's also a motive for murder. And while I have no obligation to prove motive, jurors like some explanations of why people perform criminal acts. Does that answer your question?"

"But you can't prove that the defendant knew she was pregnant. Isn't that correct?" Braxton interjected.

"Right. I don't have any proof that he knew about the child when he killed Amy," Perrin said.

"Then what is the point of trying for a second time to get his DNA?" Braxton asked.

"Because if I get his DNA, I'll know whether he is or is not the father of this child. At this point, I'm not sure how I would use that at trial. I am not even sure the court would allow me to use it. I am also not sure whether he will testify, and if he does, whether I can use it to cross-examine him. But I know this for sure, if I don't get his DNA, I won't have the option. The bottom line is that I need to get his DNA and frankly, I am not sure why we are having this conversation."

Perrin didn't know the real reason why Braxton was asking the question. She had to think of an answer that would give her some cover. Braxton said, "We lost one motion on the DNA issue and I didn't want to lose another one. I was concerned that if the court denies a second attempt to get the DNA, it would weaken our case generally."

After Perrin left, Braxton said, "We have to file that motion. We really have no choice. I must assume this issue will eventually be picked up by the media. She was pregnant, and someone is the father. There is no doubt in my mind the sharks will be pursuing the identity of the father. Those are the stories that sell advertising."

Long, the public relations guru, agreed.

"And while I don't want to make this guy an enemy," Braxton continued. "I need to look out for my own political future. I want to be in a position to say publicly that we prosecuted this case vigorously. I also don't want Perrin going rogue if this paternity issue becomes a matter of public record, which I believe it will. Whether Cardwell grants it is another issue. I'll tell Perrin it's okay to file the motion and set it for argument immediately. In the meantime, I'll have a conversation with Cardwell."

"Are we are going to file it under seal again?" Long asked.

"Yes. We can justify the secrecy based on privacy concerns."

"Are we going to tell the senator what we are doing?"

"No. I don't see the court granting the motion, and I'm really not interested in having another conversation with him on this issue," Braxton said.

Chapter Thirty-Seven

"Didn't I hear and deny that motion once in this case?" Judge Cardwell asked.

The Circuit Attorney was meeting with the judge behind closed doors in chambers to discuss a case while she was prosecuting it, a practice that was totally unethical for both the judge and the prosecutor. The rules of court as well as those of professional responsibility prohibited what is known as an *ex parte* communication. The judge is prohibited from discussing a pending case with only one of the parties. All parties must be present. Apparently, Cardwell and Braxton either were not familiar with those well-known rules, or they just didn't care to follow them.

"Yes, but that was before we filed the manslaughter charge," Braxton replied.

"You think that makes a difference and I should grant the motion?"

"Not exactly."

"Then *what* exactly? The last time I thought you didn't want the motion granted. And now you said you are filing another request for the defendant's DNA, and you want me to deny it again? I'm confused."

"Perrin is pressing the issue, and I'm concerned that if I don't file it, he could be a future problem." Braxton decided against pointing out that she needed to protect herself from future political fallout, because that also applied to Cardwell. "Frankly, I don't think it matters whether we get the sample from a technical evidentiary standpoint, but Perrin is trying the case. Ordinarily, as we did when you ran the office, I would just leave that decision up to the trial attorney. But this case is different. I am getting some push back from the senator on any DNA test for the kid."

"But that puts me in an awkward position. Last time I could justify it because you hadn't filed the manslaughter charge. This time there is a manslaughter charge. What basis do I use to deny it again, particularly since you are pressing the issue?"

"I suppose that you could say that it isn't relevant, which would be true," Braxton said, attempting to justify the illegal action.

"And I suppose that you could decline to file the motion and take the heat if this becomes public."

"That's not an option. Not only will I get shit from Perrin, but I suspect I will also hear from Sandworth. He wasn't happy when he found out we only went with manslaughter in the death of the fetus. He was pressing for a murder charge and once again accused me of political favoritism. He doesn't understand that I can't make a murder charge. He is convinced that we are rolling over on this case. Fortunately, he hasn't shared his belief with the media. At least not that I know of. And I don't want to press the envelope with him."

"I'll take a look at it after you file the motion. But you do know that this motion is a reasonable request that ordinarily would be granted." Judge Cardwell said, ending the conversation.

As soon as Braxton left the office, Cardwell was on the phone. "They're filing another motion for a DNA sample. Braxton was just in here and said she had no choice."

"I don't want that slut hooked up with our son. But at the end of the day, I just want to make sure that he doesn't take the fall for this," the unidentified individual on the other end of the call said.

"I'll figure it out," Cardwell said.

Chapter Thirty-Eight

For the second time, all parties appeared in Judge Cardwell's chambers to privately argue the prosecutor's latest motion to obtain Garner Lee's DNA. But this time, Perrin had the benefit of an additional manslaughter charge on which to hang his hat. This time the court could not justify its refusal based upon a lame suggestion that this was a criminal, not a paternity, case. This time it was needed for a criminal matter. A serious criminal matter involving the death of an innocent unborn child. Shocked by the court's last ruling, Perrin felt confident this time.

Felbin had his instructions. He needed to confess the motion consistent with the wishes of his client and contrary to his advice. He had no choice. He had to follow the wishes of his client, even if harmful. But nothing said he had to confess the motion immediately. He decided to wait for a little while to see how this played out. If Cardwell ordered the sample, as she was likely to do, he would have a point he could argue on appeal if his client was convicted. On the other hand, if she refused, he could offer the defendant's consent. Since he thought it was odd that he'd won this motion the last time, he could not be certain what Cardwell would do now.

When the argument began, Perrin went right to the point. "The last time I filed this, you said this was not a paternity case and denied my request. This time there is a manslaughter charge pending against this defendant for which a DNA sample is necessary. We believe . . ."

Perrin was unable to finish his sentence, let alone his argument, before he was interrupted by the judge. "Are you telling this court that the identity of the father of this child is an essential element of this crime?"

Uncertain where this was going, Felbin thought it was looking like this motion was heading in the same direction as the last time Perrin tried. *This was not a complicated is-*

sue. Whether the jury would ever hear the DNA results was another question. Ordering a DNA test should be a no brainer in any ordinary case. But this was not any ordinary case.

"No. I am not saying that. But . . ."

Again, Perrin was not allowed to finish his sentence before another interruption. "If it is not an essential element of the offense, why are you requesting that I subject the defendant to this intrusion? Does he not have a right to be free from unreasonable searches and seizures, and would this not be unreasonable if it is not an essential element of this offense?"

"It is not a violation of his constitutional rights. But I believe it is relevant for the jury to have a complete understanding of the relationship between the victim and this defendant. It also goes to motive," Perrin said recognizing that his motion was on a downhill slide.

"What is your position on this, Mr. Felbin?" the judge asked.

"I think you are doing just fine arguing my side of this issue. Just don't lose the argument," Felbin said sarcastically.

"Very well. Mr. Perrin, your motion is denied. Anything further, gentlemen?"

Disbelief would not adequately explain Felbin's reaction to this latest ridiculous ruling by this inept political appointee. She represented everything wrong with the way in which judges are selected in the State of Missouri and elsewhere in this country. Cardwell is the poster child for why a system that is not based upon objective testing and other criteria doesn't work. Competent lawyers are excluded from consideration, because they are not politically connected. In other words, they have not greased the palms of the politicians who influence these types of political appointments.

Felbin was now between the horns of a dilemma. Should he tell this idiot that his client would consent to the DNA sample? Or should he just do a private test that he might or might not have to turn over to the prosecutor? Obviously, since she denied the motion, he couldn't claim the ruling as error later. But his curiosity got the best of him. No reputable judge would have ruled the way this one did on two occasions. Something was going on. He decided to press the envelope. He would also be fulfilling the wishes of his client.

"Yes, there is one more thing. My client will consent to the DNA test," Felbin said.

Now, disbelief enveloped the prosecutor's face.

"Mr. Felbin, I'm not sure I heard you correctly. Your client is consenting to the test?" Cardwell asked, equally shocked by the announcement.

"Correct."

"Although I'm not completely sure if you have lost your mind, Mr. Felbin, but if you will not protect the constitutional rights of your client, the court will be compelled to do that for you. The state's motion is still denied."

"You don't have to worry about my state of mental health or the constitutional rights of my client. All you need to worry about is what you are doing in this case. I always knew that you were an incompetent political appointee, but the decisions that you have made in this case have given new meaning to the word incompetent," Felbin said, anger in his voice and on his face.

For the second time in one day, the prosecutor was in a state of shock. In his young career, he had never heard a lawyer talk to the judge like that.

"Mr. Felbin, if you continue with this diatribe, you will be held in contempt," Judge Cardwell said, anger now apparent in her voice and on her face.

"No, you won't, because you know if you do, I'm out of this case. And you have already denied my motion to withdraw. You also know if you hold me in contempt, we will have to go out into the courtroom in full public view instead of hiding behind closed doors in your chambers. So, tell me, *Judge,* are the rulings that you have made in this case the result of your relationship with Senator Lee? You know, the guy that put you on the bench. Please tell me, *Your Honor,* how close am I to the truth?"

"What you are close to, Mr. Felbin, is a contempt citation. In fact, this court finds you to be in contempt. A hearing will be scheduled after the matter of State of Missouri versus Garner Lee is concluded. And by the way, Mr. Felbin, your anticipated motion to withdraw is denied. Now, get out of my office," Caldwell said as she called for the bailiff.

"And you wonder why people have no confidence in the judiciary and why people hate lawyers," Felbin commented as the bailiff was escorting him out of her chambers.

"Well, that was entertaining," Felbin said to Perrin. "My apologies to you for that outburst. What the hell is going on here? Why is your office putting up with this political hack?"

"I have no idea," was the only thing Perrin could say.

Chapter Thirty-Nine

Before Felbin was out of the courthouse, Cardwell was on the phone briefing the same unidentified individual on the results of the hearing and warning that the defendant had volunteered a DNA sample.

On the way to his office, Felbin also made a phone call. He needed to tell his client what happened. He wasn't looking forward to that conversation.

"She did what?" Garner Lee asked.

"She denied the prosecutor's motion, and then denied it again after I told her that you would voluntarily give up your DNA," Felbin repeated.

"What do we do now?" A mixture of anger and frustration sounded in his voice. "As I have told you, I want to prove that child was mine. I want to get the test done with someone and give it to the prosecutor. We don't need a court order to do that, do we?"

Felbin was amazed at how little his client knew about the law. Although he was uncertain how Garner Lee made it through law school and passed the bar, he believed his love of Amy was genuine and that he did not kill her. But he was not so sure that he was the father of the child.

"Yes, Garner, we can do a private paternity test and we don't need a court order, like I told you before." Felbin wondered whether his client was still in shock and depressed. Sometimes he heard and understood things and sometimes he didn't. "But, again, I'm telling you this is not a smart move. We can certainly get the test done. That's not a problem. But giving it to the prosecutor is another issue. As I told you before, if we inject that issue into this case, the prosecutor will turn that around and suggest that you didn't want the child, which they will claim is a motive for murder."

Given Garner's state of mind, Felbin decided against suggesting that his client was not the father.

"They can suggest what they want, but I know that I am the father of that child. Right now, because of the publicity, that issue is hanging out there. No one has been identified as the father. Either she was a slut who fucked every guy in town or she made love with me and we created a beautiful thing. But either way, that jury is going to know she was pregnant and the father was not verified. I'm guessing that doesn't help our defense either."

Felbin couldn't argue with that. Obviously, the jury will know she was pregnant. Garner was charged with killing the fetus. Rather than ignoring the elephant in the room, perhaps the strategy was to embrace the paternity and make the argument that he loved both Amy and the child and didn't kill anyone. Jury trials are a little bit like playing roulette. You can put your chip on one number or split the bet by placing the chip on the line between two numbers. Of course, the payout on the split is not as good. But in this case, there would be no splitting the bet. Either Garner was the father, or he was not.

"I'll go ahead and set it up with the lab and let you know when you need to be there to give your sample. In the meantime, I would suggest that you tell no one that we are doing a paternity test. And that includes your parents. Do you understand?"

"I understand."

Felbin was still uncomfortable with this test. He had a bad feeling. But at the end of the day, there probably was no other choice. He needed to place his client's chip on one number and couldn't hedge this bet. But the question of paternity was not the only bad feeling that Felbin had about this case.

Chapter Forty

The speedy trial date set by the court over Felbin's objections was rapidly approaching. The defense had nothing, other than the defendant's denial. And it didn't look like it was going to get any better. Felbin continued to beat himself up for taking a case that involved Senator Lee, as he waited for his girlfriend and confidant, Melinda Evans, to arrive at the bar. He ordered a cocktail, Tanqueray and tonic with a twist of lime, telling Melissa, a bartender at C. J. Muggs, his favorite watering hole, to go light on the tonic. It had been a long day, and he needed to relax. Dinner and a drink with Melinda was the way to do that.

Halfway through his first drink, his otherwise bad mood was lightened by the sight of Melinda walking into the restaurant. She had that effect on him. Between her travel schedule and his case load, he hadn't seen her in a few weeks. He'd missed her. She was good for him, and he was good for her. Their relationship was simple and uncomplicated.

"I see you started without me," Melinda said, greeting Felbin with a kiss on the cheek and waiving to Melissa. "How was your day? Or should I say how was your day with the good senator and his family, since that seems to be consuming you lately?"

"Well, I was held in contempt of court and almost went to jail today. And that's pretty exciting and doesn't happen every day."

"What?" Melinda said, concerned about Felbin's news. "Now I need a drink," she added, as Melissa placed a Blue Moon beer in front of her, a departure from her usual. Like Felbin, her usual drink of choice was Tanqueray and tonic, at least at this establishment.

Typically, Melinda would tell anyone who cared to listen that she never drank before she met Felbin. Of course,

Felbin would respond by suggesting that she was now making up for lost time, including experimenting with shots.

"I got into it with Cardwell."

"I'm shocked," she said, as she sampled her Blue Moon. "What happened?"

"I told her she was nothing but a political hack who gave new meaning to the word incompetent."

"Oh my . . . can you be held in contempt of court?"

"Well, that's not what set her off," Felbin said.

"There's more?"

"Yeah. I suggested that her rulings were a payback for Senator Lee, who put her on the bench. That did it. Thin skin."

"Did this happen in the open courtroom with people there?"

"No, it was in chambers, because she didn't want anyone to hear her ridiculous ruling on a motion."

"Why do you do that? It can't possibly help your client."

That's one of the many things that Felbin loved about her. She was not shy about calling him out when she thought he went over the top. Generally, that would result in a discussion at the end of which Felbin would acknowledge his bad boy behavior and promise that it would not happen again. But they both knew that promise would only last until the next discussion.

"Sometimes I react without thinking," was all he could offer. A weak explanation.

"Sometimes?" Melinda pressed.

"This case is really getting to me. I'm kicking myself for getting involved in the first place. That was a mistake. But I believe this kid didn't kill his girlfriend. I really don't have any evidence to back that up. It's a gut feeling based upon my belief that he genuinely loved her."

"But I thought you believed she didn't love him and was just using him."

"That's true. But I don't believe he saw that. Or if he saw it, he ignored it. She made the rounds, that's for sure."

"What do you mean by that?"

"We know Amy had another regular visitor. Some black guy that used to visit at night and wore a hat to perhaps hide his face. But I don't think Garner knew about it. Or at least it hasn't come up in conversation, and I didn't specifically ask him about it yet."

"What difference does it make if she had another friend? She was young and single."

"A couple things. If he did know, it gives him a motive to kill her. But if he didn't know, that could put another potential suspect in play."

"But you don't have any evidence to prove either one, do you?"

"I don't have any evidence to prove someone else killed her, although I do have evidence of that nighttime visitor. The question is whether we let the jury know about it," Felbin said as Melissa brought him another drink.

"What's the downside?"

"The risk is that the jury speculates he knew about this guy, got jealous and killed her. Looking at the picture of the crime scene, it's clear to me Amy knew the person who killed her. It looks like it was a spur of the moment thing. Nothing that was planned. The prosecutor will use that against us. They can put him in that apartment at the time of the murder. He'll suggest they fought, Garner got mad, and picked up the statue and whacked her in the head."

"But won't the prosecutor bring up the visitor?"

"Don't know. It's risky for him, too, if he puts another suspect in play. I also don't know if they know about that. It wasn't in the police report. The witness who gave us this information may not have shared it with the detectives when they interviewed her. She was out of town on the day of the murder, so they probably didn't pay much attention to her."

"Let's get back to the question of why you said what you did to Judge Cardwell and got yourself held in contempt of court. I know you have no use for her, but why the outburst? What's going on?" Melinda said as she signaled Melissa for another beer.

"I told you before that I had some concerns about her objectivity in this case. She won't let me out of the case. She put this case on a rocket docket, giving me little time to adequately investigate and prepare. The good senator doesn't want any DNA done on the fetus. When the state files a routine motion to obtain a DNA sample from the defendant in a case involving the death of a fetus, it is overruled. Then when the state tries again to get the sample after the defendant is charged with manslaughter in connection with that fetus, the motion is overruled again. But here is the best . . ."

"There is something better than what you just described?" Melinda said interrupting Felbin's rant.

"Oh, yeah. This is the best. After she overrules the state's motion for a second time, I say that my client will consent to the test. That's when she loses it. After suggesting that I'd lost my mind, she still overrules the prosecutor's motion. And that's when I lost it and suggested that the fix was in. But even more incredibly, the prosecutor, after getting his ass kicked twice by this corrupt poor excuse for a lawyer, judge and human being, did nothing. He just stood there looking like a deer caught in the headlights."

"Why would you say that your client consented? I assume, you objected to the DNA test. Sounds to me like she was justified in saying that you lost your mind." Melinda appropriately pointed out.

"No, it was my client who lost his mind. He is absolutely convinced that he is the father of the child and he wants the world to know it. My instruction was to agree to the test. I held back, hoping she would order the test and I would have something I could talk about on appeal if she was wrong, although I didn't think she was wrong."

"But what if the test comes back that he is not the father?"

"Exactly," was Felbin's simple reply.

"Well, from the way you described this situation, it sounds like something is going on. But it also seems like your client is the beneficiary of her bad decisions."

"That's probably true, at least for the moment. Of course, if this is a payback for the judicial appointment, it would benefit Garner."

"Can't you turn her in if she is corrupt? Surely, there has to be an agency that deals with dishonest judges."

"There is. It called the Judicial Commission. But at the moment, I don't have enough evidence. As you might expect, it takes a lot to discipline a sitting judge. In addition, my general ethical obligation might be at odds with the interests of my client. What do I say? Excuse me, but this judge is corrupt because she is bending over backwards to exonerate my guilty client."

"It never ceases to amaze me the games that lawyers play. Both sides massage the truth and spin the facts to suit their own purposes. I can't help but wonder whether juries ever get all the facts in any given case. But at the end, there is a winner and a loser determined by the best spin artist. How do we ever know whether justice is served and the party that wins is truly the legitimate winner? Or whether that party is just the beneficiary of a better spin doctor?"

Strip away the bullshit and hit you over the head with reality. That's what she did best. Get out of the make-believe world in which you and your colleagues live so comfortably. Face reality and do the right thing. Her message was always the same. His response was always the same. The theory was great, but the execution impossible.

"The sad fact is that we probably never know. Now let's go downtown to Kemoll's and get some dinner. I'll call Joe and tell him to pick us up. At least we can end this day on a pleasant note."

Chapter Forty-One

With time growing short, a trial strategy needed to be developed. But Felbin and company had little ammunition. All the evidence pointed directly to Garner Lee. Without any doubt, through multiple witnesses, the prosecution could put him in the apartment at or near the time of the murder. When the body was discovered, there was no forced entry, and the door was unlocked. The friends of the victim would describe a tumultuous relationship between Amy and Garner. Might also include assaults. The defendant's fingerprints were in the apartment. Of course, easily explained by the fact that Garner spent time there. They were dating. What wasn't so easily explained was the defendant's print in blood on the inside of the front doorknob. At the very least, the defendant was inside the apartment after the murder. But the most damaging piece of evidence was the lie.

Felbin also had another problem. It perhaps eclipsed the evidence. It might put his client in the penitentiary for a very long time. It could push his client over the edge.

"We have two problems," Felbin told his investigator.

"Only two?" Tony Carmine said.

"The paternity test is back. Garner Lee is not the father of Amy Deland's child."

"Shit," was Carmine's immediate reaction. "How do we handle this with Garner? He was absolutely certain he was the father of that child."

"I know he was. We obviously need to tell him. But our first problem is when and how to tell him. This trial is just around the corner, and we need him focused because we may have to put him on the stand to explain the lie he told the police. The second problem is how we handle this at trial."

"Shit," Carmine repeated.

"Is that the only contribution you plan to make to this mess?"

"Plead guilty," was the second contribution.

"Thanks. You're a big help. We need to get him in here as soon as possible, to give him time to deal with this. As to how we break the news, I guess we'll just have to play that by ear," Felbin said, uncertainty in his voice.

"This creates a whole new set of issues. If that is someone else's kid this slut was carrying, our anonymous nighttime visitor is really in play. I was never under the delusion they were playing dominos during those visits," the investigator said, crudely stating the obvious.

"Ironically, our visitor and our client share the same motive, but from different sides of the room. Both may have reacted in a jealous rage. Or both may have argued with our victim on whether to keep or abort the fetus. Interesting. But that doesn't really help us. The question is what role, if any, does it play in this trial? That's the most important thing right now," Felbin said.

"We can't ignore the obvious. Our guy is charged with killing an unborn child. And our victim didn't get pregnant from a toilet seat. Either Garner or another sperm donor that hit the jackpot." Another crude observation.

"Of course, we can't ignore the obvious. Let's play out both scenarios. If we introduce the third party, we also introduce the issue of jealousy. But if we don't, perhaps the jury will assume the child is his. And why would he kill his own child?"

"The answer to your question is what you said before. He wanted her to abort, she refused, and he whacked her. But we might be able to handle that if we put him on the stand to talk about his love and devotion to her."

"Are you forgetting Amy's friends and their *love* of our client? None of her friends had one good thing to say about Garner. In fact, some even accused him of assaulting her. That won't help us," Felbin pointed out.

"Yes, but we have people who will say just the opposite. Then it'll be up to you to discredit her friends."

"I don't want to make this about who knocked up Amy Deland."

"Whether you want to or not, won't this case eventually get to that issue?"

"If this was a normal case, I would say absolutely. But given the way this thing has gone so far, I don't have a clue.

Then there is the paternity test. And if I turn it over to the prosecutor and he doesn't use it, do we? Of course, that assumes this idiot judge lets anyone use it."

"What do you mean? If it helps us, we use it. If it doesn't, we dump it."

"Not that simple. There are some ethical considerations," the lawyer said.

"Fuck the ethics. A kid's life is on the line."

Tony Carmine was a great investigator and a valuable asset to Felbin and the clients they represented. But sometimes he didn't let the rules hamper an otherwise good defense. Usually, Felbin had to reel him in and set some boundaries. This was one of those instances.

"We know that Garner is not the father. I would have a problem injecting that issue and suggesting to the jury that he is the father. On the other hand, if I don't open that door and begin the discussion, I could challenge the prosecutor's suggestion that he is not the father. Then there is the question of whether I need to turn that test over. Obviously, if we use it, I need to give it to him before the trial starts. I'm already facing a contempt and I don't need any additional time in a cell."

"Sounds like lawyer bullshit to me."

"It may be a distinction without a difference. But it allows me to sleep at night," Felbin said.

"And we certainly want you well rested for this case."

"The additional unknown here is what the prosecutor will do. How he will play this? I suppose we can't discount the possibility that Cardwell will put short pants on him if he goes anywhere near the issue, like she did when he tried to get the DNA evidence. But if she doesn't, I suspect that he gets the most bang for his buck if he suggests that Garner is not the father. That will be the most prejudicial issue for us because it injects the issue of jealousy. The idea that he killed her because she refused to abort won't play as well. And as we both know, a trial is nothing more than good theatre," Felbin noted.

"We can all agree with that. In the short time we have left, what else needs to get done?" the investigator asked.

"I want you to go back to that witness who told us about Amy's visitor and see if she can give us any more detail on that mystery man. Also, do another canvass of the apartment and the neighborhood to see if we can get anything else on him. If we can put a name and a face on this guy, we may be able to offer him to the jury as another suspect. In the meantime, I'll get Garner in here and deal with that."

Chapter Forty-Two

Ordinarily, and with criminal cases in particular, clients usually don't have much to offer and generally just get in the way. Nonetheless, criminal defense lawyers are required to recognize that the client calls the shots and all the lawyer can do is offer advice. Some clients are better than others at accepting that advice. Garner Lee was more inclined to follow his own gut, particularly where matters of the heart were concerned.

Felbin knew what he had to do. What he didn't know was whether the news would put his client over the edge. Garner Lee was absolutely convinced he was the father of that child. Couldn't be anyone else. He had no clue of what Amy Deland was really like. The signs were probably there. But like most people, he was blinded by love and emotion.

Unfortunately, now it was time not only to face reality, but deal with it. His life depended on it. He was not the father of this child. And that meant that someone else was. It also meant that someone else was in the picture. Felbin guessed Garner would overlook the possibility this guy was good for the murder and instead, focus on Amy's infidelity.

After exchanging some social pleasantries and small talk about the upcoming trial, Felbin got to the point of the meeting. "Garner, the paternity test results came back. You are not the father of that child."

Garner sat motionless, staring at Felbin with lifeless eyes. After what seemed like an eternity, he finally said, "That test is wrong."

"The test is not wrong," Felbin said in a whisper.

"We need to have another lab do another test. And if that doesn't work we need to find another lab. And if that doesn't work . . ."

"Stop, Garner," Felbin interrupted. "We will be picking a jury in a few days, and we need to deal with this now. We are not going to have another lab look at this. You are not the father of this child."

Garner put his head in his hands and began to cry.

Felbin felt sorry for his client at that moment. He was the son of a powerful and rich family. But all the money and power in the world couldn't replace the hurt Garner was feeling. He thought he was in love. He thought she felt the same. But now he knew that was not the case. And on top of that, she was cheating on him and carrying another man's child. Tough for anyone to accept, let alone someone facing a murder charge.

But there was more. The mystery visitor. The one who came with the cover of darkness concealing his identity with a hat. Garner needed to hear about that from his lawyer first, rather than during the trial if the issue came up.

"How do you know that?" was Garner's immediate response to the news of Amy's visitor.

Felbin explained the information came from a witness who lived in the building and observed the regular visits, all occurring at night. That didn't satisfy his client.

"How does this witness know this guy was visiting Amy? Maybe he was visiting someone else in the building. And even if he was visiting Amy, how do we know he wasn't just a casual friend? You don't know he wasn't." Garner was in denial. He wanted to ignore the obvious.

Felbin didn't respond immediately to Garner's questions. There really wasn't much he could say that would satisfy him. The facts were the facts, and you could ignore them, but they were not going away. Garner had to deal with it now. He needed to go into the trial with his head screwed on straight.

"Garner," Felbin began, "we both know what was happening. Amy was seeing someone else on a regular basis and she became pregnant. The child was not yours, and we don't know who the father is. That's what we have here. And you need to deal with it."

"I don't know that. I don't know any of that. Maybe she was raped, but didn't want to report it. You know that happens all the time," Garner replied.

"Okay. We'll get to the bottom of all of this. Who killed Amy and how she became pregnant. But for right now, we need to get you out from under these serious charges, and that needs to be our focus."

Felbin felt bad about being so direct. But there was no time for sugar-coating anything. He and his client needed to get ready for a trial, and there was no time to waste. He concluded the meeting by telling Garner that he didn't know how the prosecutor was going to handle these two issues. Whether he would tell the jury about the visitor and that the baby was not Garner's. In any event, the defense would be ready for whatever the prosecution tried to do.

After Garner left, Carmine said, "What the fuck. Is he delusional? This little slut has a regular nighttime visitor, gets knocked up and he is talking about rape! Is he for real?"

"He's just masking the pain. He really did love this woman. And I suspect that at some level, he knew what she was. That she was using him. Hell, her friends knew what she was, according to what they told you and the police. I also suspect that her behavior was the subject of numerous disagreements," Felbin said.

"Do you think he really did kill her? He found out she was cheating on him?"

"No, I don't think he killed her. I do think that they had an argument before she turned up dead. But I believe he went there on Valentine's Day to patch things up from whatever argument they had. He arranged to have a nice romantic dinner and then hopefully get lucky afterwards. I also think she was smart enough to conceal whatever extracurricular activity she was doing. She wasn't ready to dump him for another sugar daddy."

"Maybe, she was dumping him for another sugar daddy and he was not going willingly. He got pissed and whacked her over the head with that statue in a fit of rage," Carmine surmised.

"That's certainly possible in this case."

Although he didn't discuss it with Garner, Felbin was reasonably certain any discussion about Amy's involvement with another man or the identity of the father would not be helpful to the defense. He decided he would not inject either issue into the trial and hoped the prosecutor would not as well.

Chapter Forty-Three

Unlike television trials that are completed in less than an hour considering commercial time, trials in the real world are intense dramas requiring months of preparation. Success or failure is measured by the amount of preparation. The elimination of surprise is the name of the game. That's why pretrial preparation includes evidence and document production, as well as depositions, which most trial lawyers believe are critical to a successful outcome. Depositions are statements under oath where a lawyer asks questions, and witnesses are required to respond immediately with their responses memorialized on the record for future use. The purpose of a deposition is not only to discover what the witnesses know, but also to lock them into a story. If that story deviates at trial, the deposition can be used to impeach or contradict the witness. Conflicts in testimony reduce credibility.

Thanks to Garner Lee's family, Felbin would not have depositions in his arsenal. He would not have an expert to help explain Garner's lie. Instead, he would have to rely upon interviews that his investigator conducted with witnesses who would likely testify for the prosecution. Thanks to Garner Lee's family, Felbin's ability to prepare to defend his client had been needlessly impacted. The price for Senator Lee's demand for an immediate trial to protect his political career might very well be the life of his son.

Felbin had represented numerous politicians over the years, and it was always the same. They were above the law and could not comprehend how someone would dare to prosecute or even challenge them. But this case was different. The politician was not on trial. His only child was. In meetings with Garner's parents, it was clear that the senator's interest lay in protecting his reputation. But Felbin was surprised at the attitude of his mother. Although not overt, Felbin sensed that Cassandra Lee was even more concerned that her son's criminal charges not impact the family's political goals.

Cassandra Lee was an intelligent and well-respected lawyer from a blue blood family. Her son was awaiting trial on serious charges that could land him in the penitentiary for the rest of his life. She was no stranger to the courtroom and the consequences of lack of preparation. Yet, she was behaving like this was a traffic ticket. But at this point, Felbin couldn't worry about any of that. He needed to prepare a defense and had to go with what he had.

Immediately before the start of any trial, Felbin would meet with his investigator, to go through last minute details and ensure that nothing was overlooked.

"Did we do any good with any of the potential witnesses that Garner gave us, who could talk about his relationship with Amy?" Felbin asked Tony Carmine.

"Of the five names that he gave us, either they said that they didn't want to get involved or they claimed that they didn't really know anything that would help. Actually, one guy who wanted to be helpful, had to admit when I pressed him that he saw a lot of what he described as differences of opinion. It would be like the guy who is caught burglarizing your house saying that he just stopped by to get some decorating ideas. This guy would get his ass kicked on the stand," Carmine said.

"In other words, we don't have any witnesses to counter what her friends say about him and their relationship?"

"Not unless you want me to find a stranger off the street and pay them to say nice things."

"I'm thinking you are certainly not above that," the lawyer told his investigator.

Ignoring Felbin's comment, Carmine asked, "What are we doing with these Stoner people? Do we need to lay a subpoena on any of them?"

"How would you propose that we use them in this trial?" Felbin asked.

"Don't you think it is a little odd that this agency represented the old man and he knew our victim but said nothing about it?"

"I not only think that's odd, but remember he said he didn't even know her when I initially asked. But he changed his story when I told him that she worked for the agency that represented him. Then he said he knew who she was, but didn't know her. A bullshit distinction without a difference. But how does this help the kid? How do we use it in trial?"

"I suppose we could use it to suggest that the Lee family all knew Amy and liked her. One big happy get along family. And they never witnessed any problems between Amy and Garner," Carmine offered.

"First of all, that is not true. They hated her. Thought she was a gold digger and didn't want their son involved with her. Second, the last thing that the senator would want to do is testify in a case he wants out of his life as quickly as possible. His political career is more important," Felbin said.

Changing the subject, Carmine asked, "What are we going to do about the pregnancy thing and our mystery midnight visitor? I assume that we are not going to open either door."

"We will have to play the mystery man by ear and see how the evidence develops. With respect to the pregnancy, given some of her pretrial rulings, I suspect that Cardwell is not going to let anyone get into that, other than to allow evidence she was pregnant, and the fetus died. I suppose the jury will be left to assume Garner is the father."

"I suppose in the long run that helps us."

"I suppose so. But this whole thing with Cardwell has bothered me from the start. Her rulings are not just stupid. They are calculated to help the defendant. I assume this is payback for the appointment to the bench. I don't think it was a coincidence that she wound up with this case. I think the fix is in and she is going to do what she can to ensure that this kid doesn't get convicted."

"And what's wrong with that?" Carmine asked.

"There is nothing wrong with that if you are the defendant and the beneficiary of unethical conduct. But to those of us who have some respect for the ethics of our profession, there is a lot wrong. Do I really need to explain it to you?"

"I get it. But I'm not seeing much you can do about it. If you blow the whistle, you throw our client under the bus. What are the ethics of that?"

"True. But if I don't say anything, I might be the one under that bus. At the moment, I'm only speculating the fix is in. I can't really prove it. If I'm right, we'll see if Cardwell is smart enough to cover her tracks. Obviously, she wants to keep her license. If she isn't smart enough, we will have several different problems. How she handles the trial will tell the story. I guess for the time being, we just sit back and watch the show."

One final pretrial issue remained for the defendant's team. Should they send their client's DNA to a private lab to compare it to the DNA profile found on the statue? After some discussion of the necessity to surrender unfavorable results to the prosecutor, they decided to get the comparison done and deal with disclosure issues later.

Chapter Forty-Four

A large crowd waited in a long line outside the court-house. They were all there to see the show. The son of a big shot politician from a blue blood family on trial for murder. A black man on trial for murdering a white girl. It didn't get any better than that for the rednecks, as well as for the sceptics who believed the system was corrupt, and money and power bought justice. There was something for every-one in this trial. That's why the crowds were expected to be overflowing.

But on this day the prospective jurors would take up most of the seats in the courtroom. The curious onlookers would have to wait until after the jury was selected. In the meantime, they would need to go back home and watch Judge Judy perform her television judicial magic. A poor substitute for the Cardwell show.

Cardwell ordered a panel of seventy-five, thinking that many would be dismissed for cause, given the publicity as well as the notoriety of the defendant and his family. Of the seventy-five, close to half were black, the remainder white.

Although the victim was white, Felbin wanted a black jury. All twelve black if he could get it. The prosecutor would be looking for all white faces. In the end, there would be a mix. But the prosecutor needed the vote of all twelve to get a conviction. The defense needed only one to avoid that re-sult. Now the chess game would begin.

Because this was a murder case, each side would be allowed to eliminate six potential jurors without having to show any cause for their removal. These strikes are known as peremptory challenges. But if the bias of the juror or the inability to serve for any reason is clear, that person can be removed for cause. Under that circumstance, neither par-ty would have to use a peremptory strike. Judge Cardwell would be the final arbiter of who would be eliminated for cause.

Trial lawyers don't select jurors based on whether they can be fair and impartial. That's the last thing they want. Rather, they are looking for jurors whose life experiences make them sympathetic to their side of the lawsuit. For example, in a criminal case, the defense would be looking to eliminate people with a law enforcement background while the prosecution would argue against any removal for cause for those individuals.

It was important for the lawyers to eliminate as many potential jurors on the basis of cause as they could. That way they were not using their limited number of peremptory strikes to get rid of people who would not favor their side. Usually, after the challenges for cause had been made, all of those who remain would not be acceptable to one side or the other. The peremptory strikes can then be used to remove people who remain. But those are limited, which is why lawyers press for cause removal, which increases their ability to select a jury that is favorable to them. Just one of many games played during the course of a trial.

During jury selection, Felbin might get an idea early on as to the type of trial Judge Cardwell would be conducting. Fair or fixed? When a challenge for cause is made, the judge has the sole discretion to decide whether the juror can be fair and impartial. If not, the juror is removed for cause with neither side using one of their six strikes. A judge who is not dedicated to conducting a fair hearing for both sides can shape the jury by eliminating people for cause *without* cause.

The selection process began normal enough with the prosecutor asking the routine questions. Does any member of the panel know anything about the case, and if so, whether that information can be set aside and the case decided based upon the law that the court provides, and the evidence presented during the trial? Any crime victims? Any member of the panel or immediate family ever been prosecuted? Ever been a witness in a criminal case or in any case? Ever testified in court? Ever served on a jury before?

For the first forty-five minutes, the prosecutor moved right along. Routine questions received routine answers. The bumps in this smooth process began with the question of whether anyone knew the defendant and his parents. While no one acknowledged knowing the defendant other than through pretrial publicity, numerous hands were raised indicating knowledge of Senator Lee. No surprise there. He was a politician, perhaps the most influential in the state. But now the real question. Do you know of him or do you know him personally? The answers varied, but with most knowing of him. That presented no problem, even for Cardwell, if they could agree to be fair and impartial. Those who knew him personally, however, did create an issue.

An African American female juror indicated that she not only knew the senator personally, but he had helped her son obtain funds to assist in his education at one of the state universities. Her son was about the same age as the defendant, and she couldn't afford the tuition. Despite her relationship with the senator, she indicated that she could set aside her relationship with Senator Lee and give both sides a fair trial. Even an inexperienced prosecutor like Paul Perrin knew that wasn't the right person for this jury. He asked to approach the bench and out of the hearing of the jury panel moved to strike for cause.

When Judge Cardwell turned to Felbin for a response, he said, "The juror said she could be fair and that is what we are looking for. Merely because someone knows another person does not mean they are incapable of being fair to both sides. If we were in a small town, everyone would know everyone else both by name and probably socially. That doesn't disqualify them from serving on a jury."

"This is more than just knowing him. He was the reason her son went to college. He was the source of funding. There has to be some gratitude for that, and I don't want this trial to be the payback," the prosecutor said.

The word payback prompted Felbin to look at Cardwell. Their eyes met and for what seemed like an eternity, they silently communicated. They didn't need words. Cardwell knew exactly what Felbin was thinking.

Felbin did not respond to Perrin's point. He didn't need to.

"Your motion to strike this prospective juror for cause is denied. She said she can be fair and this court has no reason to doubt her at this point. Should another issue arise with her, I will reconsider my ruling," the judge said.

Technically, Judge Cardwell was probably not incorrect. The juror did say she could be fair. But nobody in their right mind would believe her. Felbin was concerned this might be a preview of things to come.

The questions for the people who knew the senator continued. But a pattern was beginning to develop. The people who said they knew him all stayed. The people who claimed they received favors from him, stayed. Even the people who campaigned for him stayed. But then came the people who campaigned against him, and the mood changed.

A white male indicated he supported the senator's opponent in the last election and campaigned against him. Like the others who preceded him, this gentleman said he could be fair to both sides.

Felbin decided to test the waters and moved to challenge this potential juror for cause. "Clearly, this juror cannot be fair in this case. It's one thing to say you don't support a political candidate, but quite another when you actually go out and campaign against that person. Generally, those campaigns are not friendly, but rather mudslinging contests. Just look at the animus that existed in the presidential election between Clinton and Trump. And while they pretended to kiss and make up after the election, no one believed it. The sad fact is after the insults hurled during that election, they hated each other, and that was not going to change."

Felbin's argument was weak and he knew it. But he had nothing to lose by making the argument. He also wanted to see how she would handle the issue and whether any favoritism would surface.

Perrin's response was quick and pointed. "Is he kidding? He is suggesting that this juror campaigning against Senator Lee's opponent is analogous to the Clinton/Trump race for the presidency. He is delusional and . . ."

Perrin was interrupted by the Judge. "Mr. Perrin, this court will not tolerate any disrespect to another officer of the court. Keep your comments civil and professional," she warned.

Cardwell defending Felbin's honor. That's rich. Felbin had to pinch himself to make sure he wasn't dreaming. He was hoping that Cardwell didn't expect him to return the favor.

"I apologize, Your Honor. I meant no disrespect to Mr. Felbin or anyone else. I just think his motion to strike this juror for cause is without merit," Perrin simply said, clearly intimidated by the scolding.

Without explanation, the court sustained Felbin's motion. This juror, along with anyone else who campaigned against Senator Lee, was gone. That told Felbin all he needed to know. This was payback. This corrupt judge was trying to stack the jury in favor of Garner Lee. But it was a clever move on her part, because the prosecution has no appellate rights if the defendant is acquitted. If the defendant is found guilty, he wouldn't raise this as a point of error to get a new trial, because she gave Felbin what he wanted. How can you say you are prejudiced when you get what you ask for? In either situation, her decisions would never be reviewed by a higher court.

Chapter Forty-Five

After two days, all the questions were asked, the answers given, the arguments made, and the strikes recorded. Finally, the jury was in place. Three white and three black males. Two white and four black females. Three alternates, two white males and one white female rounded out the jury that would decide the fate of Garner Lee, the only son of Senator Winston Lee. The opening statements would begin, after the overflow crowd was seated.

Felbin liked the jury Cardwell picked. Although not all black, the majority were. Many were supporters of the defendant's father and none were political enemies, at least as far as he knew. His only concern was the number of females. He would have preferred more men because the victim was white and there would be evidence of physical altercations between Amy and Garner. But at least from the standpoint of the composition of the jury, the odds of an acquittal looked good. And even if there would be no acquittal after this group heard the evidence unfavorable to Garner, Felbin only needed one to hang the jury and prevent a guilty verdict. Things were looking pretty good.

Perrin got right to it in his opening. No introduction, but right to the cornerstone of his case. "This defendant, this guy sitting right here, lied to the police when he was questioned about the murder of his girlfriend. The girl that he claims he loved. He told the police that he was not in Amy's apartment at the time of her death. *I wasn't there.* Those were his exact words. But he was there. We know that, because his fingerprints are in her blood on the inside of the apartment door."

Perrin paused, allowing those words to resonate throughout the courtroom. Continuing, he repeated, "His prints were on the inside of the door in her blood," emphasizing the word inside. "The evidence will show that he killed Amy Deland and lied to the police, claiming he wasn't anywhere near her apartment to cover up his crime. Innocent people don't lie to the police . . ."

Felbin was on his feet immediately objecting and asking for a side bar conference at the bench outside the presence of the jury. He was hot.

"Mr. Perrin just obliterated the presumption of innocence and destroyed the Constitution in the process. Mr. Lee enjoys that presumption until the state can prove his guilt beyond a reasonable doubt. But he just took care of that. The jury heard it, and you can't un-ring the bell. I move for a mistrial based upon the prosecutor's misconduct."

Felbin needed to make a record for an appeal in the event the case went south. He didn't expect to win his motion.

Perrin was stunned by the reaction of Felbin to his comment. Clearly, he didn't know he did anything wrong. His response was almost apologetic. "Your Honor, it was not my intention to prejudice the defendant in any respect with my comment. Nor do I think it had that effect. However, I think instructing the jury to disregard would cure any harm to the defendant Mr. Felbin claims occurred, without resorting to the drastic remedy of a mistrial."

Felbin had nothing else to add. He knew at this early stage he was not going to get his mistrial. Most good trial judges would want to see how this played out with a jury. If they acquitted, it would take the court off the hook. If they didn't, this issue could be revisited in post-trial motions. But this was Cardwell. Good and judge in the same sentence was an oxymoron when it came to her.

Judge Cardwell said, "Your comment is a serious constitutional violation. And I am concerned you have prejudiced this defendant beyond repair. But, at this time, I am going to overrule the motion for a mistrial and I will instruct the jury to disregard. But I will warn you, Mr. Perrin, another incident like this will have very severe consequences."

She was overruling the motion. That meant money in the bank for Felbin. The issue was not dead, but might be revisited in the event of a guilty verdict. Felbin would raise the point in a post-trial motion, seeking an acquittal, rather than a new trial based upon prosecutorial misconduct.

The remainder of the prosecutor's opening was short and free from any serious missteps. Occasionally, Felbin would lodge an objection just to screw with the young lawyer and throw him off track. Just another part of the game.

In addition to the defendant's lie, which was the cornerstone of the State's case, Perrin hammered away at the hostility between Amy and Garner to include physical violence; his presence in the apartment at the time of Amy's death; his fingerprint found in Amy's blood on the inside of the front door; and the defendant hiding out in a hotel. Of course, he avoided a comment that innocent people don't hide out. But he did say flight is an element of guilt. He concluded by talking about the poor little innocent baby that never got a chance to experience life before being brutally murdered by an enraged jealous boyfriend.

Enraged jealous boyfriend. Felbin wondered where that came from. But otherwise the opening was good. Perrin was not overly dramatic, but rather hit the high points of his case.

Chapter Forty-Six

Now the question was whether Felbin would tell the jury his side of the story or defer. In any criminal case, the defendant can give an opening statement after the prosecutor's or wait until the start of the defense portion of the trial. The strategy depends on whether the defendant will put on any evidence beyond cross-examining the prosecution witnesses. For better or worse, Felbin decided he needed to counter the damage done by Perrin immediately. But he had to be careful. He needed to deal with the lie, but not in a way that would lead the jury to believe the defendant would testify. That decision was yet to be made.

Felbin knew he had seven African Americans on this jury. All he needed was one. He had to get to them. While they couldn't carry the day completely, they could prevent a guilty verdict. He needed to convince them Garner Lee was a victim here, just as much as Amy Deland. Instead of finding the real killer, the police were content to prosecute an innocent black man, in part because they didn't like his parents. Then there was the fact he was in love with a white woman. That could be tricky. For the moment, he had to spin it to the cops and make them the bad guys and hope hostilities between the victim and Garner's parents didn't surface.

There was another problem. How was Felbin going to handle the victim? Was she an opportunistic slut who used the idiot son of a wealthy and powerful family? That was the opinion of her friends. Or at least that's what they told the police. Those same friends also suggested she was planning to dump him. That would be a slippery slope. He needed to stay away from it. And what about the regular night visitor? Would he let the jury in on that little secret, or would the prosecutor throw it out there? Perrin didn't mention it in his opening, which might mean he didn't know about this guy.

But this was just the opening statement. No need to be specific now. The decision on those issues could wait. After all, the only thing Felbin wanted to do was interrupt Perrin's flow and let the jury know he wasn't some potted plant along for the ride in the prosecutor's show.

"Let's address the elephant in the room," Felbin began. An odd and perhaps dangerous start for an opening statement. "Garner is obviously black and the woman that he loved was white. This country gives all of us the right to freely choose. That wasn't always the case," Felbin said, obviously playing to the black jurors. "Garner was free to choose Amy, and Amy was free to choose Garner. Their love was not impeded by race. Their love trumped any racial issues. They didn't see each other as black and white, and I am confident that you won't either. Instead, they were two people who were in love."

In addition to painting a picture of the loving relationship between his client and the victim, Felbin knew he was going to have to deal with prosecution witnesses who would present a very different picture of that relationship.

"The evidence will show that Amy was a popular young woman who had many friends. But some of those friends didn't like Garner. Amy and Garner did a lot of things together and spent a lot of time together. They did fun things. Maybe some of her friends were jealous. They didn't do the kind of fun things that Amy and Garner did. Or, maybe they simply didn't approve of a black man in love with a white woman," Felbin said, looking directly at the black jurors while waiting for the objection. But it never came. Maybe Perrin thought he would just highlight the comment with an objection.

"February 14, Valentine's Day. A special day for people in love. But this was a dark day for Garner. The worst day of his life. This was the day he found the woman he loved, the woman he wanted to spend the rest of his life with, lying on the floor of her apartment, lifeless."

Felbin noticed that several of the jurors looked at defendant to gauge his reaction. Almost as though on cue, Garner's eyes began to fill. Tears slowly ran down his cheeks. His reaction didn't appear staged. It was a normal reaction for a person who had lost someone they dearly loved. It should have been clear to the most casual observer that Garner Lee was in pain.

The behavior and reaction of defendants in criminal trials can have a substantial impact on jurors. Cases can be lost by inappropriate courtroom demeanor or an errant conversation in the hallway overheard by a juror. As part of the preparation process, good criminal defense lawyers school their clients on how to behave both inside and out-side the courtroom. Some tell their clients to have no reaction to anything that is said or done. Others suggest a mild rebuke to adverse testimony or evidence and tears where appropriate. But all totally agree outbursts, anger and hostility should be avoided at all costs. It's probably not a good idea to have the guy who is charged with felony assault attacking the victim either verbally or physically while testifying.

"Garner went to Amy's apartment on Valentine's Day to pick her up. They were going out for a special dinner to celebrate the day and their relationship. He made a reservation at their favorite restaurant. But there was no celebration. Instead, he found her lifeless body. Random, rambling thoughts filled his head. Who could have done this? Why would someone do this? Amy was liked by everyone. She had no enemies. She's gone. I'll never see her again. I never even got a chance to say goodbye or kiss her. This can't be happening. Is she really dead? Imagine how each of you would react if you found the person you loved, dead, murdered."

The last statement finally drew an objection. Felbin was beginning to think his opening was so boring that his opponent fell asleep.

"Objection, Your Honor. He is personalizing his open-ing," Perrin said.

That's a silly objection, Felbin thought. *Of course he was personalizing it.* Like all skilled criminal defense attorneys, Felbin was trying to do all he could to prejudice the hell out of this jury.

Silly or not, the court sustained the objection. But what could she do beyond that? They heard the comment and she could not force them to stop thinking about how they would react to confronting the death of a loved one.

Ignoring the judge's ruling, Felbin continued, "Regardless of how you would react under the same circumstances, Garner's reaction was to go into shock. At least that's what he thinks happened. The rest of his time in the apartment is a blur. He believes he touched Amy as she lay on the floor. Perhaps he even kissed her. He doesn't even remember leaving the apartment or what he did afterwards. But he does know he didn't kill her. He couldn't kill her. And they will have no credible evidence he killed her," he said, pointing to Perrin.

As soon as Felbin completed his sentence, Perrin was on his feet objecting. "Objection. He needs to tell this jury what he intends to prove and not what he thinks I can't prove. That argument is improper."

"Overruled." The ruling came quickly and emphatically. Actually, Perrin was correct. The opening statement is supposed to give the jury an idea of what a party's evidence will be. But apparently not in the courtroom of Judge Joan Cardwell.

"Speaking of the lack of credible evidence, let's talk about Garner's interrogation by the police," Felbin said, looking directly at Perrin with a gotcha expression on his face. "Mr. Perrin says he is going to prove the defendant lied," Felbin continued, careful not to use Garner's name and lie in the same sentence. "But it is what he didn't tell you that is important. He didn't tell you about how that interrogation was conducted. He forgot to mention the pressures, threats and tactics used. A black man dating a white woman, it doesn't get any better than that . . ."

"Objection," Perrin jumped out of his seat and yelled.

"Sustained," was the immediate ruling, no discussion necessary.

But the ruling didn't matter. Felbin made his point, one that would resonate with the black jurors.

"While Garner is at home still in shock from the death of the woman he loved, the police show up at his door. No warning. No notice. They just show up and walk in when he opens the door. Apparently, no invitation necessary."

"Your Honor," Perrin was on his feet again. "Can we do this without the editorial comments? This is supposed to be about what he intends to prove, and I haven't heard anything yet."

"There is no need to present any defense when the state hasn't presented any evidence of guilt," Felbin shot back.

"That's enough from both of you," Judge Cardwell said, putting an immediate end to the rancor. "I am warning both of you. You're both testing may patience. Move on."

"Yes, Your Honor," Perrin said apologetically.

No apologies from Felbin, not now, not ever. But he had to be careful he did not let his disdain for this judge spill over into the trial. The jury didn't know the history, nor could they find out.

"As I was saying, when Garner spoke to the police after they showed up at his door unannounced, he was in shock. They knew that. They could see it in his eyes and hear it in his voice. But that didn't stop them from accusing him of murder. Here he is trying to deal with his loss, having just witnessed the horror of a murder scene, and they are suggesting he is a murderer. His shock turned to fear, and his fear turned to despair. He asked them to leave his house. They refused and continued to press him. He said and did whatever it took to get them out of his house so that he could grieve privately. He didn't care about anything at this point."

Felbin continued. "They also have a murder weapon. And maybe I missed it, but I didn't hear the prosecutor tell you how they plan to connect Garner to that weapon. Oh wait, I didn't miss anything because they never did tell you how they plan to do that. And that is because they can't connect the dots. Imagine that, they have a murder, but they can't connect it to the person they have accused of murder.

"Your Honor . . ." Perrin said, but didn't have to finish his objection.

"Mr. Felbin . . ." the judge began, but likewise didn't have a chance to reprimand the defense lawyer, who continued with his opening statement, refusing to recognize his indiscretion.

"Ladies and gentlemen, the evidence will show there are fingerprints on that murder weapon, but they belong to someone else. Hopefully, before the end of this trial the prosecutor will let us all in on his little secret as to who these prints belong to."

"Objection, objection, objection," Perrin said as he jumped up.

"That's all we have for now, Judge. But I'm sure you will be hearing more from us as this show continues," Felbin concluded, as he took his seat at the counsel table. He figured he needed to quit before Cardwell held him in contempt. He knew he'd pushed both her and the prosecutor to their limits. He also couldn't talk about DNA comparison on the murder weapon, because he didn't have the lab results yet.

"Ladies and Gentlemen, we are going to take a short recess," she told the jury. "And counsel, I would like to see you in my chambers."

Chapter Forty-Seven

Felbin expected the *you better behave yourself or else* lecture. But those were usually idle threats that didn't have any teeth. She'd already used the hammer of contempt once in this case. But she knew she couldn't hold him in contempt because he could then request a mistrial and seek to recuse her. And she didn't want that. She would have to wait until the end of the trial to have a hearing and actually hold him in contempt. But Felbin knew by that then, she would be more interested in getting him out of her courtroom than continuing the fight. But, like Melinda suggested, he had to go in, keep his mouth shut and listen to her meaningless threats.

As expected, the meeting was anything but a social event. The purpose was to make it clear to Felbin that she was the boss. She was in charge. And if he stepped off the line, she would not hesitate to impose a severe sanction. Surprisingly, Felbin was able to control the movement of his lips. He didn't agree or disagree with the warning. Fortunately, the judge didn't require an acknowledgement.

Felbin's problem wasn't so much the judge, although they were never going to be best friends during the trial or after. His problem was the evidence. He did the best he could with the opening. But he understood he had problems, the most important was his client's statement, which would be refuted by the blood on the doorknob, Amy's blood. That would put him in the apartment at the time of the murder.

But the judge's lecture was not the only one he would get on this day. His client was waiting to talk to him when he came back into the courtroom. He wasn't happy.

"I want to testify. You didn't tell the jury that I wanted to tell them what happened," Garner said.

"Listen, Garner. This isn't a decision that we need to make now. You're right, I didn't tell this jury you would testify. We need to see how the evidence develops and decide at that time. Then we will . . ."

Garner didn't wait for Felbin to finish his sentence. "I thought I was the one who decided whether I would or would not testify, not you."

"That's true. You are the one who makes the final decision. But, I would hope you would at least listen to my advice. The beginning of any criminal trial is not the time to make a decision whether the defendant should or should not testify. There simply is not enough evidence on the table to make an informed decision. While we may have an idea of what evidence the state has, we don't know how that evidence will play for the jury, if and when it comes in. And an opening statement is certainly not the time to tell the jury you would be testifying."

"I want to testify, and I will testify," the defendant told his lawyer.

"STOP," Felbin's voice rising to a level noticed by some in the audience. "You are behaving like a child. Sit your ass down in that chair and keep your mouth shut. You're embarrassing yourself."

Felbin needed to get away from his client while he waited for the prosecutor to locate his first witness. He found Carmine in the hallway, reviewing some notes.

"Did you get the first in a series of tongue lashes from her royal highness?" the investigator asked.

"Yeah, threats she couldn't deliver on. No big deal. But the bigger tongue lashing came from our client," Felbin replied.

"What are you talking about? What is he pissed off about now?"

"He wanted me to tell the jury that he was going to testify."

"Are you kidding? He's dumber than I thought. He really wants to testify? He'll get his ass kicked, even by this idiot prosecutor. You know, life would be good if we didn't have to deal with the clients. What the hell are we gonna do?" Carmine said, always having a kind word for the clients.

"We're doing nothing at the moment. The opening statement is done, and we can't go back to let the jury know what he wants to do. As far as whether he testifies, that's his call. All we can do is advise him when the time comes. In the meantime, we need to prep him, because I suspect that he won't listen to us and will insist on testifying."

"Prep him? Now there's a joke. You can hand him a script and have him read it on the stand and he will still fuck it up."

"I understand that he isn't real bright. But . . ."

"Not bright," Carmine interrupted. "He's dumber than a box of rocks. Apparently, it doesn't take a lot of smarts to get through law school."

Ignoring the law school comment, Felbin said, "I believe this guy didn't kill anybody. I think he truly loved Amy and was genuinely devastated to find out he was not the father of her child. I think sincerity will come through if he testifies. Who knows whether that will trump the lie which we know they will get into evidence. Either way, we have to deal with the lie. We have a lot of problems with this case. but that's the biggest hurdle to overcome."

"Remind me again why we are involved with this case."

"Don't go down that road," Felbin said. Frustrated, he ended the conversation and returned to the courtroom.

Chapter Forty-Eight

The prosecutor was finally ready with his first witness. As expected, he led with the veteran homicide detective Sergeant Jack Sandworth. A good move. Get right to it by starting with the guy who not only had spent a lifetime on the witness stand, but was also dedicated to putting the defendant away for a long time and embarrassing his family in the process. The only risk for the prosecution was whether that hostility would become obvious and impact his credibility. But he was a pro, and that risk was worth taking.

Perrin began with the impressive credentials of the witness. 31 years as a St. Louis police officer. 18 years as a detective with 13 ½ of those spent in the homicide division. A variety of commendations accompanied those years of service, including the medal of valor, the most prestigious award in the department, and two officer of the year awards.

When he was finished impressing the jury with Sandworth's background, the prosecutor directed his attention to the victim's apartment on February 15. Sandworth, along with his partner, Detective Leroy Anderson, met a uniform officer who was dispatched after a 911 call. In addition to Officer Robert Bayer, an unidentified female, later identified as Becky Smallwood, the victim's friend, was also in the apartment.

Sandworth told the jury his attention was immediately directed to the body of a female lying face down on the floor in the living room. Her head and body were perpendicular to the front door. A bloody brass statue, which he described as the murder weapon, was located at the victim's feet. Except for the bloody statue, nothing else seemed to be disturbed in the apartment. There did not appear to be any forced entry. A large amount of blood covered what appeared to be a deep laceration visible on the back of the skull. A pool of blood and spatter were observed in various locations, both in the immediate vicinity of the body and several feet away. It did not appear there had been much of a struggle and clearly, the wounds were not self-inflicted.

"Based upon your observation of the scene, were you able to form any opinions or come to any conclusions?" the prosecutor asked.

"Yes. Amy knew her assailant," the veteran detective offered immediately, hoping to get his answer out before Felbin had a chance to object. The sign of a professional and experienced witness.

"Why do you say that?" Perrin followed up.

No objection from Felbin. The jury already heard the damaging part. He had to neutralize this point on cross, rather than highlight it with an objection here.

"Several reasons," Sandworth began. No sense rushing this answer. Nothing Felbin could do but listen. "As I said before, no visible signs of forced entry. No signs of a struggle. Nothing was broken or out of place other than the brass statue, which probably came from a bookcase adjacent to the body. I think what happened was . . ."

"No, no, no. We're not going there. You're a professional witness. You should know better than that," Felbin jumped in, reprimanding the detective.

"Sustained," the court ruled, without a Felbin reprimand for the editorial comment.

"I want to direct your attention to the inside front door of the apartment. Did you notice anything unusual on the inside of the door?" Perrin continued.

"Yes. We observed blood on the handle of the inside doorknob. And the amount was sufficient to get a print."

"Did the blood appear to be fresh?"

"Looked fresh to me."

Perrin moved to some of the investigative leg work. Sandworth explained that the time of death was between 4 pm and 7 pm on February 14. The detectives did a canvass of the other three apartments in the building to determine if anyone saw someone coming or going during that time. They located two witnesses who were leaving for a Valentine's Day dinner at a restaurant at approximately 6:30 pm. They lived on the second floor across from Amy. There were two apartments on the second floor and two on the first. They passed the defendant on the stairs as they were coming down to go out to dinner and he was going up, heading to Amy's apartment.

"Did you do anything to learn why the defendant would be at the victim's apartment at 6:30 pm," Perrin asked.

"Yes. We figured since it was Valentine's Day, he might have been coming for dinner. But since we didn't see any evidence of dinner preparation in the apartment, we figured they might be going to a restaurant. We also had a witness who indicated Amy had told her she and the defendant were having dinner together on Valentine's Day."

"What follow-up did you do?"

"We obtained a list of restaurants they frequented and started checking for a reservation. We found one. Kemoll's for 7 o'clock. The presence of the defendant in the victim's apartment around 6:30 fits the timeline."

"If I understand what you are telling this jury. We now have this defendant in Amy's building, walking up the stairs toward her apartment at 6:30 pm. He has a dinner reservation downtown at 7 o'clock. And his fingerprint is found in the victim's fresh blood on the doorknob inside the apartment. Did I understand that correctly?"

"You did," Sandworth responded confidently.

"What did the defendant have to say about all of that? Did you ask him?"

"My partner and I visited the defendant on Monday, February 15. He told us he didn't know why we were there and denied knowing Amy was dead. He told us he was not at Amy's apartment on Sunday, February 14. His exact words were *I wasn't there.* He also told us he didn't see her at all that day. He guessed the last time he spoke to her was a couple days prior to our visit. Despite Sunday being Valentine's Day, he said he had no plans to go to her apartment or see her."

"Did you think that was odd?" Perrin asked.

"Yes. It was Valentine's Day. I thought at least he would have spoken to her or made an effort to talk to her on this special day. Unless, of course, they'd had an argument and he was angry."

"Objection to the speculation, unless, of course, the detective has what we call evidence in this courtroom to back that up. Otherwise, it's just another underhanded tactic to prejudice this jury. Evidence, Detective, we need evidence, not your speculation," Felbin said, looking at the jurors sitting in the front row of the box.

"That will be sustained. Again, Mr. Felbin, I'm not going to warn you again about speaking objections," Judge Cardwell said.

"Are you at least going to instruct this jury to disregard Sandworth's speculation and warn him about presenting facts instead of his self-serving, gratuitous comments designed to prejudice this jury against Garner?" Felbin responded, this time looking directly at the witness, who began to smile.

"While you're at it, you might tell this professional witness to wipe the smile off his face," Felbin added.

"That's enough from both of you. The jury will be instructed to disregard the last answer of this witness, if you can remember it, given all the chatter and antics that followed. Mr. Perrin proceed," the judge directed.

When Felbin sat down, Carmine cautioned him about controlling his animosity toward Cardwell. "I'm thinking that you could have handled that with a little less sarcasm directed toward her. Sarcasm and hostility won't play well. Those jurors don't know she's an idiot."

Felbin just shook his head. He knew Carmine was right, but sometimes he just couldn't help himself when it came to Cardwell. He would never forget what she did to Bobby Decker.

"At the time that you interviewed him, did you know that his fingerprint was on the doorknob inside Amy's apartment?" Perrin continued.

"We did not. Otherwise, we would have asked him to explain that."

"Did the defendant claim he did not know Amy was dead?"

"Yes. We told him she had been murdered."

"What was his reaction?"

"No emotion whatsoever. It was like we had told him that she went grocery shopping," Sandworth said, shaking his head as a sign of disgust for the callous reaction of a person he believed was a killer.

"Did you have occasion to arrest the defendant for the murder of Amy and her child?"

"Yes. My partner and I arrested him."

"Please tell the jury the circumstances of that arrest."

"When we received the arrest warrant, we went to his office, thinking we would find him there. We spoke to his mother, who is also a lawyer, and she claimed she didn't know where he was or when he would be back. We left. A few days later, a St. Louis city police officer working secondary at the Ritz spotted him and told us he was staying there under an alias. We went there and grabbed him in his room without incident."

"Sergeant Sandworth, the person that you arrested and the person who told you he was not inside Amy's apartment on the day she was murdered, do you see that individual in the courtroom?"

"I do," the witness said, pointing to the defendant and describing what he was wearing.

"That's all I have," Perrin said, concluding his direct examination of this witness.

Now it was Felbin's turn. He needed to neutralize some of the damage this witness did. The entire case might depend on this cross-examination.

Chapter Forty-Nine

Felbin liked Jack Sandworth. He was a skilled witness and a worthy opponent. He had faced him numerous times in other cases. Felbin knew he had to be careful with this witness. He had to keep him on a short leash, otherwise the result could be a disaster. Sandworth had also testified for him in a matter involving a police officer facing disciplinary action. But that relationship could not interfere with his effort to discredit completely or at least mitigate his testimony on direct. Sandworth was a pro and would understand. Good police officers understood Felbin was just doing his job. Nothing personal.

"Did I understand you to say that you have been with the department for some 31 years, sergeant?" Felbin began.

"Yes, sir," Sandworth replied simply and directly. He knew where this was going.

"And you have been a detective for 18 of those 31 years?"

"Yes."

"Now, a detective position is something that is coveted in the department, isn't it?"

"I don't know what you mean coveted in the department. I don't even know what that fancy word means exactly. All I know is that I am a cop just like all the other cops in the department. No better. No worse."

Here we go. Let the games begin, Felbin thought.

Sandworth knew exactly what the word coveted meant. He also knew that Felbin was setting him up. This wasn't their first rodeo. Felbin would get where he was going. But Sandworth was going to make him earn it. He would do what he could to interrupt the flow, in the hope that he could minimize the jury impact.

"Well, let's see if I can help you out, Detective."

"Actually, that's Detective Sergeant, Mr. Felbin," Sandworth corrected.

"Thank you for that clarification, Detective Sergeant."

"No problem. I like to be precise when I testify."

So much for keeping Sandworth on a short leash.

"As do I, Detective Sergeant, which is why I am trying to clarify a portion of your direct testimony. When you testified that you had been a detective for 18 of your 31 years, you made it sound like that was a continuous 18 years. Was it?" Felbin asked.

"I simply answered the prosecutor's question, Mr. Felbin. I wasn't making it sound like anything. But to answer your specific question, no, it was not continuous."

"Do you have any idea why the department would interrupt the fine career of a great investigator like yourself?" Felbin asked rhetorically, sarcasm dotting every word.

"You know, Mr. Felbin, I have asked myself that same question numerous times. It's common for people, whether good, bad or indifferent police officers, to be moved from one assignment to another. That's the chief's prerogative, and he really doesn't consult with me. For me, I don't view it as an interruption of a career, but rather a learning experience. St. Louis is a large city filled with different police-related issues. I believe that experiencing those different issues makes you a better and more rounded police officer."

Felbin knew this was a total bunch of bullshit. But he was concerned the jury didn't know Sandworth was full of shit and might be buying this line of crap. He knew he had to counter it.

"Well, Detective Sergeant, did you embrace your transfer to a uniform and a patrol car as a learning experience immediately after you were disciplined for verbal and physical abuse?" Felbin shot back, as he looked directly at one of the black jurors.

"Mr. Felbin, I go where the chief tells me to go," the witness replied, ignoring the reference to discipline.

Of course, Felbin was not going to let that answer be the final word on this topic. "But, isn't it true, Detective Sergeant, that you were transferred from your cush plain clothes detective spot back to uniform as part of the discipline that you received after the chief found you guilty of physical and verbal abuse?"

"As I said before, transfers and assignment changes happen all the time." Again, the witness ignored the comment about discipline.

"But in your case, that transfer occurred while the discipline was imposed on the physical and verbal abuse matters. Isn't that correct, Detective Sergeant?"

"I don't recall it that way." Sandworth knew that the chief was pissed at him and the transfer was for disciplinary reasons. But he didn't exactly recall when he was moved and took a chance Felbin did not have any documents to make his point.

Felbin did have documents that reflected the dates of both the transfer and the discipline. But they were three weeks apart. Not a solid piece of information to attack this professional witness. He had to make a split-second decision, as with most issues that arise during a trial. He decided he'd made his point and needed to move on. He needed to get to the lie. The references to physical and verbal abuse were the foundation to attack the testimony about the lie.

"You said that you visited the defendant at his apartment on Monday, February 15. And I believe you used the word visited, is that correct?"

"Yes."

"Now this wasn't a social visit, was it?"

"Of course not. We were investigating a murder. There is nothing social about that."

"And actually, Garner was a suspect at the time of that visit. True?"

"Actually, he was not a suspect."

"When you arrived at his apartment, were you invited inside, or did you just simply push your way in?"

"I am sure that we had permission to enter."

"Did you hear Garner give you permission to enter?" Felbin pressed.

"I don't recall. But if he didn't want us in there, I'm certain he would have said something while we were standing at the front door or as we were entering."

"Did you know when you paid him this visit that he was the son of Senator Winston Lee and Cassandra Lee?"

"Yes, I believe we did."

"And you were acquainted with both?"

"Yes."

"In fact, you are aware that Garner's mother routinely sued the police department for alleged civil rights violations?"

"Yes."

"And you had friends on the department that she sued, isn't that true?"

"Yes."

Felbin decided he wouldn't press this issue. Instead, he would let the jury draw their own conclusions and not give the witness the opportunity to deny this was a payback.

"When you had your visit with Garner, and he told you he hadn't seen Amy on Valentine's Day or even a couple days earlier, what did you say?"

"I don't know that I said anything."

"Well, Garner told you that he and Amy were in love, didn't he?"

"Yes."

"And after he told you they were in love, you didn't press him on his statement he didn't see or talk to her on Valentine's Day like any good Detective Sergeant would?"

"No."

"Is there a reason, Detective Sergeant Sandworth, that you didn't do that?"

"No," another simple response.

"And you said you had a witness who told you Amy and Garner were having dinner together on Valentine's Day. Surely, you asked Garner about that."

"We did not." But before Felbin could ask another question, the witness added, "And the reason we didn't ask him about the dinner or seeing or talking to her on Valentine's Day was because I thought maybe they'd had a fight and they were not talking to each other."

This professional witness had just landed a punch that hurt, and Felbin knew it. Sandworth just gave Garner Lee a motive to murder, and Felbin had to deal with it now.

"In fact, Detective, not only did you ask him about this like any experienced investigator would, but you also accused him of lying, isn't that true?"

"Not true."

"And then you accused him of killing the woman he loved while you were screaming and pointing your finger, isn't that also true?"

"We didn't accuse him of anything. We were just starting the investigation."

"Hold on. You had information they planned dinner. He told you he didn't see her on Valentine's Day. You now claim you thought they had a fight and you, an experienced homicide detective, want this jury to believe you didn't ask a single question about any of this?" Felbin was livid and needed to control his anger.

"We were looking for cooperation and information, not confrontation. We didn't have enough to go after him at that point."

"Unbelievable," Felbin commented. As Perrin was standing to object to Felbin's gratuitous remark, he asked his next question. "Did Garner ultimately kick you out of his home?"

"I wouldn't put it that way. He was very nervous and really wasn't providing any information. So, we left."

Felbin knew he had to score some points on this issue. It was critical. He needed to create the impression that this experienced detective scared the defendant into lying. It was a long shot and probably crazy. But he knew if he couldn't get the job done with this witness, the defendant might have to testify to sell it. And at the moment, Felbin was losing the battle and decided to abandon this line of questioning before any more damage was done.

"Did you eventually return to the defendant's home and obtain his fingerprints?" Felbin asked, changing the subject.

"We did."

"And was he cooperative, and did he voluntarily give you his prints?"

"He did."

"And I believe you said the statue that you found was the murder weapon, correct?"

"Yes."

"And is that because the statue had the victim's blood on it and appeared to have been removed from a bookshelf near the body?"

"Basically, yes."

"And you also found fingerprints on that murder weapon, correct?"

"Yes."

"And were you able to match Garner's prints to the prints you found on that statue, the murder weapon?"

"We were not."

"Were you able to match those prints to anyone?"

"No."

"Based upon your investigation, you also expressed your opinion Amy knew her assailant, correct?"

"Yes."

"What did your investigation reveal as to how many people Amy knew?"

"I don't know."

"Do you know how many friends she had?"

"No," Sandworth said, clearly annoyed at the direction the questioning was taking.

"Can you tell us how many enemies she had?"

"Same answer. No, I can't."

"Then you are unable to tell this jury whether the fingerprints on the murder weapon are those of Amy's friends or her enemies, is that correct, Detective Sergeant?"

"That would be correct."

The inability of the prosecution to connect the fingerprint to the defendant was a strong point for the defense. But, in addition to the lie, there was another elephant in the room. Sandworth told the jury Garner had no reaction when the detectives informed him his girlfriend had been murdered. That might be a bigger problem than the lie. Felbin had a simple choice. Take the witness on or let it go.

As an experienced trial lawyer, Felbin was used to making split second decisions based upon surprises that occur during a trial. This was one such circumstance. There was nothing in any of the police reports that reflected the demeanor of the defendant. Sandworth, being the good detective he was, saved that little nugget to stick up Felbin's ass at the trial. Now, it was Felbin's turn, and Sandworth waited.

Several scenarios flashed through Felbin's head like a bullet train. He could try to suggest Garner was in shock. But in order to be persuasive and sell the point, he would need the cooperation of this witness. That wasn't going to happen. Nothing was going to work. He made his decision.

"No further questions of this witness," Felbin announced, leaving the elephant unscathed and fully visible in the room.

Perrin had a few other questions.

"Sergeant Sandworth, with respect to the print that was found on the statue, to your knowledge, was anyone able to determine the age of that print?"

"No."

"Therefore, it could just as easily have been put there by an invited guest months ago, rather than the killer?"

"That would be true. It depends on the last time it was cleaned. And we obviously can't ask Amy."

"Thank you, Sergeant. That's all the questions I have, Your Honor."

As the witness stood up, Felbin said, "I have just a few more brief questions, if I may." Rather than waiting for the judge's permission, Felbin started in. Just another sign of disdain, not for the office, but rather the person occupying it.

"Based upon your examination of the crime scene, including the location of the injury on the back of the victim's head, were you able to determine whether the killer was left- or right-handed?"

Perrin was on his feet objecting that the question was speculation beyond the expertise of the witness. To Felbin's surprise, the objection was overruled. Another example of collusion, or just ignorance of the rules of evidence?

"I don't know. That would be a question for the medical examiner. It's beyond my expertise," Sandworth said.

This guy was good.

"I will ask the medical examiner when he testifies. But right now, I'm asking you, not as a medical examiner but as a trained, experienced police officer. Will you answer the question in that capacity?" Felbin pressed.

"I can't really say."

"Well, let me take you by the hand, Detective Sergeant. The injury on the back of Amy's head, was that to the left or the right of the midline, as you are looking at her skull from the back?" Felbin asked, after handing the witness a crime scene photo.

"I would say more to the left."

"And again, taking a look at the photograph in your hand, that murder weapon that was on the floor with the fingerprint on it, would you say that was more to the left or the right of the body positioned face down on the floor?"

"I would say more to the middle."

Knowing that was the best he was going to do with this witness, Felbin announced he had no other questions.

When he returned to the counsel table, Carmine said, "He kicked your ass, boss."

"Thanks. I knew I could count on you to state the obvious," Felbin replied.

Chapter Fifty

The next series of witnesses were the haters. These were all of Amy's *friends* who disliked Garner and his relationship with Amy. Probably more than that, they hated the attention Garner showed her, the money he spent on her and the places and good times they'd had. Each of them had boyfriends who took them nowhere and spent nothing.

These witnesses also knew Amy Deland was an opportunist. She really wasn't in love with him and didn't even care about him. She was in the relationship for what she could get out of it. They also knew she was getting ready to dump him. However, in this trial they would portray themselves as the best of Amy's friends looking out for her well-being.

But Felbin had to be careful. They were dangerous witnesses, because they would provide a motive for murder.

Becky Smallwood was the first hater to testify. She told the jury her good friend, Amy Deland, didn't show up for work on February 15. They both worked for the Stoner Group, an advertising agency. It was unlike her, and Smallwood became concerned after Amy didn't respond to attempts to reach her by phone. She went to Amy's apartment to check on her after work. The front door was closed, but unlocked. She knocked, and when she received no response, she entered to find her friend lying on the floor. She described in graphic and emotional detail the scene that resulted in a 911 call. To further highlight the emotion of the moment, Perrin played the 911 tape.

No surprises so far. Felbin expected this, including the emotion from this drama queen. He also braced for what he thought was to come. But in any trial, always expect the unexpected. This case was no different.

As anticipated, the prosecutor began to question the witness about the relationship between the defendant and the victim.

"Ms. Smallwood, do you know the defendant?" Perrin began.

"Yes."

"Have you been in the company of both Amy and the defendant when they were together?"

"Yes."

"Have you been in their company more than once?"

"I have seen them together on more occasions than I care to count," Smallwood said in anticipation of sticking it to the defendant and doing her part to convict him of killing her friend.

Felbin braced for the revenge of the haters.

"On those occasions when you were with Amy and the defendant, can you describe for the jury their relationship?"

Felbin need to interrupt the flow of this line of questioning with a speaking objection. "Objection. This testimony calls for nothing more than the speculation of a witness who has never liked Garner or approved of her friend dating a black man."

That statement caused an immediate reaction from Perrin. "That is an outrageous and reckless statement. Mr. Felbin knows that is not true, and he needs to be sanctioned. He did this . . ."

Felbin wasn't going to allow his adversary to complete that sentence. "Mr. Perrin knows full well the relationship . . ."

This time the judge jumped in. "That's enough from both of you. The objection is sustained."

Sustained? Is that what she just said? Did the lawyers hear that correctly, as they looked at each other equally amazed? Was she really going to prevent this witness from describing what she considered to be the mistreatment of her friend?

"Your Honor . . ." Perrin began before being immediately interrupted.

"Mr. Perrin, I have ruled. Proceed," Judge Cardwell said sternly, anxious to move off this topic.

"But Your Honor, I need to put this on the record and explain to you the purpose of my question and the evidence I intend to elicit from this witness."

"You have made your record, Mr. Perrin. Now, please move on."

195

Perrin was speechless and in shock. His inexperience prevented him from challenging this judge. She'd embarrassed him in front of the jury. But most of all, he was upset the judge didn't even want to hear where he intended to go with his questions. All judges at least gave you the chance to explain.

Eventually, Perrin moved on to a conversation the witness had with the victim regarding her plans to meet the defendant for dinner on Valentine's Day. Her testimony in that regard corroborated that of Sandworth. She didn't know the specifics of what time and where. But she didn't have to know those details.

It was clear to this jury the defendant planned to take the victim out for dinner on Valentine's Day. Equally clear, Garner Lee had lied about his presence in her apartment at or near the time of her death.

"I would like to acquaint the jury with what kind of a person Amy was prior to her death. Can you describe her personality for the jury, please?" Perrin asked.

Felbin knew the prosecutor was headed back to the prohibited territory. He was going to try again to poison the jury with the opinion of this witness as to the relationship between Amy and Garner. But an objection at this point would not be well received by the jury. It would be perceived as an attack on an innocent victim.

"She was a kind, easy going person. She would do anything for anybody and go out of her way to help someone. I saw that numerous times."

As soon as the witness completed her answer, Felbin was on his feet asking to approach the bench.

"I suspect he is now going to try to go down the road you previously blocked. I also suspect he is going to try to elicit testimony that Amy was going to end the relationship. Of course, in addition to relevance, that testimony is also hearsay and speculative," Felbin said, while at the bench and out of the hearing of the jury.

In response to the judge's request to identify the next question the prosecutor planned to ask, Perrin said, "I plan to ask her if she can describe the personality of the defendant and any arguments she witnessed first-hand between Amy and this defendant."

"No, you're not," Judge Cardwell said succinctly.

196

"But Your Honor . . ." Perrin began, hoping to persuade her to change her opinion.

He didn't get very far. In fact, he didn't get anywhere before he was told to step away from the bench and proceed with a different line of questioning, if he had one.

For the second time, the lawyers looked at each other in disbelief on their way back to their respective tables.

Perrin announced he had no other questions for this witness. And because she didn't really add anything the jury didn't already know, Felbin told the court he had no questions.

Because he was unable to poison the jury with the volatility of the defendant and how that played out in his relationship with Amy, the testimony of the remaining haters was limited to establishing the greatness of this victim and the loss to them specifically and the world generally.

Felbin knew that was complete bullshit. Actually, these *friends* were jealous back-stabbers who recognized Amy Deland for what she was, an opportunist who used Garner for his money and his family's celebrity. They also knew she was getting ready to dump him as soon as she was able to find a suitable financial replacement to continue the lifestyle she had become accustomed to.

But painting the victim as an opportunistic slut was not going to help the defendant. In fact, it would provide a motive for murder. Felbin couldn't risk opening the door to the evidence this judge erroneously kept from the jury.

For each of these witnesses, Felbin had no questions. And the court recessed for the day after the last of Amy's friends testified.

Chapter Fifty-One

As soon as they were alone, Carmine asked, "Is she fuckin kidding? She is not going to allow that idiot prosecutor to get into the relationship between the defendant and the victim? What kind of silly shit is that? She has either been bought and paid for or she is dumber than I thought, if that's possible."

Felbin was also at a loss to understand the ruling. "I can't explain it. That testimony is clearly admissible for any number of reasons. It's like we are in a role reversal here."

In criminal cases, defense lawyers are generally critical of court rulings, arguing that they favor the prosecution. Ordinarily, that criticism is well-founded. Most good trial judges realize if the defendant is acquitted, the state has no right of appeal. On the other hand, if the jury returns a guilty verdict, the defendant will always file post-trial motions. The most common is a motion for a new trial, in which the defendant claims the court's rulings were erroneous. At that point, the court can correct any prejudice which resulted from a ruling that was actually incorrect by granting a new trial. If the trial court refuses to grant a new trial, the defendant has the additional right to take his case to the court of appeals.

"This is now the second major issue that she decided in our favor and against the state. First, she doesn't allow any DNA testing and overrules the state's motion and our motion. Both parties want DNA testing, and she won't allow it. Now, she won't allow the state to show the defendant mistreated the victim. And she won't even allow Perrin to explain what he expected the witnesses to say about the relationship between Garner and Amy. Surely, she knows where he was going with this line of questions and that it wouldn't help us."

"But what the hell do we care why she's doing this silly shit as long as it benefits us? And it is definitely benefitting us. Maybe you should tell her that you don't mind her trying your case, but you don't want her to lose it," Carmine suggested.

"She may be helping us now, but that may not last forever. I don't trust her. But more importantly, I suspect her motive is not to help us, but rather to thank the defendant's father. And if that is the case, I don't want to be in the middle of a corruption case when the shit hits the fan."

"I don't know how that would be a problem. Remember, you tried to withdraw, and she wouldn't let you out. You even accused her of corruption and she didn't boot your ass out of this case."

"She wouldn't let me out. She put this case on a rocket docket and made us go to trial without any preparation. No DNA testing. All the things the senator wanted. He is the one who wanted to keep her and wouldn't let us file a motion to move the case to another judge. I don't need a house to fall on me to figure out this is a payback. But what I don't know is whether she is doing it on her own or with the senator."

"Again, who gives a shit? A win is a win."

While winning was important, Felbin didn't take ethical shortcuts. It made him uncomfortable to think that he was part of a case that was fixed with or without the knowledge of the defendant's family. Both Cardwell and Lee were shrewd politicians. He would probably never be able to prove corruption, as both would cover their tracks. And he couldn't blow the whistle, because that would hurt his client. Felbin liked to have all the answers to all the questions, but this was one case where it would be better if he left some questions unanswered.

As Felbin and his investigator were trying to figure out what Cardwell was doing, Perrin approached, expressing his frustration. "I know that you are benefitting from these rulings, but she is over the top. She won't allow DNA testing that we both want. And now she won't let me establish a hostile relationship between the victim and the defendant. Unbelievable. Listen, Felbin, I need to have a conversation with her off the record. I would like to go back to her chambers now, to see if she will speak to me. I would appreciate it if you would come with me. I don't expect you to say anything. But she won't see me if you're not there."

It's not uncommon for lawyers to have off the record conversations with judges during a trial to address certain issues, including rulings that excluded items of evidence the jury would never hear. But this case was different. Felbin knew that some of the rulings that went against the state were simply wrong. But, clearly, they benefited his client. While he agreed to attend this meeting with the prosecutor only because he was interested to see how this young prosecutor would handle this incompetent judge, he would say nothing. Or, at least that was the game plan going in.

On the way back to the judge's chambers, Felbin was curious as to whether Perrin's boss, the elected Circuit Attorney, would also be attending this little get-together. "Will Braxton be gracing us with her presence for this meeting?" Felbin asked.

"No," Perrin said, offering no additional details.

But Felbin decided to press. "It would seem to me this would be the kind of meeting she would want to attend. In fact, I would think she should be the one to be asking the questions, not you."

"You're telling me," was Perrin's only response.

What Perrin and Felbin didn't know is that conversation was already happening. Immediately after Perrin called his boss complaining about the rulings, Braxton called the judge, her former boss. But that conversation was far different than the one Perrin planned to have.

"I received a phone call from Paul Perrin complaining about your rulings. Apparently, you wouldn't let him prove a hostile relationship between the victim and the defendant," Braxton told the judge.

"You and I both know when prosecutors don't get their way, they whine and complain. It happened when I was the Circuit Attorney, and it continues to happen. I'm not here to protect your prosecutors," Cardwell said.

"Look, Joan, I get it. I know what you are trying to do and I'm on board. But this has to pass the straight face test. Your rulings can't be ridiculous."

"You think Felbin is going to object to my rulings?"

"Felbin is unpredictable. You never know what he's going to do."

"He's not going to do anything that hurts his client. He can't. Felbin is neutralized. He has no other choice but to go along with the program. Like it or not."

"I hope you're right, and you know what you're doing."

"I do. Relax. I have to go. I have everything covered."

Chapter Fifty-Two

Mary McMurtry was Cardwell's loyal secretary. They had been together for more than twenty years. Although McMurtry was new to the judging business, she knew Cardwell better than her own children. At sixty-nine, McMurtry was nearing the mandatory retirement age of seventy. Soon Cardwell would have to find a replacement. But Cardwell knew no one could replace Mary. Not only was she loyal, she was protective. To get to Cardwell, you had to go through Mary. When Cardwell was the elected prosecutor, she would routinely turn away judges, lawyers, reporters and anyone else that she believed would annoy her boss. Most of the time she would be cordial. But there were times when a caller rudely persisted, she would react in less than a professional manner emphasizing her displeasure with an occasional *F* bomb.

Cardwell was so comfortable with Mary she would rarely close her door during both personal and professional telephone conversations. Usually, when Cardwell was the Circuit Attorney, Mary wouldn't pay a lot of attention to the calls. Most were routine business. But since her boss went on the bench, she was paying closer attention. Not because she was nosey. It helped her become acclimated with her new job.

Although most of those calls were becoming routine, there was something about the case of Garner Lee that was different. Of course, she read the papers, saw the television coverage and certainly knew who the defendant's father was. She was also well aware of how Cardwell campaigned for her spot on the bench included sacrificing an innocent police officer. Although she didn't agree with the prosecution of Robert Decker, she remained loyal to her boss. But now she listened to Cardwell's conversations in the context of that history and wondered what was going on.

Ever since the Garner case was assigned to Cardwell, she noticed the judge would either make a phone call or receive a daily phone call or sometimes two, on her private line. Because those were on the private line, she was not able to screen them. She also had no way to know who the caller or callers were and could hear only the judge's side of the conversation. The theme of the discussion was usually the same. Cardwell would assure the caller that *everything would be fine, don't worry, I'll take care of it.* Obviously, they were talking about the Lee murder case. She wondered why a judge who is supposed to be impartial, would reassure someone that things would be all right and not to worry. But she was new to the job.

After the trial recessed for the day, Cardwell placed her usual call. This time, in addition to the *I'll take care of it* assurances, she was explaining how she prevented the prosecutor from introducing some type of evidence harmful to the defendant. Why would a judge be telling someone that she protected the defendant? And who was this mystery caller? And what interest did this person have in the Lee case? She didn't need a house to fall on her to figure out that Senator Lee was involved somehow.

But this day was a little different. The Circuit Attorney called to talk about the case. That call was not on the private line. The conversation with Braxton was similar to the one the judge had with her mystery caller. From what McMurtry could gather something happened in the trial that was of some concern to both callers. Apparently, the judge had not allowed some type of evidence to be presented to the jury. But because she only heard one side of the conversation, she couldn't tell what that was.

No sooner than the judge finished her conversation with Braxton, Perrin and Felbin appeared seeking an audience with the judge.

Reluctantly, Cardwell agreed to see them. Because the door remained open, McMurtry quickly determined the subject of the meeting was the same as the phone calls. But this time, the secretary was able to hear the nature of the excluded evidence that seemed to concern people.

"Judge, I would like to talk to you about your refusal to permit me to elicit testimony regarding the hostile relationship between the defendant and the victim," Perrin began.

"I have evidence the two argued and the defendant on an occasion or two even assaulted the victim."

Cardwell listened patiently and didn't interrupt the prosecutor this time.

"This evidence is critical to my case. While by itself, it doesn't establish a motive for murder, it does demonstrate there was hostility which certainly could have led to murder if an assault escalated," he continued.

"Now you're asking me to admit evidence that allows the jury to speculate, Mr. Perrin?" Cardwell asked.

Felbin knew the young prosecutor just screwed up. His inexperience would allow this experienced former prosecutor to shut down this argument.

"No, Judge. I am not asking you to admit this to allow the jury to speculate. Evidence of other crimes is admissible to show intent and absence of a mistake or an accident. The state's position is this defendant struck this victim in the head with a statue and fully intended to kill her. And he succeeded. That makes evidence of the relationship to include arguments and assaults, admissible."

The kid was on a roll and was on the right track. Felbin was enjoying the show.

Apparently, Cardwell also knew Perrin was on the right track, because she shut him down immediately. "Mr. Perrin, I have made my ruling. That evidence will not be admitted. Is there anything else?"

"No," Perrin said, as he bolted for the open door, leaving Felbin behind. He was pissed.

"You know your ruling is absolutely wrong. I don't know what you are trying to do here, but I suspect this is some sort of payback. And you also know I can't say anything that would hurt my client. But you better hope I don't find a way. I'd like nothing better than to see your ass sitting in a jail cell," Felbin said in a calm matter of fact voice. So much for remaining silent.

Cardwell didn't respond. Perhaps she was trying to process the comments, particularly the part about a jail cell. She just watched as Felbin left the office.

Chapter Fifty-Three

When he returned to his office, Felbin answered some emails, returned some phone calls on other cases and decided he needed a drink. The next call he made was to his armchair psychologist for dinner and a drink. It wouldn't be a late evening, because he needed to do some additional witness preparation. But he also needed to relax with someone he trusted and loved.

St. Louis is the home of many fine restaurants. It is sometimes difficult to pick one. But on this occasion, since Felbin was downtown and Melinda was in the Hill section of the city, they settled on Cunnetto's House of Pasta, an Italian restaurant on the Hill.

The Hill derives its name from its geographical proximity to the highest point in the city of St. Louis. Its unique identity is shaped by the predominant Italian-American population that lives in this quaint section of St. Louis. The fire hydrants are painted red, white and green as a tribute to their Italian heritage. In addition to fine restaurants, Italian-American bakeries, saloons, delis, meticulously manicured lawns, and two bocce ball gardens attract visitors from around the country. *The Game of Our Lives,* a book and the 2005 film of the same name is the story of the U.S. Soccer team that defeated England in the 1950 FIFA World Cup. Four of the five St. Louisans who played on that team came from the Hill. But when the people who live on the Hill are not mowing their lawns, tending to their vegetable and flower gardens while enjoying the smell of freshly baked breads or snacking on salami and cheese or toasted ravioli, you will find them at St. Ambrose Roman Catholic Church, a landmark in the community.

On any given night, the line at Cunnetto's is long and parking is at a premium. The restaurant doesn't take reservations. Felbin was running late, as he needed to coordinate several things for the trial with both his administrative assistant, Jan Marshall, and Carmine as they would not be there when he returned to the office later that evening. When they finished, he asked Joe Weller, his driver and part time investigator, to take him to Cunnetto's. He was sure Melinda would be waiting patiently at the bar and having a cocktail or a glass of wine. She wouldn't be mad or even upset. A type D personality to compliment Felbin, a definite type A.

When Felbin arrived, he was greeted by Frank Cunnetto, the owner. Frank's dad, along with his brother Vince, were both pharmacists who started cooking lunches with only four bowls and three spoons between them. In 1974, they opened Cunnetto's House of Pasta. A three-foot square photograph of the two founding pharmacists hangs proudly over the bar.

"I've been reading about you. Actually, I was kind of surprised you took that case," Frank said.

"You have no idea how many times I've second guessed that decision," Felbin replied, unwilling to get into a lengthy discussion.

"I put Melinda at a table in the back of the dining room where you can have some privacy. She's patiently awaiting your arrival, as usual. I don't know what you did to deserve her," Frank joked.

"Thanks, Frank," Felbin said as he walked toward his table.

"I ordered some toasted ravioli for us. I figured from what I have been reading, you could use a little comfort food to get started," Melinda said as she greeted her dinner companion with a hug and a peck on the cheek.

Usually served as an appetizer, toasted ravioli is breaded, deep fried and served with marinara sauce. Many take credit for discovering this Italian delicacy. But most connoisseurs agree toasted ravioli was born in the Hill neighborhood of St. Louis. The most popular story claims the discovery was quite by accident when a chef at a Hill restaurant accidentally dropped meat ravioli into a deep fryer.

On this day, Felbin wasn't interested in the history of toasted ravioli. He was just interested in enjoying some as he attempted to relax from the stress of a high-profile trial. When the waitress arrived, he ordered a Budweiser draft to wash it down.

"How much time do you have for dinner?" Melinda asked. She knew he usually worked evenings when he was in trial and didn't have a lot of time to socialize and unwind.

"I told Joe I would call him to pick me up in about an hour and a half. That should help me put this day behind me, at least for the moment."

Additional conversation gave way momentarily to beer and toasted ravioli. But invariably, the conversation would turn to the Felbin's problems of the day. After all, that's why he wanted to have dinner with Melinda. She was his rock. She could put life into perspective, ground him like no one else.

Felbin didn't need a menu. He knew what he wanted for dinner. Cavatelli con Pomodoro. He ordered the same thing every time. His motto: "If it's not broken, no need to fix it".

Melinda was not quite that inflexible. She needed a menu, as she was not wedded to one item per restaurant visited. Usually, but not always, she would order Cannelloni con Salsa. But on this occasion, she decided to go with Filetto di Sogliola con Carciofi, filet of sole with artichoke hearts sautéed in a lemon, butter, white wine sauce.

"How is the new lab doing?" Felbin asked, initiating some conversation after enjoying the appetizer.

Melinda owned seven dental labs throughout the country. Her company had just opened a new one in Florida. Set up and staffing kept her busy and out of town.

"It's going okay. Lot of work. Trying to find the right people who know what they're doing is the immediate problem. I have several interviews with potential candidates next week. How is the trial going? I have been following it in the paper and online when I was out of town. But that obviously doesn't tell me the whole story," Melinda said.

Melinda listened as Felbin recounted the events of the day, waiting to offer her thoughts until he finished. "I'm not sure that I understand this. You believe this judge is fixing the case in favor of your client because of some political payback. But there is nothing you can do about that. Is that right?"

"Yes."

"Well, let me ask you this. How would you feel if your client is found not guilty because of what this judge did?"

"That's an interesting question. At one level, I would be happy. At another level, I would be upset, maybe even angry."

"Let me see if I can break this down. Are you convinced of Garner's innocence?"

"Yes."

"That part is good. But the means to that end corrupts the judicial process and is unacceptable?"

"Right."

"But there's really nothing you can do about it now and maybe ever. True?"

"Unfortunately, yes, that's true. And it is extremely frustrating. Although I must admit I'm enjoying seeing the prosecutor get his ass kicked by the trial judge. That doesn't happen very often. They are usually protecting them," Felbin said with a hint of a smile.

"You seem to be expending a lot of energy for something over which you have no control. I'm thinking you would be better served by going with it for the moment and dealing with it on the back side after the trial is over," Melinda counseled.

"That's easier said than done."

"Why did you take this case? Clearly, you had no love for his father."

Felbin wasn't expecting the question. It was a fair question and one he and others had asked several times. The obvious answer was he believed in the actual innocence of his client. But there was more.

"You're right. I had no love for his father," Felbin began. "And maybe that's exactly why I agreed to get involved. My gut told me from the outset this kid was not good for a murder. I believed he really did love Amy and wouldn't do anything to hurt her. I could see it in his eyes and hear it in his voice. It was not a role he was playing to convince me he was not a murderer. Maybe I wanted his father to understand that truly innocent people are prosecuted because of public pressure that has nothing to do with the evidence. And maybe I just wanted to get a front row seat to see his father suffer when his son was on trial like Bobby Decker, another innocent man who suffered, thanks to him."

Felbin waited to see if Melinda would say anything. When she didn't, he continued. "Then I thought maybe I was not being fair to him. I indicted and convicted him for the prosecution of Bobby Decker. But when I separated out the emotion of the Decker case, I began to think about what he really did. He was a black politician who was demanding justice as he saw it. He was protesting in a climate of racial discord between the police and his black constituents. Unfortunately, he was talking to a prosecutor who allowed her self-interests to interfere with justice. Her decision to prosecute Decker made the racial situation worse. That was her decision, not his."

"Then she was rewarded with a judgeship," Melinda added.

"And that was his first mistake. His second was demanding a quid pro quo for his son. I guess it's the goal of every politician to have a judge or two in their pockets."

"Now we have circled back to where this conversation began. You have no proof the case is fixed."

"Not yet, and maybe I never will. I guess the take away on this is you can't trust any politician of any race or gender. I suppose that's why Trump was elected. Ironically, he might turn out to be the biggest politician of all time." Felbin said.

Those were the final words on the topic. When the entrees were served, the remainder of the evening was spent enjoying dinner and avoiding any conversation related to politicians, prosecutors, judges or trials.

Chapter Fifty-Four

His client arrived early and was waiting for him when Felbin walked into the courtroom. Garner was nervous, and it showed. Understandable. He was on trial for his life. He needed constant reassurances.

At his client's request, Felbin reviewed yesterday's evidence putting a defense spin on it where he could. He needed to be optimistic when talking to Garner.

The trial was going as expected. There were no surprises. Sandworth hit all the high points. No one doubted Garner Lee was in Amy's apartment after the fatal blow was struck. His bloody fingerprints were found on the inside doorknob. The doubt would come into play with the lack of evidence connecting the defendant to the murder weapon. It was one thing to put Garner inside the victim's apartment. It was quite another to prove that he was responsible for her death. The jury would be instructed that the mere presence at the scene of a crime is not evidence of guilt. Of course, it would have been better if Garner had been out of the country at the time of Amy's death. But that wasn't the hand Felbin was dealt.

When Perrin arrived, he handed him the lab report he had received the night before. "What's this?" Perrin asked.

"It's a lab report that I just received las night. The DNA that you found on the murder weapon does not belong to the defendant," Felbin said.

"And you're giving this to me now?"

"Well, I couldn't very well give it to you before I got it."

"We need to see the judge."

Perrin complained that he had been sandbagged, and the defense should not be able to use this evidence.

"I just received the report," Felbin told the judge in chambers.

Without any evidence to support his claim, Perrin said, "He did this on purpose so we would not have time to verify the findings of this lab I assume is in his pocket."

"Oh, my. What a terrible accusation. You both will recall I was not the one who pressed for an immediate trial. You will also recall I strenuously objected to the quick setting and pointed out I would not have enough time to prepare. I would have thought *they* would have tested the DNA found on the statue," Felbin said pointing at his opponent.

"We couldn't test it because the court denied our two motions to get the defendant's DNA sample."

"If that's why you wanted it, you should have told the court that was the reason. Instead, you said you wanted it to prove some irrelevant paternity issue. You never said you wanted the defendant's DNA to compare to the DNA found on the murder weapon," Felbin replied, his voice rising.

Perrin realized he had made a mistake, a big mistake. He never did make the argument he needed the DNA to do the comparison. He was young, inexperienced, and had gotten no help from his office in this high-profile case he was thrown into. He just missed this. Of course, he also had little time to prepare his case.

Cardwell quickly adopted Felbin's position. "Had you made that argument, I might have looked favorably on your request. In all events, your motion to exclude this evidence is denied. I will, however, give you some time to have your lab verify the results from the lab Mr. Felbin selected."

Felbin knew this was a bunch of bullshit. There was no way she was going to grant that motion if there was a chance the father of the child could be determined. But now the prosecutor had Garner's DNA profile and could check it against that of the fetus to determine paternity. He just hoped Perrin would make another mistake and wouldn't think of doing that. He and Carmine had discussed that risk before they gave the lab results to Perrin. But they decided to take the chance. They felt it was important for the jury to hear there was no DNA or fingerprints belonging to the defendant on the murder weapon.

The testimony of the day began with Jennings, the two witnesses who could put the defendant in the victim's apartment building at approximately 6:30. These witnesses lived across the hall from Amy on the second floor of the two-story apartment building. On their way to dinner at 6:30, they had passed Garner on the stairs as he was walking up toward Amy's apartment. Since Felbin wasn't disputing the defendant's presence in the apartment, he had no questions for these witnesses.

The evidence technicians and the forensic expert followed and described the evidence they had gathered, including the bloody print on the doorknob, which belonged to the defendant. Felbin had no questions for the technicians, but did have some critical questions for Jim Barber, the forensic expert.

After Perrin established that the defendant's fingerprint was found in blood on the inside of the doorknob of Amy's apartment, he announced he had no further questions of this witness. That was a tactical mistake. It was now Felbin's turn.

"Mr. Barber, I want to ask you some questions that the prosecutor chose to ignore," Felbin began.

Perrin was on his feet objecting. "Your Honor, Mr. Felbin's cross-examination of this witness is limited to my direct." As soon as he finished his statement, he knew he had made a mistake, another mistake.

"He's got to be kidding. No doubt he doesn't want the jury to hear this." Felbin's response was immediate and intended to be prejudicial. He was not waiting for an invitation from the court to respond.

Technically, the prosecutor was correct. Felbin's cross-examination for this witness would be limited to the subject matter that Perrin covered during his direct examination. Although correct, the objection in this case was a young lawyer mistake. Felbin always had the right to recall the witness to ask whatever questions he wanted. Most good trial judges, however, will allow the cross to cover issues beyond the direct to save valuable trial time. This would be particularly true with this judge, who was not demonstrating a lot of love for the prosecution. As an experienced trial lawyer, Felbin knew that and took advantage of the mistake with an inflammatory comment. All Perrin could do was wait for Cardwell's ruling. That came swiftly and before Felbin could make any additional comments.

"As I was saying, I want to discuss an issue the prosecutor avoided," Felbin continued. No objection this time.

"Mr. Barber, the prosecutor asked you about a print on the doorknob. But he didn't ask you about any other prints you found. I want to direct your attention to the statue, the murder weapon. Were you able to lift any prints off that murder weapon?"

"Yes."

"You were?"

"Oh, stop, Mr. Felbin. You know that I lifted those prints. You got a copy of my report," Barber said, clearly annoyed at the game Felbin was playing.

"Would that be the same report that you also gave to the prosecutor?" Felbin responded without skipping a beat.

Barber wasn't anxious to answer that question. Instead, he was looking at Perrin who was shaking his head.

Recognizing he was not going to get a verbal response, Felbin said, "Fine. I'll take that as a yes. Now, please don't keep us in suspense. First of all, please identify the finger or fingers that you lifted."

"Thumb."

"Mr. Barber, you have been the department's fingerprint expert for what, twenty years?" Felbin asked.

"Actually, nineteen."

"And in your line of work, it is important to be accurate, precise and complete."

"Yes, of course."

"And in this case, you were accurate, precise and complete. True?"

"Yes, I believe I was accurate in this case."

"How about complete? Was your report complete for example?"

"I believe it was," Booker said, as he prepared for the follow up question that he knew was coming.

"Now let's move on to the issue that the prosecutor ignored. If you would, please tell all of us whose thumb print is on that murder weapon, Mr. Barber," Felbin pressed.

"I don't know."

"What does that mean? I thought you said your report was accurate, precise and complete."

"It is. But we don't have any prints on file we could match."

"But you do have Garner's prints on file?"

"Yes."

"And when you compared the unknown prints you got off the murder weapon to the known prints of Garner Lee, what was the result?"

"There was no match," Barber reluctantly admitted.

"In plain English, that means Garner's prints were not on the murder weapon. Correct?"

"Not that we could find," Barber corrected.

"Now let's move on to another part of your accurate and complete report the prosecutor has a copy of. When you do the analysis for fingerprints in this day and age, you also test for DNA, correct?

"That's true."

"And tell us, did you find any DNA evidence on that murder weapon?"

"Yes."

"Now, sometimes Mr. Barber, I get distracted when witnesses are answering the prosecutor's questions. Because I don't want to be duplicitous and waste time here, did Mr. Perrin mention this DNA you found on the murder weapon during his examination of you?" Felbin knew full well that the prosecutor made another mistake by ignoring this issue. Of course, he had just received Felbin's lab report.

Felbin was anxious to see how Barber would handle this. Would there be a smart-ass response designed to identify the game Felbin was playing, or would a simple negative response be the better course. Barber was no stranger to sparring with Felbin. He had done it numerous times in the past. But it is always dangerous to take on the people asking the questions, and this experienced witness knew that.

Barber opted for the simple response in the hope of moving forward quickly. "No," he said.

"Well then, let me ask this. Whose DNA is on that murder weapon?"

"We don't know, because we don't have anything in the bank that matched."

Now Felbin needed to decide whether to stop there. If he pressed the point, the witness would say he didn't have a DNA sample from the defendant. Then Perrin might take the position the defendant refused to voluntarily provide a sample, which was true, at least initially. Then the topic of paternity discussions behind closed doors might be opened. In balance, Felbin decided to settle for the answer he just got and move on. He would call his forensic expert in the defendant's case to establish that Garner's DNA was not on that murder weapon.

"Thank you for that information, Mr. Barber. But just to be clear. There is nothing that you found on that murder weapon that forensically or scientifically puts Garner Lee's hands on that murder weapon?"

"That's right."

When Felbin announced he had no further questions, Perrin wasted no time. "Mr. Barber, you said you couldn't find the defendant's prints on the statue, not that he didn't handle the murder weapon, correct?"

"Yes."

"And did you find partial prints on that statue?"

"Yes."

"And what is a partial print?"

"That is a fingerprint we don't have enough points or similar characteristics to match to a known print. The police department standard is a minimum of ten."

"And you can't exclude the defendant as the contributor of some or all of those partials, correct?"

"I can't say who they belong to."

"And the full prints you were able to find, can you tell us how long that print was on the statue?"

"I can't. It could have been a very long time or a very short time. There is no way to tell."

"For example, the print you found could have been on that statue for more than a year, is that correct?"

"Yes, sir."

"Nothing further," Perrin announced. He, too, opted to avoid the DNA issue with this witness. He didn't want to open any doors before his lab had a chance to check the findings of Felbin's lab.

Chapter Fifty-Five

The medical examiner was the state's last witness. He would establish the cause of death for both Amy and her unborn child. Felbin wasn't disputing the cause of death, but would cross-examine this witness on a different issue. There was a critical piece of evidence Felbin needed to establish through this witness. He had a thumb print on the murder weapon. But no one could say it was a left thumb. Now he needed the medical examiner to say the blow to the head was struck from the left side. Unfortunately, because of the speed with which this case was set for trial, Felbin didn't have the opportunity to depose this witness to lock in his testimony. He would be cruising through uncharted waters when he questioned this experienced expert in the presence of the jury. Always a dangerous practice for a trial lawyer. Thank you, Judge Cardwell and Senator Lee.

Doctor Phillip Long, no relation to Myra Long, the public relations director for Karen Braxton and previously for Joan Cardwell, had been the medical examiner for the City of St. Louis for the past twenty-three years. He had done thousands of autopsies and was always well prepared when he testified. This case was pretty straightforward.

Without objection, Doctor Long established the cause of death for Amy Deland was blunt trauma with a linear object resulting in a brain swell and death. He identified the statue found in the apartment as the murder weapon. Blood found on the statue was identified as that of the victim. The death of the fetus resulted from the death of the mother. He fixed the time of death between 4 and 7 pm on February 14.

Felbin didn't need to cover the cause of death for either Amy or the unborn child. Clearly, someone struck the victim on the back of the head with the statue. He would also be able to work with the 4 to 7 pm time frame. The witnesses put his client in the apartment building around 6:30 pm.

The critical issue was whether the murderer swung the statue with a right hand or a left hand. Long was no fool and would know Felbin would be coming at him on this issue. If Felbin led him down the path that the blow was struck with the left hand, Long would know his client was right-handed. This was not Long's first encounter with Felbin in the courtroom. In fact, the medical examiner's last unpleasant face off was in the Decker case. By most accounts, Felbin was the prevailing party in that battle of wits.

"Doctor Long, it is nice to see you. Unfortunately, because of the speed with which this case was set for trial, I didn't have the chance to talk to you before today. Please forgive me if I have to ask some questions that could have been answered before today," Felbin began as he shot a look of disgust at Cardwell. "Let me start with the time of death. You said that would be between 4 and 7 pm, correct?"

"Yes."

"Witnesses place Garner in Amy's building around 6:30 pm. According to your time line, Amy could have been struck with this statue two and one-half hours before Garner ever arrived, correct?"

"Well, these are estimates, and it could be a little longer than 7 pm."

Let the battle begin. This contest was like watching a pitcher trying to strike out a cleanup hitter with the bases loaded. But unlike a baseball matchup, sometimes in the courtroom there is no clear winner.

"And it could be shorter than 6 pm?" Felbin fired back.

"Yes."

"If your 4 to 7 estimate is correct, that would mean that the defendant would have been in the apartment for less than a half hour before the time of death."

"Like I said, these are estimates."

"I heard that. Of course, I would point out that these are your estimates, not mine. But if the prosecutor's witnesses are to be believed and your timetable is accurate, the defendant would have been in the apartment for less than a half an hour before the time of death, correct?" Felbin repeated.

"I don't know what the state's witnesses said or how accurate their time line was."

Clearly, Felbin was not going to get a concession on this. But he'd made his point and decided to move on.

"Doctor, I want to talk to you about the scene. Let's start with these," Felbin said as he handed the crime scene photographs to the witness. "As you can see in those photographs, the victim is face down on the floor. And according to the police report, the top of her head is ten feet nine inches from the front door and her body is perpendicular to the front door. Would you agree?"

"Yes."

"By the way, you have seen these photographs and the police report before today, correct?"

"Yes."

"And why do you look at crime scene photos and read the police reports?"

"Because I like to be fully informed," Long said.

Felbin knew that was only partially correct. "Isn't it true, Doctor Long, that those items assist you in formulating your opinions and helping the police identify the person responsible for the death?"

"That's part of it," the witness said, knowing Felbin was going to continue with this line of questioning.

"And in this case, isn't is true that that you shared some of your thoughts about who might have been responsible for the death of Amy with the police officers investigating this case?"

"I have many conversations with police officers."

He didn't answer the question. Felbin knew he was on to something.

"Well, let me ask you this. When you do your autopsy, you look for visible signs of injury, correct?"

"Yes."

"And in this case the only visible sign of injury was a fractured skull, correct?"

"Yes."

"And when you look at that picture of the victim on the floor, please tell the jury where the visible sign of injury is located on the skull of the victim."

"On the left side of the back of the skull."

"And is it your belief that this statue is the murder weapon?" Felbin asked as he handed the statue to the witness.

"It is."

"And what would you say that this statue weighs?"

"It's solid. Maybe two to three pounds. That would be my estimate."

"Pretty heavy, right?"

"I would say so."

"Now we have a left sided injury on the back of the head caused by a heavy object on a person whose body is perpendicular to and ten feet nine inches away from the front door. What does that tell you, Doctor?"

"I'm not sure that I understand the question," the witness said, clearly either unwilling or unable to answer.

Felbin was betting on unwilling. "I'm asking you if this evidence is helpful in shedding any light on the person who might be responsible for Amy's death."

"Well, it could."

Another unresponsive response. Clearly, this witness was testing Felbin's patience.

"Doctor, I am too tired to continue this dance. Doesn't this crime scene and the location of the skull fracture suggest the person who caused this fatal injury and killed Amy Deland was left-handed or at least used the left hand?"

Felbin knew he was going to get some push back on the question. He anticipated that the witness would say there was no real way to conclude that with certainty. He would make the further point that a right-handed person could have used his left hand to hold the statue and cause the fatal injury.

The witness didn't respond immediately. He looked at Felbin. It was clear he was trying to figure out how he could answer the question without helping Felbin, but at the same time without looking like an idiot. Felbin had planted the seed that the blow was struck either by someone who was left-handed or was using the left hand as Amy was walking toward the door.

"I can't say that with any scientific certainty."

Shaking his head, Felbin said, "Well, let me handle it this way. Is this the type of discussion that you would have with the police to help them solve the crime, regardless of your scientific certainty?"

"It could be, yes."

"Well, did you have this discussion with the detectives handling this case?"

"Mr. Felbin, I have a lot of conversations with police officers."

His demeanor and hesitation suggested he was lying. But there would be no way Felbin could prove it. "I'm not asking you about a lot of conversations. Just this one. Can you say with certainty you didn't discuss the question of whether the assailant was left-handed or used his left hand to strike the blow to the victim's head?"

"I simply can't say one way or the other," Long said, knowing that Felbin wasn't finished with this line of questioning.

"Would you agree that whether the assailant was right- or left-handed could be a significant piece of evidence that would help identify the person responsible?"

"It could be."

"And weren't you at least intellectually curious as to whether the individual who killed Amy was right-handed or left-handed?" Felbin obviously wasn't ready to abandon this line of questioning.

"Being intellectually curious isn't part of my job. It's what I can prove with scientific certainty," Long responded, a hint of hostility in his voice.

"Well, can you say with scientific certainty that the person who struck Amy did not use his or her left hand?"

"I think that . . ." the witness began but was interrupted by Felbin.

"Just a yes or no, doctor."

"No."

"Can you say with scientific certainty that this individual was not left hand dominant?"

"No."

Felbin knew he got all he was going to get from this witness on this issue. "Doctor, I have one final question for you. Do you know whether Garner Lee is right hand or left hand dominant?"

"I don't know."

"Did you make any effort to find out whether the defendant was right-handed before you came in here sharing your opinions?"

"I thought you said you had one final question," Long joked, causing a few jurors to smile.

"It was a two-part final question," Felbin replied. More smiles from the jury box.

"I did not make any effort to determine whether your client was right-handed."

Perrin went right at it. He knew his opponent would be pounding this left-handed drum in his closing argument. "Doctor Long, you said you couldn't tell whether the fatal blow was struck by a person using his left hand. Is that because you don't know the position of either the victim or the killer at the time the blow was delivered?"

"Yes."

"For example, if both of these individuals had been facing each other and the victim turned to go toward the door at the time the killer swung, the right hand could have been used?"

Felbin thought about objecting to the hypothetical, but decided to wait to see where the line of questioning would go.

"That's correct. And that's just one of many scenarios," Long volunteered.

And with that, the prosecution had no additional questions or witnesses, at least not at the moment.

But Felbin had a few more questions. "Wait, wait, wait," he began. "The victim and one other individual are facing each other. The victim turns, presumably to the right to walk to the door and is struck in the head. Do I have that right?" Felbin asked.

"So far, so good," Long sarcastically commented.

"But for that to make any sense at all, the assailant would have to be holding the statue in his right hand at the time they are facing each other, rather than grabbing it off a book shelf. Would you agree?" Felbin asked, knowing full well that the witness would not agree.

Long considered the question before immediately responding. But eventually said, "Mr. Felbin, I wasn't there."

"Yes, we all know that. But you said this scenario was one of many. Can you tell this jury how this scenario is possible in the absence of the assailant holding the weapon?" Felbin demanded.

"I'm not sure."

"But if the assailant held the weapon, wouldn't you expect prints and DNA to be found on that weapon?"

"I'm not sure."

Long made a mistake by agreeing with the prosecutor's hypothetical, and he knew it.

"You agreed with the prosecutor's hypothetical, and now you can't explain why you agreed?"

"I said that this was one of several scenarios, Mr. Felbin."

"I'm not asking you about several scenarios, just this one. Can you answer my question?" Felbin pressed.

"Not beyond what I just said."

No sense pursuing this line of questioning. Felbin made his point. This witness was not about to concede anything that helped the defendant. "I'm finished with this witness," Felbin said as he was returning to the counsel table.

Because Perrin needed some time to have his lab review Felbin's DNA report, he asked for and was granted a recess until 9:30 in the morning. At that time, he would decide whether he would rest his case.

Chapter Fifty-Six

In any criminal case, both parties need to make strategic decisions. Those decisions can shape the outcome of the trial and determine guilt or innocence. What jurors hear and how they hear it are important. But what they don't hear can also be important and contribute to the outcome. That includes the ever-present issue of whether the defendant testifies.

The prosecution always bears the burden of proving the defendant's guilt beyond a reasonable doubt. That burden never shifts to the defense. The defendant can sit back and offer no evidence. Do nothing. Doesn't even have to cross-examine the prosecution witnesses. If the state's evidence is insufficient to meet its burden of proof, the judge will instruct the jury it must give the defendant the benefit of the doubt and acquit.

Once the prosecutor announces that, the state rests, the defendant must make some choices. Will any evidence be offered? Will witnesses, both substantive and character, be called to testify? And the most important question. Will the defendant testify? Many of these decisions are made prior to trial. For example, if the defendant has an alibi, clearly those witnesses will be called in the defense case. But where the defense is a simple *I didn't do it,* the decision is made more difficult and will depend on a variety of factors. Defense counsel will use a cost benefit analysis. What can the defendant offer, other than a denial? And what will the cross-examination by the prosecutor look like? When the dust settles, will the defendant surface as believable? Usually, pretrial rehearsals will determine how well the defendant can withstand cross. But in the final analysis, regardless of what the lawyers think or what is recommended, the final decision on the issue is up to the defendant.

In the case of State of Missouri v. Garner Lee, there was no alibi. There was no substantive evidence that proves his innocence. The state proved beyond the shadow of a doubt he was in Amy's apartment at or near the time of her death, and he lied about it. Felbin could twist and turn that lie any way he wanted. He could suggest that the police threatened and coerced his client to the extent he lied because he was scared. Or he was so traumatized by the death of someone he loved he didn't know what he was saying. After all, the search for the truth in most trials is but the secondary unintended consequence to good theatre. Regardless of Felbin's acting skills, his client had lied when he said he was not in that apartment on the day of the murder.

Explaining why Garner was in the apartment that day was easy. It was Valentine's Day and he wanted to celebrate with the woman he loved. They would have a romantic dinner at their favorite restaurant. He made the reservation and was coming to pick her up for their date. Completely believable. Thousands of couples were doing the same thing. But why did he lie? The jury would definitely want to know. If he testified, he could tell the jury why he lied or deny he lied. If he didn't testify, his lawyer could offer to testify for him and explain the situation without the inconvenience of cross-examination.

Felbin sent his client to get a bite to eat while he and his investigator went to one of the lawyer conference rooms. They had no witnesses or evidence to present. The only question was whether the defendant should testify. Since the trial was in recess for the rest of the day, they had some time to discuss the issue and decide.

"You're not going to put that fuckin' idiot on the stand, are you?" Carmine began, never shy about sharing what was on his mind with anyone who cared to listen.

"There may be nothing to decide. Remember, he told us that he was going to testify," Felbin recalled.

"Even this prosecutor will eat him alive. How the hell is he going to explain the lie? Or is he going to say he never denied being in her apartment and Sandworth is lying?" the investigator asked.

Felbin didn't answer. Instead, he just looked out the window at the streets of the City of St. Louis, ten floors below.

Carmine continued. "If he denies telling Sandworth he never saw her and was not in her apartment, how is he going to explain the fact he didn't bother to call the police after he found her dead? Obviously, the bloody print puts him there, regardless of what he says. He's fucked whichever way he goes if he's stupid enough to take the stand. And he's definitely stupid."

"He is not a rocket scientist. That's for sure," Felbin said. "But let's look at where we are now. According to Sandworth, Garner denied both seeing Amy and being in her apartment. But a bloody print puts him inside the apartment. Witnesses put him in the apartment building around 6:30. The medical examiner establishes the time of death between 4 pm and 7 pm. Despite his denial of seeing or talking to her, he made dinner reservations for 7 o'clock in a restaurant close to her apartment. We have a left sided injury that was the cause of death and at least an inference the killer was left-handed."

"But what do they have to actually prove that he swung the statue?" Carmine asked.

"They have a lot of smoke and mirrors. But they have no one who can say he even held the murder weapon, let alone used it to kill Amy. Let's analyze it from the reasonable doubt standpoint. We have the left side injury. A print on the statue that belongs to someone other than the defendant. The medical examiner gave us a three-hour window for the time of death."

"And we only have him in the apartment for roughly thirty minutes of that three-hour spread. That's huge," Carmine injected.

"I agree. But our Achilles heel is the lie. We keep coming back to that. At this moment, I think the jury believes Sandworth, and that means Garner must credibly explain why he did what he did. He also needs to tell this jury he is right-handed."

"How's he going to explain this huge lie? Or is he gonna claim he never denied being there?"

"He's going to tell the truth." Felbin was firm with his position that Garner Lee would not lie. "His explanation is based upon a conversation with his father, he mistakenly thought he needed to deny he was in the apartment."

"You're kidding! Listen to yourself. Are you fuckin' nuts? That explanation will get him a one-way ticket to the joint. I think we are better off taking the position Sandworth isn't believable and our hero never made that statement. As far as the right-hand thing is concerned, just have him use his right hand to write out something, maybe a prayer we beat this indictment, on a legal pad when you are standing next to him doing your closing argument," Carmine suggested.

"You know that explanation did sound a bit ridiculous when I was saying it. I think you're right. We can't put him on the stand. That would be a disaster. Go see if you can find him and get him in here so we can talk."

As he waited for Carmine to return with their client, he was concerned about several things with this trial. At the moment, his focus was on whether his client would insist on testifying, as he had previously. If he did, Felbin would have no choice. Garner Lee would be talking to this jury.

Felbin didn't have to wait very long for his answer. As soon as Garner and Carmine walked into the conference room, Felbin said, "Garner, we need to make a decision on whether you will be testifying. I think . . . ."

Felbin was unable to finish his sentence before Garner spoke. "Nothing to decide. I'm testifying."

"Hold on, partner. You get up on that witness stand and they'll kick your ass all over town," Carmine said. No sugar coating. Directly to the point.

"Listen, Garner," Felbin began. "I believe that it's a mistake for you to testify. We must deal with your statement to Sandworth, and we think it's easier for me to handle, as opposed to you. They can't cross-examine me."

"I understand, and I appreciate everything you guys have done for me. I really do. I know my family has not made this easy for you. I also know we are up against it. It doesn't look good," Garner said as he hesitated and looked around the room. "I loved Amy. I didn't kill her. I need to say that on this record and in this very public trial. If the jury believes me, they believe me. If they don't, they don't, and I go to prison. But what's worse than prison is my silence with you fronting for me. If this jury is going to acquit me, I want them to do it because they believe I didn't murder the woman I loved, rather than because the evidence is insufficient. It's all or nothing, and I'm willing to take my chances."

"I know you didn't kill her," Felbin said in an effort to assure his client he believed in him. "But someone did. We have two things we need to accomplish in this case to completely clear you. The first is to make sure you are acquitted on these charges. The second is to find the real killer, to completely clear your name. But that's a story for another day. Today, we have to focus on the acquittal, and having you testify is not going to help that effort."

"I'm testifying," Garner responded as he walked out of the conference room.

"What a fucking idiot," Carmine said as he and Felbin followed their client out of the conference room.

Chapter Fifty-Seven

When the trial resumed at 9:30, Perrin announced he had no additional evidence, and with that the state rested.

A slight smile could be seen on Perrin's face when Felbin announced his first witness would be the defendant. A red-letter day in the life of this young prosecutor.

As the defendant walked to the clerk's desk to be sworn as a witness, Carmine told Felbin to check out the audience. On the most important day of his son's life, Garner's father was not in the courtroom. Neither parent had attended the trial. The absence of Garner's father was not really surprising to either Felbin or his investigator, since the soon to be gubernatorial candidate probably felt he had more important things to do. But the absence of Garner's mother was a surprise. Since she was an excellent trial lawyer, they understood why she probably couldn't bear to watch the cross-examination of her son, particularly on the question of why he lied to the police. But they could not understand her failure to attend the rest of the trial.

Felbin began with some softball questions to make his client feel comfortable on the stand. His direct examination had to be compact. He needed to get his client on and off the witness stand with minimal damage, if possible. Although Garner was a lawyer, he had no courtroom experience, either as a lawyer, or as a witness.

Felbin asked the usual type of background questions including that St. Louis favorite, "Where did you go to high school?" Garner did well explaining where he came from. He had been adopted by the Lees and didn't know his birth parents. He attempted to downplay the fact he was a kid of privilege. After all, that wasn't his fault. But now Felbin had to wander into deeper waters. And he had to be careful he didn't open any doors to evidence the court had already excluded.

"Garner, I want to talk to you now about Valentine's Day. What time did you arrive at Amy's apartment that day?" Felbin asked.

"Around 6:30 or so."

"And what was the purpose of going there that evening?"

"I loved her and wanted to spend this special day with her."

"What plans did you have for the evening?"

"I had made reservations for dinner at one of our favorite restaurants."

"Was the reservation in your name?"

"Yes."

"This wasn't a surprise visit then, she was expecting you?"

"Oh definitely, she was expecting me. It was Valentine's Day. We wanted to spend it together," he repeated.

"When you arrived at her apartment, did you pass some of the neighbors on the stairs?"

"Yes."

"If I understand your testimony correctly, you had a reservation in your name in a public restaurant and you passed neighbors on your way up the steps to Amy's apartment, is that right?"

"That's right."

"When you got to Amy's apartment, what did you see?"

"I saw her lying on the floor face down and bleeding from the back of her head. It was horrible. I ran to her. I had never seen a dead person before, but it was obvious she was dead. I started to cry. I didn't know what to do. I called my father and left."

"When you ran to her, did you touch her?"

"Yes, I'm sure I did. I'm sure I tried to find a pulse."

"When you touched her, did you get blood on your hands or any other part of your body?"

"I don't know. You have to understand Mr. Felbin," Garner began as he turned to talk directly to the jury. "I walked into the room to find the woman I loved lying on the floor. I wasn't thinking very clearly."

Good answer. So far so good, Felbin thought. Now for the big one. "Garner, there has been some testimony that when you were questioned you denied being at Amy's apartment on Valentine's Day. Is that true?"

"Yes."

"Please tell the jury what you were thinking when you did that."

"The detectives just showed up at my house early Tuesday morning. I had no idea they were coming. At the time, I was still in shock, confused, upset. I'd just lost the woman I loved. All I could think of was that I would never see her again. Based upon their attitude, I thought they were accusing me of murdering Amy. Instinctively, I guess, I just denied being there."

"But obviously, there was quite a paper trail to put you inside that apartment, and you knew that, correct?"

"Yes. I certainly knew I had made a reservation at a restaurant where the owner knows me. And the people I passed on the stairs certainly knew who I was. Clearly, they would be able to put me in Amy's apartment."

"Now, Garner, in addition to the first surprise visit you got from the detectives, they also paid you a second surprise visit."

"That's true."

"Will you tell the jury what that was about?" Felbin asked, pointing in the direction of the jury box.

"A few days later, they came back and wanted me to give them my fingerprints."

"And again, they just showed up on your doorstep without any forewarning?"

"Yes."

"What did you do?"

"I gave them my prints."

"Voluntarily?"

"Yes."

Felbin left the podium and walked to the defense table. "Can you think of anything else?" he asked Carmine.

"I think you covered it. Don't press the envelope. Just sit down and hold your breath with the rest of us," Carmine said.

"Do you think he effectively expressed his love and devotion to Amy?"

"Yeah. I think he was credible and sincere. It flowed with his testimony and didn't appear forced. But if you revisit it, it could look insincere. You're done. Sit your ass down!"

Chapter Fifty-Eight

When Felbin announced he had no additional questions, Perrin walked slowly to the podium while continuously staring at the witness. Lawyer mind games.

After slowly and deliberately arranging his notes, the prosecutor began his cross-examination. "Mr. Lee, you are a lawyer, is that correct?" Perrin began.

"Yes."

"You were accepted by a law school, went to law school and passed the Missouri bar. Is that correct?"

"Yes."

"You are a smart and well-educated guy, true?"

"I was fortunate enough to have the benefit of a good education," the witness responded, ignoring the other half of the question.

"And part of that bar examination you took was a section on ethics, correct?"

Felbin was on his feet. "What does this have to do with anything? He's not on trial for his ability as a lawyer. And by the way, he is a young lawyer who doesn't do any trial work," Felbin gratuitously added to his speaking objection.

"Overruled. But get on with it, Mr. Perrin," the court ruled.

"I did take and pass an ethics exam," Garner said.

"And truth and honesty are an important part of that examination, isn't that correct?"

"Yes, of course. I agree they are important," the witness responded without hesitation.

"And truth and honesty are part of the oath you take as a lawyer, isn't that also true?"

Felbin was back on his feet. "We will stipulate that truth and honesty are part of the bar exam, part of the oath, now can we get on with this torture? Everyone in this room knows where he is going with this. Can we get there at least before all of us are collecting social security?"

Cardwell didn't wait for a response. "If that is an objection, it is sustained. Get on with it, Mr. Perrin."

The objection had its desired effect. It interrupted the flow of the cross and more importantly short-circuited the foundation leading to the ultimate point, the lie.

The young prosecutor stared at his notes for what seemed like an eternity before asking the next question. Apparently, he had all his questions for the witness written out on a legal pad. "When you were questioned by the police, you told them you were not at Amy's apartment on Valentine's Day, isn't that true?"

Felbin started to get out of his seat to object again. But he decided against that for fear of highlighting the point. Instead, he went to a box containing defense files which were on a bench behind the counsel table. He began to pull files out of the box in a less than subtle effort to distract both the prosecutor and the jury.

"As I said before, I did say that, and I explained the circumstances."

"Yes, yes. You said you were in shock, confused and upset when the detectives visited you. I heard that. But my questions are a little different. You said the detectives came back a couple days later," Perrin said, laying another foundation in preparation for the kill.

"Yes," Garner responded simply.

"And you said you agreed to give them fingerprint samples. You knew what you were doing, and you were cooperating."

"Yes."

"Why didn't you correct the lie you told them a couple days before when you claimed to be in shock?"

The defendant's legal team didn't anticipate that question in preparing Garner to testify. And now they had to sit and wait for the response. Garner was flying without a net.

"Apparently, Mr. Perrin, you have never unexpectedly found someone that you love murdered. Not just dead from natural causes, but murdered. You can't just turn the shock and emotion off like a water faucet," Garner said without hesitation.

Good answer, Felbin thought. But he also knew this discussion was not going to end there.

"But when they asked you to give the samples, you were thinking clearly enough to agree to provide your fingerprints, weren't you?"

"I suppose so."

"And at the time you agreed to provide those samples, you knew you had already lied to the detectives. Isn't that true?"

"I don't know that I thought about it when I agreed to provide the samples."

"Well, Mr. Lee, when did you first realize that you had lied?"

"You need to do something and fast. This is on a downhill slide," Carmine whispered in Felbin's ear.

But Felbin ignored the comment. They both knew there was nothing that could be done. Their client was on his own.

"I don't know," Garner said.

"Are you telling this jury when you told Sergeant Sandworth you were not in Amy's apartment on Valentine's Day you did not know you were lying at that very moment?" Perrin pressed.

"No, I guess I knew."

"I don't want any guesses, Mr. Lee. Did you or didn't you know you were lying as soon as you told Sergeant Sandworth you were not in Amy's apartment that day."

"I knew."

"And would you agree at the very moment the detectives asked you that question, you had a choice? Either lie or tell the truth?"

"Yes."

"And you freely and voluntarily made the decision to lie, isn't that true?"

"Yes."

"And you did that to protect yourself, isn't that true?"

"I was in shock."

"We're back to that again," Perrin said, while clearly expressing his frustration with this witness for the benefit of the jury. "Let me ask it this way. Why did you lie?"

For whatever reason, Garner answered that question immediately and apparently without thinking. "My father told me it would be a problem if they could prove I was in the apartment on that day."

"Holy shit! Did he just say what I think he said? Good thing his asshole father isn't in the courtroom," Carmine whispered.

"A bit ironic he is telling the truth about why he lied," Felbin replied as he tried to conceal his surprise. Although it was the truth, the explanation was not going to play well with the jury, and Felbin knew it. This was one of the reasons he'd recommended Garner not testify.

"You're telling us your father, the state senator, told you to lie? It wasn't some instinct that caused you to lie like you said just a few minutes ago in response to your lawyer's question," Perrin continued.

"No, sir, my father didn't tell me to lie. He was just telling me it would look bad."

"Now you're telling us you lied to avoid looking guilty. To avoid looking like the person who murdered Amy, the woman you claimed to have loved."

"I DID love her. I DO love her. I DIDN'T KILL HER. AND I DON'T . . ." Garner said. His voice rising with each word he spoke, and anger clearly visible on his face.

If the prosecutor's game was to push the defendant over the edge, he came close. But Garner regained his composure, hung his head and stopped in midsentence. Felbin wasn't sure how the jury would react to the outburst. But he knew none of this was good.

In an obvious effort to further highlight the outburst, the prosecutor said, "Do you need a break, Mr. Lee?"

"No sir. I apologize for raising my voice. But I just loved her so much, and I can't get over the fact she is dead," Garner said with a tear, barely visible, seemingly forming in the corner of one eye.

Ignoring the apology, Perrin pressed on. "Mr. Lee, when you found the woman you claimed to have loved lying there in a pool of blood, did you make any effort to call the police or even an ambulance?"

Garner thought about repeating his prior answer that he was in shock. But Perrin was wearing him down. "No," he simply answered. The hollow sound of that response rattled around in his brain. Now he began to doubt himself. *Why did he leave her there? Could I have done more? Should I have done more? Could I have saved Amy?* Guilt was invading his thoughts. These were very dangerous thoughts to be harboring when you were testifying for your life.

Good trial lawyers never ask a *why* question when the answer is uncertain. But Perrin knew he had this defendant on the ropes. He figured this witness could not hurt him however he answered the question why he didn't call an ambulance or the police. And he wasn't wrong.

"I didn't know what to do. I called my father and he told me to leave the apartment. So I did. Again, I wasn't thinking very clearly," was Garner's response.

"But you were thinking clearly enough to call your father and solicit his advice," Perrin said.

"I didn't know what to do," Garner repeated.

"I'm a little confused, Mr. Lee. If you didn't kill Amy? Why would you feel the need to run instead of calling 911 for an ambulance or the police?"

"The only explanation I have is what I told you before. I was in shock and not thinking very clearly."

"But you were thinking clearly enough to follow your father's advice and *RUN*, isn't that true, Mr. Lee?" Perrin continued as he highlighted the word run with a raised voice.

"I don't know," was the only response.

Both Perrin and Felbin knew the response didn't matter. Clearly, Garner Lee ran. The jury heard that loud and clear. And because of that admission, the prosecutor would be entitled to a devastating jury instruction. The jury would be told they could consider flight to avoid criminal prosecution as evidence of guilt. Felbin knew his only hope was that this corrupt judge would refuse to give that instruction.

"I just have a few more questions, Mr. Lee. In addition to telling the detectives you were not in Amy's apartment, you also told them that you didn't know she had been murdered when they visited you two days after you were in her apartment on Valentine's Day, isn't that true?"

"Yes."

"And this would have been yet another lie you told the police who were investigating the murder of the woman you claimed to have loved," Perrin commented.

Garner offered no response.

But the prosecutor didn't need a response. "And you also lied when you told the detectives you didn't even plan to be in her apartment on Valentine's Day, knowing you were going out to pick her up for dinner."

Again, no response.

"Isn't it true, Mr. Lee, you made reservations at a restaurant to have dinner with Amy on Valentine's Day, you went to her apartment to pick her up, you had an argument when you got there, you got angry and struck her on the head with the statue, panicked and ran? Isn't that how it happened, Mr. Lee?"

"I didn't kill Amy. I loved her."

"Mr. Lee, did you know that Amy was pregnant before you went?"

"No."

Perrin wanted to ask if Garner knew whether he was the father of the child. But in light of Cardwell's pretrial rulings regarding the issue of paternity, he thought she would declare a mistrial and throw him in jail if he asked that question and injected that issue into the trial. She had denied the state's motion for a DNA sample to be used for paternity testing even after the defendant consented. She was pretty clear the identity of the unborn child's father would not be part of this trial. That was when he was asking for a DNA sample to establish paternity. But things had changed. Now he didn't need a DNA profile from the defendant. He had it.

Felbin's concern became a reality. Perrin realized he had the defendant's profile in the lab report Felbin had given him and could establish paternity. While he didn't know who the father was, he now knew Garner Lee was not. The question was whether he would use it. He knew that would draw the wrath of Cardwell. But what was she going to do? Hold him in contempt? Declare a mistrial? He was tired of getting kicked around by this judge. Her rulings were clearly slanted in favor of the defendant. Like Felbin, Perrin believed the fix was in, and Cardwell was currying favor with the defendant's father. If that was the case, imposing any sanction against him would call attention to what she was doing, because he would have to fight back to defend himself. Would she take the chance this young lawyer would take her on? Perrin decided to find out.

"Did you have a discussion with her when you got to her apartment about her pregnancy?"

"I told you, Mr. Perrin, she was dead when I arrived at her apartment."

Completely ignoring Garner's response, the prosecutor pressed his point. "Was her pregnancy the subject of your argument, Mr. Lee?"

Felbin's objection was sustained. But the jury was getting the point the prosecutor was making. Garner's denial was unnecessary.

"Mr. Lee, do you know you are not the father of Amy's child?"

As Felbin was standing to object, Garner said, "Yes."

He asked to approach the bench. But what was he going to do? The jury heard not only was Garner not the father of this child, but he also knew it. That was really damaging. The beauty of this for Perrin was that he didn't even have to use the report from the police lab he was holding back, because the defendant admitted it. Claiming Perrin sandbagged him to have the jury disregard his client's admission wouldn't work. And Felbin figured Cardwell wasn't going to declare a mistrial. That would make matters worse for her and the senator because it would highlight the very issue she'd tried to keep out of this trial. The only thing left for Felbin was to make his record and try to repair the damage.

When they arrived at the bench outside of the hearing of the jury, Felbin said, "He knew in your prior rulings, you indicated this issue was irrelevant, and yet he asked the question anyway. I'm going to move for a mistrial."

Cardwell looked at Perrin for a response.

"That was in connection with a DNA sample. There was no order prohibiting me from asking what he knew," the prosecutor said.

"Technically, he is correct. What do you want me to do beyond declaring a mistrial, Mr. Felbin? Do you want me to instruct the jury to disregard the question and the answer?" the judge asked.

Just as Felbin thought, she wasn't going to make matters worse by declaring a mistrial. Instead, she was hoping he would do a minimal amount to repair the damage and move on.

"No thanks," Felbin said. He couldn't afford to highlight the question and answer with an instruction to disregard something the jury already heard. The jury now had a motive for murder.

"I assume you were finished with this subject, Mr. Perrin," Cardwell said.

"I am," Perrin said. He knew she wouldn't do anything to him. This just confirmed his belief this case was fixed. He was going to lose.

After leaving the bench, Perrin had one final question. "Finally, Mr. Lee, where were you staying when the police finally caught up with you to arrest you?"

"I was at the Ritz."

Chapter Fifty-Nine

Felbin had a few additional questions for his client. For the moment, he was going to ignore the paternity question. "We have heard the time of death was between 4 and 7 pm. We also have the state's evidence that you arrived at the apartment around 6:30 to pick Amy up for a 7 o'clock dinner reservation. Despite that, the prosecutor suggested for the brief period you were in the apartment, you got mad and killed Amy. Garner, please give us your best estimate how long you were in Amy's apartment on Valentine's Day."

"Less than five minutes."

"And during that very brief period, did an argument start and escalate to the point where you both became upset and further escalate to the point where you became angry, grabbed a statue, somehow got behind her and struck her on the back of her head with that statue, then knelt by Amy's body, got blood on your hand, called your father and after all of that, left the apartment?"

"No, sir."

"Garner, we also heard the injury to Amy was on the left side of the back of her head," Felbin continued. "Tell this jury, are you right or left hand dominant?"

"I am right hand dominant."

"Mr. Perrin asked you why you didn't call an ambulance. But when you found Amy, did you believe that she was already dead?"

"Yes."

"How long after you entered the apartment and found Amy did you call your father?"

"Not long, maybe a minute or two. I saw her on the floor and went to her immediately, saw she was dead and then called my father and left," Garner said.

"What is the service provider for your cell phone?"

"AT&T."

"Garner, I'm going to hand you some documents that I have marked as an exhibit in this case and ask you if you can identify those."

Before the witness could answer, Perrin was on his feet requesting to see the documents the witness was just handed. Ordinarily, in a criminal case, the parties are required to exchange documents they intend to offer into evidence prior to the start of the trial. The documents Felbin just handed to his client were not provided to the prosecution. He expected his opponent to cry foul, and was not disappointed. After a quick review, Perrin was asking to approach the bench for a discussion outside the hearing of the jury.

"Judge, I have never seen these before," Perrin began pointing to the documents Felbin had just provided. "And I have no idea what this is about and what use he plans to make of them."

Without waiting for an invitation from the judge to explain, Felbin said, "These are cell phone records."

"I can see that. What is the point that you are trying to make with them?" Perrin asked, clearly aggravated by both the response and whatever it was Felbin was trying to pull.

"Well, according to your evidence, the defendant was walking up the stairs to the apartment at approximately 6:30. These cell phone records will corroborate the brief time he was in the apartment," Felbin replied, with an intentionally vague response.

"And how exactly does it do that?" Perrin demanded.

"The records show when he called his father and establishes the length of that conversation."

"Judge, these records do nothing but serve to mislead the jury. Additionally, I never saw these until he sandbagged me with them today."

"Sandbagged? These documents are responsive to your suggestion that the defendant whacked her with the statue after some phantom argument. Speaking of misleading the jury. These records rebut that ridiculous seed you tried to plant."

Not unexpectedly, Cardwell overruled the objection, allowing Felbin to present the evidence to the jury.

"Before the interruption, I was asking you to identify these documents," Felbin said as he handed the documents to the witness again.

241

"Those are my cell phone records," Garner said, after pretending to review the documents.

"Let me direct your attention to a phone call you made on February 14 after 6:30 pm. Can you tell the jury the time of that call and the person that you called?

"The time of the call was 6:38 pm. According to this record, it was a 2-minute call, and the number that I called was my father's."

Felbin had only one more question to do some damage control. "Garner, when did you first learn you were not the father of this child?"

"Just a few days ago," Garner responded, his eyes downcast, looking at the floor, and his voice low.

With the cell phone bombshell resonating throughout the courtroom and hopefully masking the paternity matter, Felbin announced he had no additional questions.

"You said you and Amy did not have any kind of an argument after you got to her apartment. But had you been arguing earlier that day or the day before?"

Now it was Felbin's turn to approach the bench to prevent his client from having to answer that question. "You already ruled he couldn't get into prior arguments," Felbin pointed out.

"He opened the door by asking about arguments on the day of the murder," Perrin said.

"I agree. You did open the door, Mr. Felbin. But we are not taking a very long stroll down this road. He can answer that question and that's it. I assume he will say yes, but we are not going to get into any of the specifics of whatever argument, discussion, disagreement or whatever else you want to call it. And Mr. Felbin, I would tread lightly on any follow up questions on this topic, lest you open another door," Cardwell said, taking delight in ruling against Felbin and admonishing him in the process.

"Mr. Lee, please tell the jury, did you have an argument with Amy earlier that day or the day before?"

Without any hesitation, Garner said, "Yes, sir. We had an argument the day before."

Perrin had not only additional questions on this topic, but he also had additional witnesses who would describe the relationship between this defendant and the woman he murdered as anything but loving. Given Cardwell's prior ruling on the issue as well as her hostility and the paternity question, he thought he should quit while he was ahead. At least the jury heard about one argument that he could use in his closing.

Now, Felbin needed to repair some of this damage. But he had to do that carefully. He could not run the risk of opening the door to allow the prosecution to put the haters on the stand.

"Garner, if I understand your complete testimony, you had dinner reservations at a restaurant for 7 o'clock and were going to pick Amy up. You got to her apartment around 6:30 and a few minutes later found her lying on the floor in a pool of blood. You then called your father and left after staying only a few minutes. Is that an accurate summary of your testimony?

"Yes."

"And at some point after the disagreement that you and Amy had the day before, did you tell her that you had made dinner reservations for 7 o'clock?"

"Yes."

"And did you tell her that you would pick her up around 6:30?"

"Yes."

With that final question and answer, Felbin indicated he had no further questions of his client. When the prosecutor said he likewise had no more questions, the court told Garner Lee he could step down from the witness chair and return to the counsel table. His testimony was now in the hands of the jury. The jurors would decide whether he was credible.

Only one more defense witness remained, the forensic expert. He would testify the DNA on the statue was not that of the defendant. Since Perrin's lab also confirmed that finding, Felbin told the court and the jury the prosecution had stipulated to that fact. With no rebuttal evidence offered by the state, the case was ready to proceed to closing arguments.

How well the defendant did would soon be determined through the sound of either the words *guilty* or *not guilty*. Both Felbin and Carmine felt the testimony of the defendant had problems. But they'd done the best they could. The record of Garner's phone call to his father established the timeline and hopefully saved the day. Although that was a complete sandbag, it would be a difficult thing for Perrin to get around. With little preparation, this young prosecutor needed to rebut his own evidence and a business record that supported the brief period inside the apartment. Despite the bumps in the road in Garner's testimony, they were cautiously optimistic. Much better than at the start of a trial they thought would be tough to win.

Despite their cautious optimism, both Felbin and his investigator wondered how their client could be so passionate in his testimony when he described his love for a woman who was impregnated by another man. Was he a good actor? Or did he love this woman so much that he could forgive an indiscretion most men would not, could not, ignore? The jury needed to believe the latter. Otherwise, a motive for murder would clearly be established.

Chapter Sixty

Before the lawyers would deliver their closing arguments, a few housekeeping matters needed to be decided. The first was a motion for judgment of acquittal. In all criminal cases, at the conclusion of all of the evidence, the defense asks the court to acquit the defendant, suggesting the prosecution did not meet its burden of proof by presenting sufficient evidence to convict beyond a reasonable doubt. That motion is routinely overruled, and this case was no exception.

The other item was the jury instructions. This is where the judge tells the jury what the law is that must be applied in a particular case. While the jury decides the facts to include, what witnesses to believe, the judge alone decides the law that must be applied to those facts. In this case, Cardwell explained the law relating to the murder of both the living and the unborn. Once the jury was instructed as to the law, the closing arguments began.

As it had been throughout the trial, Perrin's theme for his closing was the lie. After thanking the jurors for their time and attention to this case, he got right to the heart of the matter. "I want you to remember these three words: *I wasn't there*. Those three words form the cornerstone of this prosecution. That statement is dramatically different from what you heard here. The story this defendant told you today is pretty simple. He went to Amy's apartment to pick her up for a romantic Valentine's Day dinner at a nice restaurant. When he arrived, he found her lying on the floor in a pool of blood. She was dead. He then called his father, a powerful state senator, and left the apartment. That was today. But that wasn't the only story he told."

Hesitating momentarily for dramatic effect, he continued. "The story he told immediately following Amy's murder, before he had the opportunity to lawyer-up, was far different from what he told you folks here today in the presence of his lawyer and in response to his lawyer's questions. In that version, he denied even being at the apartment. His exact words were *I wasn't there.* He also said he hadn't seen Amy at all that day and had no plans to hook up with her to celebrate Valentine's Day. Of course, that story had to be abandoned and they had to make up a new one, after his fingerprint was found in Amy's blood on the inside of the doorknob. When he denied even being in the apartment, he had no idea his print would contradict that position.

"*I wasn't there.* Those three words alone establish the guilt of this defendant beyond any doubt. He murdered Amy and then had to distance himself from the scene of his crime, and that's why he lied." Pointing to the defendant, Perrin added, "This guy even denied knowing Amy was dead when the police first interviewed him. The man who left his fingerprint in Amy's blood on the inside doorknob of her apartment, denied knowing she was dead. Incredible!"

Clearly, Perrin not only was trying to highlight the fact the defendant told two stories, but he was also suggesting the second story, this one sworn, was crafted with the help of Felbin.

"We know for certain the first story is false because of the bloody fingerprint. We also know the second story is a fabrication for a couple of reasons."

Again, another dramatic pause.

"Can't wait to see how he handles this," Carmine whispered to Felbin during the pause.

"First, if true, this would have been the first story and the only story this defendant told. But instead, he chose to lie. And that alone makes the second story also a lie. But there is more."

"There better be more, because that's not going to carry the fuckin' day for him." Another editorial comment in the unique style of Tony Carmine.

"Throughout his testimony, you heard about a loving relationship between him and Amy. He loved her and would do nothing to hurt her, let alone kill her. Nowhere in that testimony did you hear one word about any problem in the relationship."

Felbin moved to the edge of his seat. He wasn't sure where Perrin was going with this. He needed to be ready to cut him off, if he ventured into unauthorized territory. But at the moment, he was on safe ground. He could comment on that one argument.

"It was not until I brought it up at the end of his testimony that you learned for the first time that this loving couple had a fight. And that fight was just one day before Amy turned up dead. The very day before this defendant showed up at her apartment and lied about being there, they had a fight. And then she was dead. No more fights. Garner Lee ended that fight.

"Why do you think they didn't bother to tell you about this fight? One reason is they knew this information would destroy the image of the loving, problem free relationship. But, of course, it is not uncommon for couples to have fights. However, this fight happened a day before Amy was murdered. That is the real reason they wanted to keep this from you."

Felbin glanced at the jury to see if he could read the reaction. Nothing. Poker faces. All twelve. If Perrin was scoring points, Felbin couldn't tell.

Perrin had to decide how he was going to play the pregnancy. The jury heard the defendant was not the father. She was cheating on him. That would be devastating and certainly a potential recipe for murder. He testified he didn't know about the pregnancy until a few days ago. While the jury was free to believe or disbelieve that, it did make some sense, considering the other evidence in the case. If he knew it before the day of the murder and that was the reason for the fight, why would he be picking her up for dinner? Perrin decided to stay away from the pregnancy and let the jurors put it where they wanted, hoping they would conclude this was the basis of an argument that led to murder.

"Now, let's put that fight together with the defendant's presence at the apartment, the reservation at the restaurant and the phone call to his father. Let me paint the picture for you," Perrin said, pausing again while looking directly at the defendant.

"Where the hell is this going?" Carmine asked Felbin.

No response. But Felbin was wondering the same thing.

"There is evidence here the defendant and Amy had a fight the day before she was murdered. But there is no independent evidence the fight had been resolved. There is no independent evidence Amy even knew about the dinner reservation or agreed to go to dinner with the person she was fighting with one day before.

"I would suggest to you the reason the fight was withheld from you was because the fight was not over when Garner Lee just showed up at Amy's apartment. Or it restarted. She refused to go to dinner with him. He became enraged. Grabbed an object. Swung it as she was walking away from him. Struck her in the head. And you know the rest."

Garner began to react to what he was hearing. He didn't like the prosecutor's theory. "That's not true," Garner said. But Felbin settled him down before the judge and the jury became involved.

"The evidence in this case is clear. The defendant was in the victim's apartment. He lied about being there. His bloody fingerprint was on the inside doorknob. The blood on the defendant's hand belonged to Amy. When he found the woman he claimed he loved, he did nothing to help her. He didn't call 911 for an ambulance or the police. Instead, he called his powerful father for help. And that was to help him, not Amy. Then he fled the scene. In addition to lying and fleeing the scene, this defendant also hid after he was interviewed by the police. At the time of his arrest, he was found hiding out in a comfortable room or maybe even a suite at the Ritz."

That last statement about the Ritz did result in furrowed brows from three of the jurors. Felbin knew from the outset this was going to be a problem. During any trial, the lawyers are never sure what piece of generally irrelevant evidence is going to upset a juror. In this case, the defendant hid from the police. That much was clear. Whether he was hiding in a tent in the woods or the Ritz was totally irrelevant. The point was, he was hiding. The place didn't matter. Or at least shouldn't matter. But Felbin knew it would matter. The Ritz would suggest this kid of privilege was avoiding arrest for the murder of his girlfriend while continuing to live a life of luxury.

"Ladies and gentlemen, this defendant," Perrin said as he pointed at Garner, "fled the crime scene and then hid. As the court instructed you, flight to avoid criminal prosecution can be viewed by you as evidence of guilt. In other words, if you did nothing wrong, then you have no reason to run. In this case, Garner Lee did something wrong. He killed Amy Deland. And he also killed her unborn child. He took two lives. Two innocent lives. Her child would never celebrate a birthday. Her child would never get married. Her child would never have children. Her child would never be able to enjoy life."

Felbin was not sure whether the jury was picking up on the repeated references to *her child*. The point of the reference was obvious, at least to Felbin. Perrin was subtly reminding the jury that Garner Lee was not the father of that child. He was hoping the jury would then speculate that this infuriated the defendant, led to an argument, and ultimately to Amy's death. Since there was no evidence to support this theory, all the prosecutor could do was hope they picked up the innuendo. And all that Felbin could do was hope they didn't.

"Understandably, he had a reason to run both from the scene and afterwards," Perrin said as he tried to make eye contact with each juror. "But now it is your job to make sure Garner Lee doesn't run again. He needs to be put in a place where he will never run again. That place is the penitentiary. Each of you took an oath. You promised that if I proved this defendant's guilt beyond a reasonable doubt, you would find him guilty. Well, I lived up to my end of the bargain and now it's your turn. I'm confident you will return verdicts of guilty for both Amy and her defenseless unborn child. Thank you."

Chapter Sixty-One

"Ladies and gentlemen without any doubt, the state has proven Amy Deland was tragically murdered. But they have failed to prove who is responsible for that murder," Felbin began, skipping the phony appreciation for their time and attention to this case.

"Let me talk first about what we know. According to the medical examiner, the state's witness, Amy died sometime between 4 and 7 pm on February 14. She was struck with a statue on the left side of the back of her head. That blow was fatal. The murder weapon was the statue. Fingerprints were found on the statue and on the inside of the front doorknob. The fingerprints in blood on the doorknob were Garner's. The fingerprints on the statue, the murder weapon, did not belong to Garner. The DNA recovered on the murder weapon also did not belong to Garner. The state's witnesses said they saw Garner walking up the stairs to Amy's apartment at 6:30 pm. Garner called his father at 6:38 pm, and according to his cell phone records, that call lasted two minutes. That is what we know for sure.

"Now let's combine what we know for sure with the reasonable inferences you can draw from all of the evidence. The timeline here is critical. Amy was killed during a three-hour window, according to the state's evidence. Also, according to the state's evidence, Garner didn't arrive at the apartment building until 6:30. Garner called his father at 6:38. We know that from the cell records. That means if you believe Garner killed the woman he loved, he had to do it in eight minutes. Let's analyze that.

"If that happened, one of two things occurred. Within eight minutes, Amy or Garner started an argument that escalated to the extent that Garner hit her with a statue and killed her. Or Garner came to Amy's apartment with the intent to kill her and no argument occurred. He just entered the apartment, grabbed the statue and hit her over the head. Now, let me explain why both of those scenarios didn't happen. And I will use the state's own evidence to do that.

"In order to show you Garner was in Amy's apartment, they proved Garner had made a Valentine's Day dinner reservation in his own name at one of his favorite restaurants. If Garner planned to kill Amy, why would he make a dinner reservation in his own name? Also, why would he carry out his plan on that particular day, knowing he passed her neighbors on the stairs going to her apartment? The simple answer to these questions is no one would do that. That credible evidence provided by the prosecution rebuts the theory Garner had planned to kill the woman he loved.

"Now let's look at the theory someone started an argument that resulted in Amy's death, all within eight minutes or less. Is that physically possible? Of course, it is. But is that reasonable? The evidence in this case suggests it is not. Again, the same problem as with the planned murder. Garner made a reservation in his name and passed the neighbors on the way to the apartment. Do you really think that he would be stupid enough to murder someone under those circumstances? I would be the first to tell you that lawyers aren't the smartest people. But we are not that stupid, and neither is Garner.

"I am sure all of you have had arguments with your spouse or significant other. I know I have had my share. My experience is that most arguments begin with a look or a comment and escalate with additional rude and inappropriate comments. An argument that escalates to murder in eight minutes or less. while possible, is just not probable or reasonable. And remember, you would have to be convinced beyond a reasonable doubt this argument happened that quickly and resulted in murder.

"Apparently, they want you to believe Garner became outraged in this short period of time and grabbed a statue off a bookshelf and immediately hit Amy in the back of the head as she walked away from him. But remember that fatal injury is to the back of her head on the left side. The left side," Felbin repeated for emphasis. "But Garner is right-handed, and this statue is very heavy. If this occurred the way they want you to believe it happened, doesn't it make more sense that whoever did this would use their dominant hand to inflict the fatal blow?

"The other thing that creates substantial reasonable doubt is the inability of the prosecution to identify the fingerprints and the DNA they found on the murder weapon. This is critical. They want you to believe Garner hit Amy with that statue, but they can't explain how he left no scientific evidence of any kind on the murder weapon. We know that the statue wasn't wiped clean, because then no prints or DNA would be detectible."

Felbin knew he had some good points to establish reasonable doubt, particularly the lack of scientific evidence. Thanks to television shows and movies, jurors were increasingly demanding scientific evidence to convict. And in any criminal trial, all the defendant needs is reasonable doubt. Not all doubt or innocence, but rather reasonable doubt of guilt.

But Felbin needed to address the two most damaging issues. If this jury was going to convict, it would be because his client lied to the police and fled. And if that is not enough, he was arrested at the Ritz. Not some flea bag motel. The Ritz. What was he thinking? Or maybe the better question is what were his parents thinking? He saw the reaction of some of the jurors when the prosecutor hammered this issue in his closing. But what could he say about that? He couldn't deny he was found at the Ritz. He needed to confess, avoid and spin the issue and hope he could carry the day.

"Ladies and gentlemen," Felbin continued, "we need to talk about the eight minutes he spent in Amy's apartment. Clearly, he was in her apartment. Equally clear, he admitted here under oath telling the police he was not in the apartment on February 14th. We don't deny that and never have. But let's put it into perspective. As they should, the police appear at Garner's home shortly after Amy is found dead. At that time, he is in shock. When he passed those residents on the stairs, he thought he was going to have a romantic dinner with the woman he loved on this special day. Instead, he found the woman he loved on the floor of her apartment, covered in blood, and dead. All kinds of thoughts ran through his head as he knelt by her lifeless body. There would be no Valentine's dinner. There would never be any other dinner. He would never see her again. He would never hold her again. On top of that, for some unexplained reason, someone took her life. Confused and in shock, he called his father, who told him to leave the apartment."

With the advice Senator Lee gave to his son echoing throughout the courtroom, Felbin glanced at Carmine, who nodded, approving the direction the argument needed to take. Don't blame the kid. Blame his father, who was more concerned about his political future than his son's life. After all, everyone hates politicians.

"Ladies and gentlemen, that advice was bad. But that wasn't the only bad advice he gave him. He also told him it wouldn't be good for him to admit being in the apartment. Frankly, I'm not sure who he was talking about. Not good for his son or not good for the father's political future, if his son was in the apartment of a woman who had been murdered."

The reporters occupied the entire first row of the courtroom. All began to take copious notes when Felbin threw Senator Lee under the bus. He knew that would be a substantial part of the stories they would be filing. And the senator would not like it. But Felbin didn't care. He was representing his son and couldn't care less about his father's political future. In fact, Felbin wouldn't mind at all if his words contributed to the political demise of the good senator.

"In fact, let me restate that," Felbin continued. "I believe that bad advice was designed to protect a political career; Senator Lee's political career and his future efforts to become our governor. I doubt having your son accused of murder would help that future campaign. And so it was that his son, who was in a state of shock, having just lost the woman he loved, mistakenly followed that bad advice. When he left the apartment without contacting the police, he was following his father's advice. When he told the police he was not at the apartment, he was following his father's advice. When he went to the hotel, he was following his father's advice." Felbin was on a roll.

"The prosecutor made a big deal out of the fact that Garner was arrested at the Ritz. But I think that makes my point. Do you really think that left to his own devices, this young man would have picked the Ritz? Or was it his father who selected both the hotel and made the decision to keep his son away from the police and his own political career? But there is one thing Garner did on his own. He voluntarily gave the police his fingerprints. That was one area where the senator did not offer advice.

"Let me say just a few things with respect to the manslaughter charge involving the tragic death of the unborn child. Garner did not kill Amy and therefore, did not cause the death of the unborn child. Whoever killed Amy, also killed the child. That much is clear. But even when that person is ultimately found, the state will have to prove the murderer knew that Amy was pregnant and therefore, knowingly caused the death of that fetus. That is a heavy burden, but one we don't have to worry about here.

"Did Garner make mistakes? You bet he did. His biggest mistake was following his father's advice. But that does not mean he murdered anyone. And certainly, the evidence presented in this case doesn't prove beyond a reasonable doubt that Garner killed the woman he loved and the unborn child. We know that you will agree and return verdicts of not guilty."

Chapter Sixty-Two

Felbin, his investigator and his client left the court-house through a back door to avoid the media, and retreated to his office to await the verdict. This is the worst time for any criminal defense lawyer. Nothing more can be done. And now the second guessing begins. What was missed? What could have been handled differently? Was the cross-examination effective? Was the closing effective? Was it credible? Did it establish reasonable doubt? And this case was no different. With the client secured in another room, Felbin and Carmine began the postgame analysis.

"Do you think we covered the lie?" Felbin asked his investigator.

"I think we did the best we could," Carmine said.

"But was it enough to carry the day? Because we both know, this verdict is going to turn on why he spoke three simple words: *I wasn't there.* Perrin made this the smoking gun of his case, as we knew he would."

"Well, you put it on that piece of shit old man of his, which is where it belonged. There is no doubt in my mind that if that slime bucket told Garner to jump off the arch, he would have, at least at that point in time."

"I know that, but the question is whether the jury will buy the argument and give the kid a pass on the lie," Felbin said.

"The problem is that we know Garner is a dumb shit, but the jury doesn't know that. All they see is a kid of privilege who is also a lawyer. And while we know lawyers aren't the smartest people on the planet and may even be dumber than politicians, those jurors may not know that," Carmine added with a smile.

Felbin didn't react to Carmine's attempt at humor. He was concerned. He knew going in that the case would be tough due in part to his client's own doing. How many times had he told clients to keep their mouths shut? The penitentiary is filled with people who tried to talk their way out of a criminal investigation. At the time they are being grilled by the police, criminal suspects don't understand that if they say nothing, their silence could never be used against them. The jury would never hear that they refused to talk. Courts uniformly have ruled that in criminal cases, defendants cannot be punished for exercising a constitutional right.

While Garner was not necessarily trying to talk his way out of the penitentiary, he was trying to eliminate himself as a suspect. He did say something and usually that something would be incriminating at some level. In this case, the statement was a lie, and the prosecutor could prove it. Felbin believed his client was scared, felt intimidated and was following his father's advice. But he was also certain his father or at least his mother, a skilled litigator, told him not to speak at all. Unfortunately, he didn't follow that advice. And now Felbin had to explain that mistake. He'd done the best he could, but wasn't sure it was enough. Soon he would know.

"I just don't have a good feeling about this, Tony," Felbin said. "I absolutely believe Garner didn't murder Amy. There are too many unanswered questions. Maybe we should have injected the mystery man and made him our prime suspect. The police knew nothing about this guy and never investigated this aspect of the case."

"That's because Sandworth was too busy trying to put a case on the son of a corrupt politician," Carmine said.

"Well, that's probably true. Maybe a little payback for his role in Bobby's case. But Jack Sandworth is a good cop and I believe if we gave him this information, he would have followed up to see where it went."

"Unfortunately, that road may have led him back to our client. That little slut, Amy, was banging some dude, Garner found out and offed her. That was the risk we discussed before. And that's why we decided to stay away from that. I think we made the right decision. It was just too risky and could have easily backfired."

"I guess you're right. But I can't . . . " Felbin was unable to finish his thought as his client appeared at the door to his office.

"I'm sorry to bother you. But I just wanted to tell both of you I am grateful for all that you have done for me. I know I screwed up. And I know you did the best you could to explain why I screwed up. Regardless of the outcome, I just wanted to thank both of you. I know you did your very best to explain the bad situation I put you in. I also wanted to say again, I did not kill Amy. I loved her. Still do, even after what she did. It's important to me that you believe that," Garner said.

"We do believe you," Felbin began. "That's the reason we agreed to represent you. You're right. We do have your statement to deal with. We all knew that from the start. But this jury has a lot of other pieces of evidence that establish reasonable doubt. Let's just hope those other issues carry the day for us."

"I have a question," Carmine said. "I'm having trouble wrapping my arms around your current feeling about Amy, given what you now know. How does that work?" For a change, Carmine selected his words carefully in raising this delicate issue.

Garner didn't answer immediately. He was obviously trying to frame his response with words that would allow Carmine and everyone else understand his feelings. "When you first told me she was carrying another man's child, I was devastated, and didn't want to believe it. I finally decided I didn't know the circumstances and perhaps never will. I concluded I could continue to beat myself up, or I could move on. I decided to move on and focus on what I believed our relationship was before she died. That was the only way I could keep my sanity. And so I focused on my love of her. Perhaps if I could find the real killer, I might get some answers."

Although he didn't respond, Carmine wasn't buying the explanation. Guys in Carmine's world were not that forgiving or forgetting about a woman who not only cheats, but gets pregnant in the process.

While Felbin was busy second-guessing himself about how he handled the trial, and Carmine was trying to understand their client's explanation, the court was also busy on the phone providing someone with an update. With the door to her chambers open, Cardwell could be heard describing

Felbin's closing argument. In particular, she emphasized that portion of the closing dealing with the involvement of Senator Lee.

It was not unusual for Cardwell during her short time on the bench to have telephone conversations with people, mostly lawyers and other judges, on pending cases. It was also not unusual for Mary McMurtry, her secretary, to over-hear those conversations. However, there was something odd about this one, and others the judge had, in connection with the Lee prosecution. Although McMurtry was only hearing one side of this conversation, those statements she was hearing almost seemed apologetic. "I don't know." "I couldn't." "I tried." She didn't know what to think. But she knew this case would be different, starting with Felbin appearing before the woman he so unabashedly criticized both publicly and privately. She was not disappointed. But she was not going to risk her job seeking answers to some of the unusual things she witnessed. It really was none of her business anyway. Or so she rationalized.

Carmine's conversation with Garner was interrupted by a phone call. The firm's receptionist announced that Senator Lee was on the line. Felbin hesitated. He figured he wasn't calling for an update on the trial he was too busy to attend. If he wanted that, he would have called his son, given his strained relationship with his client's father. He also knew the senator wasn't calling to thank him for his efforts. That just wasn't in this guy's DNA. That left only one thing. He'd heard about the closing argument and he wanted to bitch.

After pressing the speaker button, Felbin wanted to be the first to speak. "Senator Lee, we missed you at the trial. Was there some reason you were unable to attend this life or death event for your son?"

That would certainly set the tone for the conversation. But at this point, Felbin didn't care. The man's behavior during this entire matter had been anything but paternal. Felbin always understood that Lee was a politician. Although he didn't appreciate it, he also understood his involvement in the Decker case. But his behavior in a case involving his son's life was inexplicable.

"Am I on a speaker phone?" Lee responded.

"Yes, you are. Your son and Tony are here."

"Take me off the speaker," the senator demanded.

"No. What you have to say to me can be heard by Garner and Tony."

Senator Lee was not used to hearing people saying no. "Then I'll talk to you later, you fuckin' prick," Lee said as he abruptly hung up.

"I'll be looking forward to that," Felbin told his client and investigator.

Chapter Sixty-Three

There is no real way to know what jurors talk about when they go behind closed doors. After the instructions are read to them in open court, they are taken to the deliberation room. Opinions are split whether juries follow those legal pronouncements. Most lawyers believe that juries at least try to follow the law. However, the instructions can be so complex, confusing and convoluted even the lawyers trying the case have disagreements on the meaning of the law that should be applied. However, regardless of the complexity, juries don't decide the law that controls the case. That is the job of the judge. The job of the jury is to decide the facts. Juries decide who is telling the truth and who is lying. Which witnesses are worthy of belief and which are not. They then apply those facts to the law the court has given them.

Garner Lee was charged with murder second degree relating to the death of Amy Deland. For that offense, Cardwell instructed the jury if they found beyond a reasonable doubt Garner knowingly caused Amy's death or with the purpose of causing serious physical injury, Garner caused Amy's death, they should find him guilty.

The death of the unborn child was a little different. In that case, Garner was charged with involuntary manslaughter. The court instructed the jury that to find the defendant guilty of involuntary manslaughter, the state needed to prove beyond a reasonable doubt he recklessly caused the death of the unborn child. The court additionally told the jury that in Missouri an unborn child is a person for purposes of the offense of involuntary manslaughter. While the law is clear, attitudes toward criminalizing the deaths of unborn children are far from settled. While potential jurors are questioned regarding their thoughts on such controversial issues, the lawyers are never certain they are getting candid responses to these questions. Criminal convictions have been reversed based upon undisclosed prejudices. Felbin was hoping the twelve people who would be deciding the fate of Garner Lee had provided truthful responses to questions posed during jury selection.

Invariably, after the closing arguments, the courthouse gadflies and lawyers alike are abuzz with prognostications as to how long the jury will be out. This is particularly true in high-profile cases. Generally, the certainty of the prediction can be measured by the monetary risks proposed. Regardless of the amount, there is never a shortage of takers. Apart from the length of deliberations, there is also an economic reward for successfully predicting the winner.

Court personnel are notoriously bad when it comes to selecting winners. If they predict a defense victory, the smart money goes on the prosecution. Judges are not involved in these games of chance. And the lawyers who tried the case and particularly those lacking confidence in a favorable outcome, view such games of chance as poor form. Betting for or against your client is probably not a good idea, and a practice that might be disfavored by the ethics lawyers.

But the things that apply to most lawyers usually don't apply to Felbin. He was always in the game. Regardless of what he really thought the jury would do, he was always willing to bet the family farm on a successful outcome for his client. In fact, depending on the age and experience of his opponent, occasionally, he would solicit a small wager before a single witness took the stand. No such offer was ever accepted. And it was doubtful such tactics were an effective intimidation tool. But it gave him great pleasure at the end of the case when his client was in the winner's circle.

After the jury left the courtroom but before Cardwell left the bench, Felbin approached the young prosecutor, shook his hand, congratulated him on doing the best he could with what he had to work with. And he wasn't talking about the evidence. Rather, his reference was to a judge who was either totally stupid or absolutely corrupt. He was betting on the latter. But Perrin got the worst of it. He had to smile and take it because his boss was her friend. And there would be other cases in Cardwell's courtroom. He thought about putting a small wager on the outcome to pimp the young prosecutor, but decided that would be cruel and unusual punishment. This was one of those rare instances when Felbin was able to control his politically incorrect behavior.

As the minutes passed, Felbin began to think about the phone call with his client's father. Win, lose or draw, he wondered what this young man's life would be like with a father like that. Felbin had no love for any politician and felt that at some level, they should all be in the penitentiary. But this was a father whose son was on trial for murder, and all he cared about was his political future. And his mother. Where was she through all of this? She was an excellent trial lawyer. Not a politician. But, for whatever reason, she seemingly abandoned him as well. Felbin understood the father's behavior. He had seen many who were cut from the same cloth during his career. But a mother abandoning her child. That was unique. In fact, it was so unusual Felbin began to wonder whether he and the defense team missed something. They were persuaded their client was innocent. But maybe Garner's mother knew something that they didn't. Or, perhaps she was more interested in becoming the First Lady of Missouri than in the future of her only child. Not many answers, but a lot of questions and concerns in this case.

Felbin's mental ramblings were interrupted with an announcement that the jury had a verdict. At least one question would soon be answered.

Chapter Sixty-Four

Felbin, Carmine and Garner rode the short distance to the courthouse in silence. There was really nothing else to say. All the evidence had been presented and the arguments made. The case was in the hands of the jury, and they had made a decision. It took less than three hours to decide the future of Garner Lee. Although scientifically unsupported, the general, most popular courthouse theory is the shorter the deliberation, the greater the chance of a not guilty verdict. The thought is that depriving a person of his liberty is a serious matter and should not be decided quickly.

In less than an hour, the suspense would be over. Garner would know whether he would be spending the majority of the remainder of his life behind bars. But for Garner, it was never about whether he would be locked up. It was always about people believing he didn't kill the woman he loved, or at least thought he loved.

In criminal cases, the only two options juries have is to return a verdict of either guilty or not guilty. If the prosecution has failed to offer evidence to prove its case beyond a reasonable doubt, the court instructs the jury to give the defendant the benefit of the doubt and return a verdict of not guilty. That does not necessarily mean the defendant is innocent.

Garner Lee was not looking for a not guilty verdict. He wanted a complete exoneration.

Felbin knew what his client wanted. But he also knew Garner, like other innocent people who had to defend themselves against criminal accusations, was never going to get what he wanted unless he was able to find the real killer. But that was a long shot. And even then, there would be no guarantee of complete exoneration. Garner might soon be joining that small group of criminal injustice veterans that included Bobby Decker and Sergeant Tom Cannon. At least that was Felbin's hope.

As their vehicle approached the courthouse, they could see television cameras, reporters and onlookers occupying the twelve steps leading to the front door. All were waiting in anticipation for the verdict of the son of a wealthy power-broker. While Felbin had no idea what the verdict would be, he was sure of one thing. Senator Winston Lee would not be among the onlookers on the steps or in the courtroom.

"Is there someplace I can drop you to avoid this mob scene?" Joe Weller, Felbin's driver asked.

"No, unfortunately, we have to walk through them. Our security people are over there at the corner in the SUV. Drop us there and they can walk in with us," Felbin said.

Turning to Garner who was sitting next to him, Felbin said, "Obviously, the crowd has gotten larger. When we get to the steps, the security people will lead the way. I want you to stay between Tony and me. We are going to move quickly, but we aren't going to run. We are also not going to hide our faces. The reporters will be shouting questions. Just ignore them. Nobody is going to say anything. We will have plenty of time to comment after the verdict. Let's go."

The walk up the steps was without incident, other than annoying questions shouted by reporters who knew there would be no responses. The courtroom was also packed. Every seat was taken. To his credit, Garner was not un-nerved by the crowds. He walked with his head held high, silently announcing his innocence.

Paul Perrin was already seated at the counsel table when the defense team entered the courtroom. He was alone. The files that had previously covered the prosecution table were now gone. The work of the lawyers was done and soon the winner would be declared. Felbin noticed that Perrin was nervously tapping his foot, probably unconsciously. This was the worst part of the trial, waiting to hear the jury foreperson announce the result with either one word or two words.

Garner took the seat he had occupied during the trial. Felbin was on his left and Carmine was on his right. Silence filled the room as everyone awaited the appearance of the judge and the jury.

Every criminal case involves one or more defendants and victims. Usually, the families of those parties attend the trial. But this case was different. Neither the family of the defendant nor the victim attended any aspect of the trial, a point noted in media accounts as the trial progressed.

After what seemed like an eternity to both Felbin and his client, the jury began to file in. Another popular courthouse theory involves the way jurors take their seats in the jury box after they have announced a verdict has been reached. If they enter the courtroom and take their seats with their heads down, unwilling to look at the defendant, the verdict is guilty. But this jury apparently didn't get the memo, as half looked at the defendant while the other half looked at the floor.

Another delay, as everyone waited for the judge to enter the room. As Judge Cardwell came into view, the bailiff commanded all to stand. This was a tradition that existed in every courtroom in the country. Although Felbin knew the custom was designed to show respect for the court and not necessarily the individual occupying the position, it bothered him to be required to stand as Cardwell entered the room. He knew how she got there. Nonetheless, he complied.

"Has the jury reached a verdict?" Judge Cardwell asked the jury generally.

A black female seated in the fifth seat of the first row stood. "Yes, we have, Your Honor," she said.

This was the foreperson selected by the other jurors. Felbin recalled that she was a social worker who had a master's degree. Felbin was encouraged. Probably a bleeding-heart liberal, which should be good news for the defense.

The foreperson handed the verdict to the bailiff, who in turn gave it to the judge. After silently reading the decision, the judge handed the document to the court clerk, with directions to publish the jury's decision.

Felbin and Garner rose to receive the verdict. The prosecutor remained seated, as usual.

The clerk began to read the verdict. "In the matter of the State of Missouri versus Garner Lee, as to count one of the indictment, murder in the second degree, we, the jury, find the defendant, Garner Lee, guilty. As to count two of the indictment, involuntary manslaughter, we, the jury, find the defendant, Garner Lee, not guilty."

Chapter Sixty-Five

Guilty. The word vibrated around the room. But unlike most high-profile cases, there was no verbal reaction from the crowd. Just silence, while people thought about what would happen next. It wasn't often that the son of a powerful politician was found guilty of murder.

The relationship between Cardwell and Senator Lee was also well known. But the coverage thus far had only scratched the surface of that relationship. Felbin had noticed that and wondered why. The case was now out of the hands of the jury and squarely in the lap of the judge, who would decide an appropriate sentence. Felbin knew that if that sentence was in proportion to others for the same offense, the relationship might never be mentioned. However, he also knew that if there is leniency perceived at any level, the relationship would be headline news. Once again, Garner would get screwed by his father.

After the verdict was read, Garner sat motionless, staring at the clerk who read it. It was like he was having an out of body experience. He had just been found guilty of murdering his girlfriend. He wouldn't have to worry about people believing he was guilty of murder after he was acquitted. Now, a jury convicted him, and no one would doubt he was a killer.

Felbin needed to talk to his client. But first, the court needed to decide whether Garner would remain free on a bond pending further proceedings and sentencing. That issue was quickly resolved after the court announced that the million-dollar bond previously posted would be sufficient. No revocation or increase in the amount would be necessary. Now he needed to get his client out of the building and back to his office. The back door through which they escaped to go back to the office was locked. They had to go out the front door this time. Felbin was sure that was a payback by someone who didn't like Garner's father.

One of the jurors was waiting in the hallway to talk to Felbin. In state court, the jurors are free to talk about the case with the lawyers after the trial is over. "Mr. Felbin, I just wanted to tell you that I thought you did a good job."

"Thank you. But apparently it wasn't good enough. What happened in there?" Felbin asked.

"Primarily, it was his statement. We simply didn't believe that someone who loves another person like he said he did, would just leave her there and not call the police or do something, anything, after he found her. But, if he did actually kill her, he would most likely flee and then lie to cover it up. I just wanted to tell you that you did the best you could, and I would definitely call you if I ever get into trouble," the juror said.

"Thank you, sir," Felbin said as his security team suggested that they move on. The crowded hallway was not the time or the place to be having lengthy conversations with jurors, or anyone else.

Once again, the steps of the courthouse were lined with reporters and onlookers. As Felbin and his client, flanked by security, tried to negotiate their way through the crowd, the questions began. "Do you have any comment on the verdict, Garner?" "What's the next step, Mr. Felbin?" "Will you be appealing the verdict?" "Why weren't your parents at the trial, Garner?" "Do they think you murdered Amy?"

The last question could not be ignored. Turning to the reporter who asked the question, Felbin said, "That question suggests you slept through the closing argument. I thought I made it perfectly clear the only thing Senator Lee cared about was his political future, not his son's innocence. I suspect Garner's murder charge was not a career enhancer for him. He abandoned his only child. I know one thing for certain. People may be stupid enough to make him the governor of this state, but he will never win a father of the year election. I hope that answers your ignorant question."

While Felbin was fielding questions from the reporters, Cardwell was in her chamber, also answering questions. The unidentified caller wanted to know what happened. Promises had been made, but not kept. Cardwell was sure there would be a price to be paid.

As with the earlier trip to the courthouse, Felbin, Garner and Carmine rode back to the office in silence. When they arrived, the receptionist escorted Garner to one of the conference rooms, while Felbin went into his office with his investigator.

"Where do we go from here?" Carmine began.

"We file a motion for a new trial and ask her to revisit the motion for judgment of acquittal we filed at the close of all of the evidence," Felbin replied.

"What are the chances?"

"Not good. Throughout the trial she screwed the prosecutor, not us. The problem is now we have nothing to complain about in the court of appeals."

"Do you think Daddy is going to file another motion to fix with her, since she fucked up the first one?" Carmine asked.

"That will put his relationship with Cardwell on the front page as a headline. The media hasn't really touched that so far. She was able to hide what she was doing throughout the trial with technical evidentiary rulings only we knew were wrong. But if this kid gets some kind of favorable treatment after the jury has found him guilty, these sharks will crucify both of them. And I'm sure he doesn't want any part of that and will be content to sacrifice Garner again for his own political future."

"I assume probation would be out of the question for the same reason."

"Yeah. This is a murder case. People don't get probation in murder cases. Let's go in and talk to Garner."

When Felbin and Carmine entered the conference room, they found Garner staring out the window. They had seen this before. Felbin waited for a moment before beginning to speak. "Listen, Garner, this isn't over. Not by a long shot. Our next step is to file a motion for a new trial."

Without turning to face them, Garner said, "It's over for me."

They knew exactly what he was talking about. And it wasn't the sentence he would receive. "Garner, look at me," Felbin commanded. After his client turned to face him, Felbin said, "Things just got a little harder, that's all. I told you before that we need to do two things. Clear your name and find the real killer. We know someone killed her, and we are going to find him. We were hoping this jury would walk you and we could then get on with the second part of the game plan to find the real killer. But that didn't happen yet. But it will."

Garner listened to what his lawyer was saying. But when Felbin was finished talking, Garner lowered his head and repeated, "It's over for me."

It was obvious to both Felbin and Carmine they were not going to get very far with Garner right now. They just needed to proceed with the case and file whatever motions were necessary. They were convinced Garner's attitude would change because he was innocent, and he didn't want to be branded as a murderer, particularly of a woman he had loved.

Chapter Sixty-Six

The media coverage following the trial was relentless. It was obvious Senator Winston Lee was not the choice of the St. Louis media to become the next governor of the state. Unfortunately, the son was suffering for the sins of the father. Although Garner was acquitted of the death of the unborn child, the news coverage suggested he murdered both Amy and her child.

Garner was still trying to deal with the trial, the verdict and what remained of his life. He stopped reading the newspaper and watching television. But he was seeing a psychotherapist, which was helping. Carmine was keeping an eye on him while Felbin and the lawyers in his office prepared the motion seeking a judgment of acquittal or a new trial.

Eventually, Garner Lee and his father became yesterday's news and the reporters found a new sensational story to cover. Of course, their interest would be rekindled when Cardwell heard Felbin's motion and sentenced the defendant.

With little hope of success, Felbin made the final changes and filed his motion for a new trial, after which he headed for Florida. It had been a long and stressful month. He needed a break and a little change of scenery. He and Melinda have a place on the beach in Ormond Beach, the former winter home of John D. Rockefeller. It is a perfect place to relax and reflect.

When his private plane touched down at Daytona International Airport, which was next door to the Daytona Speedway, the home of the Daytona 500, the evening sky was blue with few clouds, and 72 degrees. Although it was still winter and cold in St. Louis, with snow and ice still visible, the winters on the east coast of Florida were warm and comfortable.

Before heading home, Felbin and Melinda needed to stop for a bite to eat. The Beach Bucket was a favorite flip flop bar and restaurant in Ormond Beach, just a few miles from their condo. They found a table on the beach and ordered a pitcher of Bud Light to get started. Except for a lone surfer determined to catch one more wave, the rest of the beach was empty as the sun began to set. Shrimp boats dotted the horizon, floating aimlessly on a calm sea. After a couple salads, chicken wings and several beers, Melinda and Felbin were ready to go home and fall asleep to the rhythmic sounds of the waves breaking in the Atlantic Ocean from their eleventh-floor beach side condominium.

The morning came early for Felbin. He couldn't sleep. The fate of Garner Lee consumed his thoughts. While Melinda slept, he went into the kitchen to get the coffee started and then down to the gym on the first floor of the building overlooking the beach and the ocean. A vigorous workout would take his mind off Garner. He turned on Fox 35 out of Orlando to watch the local news. The anchors along with the weatherman on the Good Day Orlando morning show were friends and had great chemistry. He also knew that this news cast would not contain any story about Garner Lee or his father.

As he began his workout on the elliptical machine, Jamie King, the Fox 35 weatherman, was predicting sunny skies, slight wind from the southeast and a high of 78 degrees. A perfect day for either golf or the beach. Melinda would make that call. The sight of the orange fireball rising from the ocean viewed from his workout machine took his mind off everything. It was a magnificent sight.

"Good morning. Did you have a good workout?" Melinda asked when Felbin returned to their unit.

"Great. Did you see that sunrise? Magnificent. Of course, not as good as the total eclipse of the sun that we witnessed in St. Louis," Felbin said as he poured a cup of coffee.

"Nothing will ever compare to that."

They were referring to the time that the moon covered the sun completely and could be seen in various cities throughout the Unites States as it traveled in a path from Oregon to South Carolina in a period of ninety minutes. The last time the phenomenon had occurred was in 1918. St. Louis was one such city that was able to view the totality of the moon covering the sun. Daylight turned to darkness, the temperature fell, the cicadas began to chirp, the dusk to dawn lights went on, and some of the planets could be identified in the two minutes and seventeen seconds of darkness. It was truly an incredible sight that might not be repeated for another hundred years.

"Did you also see the dolphins? There were about five of them going south and not very far off shore."

"No. I missed that."

Dolphins are a common sight. They usually travel in groups and swim rhythmically, their bodies appearing momentarily above the water at various intervals. Occasionally, they will jump, their bodies thrust completely out of the water into the air.

Surf fishing is another common sight along the beach. The lines are usually baited with shrimp and cast out beyond the breaking surf. These individuals, both men and women, sit patiently in lawn chairs waiting for their poles to bend, signifying a bite of some kind. The occasional shark will cause the vacationing beachcombers to stop for a look and perhaps a picture.

After a walk on the beach, Melinda and Felbin spent the rest of the day on the beach, enjoying the sun, watching the surfers negotiate the waves and taking a nap or two. It was a relaxing day for Felbin, free of reporters, judges, prosecutors, politicians and clients.

For dinner, they made reservations at Mario's, an exclusive Italian restaurant in Ormond Beach, not far from their condo. They had a private table in the corner of the restaurant, where they started the evening with a bottle of Merlot while they glanced at the menu they had seen numerous times before. This evening they shared appetizers of a stuffed artichoke and lobster ravioli. For her entrée, Melinda ordered shrimp scampi, and Felbin had his favorite, veal Marsala. For the most part, the conversation consisted of catching up with one another, since Melinda had been out of town, and his time was taken up with Garner Lee. But eventually, the conversation would turn to the Garner Lee trial, a topic they had intentionally avoided for the past two days.

"What's going to happen to Garner now that he has been found guilty?" she asked, initiating the discussion of that topic.

"We filed a motion for a new trial and she has to rule on that. Then we are on to the sentencing," Felbin answered.

"What are the chances of getting a new trial?"

"Not very good. We have some things we can talk about, but nothing that would justify a new trial or an acquittal. The problem here is the jury decides the facts and who they want to believe. The jury decided the facts in this case were sufficient to return a guilty verdict. They obviously didn't believe Garner. No judge or appellate court is going to reverse that decision."

"Then he goes to jail?"

"Yes. He goes to the penitentiary, and we file an appeal to ask the appellate court to give us a new trial."

"Do you really think this judge would put him in jail? I thought you told me that Garner's father put her on the bench."

"I did tell you that. But now a jury found him guilty of murder. She can't overlook that and put him on probation. The press would fry her. She did what she could to fix the case during the trial with her ridiculous one-sided rulings designed to benefit the defendant. But despite her help, we lost, and I feel bad about that," Felbin said as the waiter poured the remainder of the wine. They ordered another bottle.

"You think he's innocent, don't you?"

"There is no doubt in my mind he's innocent. Although he made that stupid statement thanks to his father, the rest of the evidence just doesn't add up. The fingerprint on the murder weapon is not his. How could he use that to kill Amy and not leave a print, particularly since one is there? I could understand if no prints were found. But that's not the case. They also found DNA on the murder weapon which also belongs to someone else. I'm going to guess the DNA and the fingerprint on that statue belong to the person who killed her. And that person is not Garner Lee. In addition to these types of things, I believe he is sincere when he says he loved her."

"Did she love him?"

"I think she was an opportunist. She used him for his money and family name. According to her friends, it was only a matter of time before she found another sugar daddy and dumped him, which would have pleased his parents.

They had no use for her. I think they understood what she was. but he was truly in love and didn't see that or didn't want to see it. But then she turned up pregnant at the time of her death and Garner was not the father."

"What? Are you kidding? Did he know that?"

"Not until we told him."

"Wow. How did he react?"

"That was the interesting part. At first, he was in denial. Then when reality hit him, he rationalized. But I think before he knew about her extracurricular activities, he truly loved her. It's hard to tell what he is really thinking now."

"If the evidence at trial didn't add up, how did the jury convict him? I assume they thought the evidence was sufficient," Melinda said, challenging Felbin's belief in his client's innocence.

"Frankly, I'm not sure how much of the evidence they looked at. I think they couldn't get past the lie. The explanation that his father gave that advice apparently didn't persuade them. One of the jurors waited for us in the hallway of the courthouse. I didn't get to have much of a conversation with him, because the security people were pushing us out the door. But he did tell me that the jury thought if he just happened to find her he would have called the police or done something. He wouldn't have just left her there. But if he actually killed her, he would have fled and lied about being there."

"That make sense to me," Melinda said.

"I agree until you factor in the father. The bad advice he gave benefitted him and not his son. He was worried his political career would take a hit if his kid was found in the apartment of a dead white woman. So, he told him to get out of the apartment. And while he didn't specifically tell him to lie to the police, that was the theme he was initially communicating. Garner picked up on that theme and instead of keeping his mouth shut, he told the police he wasn't there."

"But he's a lawyer and should know better."

"He is someone who has a law degree. That doesn't mean that he is smart. I suspect his father pulled some strings and got him into Mizzou law school. He isn't the brightest bulb in the box. We knew from the start this lie was going to be a problem. Then we wind up in front of

Cardwell and the case is tried in record time, limiting our ability to prepare. His father needed to get this off page one and had his puppet Cardwell push us out to trial."

"Well, I hope it works out for him, particularly if he is truly innocent," Melinda said ending this discussion.

The evening ended with bananas foster that they split.

The remainder of their week in Florida was spent relaxing in the sun. But never far from Felbin's thoughts was the future of his client.

Chapter Sixty-Seven

The day Garner Lee would learn his fate arrived. The jury returned a guilty verdict and now it was time for the court to pronounce a sentence. The range of punishment available to the court for the offense of murder in the second degree is 10 to 30 years or life. Because of the relationship between Cardwell and Senator Lee, Felbin expected the sentence would be the statutory minimum, 10 years. But the question was whether she would have the audacity to suspend the imposition of that sentence.

In Missouri, a criminal conviction consists of a plea or a finding of guilt plus the imposition of a sentence. If the court suspends the imposition of that sentence, no term of confinement is imposed. Because the second necessary element is missing, the defendant is not convicted of a crime.

Another sentencing option is a suspended execution of sentence. Under that scenario, a specific period of incarceration is imposed, but the defendant does not serve the time. However, the defendant is convicted of a crime.

In both cases, the defendant is placed on probation with certain specified conditions. If those conditions are not meet, the probation is revoked with varying consequences. If a suspended imposition of sentence has been imposed, the court is free to sentence a defendant to any term of years authorized by the statute. But where the execution has been suspended, the court can only incarcerate for the term of years originally imposed.

With the guilty finding, Cardwell now had a real problem. Because her efforts to manipulate the evidence in favor of the defendant had not resulted in an acquittal, she was faced with the prospect of having to incarcerate the son of the man who put her on the bench for a period of at least 10 years. Or she could put him on probation and run for cover. Not ideal choices.

But first, the motion for a new trial must be argued. Because it was the defendant's motion, Felbin began the argument. His initial focus was on the evidence or the lack thereof. He suggested that his renewed motion for judgment of acquittal should be sustained, because the evidence was insufficient to support the element of murder second degree. No new trial was necessary. He didn't spend much time on that because he knew this argument was going nowhere, even with this judge.

Next, he moved to some legal arguments, which included errors the judge made during the trial. Of course, these were sparse because Cardwell erred on the side of helping the defendant throughout the trial. But there was one ruling she made that was averse to the defendant. Felbin's motion for a mistrial based upon prosecutorial misconduct was overruled after Perrin told the jury during his opening statement that "Innocent people don't lie to the police." Felbin quoted the statement verbatim. He argued the statement obliterated the presumption of innocence and was an unfair comment on the defendant's 5th amendment rights. He reminded Cardwell she was concerned at the time he had poisoned the jury and prejudiced the defendant beyond repair with a statement that violated the constitution. He then suggested the verdict based upon inadequate evidence was proof the jury had been tainted by the prosecutor's misconduct.

This was about the only real issue that Felbin could hang his hat on. And although he objected to the statement at the time, even he did not believe there was anything wrong with the comment. The problem was Garner had not chosen to remain silent. Instead, he made a statement which happened to be false. And even if there was a prejudice problem with the comment, Cardwell cured it when she told the jury to disregard. Felbin knew a mistrial would not have been appropriate. But Cardwell was indebted to the senator. Maybe, now, she would give Garner another opportunity to persuade a jury he didn't kill the woman he loved, by sustaining the motion for a new trial.

Perrin made short shrift of the motion for judgment of acquittal based upon the lack of evidence. In a manner similar to a closing argument, he carefully detailed the evidence that proved the defendant's guilt beyond a reasonable doubt, starting with the lie. Most of his argument was designed to influence the sentence Lee would receive, as well as the future news coverage. Perrin knew this judge would not sustain Felbin's motion and acquit the defendant after a jury convicted him. But he was not as certain about the sentence. He was concerned that Cardwell, given some of her decisions during the trial, might put him on probation. Although his boss directed him to take no position with respect to punishment, Perrin intended to ask for a life sentence.

The mistrial request based upon a statement that Perrin made was a different matter. At the time, Perrin was stunned when Felbin jumped out of his seat and objected. He did not believe he had done anything wrong. But in order to avoid a mistrial, suggested the court instruct the jury to disregard the comment. Upon further reflection, he was convinced there was nothing improper about his statement. The fact of the matter was Lee did lie to the police. He chose to make a statement rather than remaining silent. He told Cardwell the purpose of the lie was to mislead the police so they would not find out he was in the victim's apartment. That, he argued, was evidence of guilt.

The situation would have been different if the defendant had not made any statement. A comment under those circumstances would have been improper, because he would have been commenting on the defendant's constitutional right to remain silent. That would have warranted a mistrial, he admitted. But he told Cardwell she made the correct decision at the time by refusing the request for a mistrial and instead instructing the jury to disregard his comment. He pointed out that ironically the only harm that occurred with her instruction was to him.

Sometimes judges ask questions during motion arguments on points they don't understand. Cardwell asked no questions of either lawyer. Presumably, she understood the arguments from both sides. Of course, Felbin had a different opinion of the ability of this judge to understand anything.

Since neither side requested any additional time to file anything else in support of their positions, the court was free to rule. Judge Cardwell could make the decision on the spot, or she could take the case under advisement and enter an order later, when the parties would not be staring at her. Ordinarily, in criminal cases where the court is going to overrule the motion for a new trial, the decision is made immediately following the argument. A sentence can then be imposed without further delay. In those rare instances when a court is inclined to sustain the motion and grant a new trial, the matter is taken under advisement. This is to allow the court to be certain a ruling made during the trial necessitated a do over. Most judges don't relish acknowledging their own mistakes and are reticent to expend additional time and money on a new trial.

In the case of State of Missouri versus Garner Lee, Judge Cardwell told the parties she was ready to rule if neither side had anything else to say. When both sides indicated they had nothing else to add, Cardwell said, "I want to thank both of you for your arguments. They were helpful in resolving this complicated issue."

Felbin wondered what she talking about. In his view, there was nothing complicated about this. There was sufficient evidence to sustain the guilty verdict. And there was nothing improper about the prosecutor's statement. She needed to get on with it. Overrule the motions and get on with the sentencing, where everyone could see the political payback when Garner Lee was put on probation.

"This case has been both complicated and tragic. A young lady lost her life. An unborn child lost his or her life. The jury heard all the evidence that was presented and entered verdicts of both guilty and not guilty. While reasonable minds can certainly differ on what is or is not credible evidence, the jury in this case collectively decided which witness to believe and which not to believe. That was their job, not the court's. The evidence in this case was circumstantial. The state presented no witness who actually observed anyone striking the victim with a statue. Instead, they relied upon the circumstances of the defendant's presence at the scene and his subsequent false statements as well as other evidence. While not the strongest case, the evidence is sufficient to support the jury's verdict. Therefore, I am going to deny the defendant's renewed motion for judgment of acquittal."

No surprises there, for Felbin or the prosecutor. But Felbin was sure Perrin could do without the editorial commentary. Felbin hoped she was playing to the press and laying a foundation for probation instead of penitentiary time.

"Now, with respect to the motion for a new trial," Cardwell began. "The court's job here is to determine whether any mistakes were made during the trial. Judges are called upon to make spit second decisions during the heat of battle. Time is not available to thoroughly research every issue that arises. After the trial, when the dust settles, the judge reviews those decisions to see if there is any error and if so, whether it is prejudicial to the extent a new trial should be ordered."

Felbin wanted her to get on with it. Stop the torture. Just overrule the motion, deny the new trial and get to the sentencing. Stop the bullshit. She was not going to fool the reporters. Felbin believed they knew exactly what she was and how she got to her position. If she put his client on probation for a murder, they were going to figure it out.

"I have carefully reviewed each of the rulings that I made during the trial. Based on that review, I have decided I made at least one mistake. Please remember, I am relatively new to this job and the learning curve is incomplete . . ."

As Cardwell was speaking, Carmine leaned over and whispered to Felbin, "Where is this going?"

Felbin's only response was a shrug of the shoulders. He had no answer to that question.

"I believe I erred when I refused to sustain the defendant's motion for a mistrial after the prosecutor made the remarks we have been discussing here today. Given the fact that this was a relatively weak circumstantial evidence case, I am not persuaded those remarks did not alter the outcome of this trial and resulted in a guilty finding . . ."

"She's going to give us a new trial. Unbelievable," Carmine told Felbin.

No verbal or physical response from Felbin. He was just waiting for all the shoes to drop. Nothing surprised him with this judge.

"As a result, I am going to revisit the request for the mistrial made by the defense. And I will sustain that request to the extent I am granting a new trial." Cardwell continued over the voices in the audience, which were becoming louder in reaction to her ruling. "But that new trial will be unnecessary, because I am finding that the mistrial was necessitated by prosecutorial misconduct. As such, jeopardy attaches and the case against Garner Lee is dismissed with prejudice, meaning that he can never again be tried for this offense. So ordered. The court is adjourned." And with that, Judge Cardwell left the courtroom.

The entire room fell silent. The parties and spectators alike were in a state of shock as they watched the judge leave the bench. The silence was broken when Carmine said to Felbin, "What the fuck just happened?"

Felbin didn't respond immediately. It was only after his client repeated the question asked by the investigator, that Felbin said, "She just acquitted you of the crime of murder and you're free to go."

"How can that be? I thought we wanted a new trial," Garner said.

"We did, and she gave us that. But she found that the prosecutor's statement constituted misconduct, which caused the mistrial. The penalty for that misconduct is a permanent dismissal of the charge."

When he finished that sentence, Felbin looked at Perrin, who was still seated at the counsel table. He hadn't moved. He was frozen in place, his face expressionless. Felbin wasn't even sure he was breathing. You couldn't tell from across the room.

Felbin had witnessed judges do some unethical, nasty and inappropriate things. But this one might very well top the list. Perrin did nothing wrong, yet he was taking the hit for a political payback by a corrupt judge. This was wrong on so many levels. Felbin had to do something. But what could he do? He had no proof of corruption. This simply could have been the decision of an idiot.

Chapter Sixty-Eight

For several weeks following the court's post trial decision, the media had a feeding frenzy. The coverage focused primarily on the relationship between Joan Cardwell and Winston Lee and left little doubt that her decision was a payback for a judicial appointment. This type of publicity wasn't helping the senator's political future. While he had a base that would remain loyal to him regardless of what he did, the race for governor involved the entire state, not just his senatorial district. The news of this case had spread throughout the state.

Editorials suggested the total elimination or at least a greater system of checks and balances on the role politics plays in the appointment of judges. Discussions on radio and television talk shows explored a variety of solutions, none of which were perfect or a complete resolution of the issue.

Many of these discussions focused on the process of selection of judges. In the city and county of St. Louis, judges are selected through the Non-Partisan Court Plan. In that plan, the governor makes the selection from a group of three individuals provided by a vetting panel consisting of three lawyers, three non-lawyers appointed by the governor and the Chief Judge of the Missouri Supreme Court. While the creation of this plan was an effort to remove politics from the appointment process, many would argue the effort fell short of accomplishing its purpose. Critics of the plan suggested that pay-to-play still existed, but was simply disguised. In support of their position, they pointed to substantial political contributions made directly or indirectly by judicial candidates, as well the lack of experience, intelligence and temperament by those ultimately chosen.

Replacing the plan with a general election by the people was quickly eliminated by those involved in these public debates, as this would increase rather than decrease political involvement. Much of the discussion over the weeks and months following the Lee decision centered on establishing objective criteria for the appointment of those entrusted with the interpretation and enforcement of our laws. Some believed testing similar to bar examinations, along with interviews and focus groups conducted by an independent agency would objectively identify academic qualifications, judicial temperament and the experience of candidates. That would be a start. In the end, because of the complexity of the issue, the only thing these discussions produced was a consensus that more work was needed to select the best and the brightest for the bench. But all were in agreement about one thing. They credited both Cardwell and Senator Lee for at least starting the discussion.

Felbin had his own ideas how to select the best and the brightest for the bench objectively. But this was not the time for his thoughts to be made public, despite several invitations to participate in the debate. While the focus was primarily on Cardwell and the senator, his client was also in the mix. Garner Lee was viewed as the third-party beneficiary of a corrupt system. Felbin believed his client was innocent. He also believed the case was fixed. No rational judge would have done what Cardwell did. But he couldn't prove either one. As a result, Garner Lee, although a free man, wore the scarlet letter *M.*

After the shock of Cardwell's decision subsided, Felbin met his former client for dinner at an out of the way restaurant outside of St. Louis metropolitan area where they would not be recognized. Felbin knew he had to have a conversation with Garner, but it had to wait until he was ready.

The evening began with a warm greeting, a man hug and a few drinks to relax the moment. Felbin ordered a gin and tonic. Garner had a double scotch on the rocks that he consumed quickly and immediately ordered a second.

"It's good to see you, Garner. How are you doing?" Felbin began.

"I'm doing the best I can under the circumstances," Garner replied.

Felbin knew Garner was having a tough time. He wanted desperately for people to believe he was innocent. An acquittal based upon the lack of evidence is a loss. In Garner's mind, people believed he killed Amy, the state just couldn't prove it. But here the situation was worse. The jury found him guilty and the judge thanked his father for her job by setting him free. "Talk to me. Tell me what you're thinking and feeling. I want to try to help you get through this," Felbin said.

"Help me? Nobody can help me, it's too late for that. The jury said I killed Amy, and a dishonest judge helped my father. People believe I'm a murderer who fixed it politically. How can you help me with that?"

"You're right, I can't help you with that. And there is nothing you can do about that. But you do have something going for you that no one else has."

"What's that?"

"You know you didn't murder Amy. That means there is someone out there who did and has not been caught. The police and the prosecutors believe you are guilty. Everybody believes you're guilty. Nobody will be looking for the real killer, because that person has been identified. The real killer can relax, since the case is closed. You need to stop feeling sorry for yourself and we need to go find the real killer. That's the only way you will be completely vindicated. The sad truth is, if that never happens, you will always be identified as a murderer."

Garner didn't react immediately. He was thinking about what Felbin had just said. He knew the lawyer was right. He also knew Felbin believed he was not good for this crime. Otherwise, he would not be willing to help. That would be a waste of his valuable time. Finally, he asked, "How do we find the real killer?"

"I don't know yet," Felbin said, as he motioned for the waiter so they could order dinner.

Chapter Sixty-Nine

In the months that followed, Felbin and Carmine reviewed every piece of paper in the Garner Lee case: police reports, medical reports, DNA profiles, lab reports, witness statements, everything. They were looking for something, anything that would lead them to the real killer. All dead-end streets, nothing new.

Carmine decided to check with some of his buddies at the police department to see if anything was overlooked. He knew what Jack Sandworth's position was. Garner Lee killed Amy Deland. There was no question about it. But what did his partner, Leroy Anderson, think? He never testified in the trial, and the defense had no time to take his deposition, thanks to Cardwell. To his surprise, Anderson did not share his partner's certainty about Garner's guilt. While he thought Cardwell's decision was outrageous and a miscarriage of justice, he was not certain the prosecution had enough evidence to convict. Of course, he was speaking from a police, rather than a judicial, legal perspective.

"Listen Tony, I'm not saying this guy is innocent. I'm just saying I have some concerns. This was not an airtight case. We have prints on the murder weapon that don't belong to your client. Thanks to you, we have DNA that doesn't belong to your client. We know he didn't wipe the statue clean, otherwise, we wouldn't have any prints. But then the idiot left his print in blood on the inside doorknob," Anderson said.

"There is no doubt this kid is not bright," Carmine agreed.

"We figured that out when we paid him a visit. Frankly, I will deny I said this, but I think Jack intimidated him and took advantage of the fact he lost someone he cared about, at the least. And he made a statement that turned out to be a lie, which led to his downfall. That's how I saw it. But, of course, as you know, that's our job. If we didn't turn up the heat on people, we wouldn't solve anything."

"But then he volunteered his prints," Carmine offered.

"Yes, he did. I was surprised he did that."

"Usually, people who are good for the crime, don't volunteer information they know, or at least think, might get them indicted. If he whacked her with that statue, he surely would know his prints might be on it. Unless he is totally stupid, he wouldn't be giving up his prints without a fight."

"I agree. You know, in the short amount of time that we spent with him, I just felt like he didn't feel right for this murder. Call it instinct or whatever. And there was also something else..." Anderson said, stopping in midsentence.

"What?" Carmine demanded.

"This has to be off the record."

"Agreed," Carmine said, anxious to hear what the detective had.

"According to the medical examiner, the perpetrator was either left-handed dominant or used his left hand to kill her."

"Son of a bitch. That wasn't in the autopsy report and that prick, Long, danced the dance with Felbin when he went after him on this point."

"It wasn't in the report because Jack suggested he keep it out."

Carmine was clearly upset by what Anderson just told him. "That's fucking unbelievable. We can argue about whether it should be in the autopsy report. I happen to think it belongs there. But that prick lied when he said he never talked to you guys about this issue and could not, or would not, offer an opinion. He is nothing but a rubber stamp for the prosecution. This is not the first time our office has had a problem with him and his biased conclusions."

"I suspect when you were on our side of the fence, your opinion was a bit different."

"Fair enough. Thanks for the talk, Leroy. Let's keep this little chat between us."

"Agreed. If I hear anything else, I'll give you a call."

Although Carmine appreciated the detective's candor, the policeman really didn't give them anything they could use to further the investigation of who killed Amy. Whether the medical examiner was less than candid in his trial testimony was irrelevant at this point. They already knew the killer was either left-handed or had used his left hand. Most likely, given the weight of the statue and the location of the body and head injury, the assailant was left hand dominant.

Chapter Seventy

Several more months passed with no progress. The media attention was minimal but the frustration of Felbin and Carmine was increasing in proportion to their client's depression. On a regular basis, Garner would call the office asking if there was anything new and repeatedly he would be disappointed. But now there was a different problem.

It was 7:14 pm one evening. Melinda and Felbin were having dinner at LoRusso's when his cell phone rang. They had just ordered cocktails, escargot and toasted ravioli appetizers. Ordinarily, when he was at dinner, he would allow a phone call to go to voicemail and check the message later. But this was a call from Garner, who seldom contacted Felbin on his cell phone and never during the evening. Something must be wrong. And it was. Garner was calling from jail. He had been arrested. "I was arrested for DWI," Garner said.

"Where are you?" Felbin asked.

"In Ladue."

Ladue is a wealthy suburb in St. Louis County.

"Did you take the breath test?"

"No, because . . ." Garner began before he was interrupted by Felbin.

"Garner, this will be a taped line. Please just answer my questions. Nothing more. What is the bond?"

"500."

"Do you have the cash?"

"No."

"I'll send Tony over with the cash and to give you a ride home. Get a good night's sleep and come into the office in the morning so we can get this straightened out."

"Thanks," Garner said ending the conversation.

"What's going on?" Melinda asked.

"Garner was arrested for driving drunk," Felbin said shaking his head. "If that kid didn't have bad luck, he wouldn't have any luck."

"This whole thing has taken its toll. I assume he is drinking pretty heavily," Melinda commented.

"He has been depressed, because we have made no progress in trying to find the real killer."

"Do you think you will ever find that guy?"

"It's not looking very promising at the moment."

"What happens to him if you can't get this thing solved?"

"I don't know. He's hanging on by a thread right now. He is seeing a shrink, but I'm not sure that's helping. I think the only reason he is hanging on is because we have been positive in our conversations with him. We keep telling him we are going to get this guy. But as soon as he figures out this case will never be solved, I'm not sure what he will do."

"Is he working? Doesn't he work for his mother's firm?"

"Both his mother and his father are at the firm. His mother's family started it. But he has taken a leave of absence to get his head straightened out. Obviously, the firm doesn't appreciate the adverse publicity."

"I can understand that. But isn't his father responsible for a lot of that bad press?" Melinda pointed out.

"He is. But he's pretty upset with both parents. They didn't approve of Amy and discouraged the relationship. He blames both of them for that, and his father for the bad advice he foolishly followed that got him convicted. And he blames his mother for her lack of support. Not exactly a loving family dynamic."

"I see his father is pursuing his goal to be the next governor," Melinda noted.

"Yes. Apparently, now that the reporters went on to other stories, I guess he feels he weathered the storm with Garner, as well as his relationship with Cardwell."

"How is Garner reacting to that?

"As you might expect, it's upsetting. Right now, there is no love lost between the father and his son. His father took care of this case and fixed it under the table, which is what corrupt politicians do. We all know that. On the one hand, Garner is the beneficiary of that corruption. But on the other, he is the victim. And right now, he is feeling more like a victim. He believes his life now is no better than it would have been, had Cardwell sentenced him to an extended penitentiary stay. In fact, it might be worse now," Felbin said.

Melinda knew Felbin felt sorry for this young man and blamed himself for the loss. But everyone had to move forward to wherever that took them. "Let's order some dinner and enjoy what's left of this evening. You will be able to work out Garner's driving problem tomorrow," she said.

Chapter Seventy-One

Garner was waiting in the conference room. He had arrived before Felbin and looked like hell. He was unshaven, wearing a white dress shirt and khaki pants that looked like he slept in them, assuming he had gotten any sleep. By the time Ladue released him, it was 2:30 am.

Felbin grabbed Carmine and they headed into the conference room. "You look like you could use some coffee," Felbin said, as he picked up the canister of regular coffee from the credenza and began to pour it into a mug that contained the firm logo. "Do you use cream or sugar?"

"No, black is fine. Thank you," Garner said, accepting the mug.

After pouring a cup for himself, Felbin said, "Tell me what happened."

"I had a couple drinks and a salad at Lester's. I was by myself at the corner of the bar out of the way, so I didn't have to deal with anyone. I decided . . ."

Felbin interrupted the story. "How many drinks is a couple, and what were you drinking?"

"I was drinking vodka martinis and probably had three. I decided to leave Lester's and go someplace else and maybe have another one or two. I was feeling sorry for myself again. I was heading down Clayton Road when I saw the red flashing lights come on behind me. I was watching my speed because I'd had a couple drinks, and this was Ladue. I didn't think I was speeding. When I pulled over, the cop came up to the car and said Good evening Mr. Lee. I thought since he knew my name and I was in Ladue, this could be a major problem."

Ladue is a wealthy suburb in St. Louis County. Its police department has been the subject of criticism, as well as media coverage, for a practice known as DWB, driving while black, which involves stopping African American drivers without probable cause. The city adamantly denied the practice, while civil liberty groups were just as adamant in their opposition to and condemnation of the practice. In the meantime, Garner Lee, a black man who'd recently walked on a murder charge, found himself in the unenviable position of having to defend a DWI charge that resulted from an arrest in Ladue. There could be little doubt this incident would become headline news and stir the racial debate.

"Did you ask, or did he tell you, why he pulled you over?"

"Yes. He told me I had a taillight out and invited me to take a look. I did, and sure enough, the right taillight was out. Then he gave me the finger to nose, walk a straight line and the alphabet tests and said I didn't do very well. He asked me to take the breath test. I refused, and here I am in another mess. The only difference is that this one I'm good for."

"Did you know that taillight was out when you drove after drinking those martinis? I thought your car was relatively new. Less than a year old," Felbin said.

"I didn't have my car. I had a little fender bender and took it to a friend to do the repair. In the meantime, I had to use one of the vehicles from the firm because he didn't have a loaner to give me. I got a little push back from the firm because I am currently on a leave of absence. But the office manager likes me and probably felt sorry for me. She gave me a car to use."

"What kind of a vehicle was this?" Carmine asked.

"It's a Chevy SUV of some kind. Not sure of the year. It's not a new car and nothing fancy."

"What about the color? What color is it?"

"Black."

Carmine had some other questions about the vehicle, but decided to save them for another time.

"Did they give you a court date?" Felbin asked.

"Yes. It's on the ticket," Garner said as he handed the ticket to Carmine. "What's going to happen now?

"We are going to have to wait and see what the police report says. I assume you failed the field sobriety tests. We are going to have two problems, one criminal and one administrative, dealing with the suspension of your driver's license, since you refused the breath test."

"I don't care about the license. Am I going to jail?"

"Ordinarily, I would say no. First time offenders generally get probation. Of course, you are anything but ordinary. I don't think we are going to have a problem, but we
will address whatever comes up."

"What do I do now?" Garner asked.

"Nothing. I assume there will be some media coverage,
and we will handle that. If you are contacted by any reporter, just send them to us. You ought to know that drill by
now. Did you tell your parents about this?"

"No. My father and I aren't communicating very well.
I haven't been spending much time at the office. They are
telling people I'm on a leave of absence. But when I do go
in, I try to avoid him. Unfortunately, he has been spending
a lot of time in the office. I assume he is probably trying to
put the pieces of his campaign for governor together after I
blew it up by murdering my girlfriend."

"Has he said that to you?" Carmine asked.

"Not directly. But I know that's what he thinks. I'm
sure he also believes if I had listened to him and my mother
and dumped Amy, this wouldn't have happened."

"Well, looks like your father is going to find out about
this sooner rather than later," Felbin said, as his receptionist handed him the morning paper. Below the fold on
page one was a story about Garner's arrest. The story was
mostly background on the murder case and brief on details
about the DWI, probably because the reporter hadn't had a
chance to talk to anyone yet.

Just as Felbin finished his sentence, Garner's cell
phone rang. It was his father. Felbin told him to put it on
the speaker.

"What the fuck is this? Another arrest?" the senator
shouted, thinking he was speaking only to his son.

"If this is how the conversation is going to go, then it
will be short," Felbin replied.

"Who the fuck is this? Is this Felbin?" Senator Lee
asked.

"It is, and if you can't have a rational, calm discussion,
this call will end right now," Felbin added.

"Fuck you, Felbin. I'm talking to my son, not you."

"Goodbye, Senator. Please call back when you learn
how to behave," Felbin said, as he pushed the button that
ended the call.

For the next few minutes no one spoke. No one had to. Garner stared out the conference room window, looking at nothing in particular, while Felbin and his investigator looked at each other. Garner didn't need this aggravation in addition to everything else happening in his life. And there was nothing anyone could do to make it any better.

After Garner left the office, Carmine told Felbin he had to check something. When Felbin questioned what that was, the investigator was evasive. "I just need to look at something in the murder file. I'll come down to your office," Carmine said as he left the conference room.

Chapter Seventy-Two

When Carmine entered Felbin's office a short time after the conference with Garner ended, he was holding a document. Felbin had no idea what it was or how it related to the current DWI case. But Carmine was excited about what he found. "Garner said something that jogged my memory about an interview I did with a witness in the murder case. I went back and checked the file and pulled my interview with Clara Carson. She was the 86-year-old lady who told me all black people look alike, and Garner killed Amy. Of course, she had no way of knowing that, but considered herself the self-appointed mayor of the building and knew everything going on. She lives on the first floor and positions a chair by her window, so she can see everyone coming and going."

"Sounds like a nut job to me," Felbin said.

"Well, she is, and I didn't put much stock in what she said or her theories. But I did make a note of one thing she said. She is the one who told me Amy had another regular visitor who would arrive under the cover of darkness wearing a baseball hat. She would witness that because of her seat by the window. Despite her claim that all black people look alike, she was clear this visitor was not Garner."

Felbin wasn't understanding what Carmine was trying to tell him. "I remember her and her statement about the visitor. We had to make a strategy decision as to whether we wanted to use any of that in the trial. But what does that have to do with his current drunk driving mess?" Felbin asked.

"It doesn't have anything to do with that, but everything to do with the murder case. Carson told me that Amy's visitor drove a black SUV type vehicle with a right rear taillight that was out."

It was like someone turned the lights on in Felbin's head. "And Garner was driving a black SUV with a right taillight out that he borrowed from the firm. Coincidence?"

"I don't believe in coincidences. How many black SUVs with a right taillight out that are connected to both Amy and Garner's law firm can there be? In addition to the vehicle, Clara also says that she saw a black male who apparently doesn't want to be identified visiting at night and wearing a hat that Carson believed was pulled down to cover a portion of his face. This guy obviously didn't want anyone to know he was there."

"And we have Senator Lee connected to the firm that Amy worked for," Felbin added.

"Which was a small little detail the good senator forgot to mention. Your son is in a relationship with a girl you know because she works for the public relations firm that represents you in your political campaigns. You're not happy about that relationship and encourage your son to dump her. She turns up dead. Your son is accused of murdering her. And you forget to mention to your son's lawyer that you know this woman! Not buying that. This prick is involved somehow in Amy Deland's death," Carmine surmised.

"I agree, but we have nothing but innuendo to connect him."

"Since that vehicle is owned by the law firm, do you think that Garner would know whether his father has used it? Perhaps there is some type of log that would show who had the vehicle and when they had it. But the problem is if I ask him if his father drove it, he'll probably want to know why I'm asking. Given everything else, I don't think it's a good idea to tell the kid we're thinking his father might have killed his girlfriend."

"Yeah, that could be a problem," Felbin said. "Since we don't have access to their records, I don't know of any way to get the information, other than to ask either Garner or the senator. Personally, I would prefer to ask Garner."

"Okay. I'll call him and ask. What do I say if he wants to know why I'm asking?" Carmine asked.

"Just ignore the question. If he presses, just tell him I want to know, and you don't know why."

In just a few minutes, Carmine was back in Felbin's office with the answer. "He said his father regularly drove that vehicle to Jefferson City. Apparently, his father didn't think his Mercedes was a vehicle that would be embraced by his blue-collar base. Everything the guy does is designed to further his political career at the expense of everyone else."

"Where is the vehicle now?" Felbin asked.

"Either Garner has it or it's in the tow lot. I suspect he has it. He probably picked it up on his way over here this morning."

"Let's find it. Take a picture of it and show it to the Ms. Carson to see if she recognizes it."

"Will do," Carmine said.

Chapter Seventy-Three

Clara Carson was not sure, but thought it was the same vehicle Amy's mystery man drove. That was good enough for Felbin and Carmine. Now, they needed to figure out what the next step would be to determine whether Senator Lee was that man. They knew they couldn't simply ask him. He would just lie.

"Do we bring Garner in and let him know what we found out so far?" Carmine asked.

"I don't think we need to involve him just yet. But I think we need to involve his father," Felbin replied.

"How do you plan to do that, particularly since you two are so tight?"

"I plan to call him and schedule a lunch or breakfast meeting."

"And why would he want to meet with you, particularly after the last conversation you had?"

"Because his kid is back in the news and he doesn't know if I am going to drag him back into the mix. He wants to be the governor and doesn't want anything to stand in the way of that. I will suggest to him we need to coordinate the public statements, and I need his help."

"What's plan B?" Carmine asked, not convinced Felbin's idea was going to work.

"I suppose I can tell him I have some information that he visited Amy at her apartment at night. I'm guessing he will not want his wife to find out he was making house calls at the apartment of a young female who happened to be dating his son. And more importantly, he will not want his political opponents to learn he regularly visited a female who is now dead."

"Wow. Not sure if it will get him to a meeting with you, but it will certainly get his attention. But if you are going to go down that road, don't we have to let our client know what we have before your meeting?"

"No, because I am betting he is not going to mention anything to Garner in advance of the meeting. In the first place, they are not exactly on good terms. And secondly, the last thing he will want is to have a conversation with his son about his nighttime visits to Garner's girlfriend's apartment."

"I have some questions," Carmine said. "Do you think he was the nighttime visitor?"

"Yes. He knew Amy, worked with her. And as you said, he was less than forthcoming with that information during the time his son was charged with murder. I suppose he was playing the odds we wouldn't find out, which demonstrates how incredibly stupid he is. Yes, I believe he was the visitor. The question is, why he was visiting. And it doesn't take a rocket scientist to figure out what he was doing there."

"Which leads to question number two. Do you believe that he is the father of her child?"

"That I don't know. Clearly, Amy was no saint. She was an opportunist. If she was screwing two thirds of the Lee family at the same time, it's hard to tell who else she was involved with."

"And in the unlikely event you get him to a meeting, what do you plan to tell him?"

"Don't know. Need to play that by ear and see how the chat is progressing."

Chapter Seventy-Four

Senator Lee accepted Felbin's invitation to have a luncheon meeting. He was persuaded the discussion would center around the issue of publicity on his son's new criminal allegation. No threats were necessary, which again proved the point that politicians would do anything to avoid bad press, including breaking bread with someone who gave them indigestion.

There were three stipulations for the meeting. It had to be held in a location that afforded privacy, only Felbin and the senator would attend, and the meeting could not be recorded. After the closing argument, it was not politically expedient for the senator to be seen in public with Felbin. A private room at Westborough Country Club, where Felbin was a member, was arranged.

The meeting began with the exchange of some awkward pleasantries. It was obvious these two did not like each other. Both spent little time looking at the menu, and ordered salads with iced tea. Felbin eased into the discussion while they ate. He told the senator he needed some ideas how to handle the publicity surrounding the DWI. Initially, Lee's position was that he had nothing to do with the arrest and wanted to be kept out of it. He wanted Felbin's assurance that would be the case. It was obvious this was the reason he agreed to attend the meeting. "My son and I have not been speaking lately. But I'm sure you know that. I had nothing to do with his drinking and driving, and I want to be sure my name does not come into this," Senator Lee said.

"You're his father, and he has your name. To that extent you are involved," Felbin responded.

"There is nothing I can do about that, as much as I would like to. But other than that, I don't want any bullshit from you that somehow I was responsible for him drinking or getting drunk. I had nothing to do with that, or him, for that matter."

Felbin needed to control his temper. He was ready to respond in a way that would surely end the meeting. But he had to be smart about it. He was on to something and didn't want to blow it. The senator had just given him a window of opportunity to expand the discussion. "Well, in addition to being his father, you are involved in another way, Senator. A vehicle that is owned by your firm was seen at Amy's apartment on numerous occasions. What do you know about that?"

The reaction was instant and obvious. Lee was hiding something. It was clear to Felbin, Lee knew exactly what he was talking about in connection with this vehicle. He took several sips of his iced tea to give him time to regain his composure and to think about his response. Finally, he said, "Garner was dating her and had access to this car. I'm sure that he drove it there."

"No, Garner never drove that vehicle to Amy's apartment."

Now the senator needed to ask a question. "How do you know this vehicle belongs to the firm and was at her apartment?"

Felbin was not about to answer any questions. He was there to ask the questions. "Now it's my turn to tell you I don't want any bullshit from you. Why don't you tell me what that car was doing at the apartment of a woman who worked for you?"

"Fuck you, Felbin. I knew this meeting wasn't to discuss publicity issues," Senator Lee said as he threw his napkin onto the table. "I don't know what you are suggesting. But that shit better not find its way into the public domain, or you will be sorry, you prick," Lee said as he rushed out of the room.

"That's Mr. Prick, Senator," Felbin said, as he removed three bags from his jacket and carefully placed the iced tea glass, fork and napkin that Senator Lee used in each bag.

Chapter Seventy-Five

The investigation into who killed Amy and why wasn't going very well. Carmine had interviewed the neighbors again, as well as the people Amy worked with. Other than Clara Carson, the neighbors were not able to identify any additional male visitors. In fact, most indicated if she was involved with anyone other than Garner, they would probably know. Of course, Carmine knew that wasn't true, since they didn't know about the nighttime mystery man.

The people she worked with, as well as friends that Carmine contacted, expressed a similar opinion. Although she was described by most as a social climber interested in wealth and status, no one knew of anyone other than Garner that she was involved with.

The interviews with neighbors, friends and coworkers led Carmine back to the point of beginning. He had only one potential suspect—the nighttime visitor. Based upon his training and experience as a retired police officer, Carmine knew Amy Deland was murdered by someone she knew. There was no sign of forced entry or a struggle, and nothing was taken.

But this day was different. They caught a break in the case. Where it would ultimately lead, Carmine wasn't sure. "This loser is ours. We have him by the balls, and I can't wait to squeeze," Carmine said, as he walked into Felbin's office.

Felbin knew exactly what he was talking about. "You got the results?" he asked.

"Yes, I do. The guy at the lab just called and said that Senator Winston Lee is the father of Amy Deland's child."

Felbin had sent the fork, napkin and glass Felbin borrowed from the Westborough Country Club that contained the DNA of Senator Lee to a friend at a lab for a paternity check. Although it was not an official analysis, it was enough to move to the next step. The result really wasn't a surprise to either Felbin or Carmine, given the information they had about the vehicle. But now the question was what to do with the information. They knew they had to involve the client at this point.

Felbin asked his secretary to contact Garner and ask him to come into the office as soon as possible. There was no sense in delaying the unpleasant task they faced. While they waited, Carmine said, "In all my years in this business, I don't know that I have had to do anything worse than this. And that includes telling people that their loved ones were dead."

"Just when you thought things couldn't get worse for this kid, this happens," Felbin said.

"What do we say to him?"

"We tell him straight what we have. We give him all of the details and don't leave anything out."

"I'm guessing he will be pissed because we didn't tell him about the meeting with his old man, seizing the restaurant items and running the paternity test."

"If he is pissed at anyone, it will be his father. As far as running the paternity test without telling him, my position is this is just a preliminary, unofficial test, and we will seek his approval to run it officially. Obviously, we are not going to release this result publicly."

"Are you sure your buddy's conclusion Senator Lee is the father of this child is correct?" Carmine asked.

"I'm positive his conclusion is correct. The only problem is that my friend did this as a favor for me. He won't be in a position to testify if we need that, in part because his lab didn't know he did this for me. He is also a good friend, and that would potentially impact his credibility and impartiality. We are going to have to use another lab do a formal analysis. We can probably send it to the same lab we used before.

"I certainly hope this doesn't push this kid over the edge," Carmine said. But he knew this was only part of the problem they had. Simply because the senator was involved with Amy did not mean he killed her. Like Garner, he might not have known she was pregnant. "Although this development could potentially ruin his political career, it doesn't prove he is a killer."

"That's true. In fact, it may not even ruin his political career. Donald Trump was elected President of the United States after his so-called locker room conversation with Billy Bush talking about groping women was made public on the television show Access Hollywood."

"But Trump is a crude idiot who objectifies and has no respect for women. He is not a potential suspect in a murder case."

"This development certainly puts the good senator in the crosshairs. It gives him a motive to kill her, and that makes him more than just a person of interest. He is a suspect, at least as far as I am concerned," Felbin said.

"Since we have his DNA and can connect him to the victim, why don't we check the statue to see if his DNA is there? That would certainly seal his fate," Carmine said.

"Not yet. I want to see where this goes first and see if he makes a mistake. Getting a paternity test is one thing, but putting his DNA on a murder weapon is different. I don't feel compelled to turn the paternity thing over to the prosecutor yet, but I think we would need to give them the lab result if he is on the murder weapon. And right now, given this guy's influence, I want to keep what we are doing in house," Felbin said.

The conversation Felbin and his investigator were having was cut short by the announcement Garner had arrived.

Chapter Seventy-Six

As Felbin had said, there was no other way to do this unpleasant task other than straightforward. It was what it was, and no amount of sugar coating was going to change that. "Garner, we have a development we wanted to discuss with you," Felbin began. "I had a meeting with your father a couple weeks ago and I obtained a DNA sample from him. I sent it to a friend who works in a lab to give me an unofficial opinion on whether your father is the father of Amy's child. We just got the results today, and he is the father of Amy's child."

When he finished, Felbin felt horrible. It was like he hit this young man on the head with a sledge hammer. But it had to be done, and there was no one else to do it.

Garner sat in silence, staring at nothing. They had seen this look before when he learned he was not the father of the child the woman he loved was carrying. But this time it was different. This time he learned his father was involved with the woman he loved; involved sexually and was the father of her child.

Ten minutes passed without a word spoken by anyone. Finally, Felbin decided to break the silence. "Garner, we have to talk," he said.

No response. No eye contact. Garner continued to stare at nothing. Felbin wasn't even sure he heard what he said to him. Felbin repeated, "Garner, we have to talk. We need to decide what to do next. I can't begin to understand how difficult this is. But we must move on. We have an agreement we are dedicated to finding out who killed Amy. And, as hard as this might be for you, your father is a suspect, given this latest development. We have to deal with that."

Finally, Garner calmly said, "Don't worry, I'll deal with that."

Felbin didn't know what he meant by that. Although he'd had his share of youthful scrapes, Garner was not a violent person by nature. But this was no ordinary situation. And his calm demeanor after what he was just told was also extraordinary. Most people would not only be angry, but would also clearly show that anger. "I hope you are not talking about doing anything stupid," he said.

"Depends on what you mean by stupid," Garner said, again in a calm voice.

"I mean I hope you are not planning to physically harm him."

"No. That would be too easy for him. But I will harm him. He took the most important thing in my life away from me, and I plan to do the same for him."

Felbin knew what he meant. He didn't need to have him explain. The most important thing to Winston Lee was his power as a politician, and Garner planned to bring him down. "We have some more work to do before we can bring him down. While he is the father of Amy's child, that doesn't mean that he killed her."

"Oh, he killed her all right. And I plan to announce that to the world. I also plan to have a conversation with my mother and destroy his marriage. She was too good for him anyway. She has all the money in the family and is the one who finances his political ventures. When she finds out what he did, she will cut off the money and probably cut his balls off. He will be living on the street by the time this is over."

"Garner, we need to prove he killed Amy, and that has to be done with evidence. We don't have that evidence just now. All we can prove is he was involved with her and got her pregnant," Carmine added.

"You're going to tell me this married man is screwing some young white girl he gets pregnant and he is not going to kill her to protect his precious political career? My mother funds all his political shit. He has no money of his own. And I'm pretty sure they have a prenup agreement where he gets nothing if they get divorced."

"We agree with that. That's what makes him a suspect. But we still have to prove that," Felbin said.

"And remember we were concerned about a similar motive when you were on the hot seat. We were worried if the jury found out that you were not the father, it gave you a motive to kill her because she was fucking someone else.

The problem in both cases is there is no proof either of you knew she was pregnant," Carmine added.

"I know one thing for sure right now. He is the father of a child whose mother was murdered. That should kill both his marriage and his political career," Garner said.

Felbin needed to get the conversation back on track. They had a piece of evidence, and they needed to figure out how to deal with it. "Garner, I know you are upset and angry. I get that. But we need to decide the next step to see if we can get the evidence necessary to prove who killed Amy. I assume you are still interested in doing that."

"I'm not sure."

"Well, I'm interested in that, whether or not you are still on board. I think the next step is for me to have another conversation with your father," Felbin said.

"What good will that do? You think he is going to admit he killed Amy?" Garner asked.

"I don't know if it will do any good. But I need to turn the heat up and maybe he will make a mistake. It's usually not the original crime, but rather the cover up that brings people down. Up until now, your father hasn't had to do anything. You were the one charged with the murder, and all he had to do was fix the case so you wouldn't be convicted for a crime he committed. But in the meantime, I want you to promise me you won't say anything about this to anyone. And most of all, you won't go public with the pregnancy issue."

"I can't promise that."

"Well, I can't stop you. But I'm telling you, you will seriously jeopardize any chance we have of solving this murder. And remember, Amy was a woman you loved very much."

Garner did not respond to Felbin's comment immediately. It was obvious that the phrase *loved very much* was rattling around in his head. Finally, he said, "I have to go."

When he left, Carmine turned to Felbin and said, "What do you think he's going to do?"

"I really don't know," Felbin replied.

Chapter Seventy-Seven

Felbin wasted no time in contacting Senator Lee. He needed to get to him before his son did, whatever he was going to do. At first, the senator refused to speak to him. However, threats of publicity finally brought him to the phone. "Senator, I realize our last meeting did not end well. But I need to have another conversation," Felbin said.

"Well, talk away," Lee responded.

"No, we need to have a face to face. What I have to tell you cannot be done over the phone."

"I really don't have any interest in meeting with you. You threatened to publicly release something. What is it?"

"That's what we need to discuss. I will just say this. The information I have, if released, has the potential to totally ruin your political career. But I will promise you between now and the time we meet, I will not release anything to the media. If you refuse to meet, there will be no guarantees."

"Is this about the girl who was killed and some car at her house again?" the senator asked in a way that suggested he'd had no relationship with or even known Amy Deland.

"No. Are you going to meet me? Yes or no?"

"Under the circumstances, you give me no choice."

"Fine. Same place. Same rules. I'll get us a private room and meet you there in an hour."

"He's actually going to meet you again?" Carmine, who was listening, at least to Felbin's side of the conversation, asked.

"Like the politician he is, he understands he can't run the risk I will release what I have to the media."

"Shall we bug the room?"

"No. I told him the same rules would apply, and that means no tape recording."

"You may be sorry if this jackass gives you something and then later denies it, as you know he will."

"I'll take my chances. I've got to get going. I don't want to be late."

As it turned out, the senator was the one who was late. His hostility was apparent from the moment he walked into the room. "What is this all about? I don't have all day to spend with you," Lee began.

"Nice to see you again, Senator Lee," Felbin said sarcastically. "Let me get right to the point, so I don't waste your valuable time. You are the father of Amy Deland's child."

Like his son, Senator Lee reacted to the news like he had been hit on the head with a sledge hammer. Felbin could tell Lee was trying to process what he was just told. "How do you know that?" he finally asked.

"Because we did a paternity test and compared your DNA to the fetus."

"That's bullshit, and you are lying. Where did you get my DNA?"

"From the fork that you ate lunch with, the napkin you used to wipe your mouth and the iced tea glass you drank out of."

"You fuckin' prick."

"Senator, name calling is not going to get us anywhere. I have a lot of questions, but let's start with you explaining your relationship with Amy."

"I don't have to explain anything to you."

"Do you deny you had a relationship with her, and you might be the father of this child?"

"I absolutely deny I had any relationship with her, other than she was some type of clerk in the public relationship firm I used. Your paternity test is wrong. I don't know who did the analysis, but they don't know what they are talking about. In the meantime, if you put that out there," Lee said pointing to the window, "I will sue your ass, along with the person who did the test, assuming you are not lying about that, too. Do you have anything, else or are we done here?"

Felbin decided to push a little harder. "I believe not only are you the father of her child, but you also killed her after you found out that she was pregnant."

Without hesitation, Lee said, "I did not kill anyone. I told you, I had nothing to do with her. I had no relationship with her, sexually or otherwise. I would have no way of knowing she was pregnant and you can't prove otherwise. Again, if you put this bullshit out there, I will sue you."

"Actually, there is a way that I can prove that. DNA was found on the murder weapon. It was not Garner's. Now that we have your DNA, we can check to see if it's yours."

"Go ahead. Check it. Actually, if you want to check it, I'll pay for the test." Lee was adamant in his challenge. "I told you I didn't have a sexual or any other romantic relationship with her, didn't visit her at her apartment at night or any other time, and I certainly didn't kill her. Frankly, your client had more reason to kill her than I did."

Felbin ignored the last comment, but then said, "I never said you visited Amy's apartment at night. The only way you would have known is if you were that visitor."

"You did tell me that. This meeting is over. Send the bill for the DNA test to my law office, and I will promptly pay it. If you need the payment in advance, I will be glad to do that as well. In the meantime, I will repeat: if you release any of this, I will own you," Lee said, as he headed for the door. Another abrupt and angry departure.

Felbin knew the senator was an accomplished liar. After all, he was a politician. But encouraging a DNA test of the murder weapon and even offering to pay for it was risky. If his DNA was found on that statue, there would be no explanation that would pass the straight face test. And it would be a significant piece of evidence that would put him in the penitentiary for the murder of Amy Deland. But Felbin also knew Lee was lying about the paternity issue. While he might not have known Amy was pregnant, there was no doubt he was the father of that child.

Chapter Seventy-Eight

By the time Felbin returned to his office, a phone message was waiting for him from another member of the Lee family. This time Garner's mother, Cassandra wanted a meeting as soon as possible. Felbin instructed his secretary to make the arrangements for the afternoon.

In the meantime, Felbin met with his investigator to bring him up to date on his conversation with the senator. "He denied everything. He was not the father, didn't have a romantic or sexual relationship with her, had never been to her apartment, and certainly didn't kill her."

"You accused him of killing her?" Carmine asked.

"I did. His reaction to that was interesting. On the paternity issue, I could tell he was flustered. That took him by surprise. It was like I punched him in the stomach, and he had to take a minute to catch his breath. But when I accused him of murder, there was an immediate denial. No hesitation."

"No shit. If you accused me of murder and I was good for it, I would deny it immediately, too. No hesitation."

"This was different. His demeanor was different. I don't think he was lying. Then he challenged us to do a DNA test on the statue."

"He wants a DNA test? Is that a bluff?" Carmine asked in amazement.

"That's what he said. He also offered to pay for it," Felbin added.

"Of course, he's a professional liar, and as a politician, he's a risk taker. I think he's bluffing. We know he's lying when he says he wasn't screwing her, because the DNA says he knocked her up," Carmine said.

"I hear you. But this is a huge risk, because if his DNA is on that murder weapon, he has no way out."

"That's not true. He would then be forced to admit he was banging her, was frequently in her apartment and during one of those visits, he came out of the bedroom and touched the statue. He might even claim the statue was one of their sex toys," Carmine said facetiously.

"And who would believe that?"

"The same people who believe all of the other shit these politicians put out."

"My guess is if we do the test, his DNA will not be on that statue. He's not stupid, and wouldn't run that kind of bluff."

"What are we gonna to do?"

"We have his DNA and we can run a test anytime we want. Although we have him up against a wall, I think I want to take him up on his offer to pay for the test and see how he reacts and whether he backs off. Get a cost from a lab that we have never used before and we will send it to him. My guess is he will pay for the test."

"My guess is that he is full of shit and won't pay."

"We'll see. By the way, his wife is coming in later and I want you to sit in on that."

"What the hell is that about?"

"Don't know."

Chapter Seventy-Nine

Cassandra Lee arrived on time, dressed as though she was appearing before the United States Supreme Court. Her tailored navy-blue suit was simple but elegant, and accented by jewelry that was not overstated. She was an attractive woman who needed very little makeup to cover imperfections. She was intelligent and personable. But she could also be cunning and deadly, particularly if you were on the other side of a lawsuit or disagreed with a position she had taken. She earned her reputation as an aggressive litigator, mostly in civil rights cases, her specialty. But there were those who would say she could not be trusted. Her word was not necessarily her bond. People were usually evenly divided in their opinion of her. You either loved her or hated her. There was no in between.

"Thank you very much for seeing me so quickly," she said, extending her hand to Felbin.

"You're welcome. I believe you know my investigator, Tony Carmine," Felbin said.

"Yes. Nice to see you again, Mr. Carmine," Lee said, again extending her hand.

"What can we do for you, Ms. Lee?"

"This is very upsetting and embarrassing. But before I discuss the details, I have to be sure our conversation will be protected by the attorney-client privilege. I believe it is, but I would like you to confirm my belief."

"Yes, it would be protected by the privilege," Felbin replied.

"And that would also apply to Mr. Carmine, since he is your investigator, is that correct?

"Yes, that would also apply to him, or to any of our other investigators."

"Thank you. I don't know where to begin," she said, her voice cracking and eyes beginning to fill with tears. Clearly, she was upset, but trying her best to hold it together.

"Take your time. Would you like something to drink?"

Taking a Kleenex out of her purse and wiping her eyes, she said, "No, thank you." Hesitating to regain her composure she began again, "I had a most disturbing conversation with my son. I am quite confident you know the details of that conversation and what I am about to repeat here."

Felbin and Carmine sat in silence, declining to react or comment on her suggestion they knew what Garner had told her. But clearly, they knew what was coming.

When they didn't react, she continued, "My husband was cheating on me. While that is bad enough, he was cheating with the woman who was murdered. On top of that, he impregnated her, and that child was the subject of Garner's criminal charge. I know that you know all of that. I just had to say it out loud. I wanted to hear what that sounded like, perhaps in the hope this was not real. But I did hear what I just said. My husband conceived a child with a woman who was murdered." Her eyes began to fill again.

"Did you know Amy Deland?" Felbin asked.

"No, I didn't know her. I would see her occasionally at various functions, but I really didn't know her. I doubt I have spoken five words to her."

"Did you know she worked for your husband's public relations firm?"

"Only after Garner began to date her."

"And it's our understanding both you and your husband didn't approve of that relationship. Is that correct?" Carmine asked.

"That's true. I did not think she was good for him and as you know, I did not make a secret of that."

"Why didn't you think she was good for him?" Carmine pressed.

"Because I thought that she was a gold digger, an opportunist who was using him for what she could get. I had my investigator look into her background when they began to date."

"Did your husband know you had her checked out?" Carmine asked.

"No. I didn't tell him, and told my investigator no one else needed to know what he was doing."

"What is it you need from us, Mrs. Lee? You know we don't do divorce work," Felbin said.

"I know that. I am not here for that. I am here for some criminal and public media protection. I am not sure where this is going. Obviously, as the father of this child, my husband potentially becomes a suspect in the murder of this girl. Then I suppose Garner and I are thrown into it as well. Additionally, there is that whole thing about the way Garner's case ended. I am sure people are looking into the relationship between Cardwell and my husband and whether this was a payback for her appointment to the bench. Garner and I are not interested in being dragged into the middle of that either."

"Do you know of any current investigation into either Amy's murder or Cardwell's acquittal of Garner?" Felbin asked.

"No, other than your efforts to find the real killer to totally exonerate Garner, for which I am grateful. But I believe my husband will be publicly identified as the father of that child sooner or later. He is planning a run for governor and dirt like this always gets out. When that happens, I suspect several investigations will occur and Garner and I need some legal protection."

"Why us? There are plenty of good criminal defense lawyers in this town," Felbin said.

"Because not only are you an excellent litigator, but you also know this case. And you believed in Garner. You knew he did not murder that girl, and that he was accused of that, thanks to his father. I cannot think of anyone else, other than myself right now, who dislikes my husband as much as you do."

"I certainly understand your need for representation. I don't see any conflict between you and Garner, and we certainly don't represent your husband. We would be willing to undertake your representation, assuming this matter proceeds as you predict. I will have my secretary prepare the necessary paperwork and bring it in for you to sign."

The paperwork Felbin mentioned was a standard engagement contract which defines the attorney-client relationship and the duties and responsibilities of both the attorney and the client, as well as all financial obligations.

While they waited for the paperwork, Lee asked Felbin, "Do you think my husband murdered that girl?"

Felbin, struck by the impersonal references to Amy Deland, said, "We don't know. The only thing we know for sure is that the senator is the father of the child. But we will continue our search for the real killer, because Garner deserves to have his name cleared. Clearly, this was not some random murder or a botched burglary. There was no forced entry, and nothing was taken. She knew her assailant, or at least felt comfortable letting the person into her apartment. We promised Garner we would not give up the search until the real killer was identified."

"I agree, even if it turns out his father is a murderer. The killer needs to be identified, not only to serve the interests of justice, but also to vindicate my son, who has been devastated by all of this. But while I am upset with my husband, I truly do not believe he is a murderer. That would be devastating for all of us."

Felbin decided against telling his new client his plan to call her husband's bluff on the paternity test. He didn't think she needed to know that information at the moment.

Cassandra Lee carefully read the engagement agreement Felbin's assistant presented to her. She had no questions. After signing the document, she said goodbye to Felbin and his investigator.

Chapter Eighty

A week passed with no response from Senator Lee regarding the laboratory bill for the DNA analysis of the murder weapon Felbin's office sent to him. Another conversation was necessary. But this time, there was no return call, and there would be no additional discussion, at least not with Senator Lee.

Carmine was thrilled Lee would not pay for the analysis. He was right, and his boss was wrong. "I told you this was all a bluff. This loser had no intention of subsidizing that review. And that's because he's as good as gold for that murder. What do we do now?"

"We do what we planned to do after we gave him the chance to step up to the plate. We have a lab do the analysis, and we pay for it," Felbin said.

"Which lab?"

"Like we talked about before, we need to pick one we have no connection to and we have never used before."

"Should we send it to your guy to do an unofficial analysis, because any lab we pick is going to take some time to get us the result?"

"That would certainly speed up the process, if he is willing to do me another favor. I broached the subject with him before when he did the paternity test, and he was not enthusiastic. I didn't press it with him, but I can revisit it."

"Let's say your friend says there is a match. Do we take it to Lee, then?" Carmine asked.

"That's a good question. I . . ."

"I always ask good questions. It's just you don't always recognize a good question," Carmine interrupted.

Ignoring the comment, Felbin continued with what he was about to say. "I think that we go to him first and, like the paternity test, judge his reaction. But here's the problem. If we take it to a lab and the result indicates his DNA is on the murder weapon, we will need to turn that over to the prosecutor. I think that is our ethical obligation. But, as I have said before, I don't trust anyone, given this guy's influence."

"Here we go with that ethical bullshit again. Why is it everyone else can engage in as much fuckin' unethical and even criminal conduct, but we have to play by the ethical rules?" Carmine asked.

It was obvious Felbin was trying to figure out a way to determine whether the senator could be connected to the murder weapon. But he didn't want to turn the information over to the prosecutor before he was ready, and satisfied the case would not be fixed for a second time. He also didn't want to be accused of withholding critical evidence in a murder case. An unofficial lab result from his friend, although not foolproof, might get Felbin where he needed to be. While it might be a distinction without a difference, Felbin decided to take a chance. "I will contact my buddy to see if he will give us an unofficial analysis. We can then go to a lab we have never used before and get an official one," Felbin finally said, much to the delight of his investigator.

"What about Garner, do we tell him what we are doing?" Carmine inquired.

"I don't think we need to do that. He is in an emotional state, and I'm not sure what he will do with the information. Obviously, he didn't follow our advice about not talking to anyone."

"Yeah. What's that about? I'm surprised we haven't seen this as headline news."

"I suspect he went to his mother first because he could hurt his father very badly there without putting his own name into the headline. Any public story about the pregnancy is going to involve him, even to the point of fueling speculation he killed Amy in a jealous rage after he found out about his father's involvement. I think his concern about publicity will be helpful to us. It should prevent him from running his mouth to the press while he comes up with a solution for his own problem."

"How long do you think your friend will take to get us the result?"

"Don't know, but I'll make the call right now."

Chapter Eighty-One

Once again, Felbin prevailed on his friend for another off the record favor. The result came back quickly and although unofficial, exonerated Senator Lee. That was a surprise to both Felbin and Carmine. The real question is how Garner was going to react, having been convinced his father not only impregnated his girlfriend, but also killed her.

The hastily called conference with Garner began with casual greetings. But Felbin did not spend a lot of time chit-chatting. He got right to the point. "As you know, we have your father's DNA. We sent that to a lab to determine whether his DNA is on the statue that killed Amy. The result we got back is that his DNA is not on that murder weapon. In my opinion, he is not a suspect in Amy's murder."

Felbin watched Garner's reaction. It was different from when he learned his father impregnated the woman he loved. This time he reacted like he knew this was coming. Like he knew his father did not kill Amy. Or maybe he was just tired. He'd lost the woman he loved. He was accused of murdering her. He was found guilty and then acquitted by a corrupt judge, thanks to his father. It turned out that the woman he loved apparently didn't love him the same way he loved her. His father was sexually involved with her, and gave him a brother or sister. He was now estranged from his father, and his family was shattered. Felbin understood these events were more than anyone could endure. But he also understood his client had to put this behind him and move on. The task of finding the real killer of Amy Deland remained.

"What now?" Garner asked.

"We continue with our search for the real killer. Frankly, given the information we had about the pregnancy, we thought we were on to something with your father. Interestingly, when we told him we could do a DNA test on the statue, he not only challenged us to do the test but offered to pay for it. He told us to send the bill to the law firm and he would pay it. After we sent him the bill, he refused to pay for the analysis. I had a friend do an analysis and give us his unofficial opinion."

"He didn't refuse to pay for the test, my mother did," Garner said.

"How do you know that? I thought you weren't talking to your father," Carmine said.

"I'm not. My mother told me."

"How did you come to have a conversation with your mother about this?" Felbin asked.

"Apparently, she found the bill, or my father showed her the bill, and she came to me to discuss it."

"Was that before or after you told her about the pregnancy?" Carmine asked.

"After."

Carmine and Felbin looked at each other, somewhat confused by what Garner was saying. "What did she say to you?" Carmine continued.

"She said he had gotten a bill from your firm for a DNA test on the murder weapon. She wasn't sure where all of this was going and was concerned about what would happen if there was a DNA match on the statue. I told her this was all about finding out who killed Amy."

"And how did she respond to that?" Felbin asked.

"She said she did not see any future in that and, as a family, we needed to move on. Amy was dead and there was nothing we could do to change that. Finding the real killer and proving it with irrefutable evidence was a long shot. And without that, people would continue to believe I was a killer who got off because the case was fixed. Pointing the finger at my father would ruin his career, and ultimately our whole family."

With his confusion turning to disbelief over what he was hearing, Felbin said, "Garner, let me ask you something. As far as you can tell, are your parents getting along now? Is there any fallout or hostility after your mother learned of your father's infidelity?"

"None whatsoever. She is not kicking him to the curb, like I thought she would, which really pisses me off. It's like we have to protect his reputation, and the reputation of the family, and her blue blood law firm. I guess she wants to be the First Lady of Missouri, and maybe even of the United States. At the end of the day, money, power and status are really all that matter to most people, and apparently she is no exception."

Both Felbin and Carmine were confused. This was different from what his mother had told them and different from what Garner expected. Now, he was at odds with both his mother and his father at a time when he needed both parents.

"I'm sorry about all of the unpleasant issues in your family. At some level, I can understand why your mother would want to generally protect the entire family. I doubt it is because she wants to be the First Lady of anything. Rather, publicity about what your father did would be devastating for all of you," Felbin said, in an attempt to soften Garner's anger toward his mother.

Regardless of what was going on in in the Lee family dynamics, the question was whether Garner wanted to continue the pursuit of Amy's killer. "However, we still need to find the real killer," Felbin continued. "I disagree with your mother. I believe we can find irrefutable evidence that will identify the killer. Remember, we have DNA evidence on that statue. Once we match that, we will have our man. And you will be completely exonerated because people believe in the science of DNA. In the meantime, I assume you are not following your mother's advice, and we will continue with the search," Felbin said.

"I absolutely want to proceed. Regardless of what she and my father said and did to me, I want to know who killed her. And then I will be exonerated, have some closure and can move on with the rest of my life. We can evaluate what it will do to the family after we identify the person who killed Amy."

Chapter Eighty-Two

The conversation between Garner and his mother raised concerns for Felbin. That conversation seemingly contradicted what his mother told him and Carmine when she was looking for representation. In all events, Felbin needed another meeting with his new client.

This time when she arrived at the office instead of dressed for an appearance before the Supreme Court, it looked like she had been to another court; Centre Court at Wimbledon. Looking like an ad for Nike tennis apparel, Cassandra Lee wore a hot pink tennis dress, white tennis shoes and a white head band, all with the Nike swoosh logo. A small amount of perspiration had replaced whatever little makeup she was wearing. Diamond stud earrings, which Carmine estimated at about a carat each, were the only noticeable jewelry she wore. The plastic bottle of Ice Mountain water she carried was the only thing without the Nike logo.

"I see you are coming directly from court," Felbin said, hoping to begin the meeting on a light note. This lady was a very smart lawyer. He needed some answers to the advice her son said she had given him. But he also had to be careful he didn't alienate her. Garner needed to find out who killed the woman he loved, and everybody needed to be on the same page with that effort.

"I am so sorry. I usually don't go to meetings like this, but my match went longer than expected and I didn't want to be late. I came here directly from the court; that is, the tennis court. I didn't even have a chance to shower," she said, smiling and taking a drink from her water bottle. "The club championship mixed doubles tournament is underway, and my partner and I are defending our title. This was an important quarter final match. Again, sorry for the attire and the sweat."

"You look fine. We don't stand on a lot of formality around here." Felbin said.

"Good to know. Maybe the next time I come, I'll exchange the tennis outfit for a jogging suit," she joked.

"I at least hope you won your match."

"Yes, we did. My partner and I are hard to beat, not so much because we are good, but I'm left-handed and he's right-handed. We are able to cover a lot of the court with stronger forehand rather than weaker backhand shots."

This was a good start. She seemed to be relaxed and happy, perhaps because she'd won her match. Felbin knew that wins were a big part of this lady's life.

"I wanted to talk to you about a meeting we had with Garner. He told us you had a conversation with him and suggested he abandon his pursuit of the person who killed Amy. He said . . ."

Before he had a chance to finish his thought, Cassandra Lee said, "My training as a lawyer has taught me to do a cost benefit analysis for issues like this. And when I balanced the benefit of pursuing this woman's killer against the cost to my family, that pursuit comes in second place in a two-issue race. As far as Garner is concerned, he is a black man who was involved with a white woman who was murdered. There are those people who will always believe he killed her, regardless of the evidence. Unfortunately, that is the world in which we live. I don't think you will ever be able to prove beyond any doubt who killed her."

"When we met previously, I was under the impression you were in favor of pursuing this investigation," Felbin said.

"Well, I am sorry if I left you with that impression. That was not my intent."

Felbin knew this was false. Her position now was completely different from when they'd last met. But debating the issue would not be beneficial. Instead, he decided to go down a different road. "Mrs. Lee, Garner told us you refused to allow your law firm to pay for a DNA test that was designed to determine whether your husband's DNA was on the murder weapon."

Lee confirmed it was her decision to refuse to pay for the test, which led to another question.

"Did you know it was your husband who challenged us to do the test and offered to pay for it?" Felbin asked.

"Yes." She didn't elaborate and instead took another drink of water.

Since Garner did not know his father had offered to pay for the test, her husband must have told her. And if he told her, then she would obviously have concluded, as did Felbin, he was certain there would be no match. Why then would she not authorize the test? Felbin decided to ask.

"Because it would have been a waste of time. I told you before I knew my husband did not kill that girl," Cassandra Lee said emphatically.

That wasn't how Felbin remembered their previous conversation. When they first met, she said she did not believe her husband was a murderer. Now she was saying she knew he didn't kill the girl. This was the second time she'd contradicted her prior statements. Something was not right here. "Have you spoken to Garner since he was here?" Felbin asked, determined to get some answers that made sense.

"No."

"Can I assume then you don't know we paid for a DNA test on the murder weapon and your husband's DNA wasn't on it?"

"No, I did not know that."

"During our initial conference, you indicated you were concerned about being dragged into a murder case once it gets out your husband was involved with Amy," Felbin said, avoiding the reference to the pregnancy.

"That's true."

"But now we know his DNA is not on the murder weapon, that concern should no longer exist."

"Mr. Felbin, you know as well as I do that simply because his DNA is not on the murder weapon, does not mean he can't be charged. He has a big target on his back. And you also know the best way to squeeze a plea deal is to threaten to indict a family member. Since Garner has been acquitted, that only leaves me. In addition, we have a black man running for governor and a dead white woman. There is also the matter of the perception Garner's case was fixed by Cardwell and my husband as a payoff for her appointment to the bench."

Felbin knew prosecutors were not above at least threatening to indict a family member, if they could get a plea out of the primary target. That tactic was once used to obtain a plea from a sitting Missouri attorney general who was running for governor. Felbin also knew that prosecutors didn't like to lose, particularly in high-profile cases. No DNA on the murder weapon made a prosecution of Senator Lee highly unlikely, and Felbin knew Cassandra Lee knew that. "What is your current relationship with your husband?" Felbin asked directly.

"Frankly, Mr. Felbin, I don't see that as being any of your business. I didn't come here to discuss my domestic issues. But since you asked, I will tell you I have no immediate plans to file for divorce. If I file, I know it will become headline news, and I want to avoid that. As a result, I am going to hang in there until we can finally put those matters behind us. Although doubtful, maybe we can even salvage our marriage. After all, he is not the first guy who cheated on his wife," she said. No tears this time.

The conversation with his new client was not going anywhere and Felbin knew it. After she left Carmine said, "What the fuck was that?"

"I have no idea. She did a one hundred eighty degree turn from the last time she was here," Felbin said.

"She's a fuckin' con. That poor me show she put on last time complete with all those tears and emotion was bullshit. It was part of the con."

"Why would she need to con us? If she needed legal representation, we had no problem doing that as long as there was no conflict with our representation of her son. And we certainly were not going to represent her husband, as she well knew. None of this is making any sense."

"She has to con us because that's how she lives her life," Carmine said. "She comes in here all pissed off at her cheating husband. She wants to find the killer to exonerate her son. And now, she is concerned about the political future of her family and claims she never was in favor of any investigation. This isn't adding up for me." Suddenly, Carmine stopped and stared at his boss. "Did she just tell us that she is a left-handed tennis player?"

"That's what she said. Why?"

Carmine continued to stare at Felbin. Clearly, he was trying to reconstruct something in his head. Finally, he said, "Holy shit." After pausing again to collect his thoughts, he continued. "When she was in here last time, did you notice how she signed the client contract?"

"I didn't pay any attention."

"I ordinarily don't pay any attention to that either. But for some reason, I watched her sign the document. She signed her name with her left hand. And I can't tell you why, but for whatever reason, I didn't think of her as a lefty. Now we know she also uses her left hand to play tennis. And this left-handed person doesn't want us to continue looking for Amy's killer. The Amy she hated."

"And we know Amy was struck from behind by either a left hand dominant person or someone using the left hand. We concluded it probably couldn't be a right-handed person using the left hand, because the statue is too heavy. We also know Amy probably knew or at least was familiar with the person who killed her, and that's why she let them in her apartment."

Carmine agreed with what Felbin was saying. It all made sense. Cassandra Lee didn't want her son dating Amy. She viewed her as an opportunist and most likely something even less flattering, particularly now she'd found out Amy and her husband were playing house. When speaking to Felbin, she never tried to disguise her feelings about Amy and always referred to her in an impersonal, third person manner. She discouraged her son from pursuing the real killer. And now, they discovered she is left-handed.

"This is all good circumstantial evidence, but we need something else," Felbin pointed out. They both knew what that something else was.

Carmine put the Ice Mountain water bottle that Cassandra Lee left behind in a bag. Felbin would prevail upon his lab friend to do one more favor.

Chapter Eighty-Three

Felbin needed another meeting with his client, Cassandra Lee. This time it was a little more difficult to arrange, with Lee blaming her busy trial schedule. But finally, it was arranged and when she arrived, the receptionist immediately showed her to one of the conference rooms where Felbin and Carmine were waiting. In front of Felbin was a thin file folder that contained information on their new client.

This meeting would be different from the other two. Lee took immediate control, bypassing the customary preliminary greeting pleasantries. "I assume you had the water bottle I left behind DNA tested," she began.

Surprise would not begin to describe the look on the faces of both Felbin and Carmine.

"Why would you say that?" Felbin asked.

"Because that is what you did with my husband when you met him at your country club."

"Who told you that?" Carmine asked.

"My husband did. And I thought it would be a good idea if you also checked my DNA to see if it was on the murder weapon. That is why I left the water bottle in your conference room. I wanted to give you the vehicle to do that within the confines of our attorney-client relationship. And that is why we are having this meeting, is it not?" she asked. But no response from either Felbin or Carmine. They were speechless. Her demeanor was no longer that of a woman scorned, deeply hurt, betrayed by the infidelity of a spouse and trying to protect herself and her son. This time she was arrogant and confident. "Do tell. What did you find out about my DNA?"

"Your DNA is on the murder weapon," Felbin said and left it at that, to see how she would respond.

"Of course it is," she said.

"What the fuck is going on?" Carmine whispered in Felbin's ear. But with Lee's last response, Felbin was beginning to understand what this very smart lawyer was doing.

"You murdered Amy Deland," Felbin said.

"I certainly did. That little whore got what she deserved."

Felbin thought he knew the answer, but thought he would ask the question anyway. "Why?"

"I will tell you exactly how it happened. I went to her apartment to offer her money to stay away from my son. I knew they had dinner plans for Valentine's Day and I wanted her to cancel them and end the relationship. I didn't intend to kill her. As I told you, I did not think she was good for him. She was an opportunist. She turned the money down. She said it was not enough and wanted more. I told her that was all there was and there would be no more. I told her to take it or leave it, but if she left it, I would make her life miserable."

"How did you plan to make her life miserable?" Carmine asked.

"I told her I would get her fired from the public relations firm my husband uses and she would never get another job in Missouri or anyone else for that matter. She told me that was not going to happen because she was fucking my husband, in addition to my son. Then she told me she was pregnant and believed my husband was the father. I doubt she really knew who the father was, but I lost it at this point. We were standing next to a bookshelf. When she turned to walk toward the door, I grabbed the statue from the bookshelf and hit her in the head as hard as I could. She went down. I dropped the statue and left."

"Did you know she was dead when you left?" Felbin asked.

"I didn't know for sure. But I hit her as hard as I could, and the statue was heavy, as you know."

"Did you intend to kill her when you grabbed that statue?" Carmine asked.

"I think that I probably did at that point because I was so angry."

"That could be a real problem for you criminally," Carmine said.

"Actually, it won't be a problem. When I signed your client contract, I saw you watching me," she said, pointing to Carmine. "You saw me use my left hand. I knew from the newspaper coverage of the trial your theory was the killer was left-handed. When I spoke to Garner about abandoning the pursuit of the real killer, he refused, and he told me how dedicated you were to solving this murder. You told me the same thing when I first met with you. I knew no one else was looking for the real killer. The police thought they had their guy when they arrested Garner and closed their file after Cardwell acquitted him. And the Circuit Attorney doesn't care."

Felbin and Carmine couldn't believe what they were hearing. This woman was calm and coherent while confessing to a murder, and all they could do was listen. What they were witnessing was a stark contrast to her Academy Award performance the first time she'd come into the office.

As Felbin and his investigator listened without comment, Lee continued. "You also mentioned this was not a random criminal act because there was no forced entry, and nothing was missing from her apartment. You theorized this little whore knew the person who killed her. That certainly reduced the pool of suspects. With the pregnancy caused by my husband, I realized it was only a matter of time before you would be looking at me. That is why I came here and hired you. I needed to establish that comfortable attorney-client relationship. After that, I just helped you along with your investigation. I had to have you get my DNA off that water bottle. I knew your investigator here saw me sign your contract with my left hand. To focus your attention on me, given your theory the killer was left-handed, I mentioned I used my left hand to play tennis. I figured with my sudden change of position on your investigation, you would be able to put it together and at least test the water bottle. By the way, I lied about my tennis match that day. There was no match."

"I assume when we saw you last time, you knew we had your husband's DNA tested, despite your refusal to pay for the test," Felbin said.

"I didn't know for certain. I figured, given your dedication to the cause and your disdain for my husband, you would not let payment stand in the way of your efforts to prove he committed this murder. Of course, I knew his DNA would not be on that statue unless they were using it as a sexual object," Lee responded, without any emotion whatsoever.

Cold. This lady was absolutely cold and detached from the murder of another human being she'd committed.

"As long as this is true confessions, what about Cardwell?" Felbin asked.

"What about her?" Lee responded, knowing full well what Felbin was asking.

"You were the one who fixed the case." Upset by what he was hearing, Felbin decided to skip the question and go directly to the accusation.

"I would not say I fixed the case, rather I suggested to this good judge what the law is."

"Or what the law should be, according to the outcome that you needed," Felbin added.

"I was not going to allow my son to go to the penitentiary for a murder I committed. I arranged to have Cardwell get the case. I knew she owed us for the appointment . . ."

"You mean owed your husband," Carmine injected.

"No, I mean owed us. Because he was a high-profile politician with a large following, Senator Lee was out in front on the Decker case. But I was the one behind the scenes pulling the strings. My husband talked to Cardwell about the Decker case, but I was the one who made the promises to her and then followed through. I promised my husband would get her a judgeship if she prosecuted that cop, Decker, who executed a young black kid. I needed that prosecution for my various civil rights claims against the St. Louis Police Department, and also because I represented the dead kid's family. Of course, you didn't know that, because the lawsuit never materialized. Frankly, after reviewing the evidence you presented during the trial, I was concerned about my ability to prove Decker had hit the kid with his flashlight. And I didn't want to take the heat if I couldn't. I needed a conviction, and didn't get it, thanks to you," Lee said pointing to Felbin.

"Not thanks to me. You and I both know Decker didn't murder anyone. You and your husband pressured Cardwell into prosecuting Decker because of the Tom Cannon case. He was the white sergeant who was accused of assaulting a mentally challenged young black man in his own home. I'm sure you recall that case. And people were upset because Cardwell screwed up and allowed the case to be tried outside of St. Louis. The officer was acquitted by an all-white jury and then along comes the Decker case. Another white cop arresting a black suspect. This time the suspect died, and you were not going to let this cop get away with that. As a result, Cardwell charged Decker with murder before she had all the evidence, thanks to you. And then after all the evidence came out during the trial, you found out Decker didn't kill anyone. He was as innocent as your son."

"I don't know that," Lee said. A simple denial. No need to explain.

"And so, when Garner was charged with murdering Amy, you were the one who collected on the debt Cardwell owed you after she prosecuted an innocent police officer," Felbin said.

"Like I began to say, I was the one who arranged for her to get the case. And after she did, I had numerous conversations with her before, during and after the trial. I knew what the outcome would be, so we wanted a quick trial. I wanted to get Garner out from under this as soon as possible. And of course, my husband didn't need this for his campaign for governor. You really didn't need the time to prepare, Mr. Felbin," Lee said, pausing to look at Felbin. "Cardwell kept me informed on what was happening during the trial, because we decided not to attend. It was only when the paternity issue surfaced at the trial that my husband became involved and had some conversations with the good judge."

"I suppose you thought the jury would acquit," Felbin said.

"I thought Cardwell could control the evidence, and Braxton was supposed to control the young prosecutor she assigned to the case. The result should be an acquittal. We didn't count on Perrin going rogue. Of course, I would have preferred Braxton decline to prosecute in the first place, but that didn't happen. Apparently, Sandworth took it to one of her assistants, who issued the charge without her knowledge. She will pay a price for her inability to control her subordinates."

Felbin knew the fix was in from the start. He just couldn't prove it. Now, his own client was admitting she fixed the case on behalf of her son. But he was curious about one thing. "Was it your idea to revisit the mistrial issue and then sustain it, but acquit Garner based upon prosecutorial misconduct?"

"Of course it was. Do you think that idiot Cardwell would have thought of that? At first, she was just going to put him on probation. But that wasn't acceptable to me. Then she was simply going to sustain your motion for judgment of acquittal. I didn't think that gave us enough cover. I thought putting it on the prosecutor was a better plan. That was also payback for Perrin going rogue. Since Karen Braxton was okay with the idea, Cardwell went with it. Because Perrin wasn't real cooperative with her during the trial and made her life miserable, she didn't mind throwing him under the bus. It was my understanding she was either going to fire him or force him to resign. I heard recently he quietly resigned."

"Did you also control all of the evidentiary decisions Cardwell made, including her refusal to require a DNA sample for a paternity test?" Felbin asked.

"Not all of them. That one I did, along with my husband. Obviously, my husband had an interest in making sure that details of the pregnancy didn't come out. Although I doubt this little slut told him she thought he was the father, I am sure he thought there was that possibility. At the time, despite what she told me, I thought Garner was probably the father, and I didn't want the publicity my son fathered a child with this tramp on top of everything else. Of course, if she was right and my husband was the father, it would have been devastating for Garner in more ways than just the trial."

"And I suppose you counted on Cardwell to keep all the paternity issues out of the case," Felbin said.

"Yes. But I didn't count on Garner's demand for a public airing of the issue. I suppose I didn't realize how much he cared about her." Lee was unable to use the word *love* in connection with the relationship between her son and the woman she'd killed.

"And you didn't count on our lab comparing the DNA on the murder weapon to Garner's."

"No, actually I did count on that. I obviously knew there would be no match. I also knew you would need to send the results to the prosecutor since you wanted the jury to hear the evidence. What I didn't count on was Perrin checking the paternity once he had Garner's DNA. Braxton claims that she didn't know he did that. Of course, his job was made easier when Garner admitted he knew he was not the father."

"Does your husband know you murdered Amy?" Carmine asked.

"The only people who know what I did are you two," Lee said, referring to Felbin and his investigator.

"I guess you think you committed the perfect crime," Carmine said.

"I wouldn't say the perfect crime, Mr. Carmine. But I am feeling pretty comfortable at the moment. You can't continue to investigate this or make any public comments, because you know where it will lead. Your search for the killer is over. We all know the police and the prosecutor have no interest in doing any additional investigation. Looks to me like we are at the end of the road."

"What about your son?" Felbin asked.

"What about him?" she responded, answering a question with a question.

"He was convicted for a murder you committed."

"He was acquitted of that crime."

"Technically. But everyone knows how that happened and no one believes he is innocent."

"Well, perhaps you should have done a better job for him, Mr. Felbin. But in any event, we are already looking for a house for him in another state. He will be just fine."

With that remark, Felbin stood up and said, "Get out of my office."

As she was leaving the conference room, she turned and said, "Remember your oath. Not a single word that jeopardizes our relationship."

Felbin responded to her comment by slamming the conference room door.

Chapter Eighty-Four

"You're not going to let her get away with that, are you?" Carmine asked.

Both Felbin and Carmine couldn't believe what they just heard. A woman, their client, had just confessed to a murder. A murder her son was accused of committing and for which he was prosecuted and convicted. She bought a judge to fix the case and ensure that her son would never be convicted and spend any time in the penitentiary. Then she hired her son's lawyer, who was dedicated to finding the real killer in an effort to exonerate her son. By hiring the only person who had any interest in turning over all the rocks, she effectively killed the investigation by cloaking herself in the attorney-client privilege.

"What is it that you think I can do? Perhaps I can call the corrupt Circuit Attorney. Or better yet, call the corrupt judge and turn her in," Felbin responded, his voice filled with anger and sarcasm. "It's over. She won. She outsmarted us."

"What do you mean, she won? This fuckin' bitch just admitted to a murder and bribery. And I didn't spend a career in law enforcement to let people tell me to my face they murdered someone and then walk away. It didn't happen then, and it's not happening now."

"A different set of rules apply to you now. You're working for a law firm, not the police department. As I explained to you numerous times, we have ethical rules."

"And as I explained to you numerous times, I don't give a shit about your ethical rules. Those aren't the Carmine rules. The Carmine rules don't allow someone to confess to a murder, say *fuck you; there's nothing you can do about it,* and walk away."

Tony Carmine was a cop, and a good one, at that. But he didn't understand or perhaps understood but refused to accept the rules of the legal profession. Legal reality was about to come crashing down on Tony Carmine's world.

"Tony, listen. I don't want to lecture you, but you have to understand some things. Once she came into our office and had a conversation with us, certain rules applied, and protections occurred. She wasn't talking to us at some cocktail party. She was consulting us for legal help. That conversation then gets some protection, regardless of whether she hires us."

"You're telling me we couldn't repeat a conversation we had with her where she doesn't even hire us?" Carmine was confused.

"Yes. But she did more to ensure we were silenced. She hired us. And when I say us, that includes you. Remember how careful she was during that meeting?"

Carmine shook his head.

"The first thing she did was solicit an agreement from us that any conversation with both you and me, was protected by the attorney-client privilege. And this was before she retained us. We agreed that all conversations were protected. Then to further ensure that protection, she hired us and signed a retainer agreement," Felbin said.

"But she hired us under false pretenses," Carmine said, looking for a reason to get around the attorney-client privilege.

"Tony, Tony, Tony. People lie to lawyers all the time. It doesn't matter. They are still protected by the privilege. They can lie to us, we just can't lie to them. But nice try."

"Okay. I get it that you can be in trouble if we report this confession to law enforcement. But what are they going to do to me if I take it to someone like Sandworth? Are they going to take away a law license I don't have?"

"Obviously, they can't take away something you don't have. But this is what the court can do; suppress whatever evidence you give Sandworth or anyone else. She was very smart in this way as well. She left a water bottle so that we would run her DNA and we, as her lawyers, would discover evidence that she committed a crime. That puts it within the privilege, because we can't do anything that harms the client. And obviously, putting her DNA on a murder weapon harms her."

"You're telling me your silly rules don't allow us to report a crime or evidence of a crime?"

"Not exactly. Let's say that Cassandra Lee came into our office and said she was going to kill Amy Deland. We could report that to the police to prevent the crime from occurring. But that's not what happened here. She had already committed the crime. Amy was dead. That gives Lee, or anyone else who committed a crime, certain protections in addition to the attorney-client privilege. In fact, as you well know, the police also have rules. Lawyers aren't the only ones who have to play by a set of rules. If you get a confession that violates the rights of the suspect, you can't use it against that person."

Carmine wasn't getting the answers he wanted. And with each answer, he was becoming more and more frustrated. "What about that piece of shit Cardwell? Can we at least report her to some judicial commission?"

"Sure, we can. And what do we use to prove a case of corruption?" Felbin asked, equally frustrated.

"The admission of Lee. It's my understanding these hearings are confidential. We wouldn't be doing anything to hurt our beloved client."

"Doesn't matter. We can't disclose her statements to anyone unless she consents. And I can't see her doing that anytime soon. In addition, I suspect she would deny she admitted to us she fixed a murder case."

"This is total bullshit. They lie, cheat and murder and get away with it. But we have to play by the rules. Suppose I just leak it to Sandworth or a reporter I know."

"You know my answer. If we do, we are no better than they are."

"What about Garner? Can we at least tell him what's going on? That his mother is a fuckin' killer."

"I think you also know the answer to that. But I'll give it to you anyway. No."

"He has to live the rest of his life not knowing who killed the woman he once loved? And on top of that, people will continue to believe he is the one who killed her, while his mother goes on to live her perfect life."

"That's probably the worst part of this whole tragedy. There is a lot of injustice and corruption in the world. This state isn't unique in that regard. Most, I suspect is caused by politics or corrupt politicians at some level. I suppose we would all be better off if we could remove politics and political influences from every aspect of our lives, including the judiciary. But for the moment that's not happening, and we must do the best we can to live with it."

"You do know that I will not rest until this lady is in the penitentiary," Carmine said.

"I know that, Tony," Felbin said, as he turned off the lights in the conference room.

About the Author

Chet Pleban is a St. Louis attorney with over 40 years of both civil and criminal trial experience. Many of his cases are high-profile and involve law enforcement officers who find themselves on the wrong side of the criminal justice system. In addition to his criminal practice, he also represents people who have suffered serious physical injury and those whose employment was wrongfully terminated.

In addition to his law practice, Pleban also provides legal commentary for radio and television outlets as legal issues of importance arise. He has been a guest lecturer at St. Louis University, Washington University, the University of Missouri as well as many of the local high schools, and regularly teaches Continuing Legal Education classes in Missouri and other states.

His first novel, *Conviction of Innocence,* was a fictionalized account of a St. Louis police officer he represented who was accused of murdering a burglary suspect. The book was a three-year project that he wrote while spending the winter months in Florida away from not only the St. Louis weather but also the demands of a busy law practice. While continuing to write during the Florida winters, Pleban divides his time during the summer months between his home in St. Louis where he continues with his active law practice and his summer home at the Lake of the Ozarks.

WEBSITE: wwwconvictionofinnocencebook.com
TWITTER: https://twitter.com/ChetPleban
FACEBOOK:
https://www.facebook.com/profile.php?id=100004256177967

www.ingramcontent.com/pod-product-compliance
Lightning Source LLC
Chambersburg PA
CBHW060418030726
47495CB00003B/632